Dedicated

to

Audrey

Whose dedication and tireless effort made this book possible.

Rogue Wildcatter

Happy reading and best regards!

Dub Hicks

Printed in the United States of America
by Princeton Academic Press, Inc.
3175 Princeton Pike
Lawrenceville, NJ 08648
609 / 896-2111
First Edition

Publisher Acknowledgement

ICAN Press would like to acknowledge the following contributors for the production and marketing of this publication: Dahk Knox, Josette Rice, Marian Denson, Steven Fellwock, Patricia Godsoe, Tammi Becker and Tina Prato.

Book Cover Illustrated by Jan M. Lowry

Disclaimer

This document is an original work of the author. It may include reference to information commonly known or freely available to the general public. Any resemblance to other published information is purely coincidental or accidental. The author has in no way attempted to use material not of his own origination. ICAN Press disclaims any association with or responsibility for the ideas, opinions or facts as expressed by the author of this book.

Printed in the United States of America
Library of Congress
Cataloging-in-Publication
ISBN: 1-881116-39-5

FIRST EDITION

Rogue Wildcatter

By

Dub Hicks

Publisher in the United States of America
by ICAN Book Publishers, Inc.
616 Third Avenue
Chula Vista, CA 91910
619 / 425-8945

Table Of Contents

Chapter One

From Houston To Conroe

The flight from Caracas had been uneventful. A strong tailwind had decreased our usual flying time by half an hour. I decided to ride into Houston by limousine and not wait for my prearranged ride. Enroute my mind roamed into the recesses of the past. I was in a pensive mood brought about by recent happenings.

The limousine stopped at the west entrance of the Mullen Tower. Five passengers made their exit while I sat immobile and completely impervious to my surroundings. I have been in a veritable trance during the thirty minute ride from the airport.

"Where to sir?" asked the driver. His query startled me, bringing me back to reality. I quickly opened the door and emerged tipping him generously, then entered the building.

"What was the matter with me today?" I asked myself as the bank of elevators were there before me. I punched the "up" button. As the doors opened on the thirty-first floor, I was suddenly gripped by a weird feeling I was somewhere else until I saw before me the sign on the frosted glass: "Hugh McCulloch Enterprises." That was my name and I was opening my office door seeing the smiling face of my secretary, Diana Krist. She gave me her usual cordial greeting.

"Welcome back, how were things in Venezuela, Mr. McCulloch?"

"Everything is straightened out Diana, the government accounts are now up-to-date."

Diana was very efficient, possessing many of the attributes that capture attention. Men especially noticed her eyes first—they were a special hazel color reminding me of a mellow, ripe apple. Her hair was always perfectly coiffured, these were the things that merited first notice when Diana was sitting. If she was standing the attention centered on her figure. It could not be regarded casually, it demanded and received a second and third appraisal. If her body was draped in a potato bag, she would still exude the essence of Haute cöuture. Along with all these assets, her presence activated dormant glands in old men, and started their juices flowing. She was an asset to my firm, and the only employee ever causing me to question the sagacity of my iron clad rule of never seeking solace, or hanky panky from or with an employee.

Her welcome and sincerity coupled with the lilt in her voice could be likened to the tinkle of the silver servants bell.

Damn, it was hard to be businesslike with her.

"I could have used your presence to soften up the crusty, hard sell bastards I was dealing with. But all in all, everything went as anticipated. I hope you managed to keep your army of suitors at a respectable distance while I was away."

I hurried on before she answered in the negative, while she called out, "Mr. Harry Benbow has been trying to contact you the last two days. He left a number where you may call him."

I wended my way to my private office, taking the direct route to avoid any conversation with my legal secretary, Penelope Herring, whose office was situated about fifty feet from the entrance. It wasn't that I did not like Penelope, but just a feeling that was encompassing me, a desire to get into my office, close the door, meditate and review the events of the past few days.

I swiveled the executive chair around, letting myself down into the soft confines of its comfort. I found myself surveying the office as if I'd never seen it before. My eyes first gazed intently at Audrey's portrait, she seemed more beautiful and desirable than ever. The genuine Ming vase enhanced the painting above it, "Heaven in Waiting"—the Heaven being a voluptuous nude woman sitting side view with her knees drawn-up with her chin resting on them; an expression of longing had been captured perfectly in her eyes. I had often wondered what she was longing for, but had never settled on any acceptable condition. Her breasts did not project outward, but upward and I'd always believed the artist was trying to convey some message to all who beheld the painting.

As I surveyed my surroundings, my thoughts began to unravel into the distant past. Some mental force within started exerting a feeling of guilt through my whole being, an inner voice told me my conscience was taking over my thoughts. This I did not want as I had always been an entrepreneur, a brigand, and would cheat to gain my end and could always rationalize any action that I committed to further my gains.

Maybe this feeling was an aftermath of my last meeting with Carmen Bolivar in Cabimos, truly a night to remember, just eight years ago. Perhaps just carrying the pouch containing the bark of the Cauca tree had an effect on my thinking, but she had said to chew a small portion of it. I recall her words vividly; they were words of wisdom.

"Life is a procession of problems; the struggle we know as life, sometimes overpowers our will to fight. Having your past pass in review will help you face the future, and will clear the mind; your problems will have become less of a burden."

If ever anyone needed to clear their mind it was me and right now! Everything else Carmen Bolivar had told me was true, by God! I'd find out about this Cauca bark!

I took the pouch from my pocket, removed an inch long piece of the bark and started chewing it slowly.

Almost instantly the thought occurred to inform Diana to not accept any calls or disturb me until told to do so. This I did as I continued to chew the bark.

My lips were beginning to tingle slightly, the design on the vase across the room began to appear with the clarity of being magnified.

A feeling of total relaxation overcame me and I suppose I went to sleep. I do not know the state I was in, except I had no control over my mind. I drifted into

THE PAST—THE PAST—the past—the past—.

The day was a hot summer day and I had awakened with the thought of getting Harry Benbow and going to the swimming hole. After a breakfast of hot biscuits soaked in coffee, then covered with milk gravy, I dressed in my denim shirt and bib overalls turned up to my knees.

I purloined two onions, some bacon, and a can of pork and beans from our cupboard, and headed for Harry's house.

Harry had the chore of milking each morning, so I sat on a bale of hay while he kneaded the teats of old Bess. He could really make that milk squirt, and occasionally he'd tilt a tit in my direction, giving me an eye full, while I, in turn, would punch the cow in the flanks. She'd kick like hell, and switch her tail, stinging Harry's face. One time we were cavorting like this and the cow kicked the almost full pail of milk over. We watched it disappear into the hay on the ground, as a result, Harry got a licking so we eased up on the horse play for awhile.

The creek we swam in was about two miles north of town. We followed a sandy road for about a mile and a half, then left the road crossing at Mr. William's farm, then onwards through some woods to the swimming hole. In the summer before noon, the cool sand of the road was such a pleasant balm to bare feet, as we'd walk along in the ruts with eyes keen as a hawk's, observing everything that moved—be it a bird, snake, lizard or horned toad. We'd leave the road to cross Mr. William's farm with an ulterior motive in mind. He grew the most fabulous, largest, sweetest watermelons in the world. Viewed with boyish elan they appeared to be at least a yard long. It required quite a bit of strength and determination to convey one of them for almost a mile to the creek, it was tossed in the water for two or three hours to cool, during which time we were enjoying a swim. We'd convince ourselves the melons were ice cold, then break them open. Being of such size and usually having two of them, we'd only eat the heart, and discard the remainder. Later in the afternoon we'd build a fire and cook our grub, usually consisting of fried potatoes mixed with chopped onions, and pork and beans with bacon. Most times we'd bring fishing lines and hooks, catching grasshoppers for bait on the way. We'd catch small perch about three inches long, string them, and by the end of the day they were as dry as beef jerky. I'd take mine home to fry, always with my mother expostulating, concerning the odor resulting from my fouling up the kitchen. But when done, to me, they were more to be desired than Trout Almandine at Antoine's in New Orleans!

Mr. Williams devoted a lot of time and labor to produce his melons for the purpose of selling them, with no thought of donating them to anyone. He had seen evidence several times of our forays into his patch and did not relish the idea of us helping ourselves to the best watermelons in the field. It was always our quest to seek out the largest ones, give them the thump test to see if they were ripe.

The melons were always planted between rows of corn, the corn providing a suitable cover of our nefarious operation, thus swiping melons became a conquest as well as being tasty eating.

The finger of fate pointed to us one sunny hot morning on the way to the swimming hole. We were in the watermelon patch, tromping around oblivious to everything but our search for two of the largest ones. We were bending over when farmer Williams, seated in some tall grass at the end of the row partially concealed, resorted to effective action in stopping the pilferage of his melons. He had armed himself with a 410 gauge shotgun, equipped with some shells that he had extracted the lead pellets from, then packed the vacancy with salt bacon. Fate was with me as he selected Harry's boyish rump for his target in lieu of mine. As Harry was bending over, the seat of his overalls were stretched as tight as a drumhead. Mr. Williams fired both barrels at the cheeks of Harry's butt and scored a bull's-eye. We departed swiftly not caring to be slowed with the burden of a melon.

When we reached the swimming hole, Harry could hardly wait to appraise the results of being shot in the rump with the fat meat. He peeled off his clothing surveying the effects of farmer William's marksmanship—he had scored "expert"—as Harry's butt had two big blisters, red as a morning rose! He hurriedly dived in the pool to cool-off his rear.

We sought other locations for melons, but there were none in the area that were accessible due to location. All the melon patches we scouted after Harry's "hot seat," were in close proximity to the grower's house, and usually in full view of the grower and a dog or two.

We were living in a small town in Central Texas that boasted a population of about twenty-five hundred. The populace being reliant on one of three vocations for a living: railroading, bootlegging, or farming. I'd say the three activities supported approximately eight hundred people each.

In September, of the last year we lived there, a carnival had set up in what could be considered a park—along with various rides, they were presenting a rodeo, complete with bucking broncos, wild bulls, and a motley array of so called cowboys. The rodeo performed afternoon and night, so Harry and I could find no valid reason to attend school during that week, lest it interfere with the important work we had assumed with the rodeo. We had been given the privilege of feeding the spirited horses, the mean, vicious bulls, and cleaning up the manure in the walkways surrounding the arena. We performed our duties with alacrity, being paid each afternoon with four passes each. We were given carte blanche privilege to enter and leave as we desired.

We sold the passes easily for twenty-five cents apiece. We were not only occupying a status station in the other kids eyes, we were in the money!

The carnival dismantled on the weekend and departed. Harry and I were facing an old maid school principal Monday morning. I could hardly sleep Sunday night, having seen the result of this principal's ire on several occasions. Playing "hookey" was considered a capital crime by her standards. Her usual procedure in dealing with miscreants, bordered on the sadistic, as it resulted in the usual six to eight swats on the rump with a perforated white pine paddle, one half inch thick, and twenty inches long. If there were more than one to receive the punishment, she brought them into her office as a group, so that the poor bastard whaled first would present an eye-popping scene to the rest waiting their turn. Harry and I compared our polka dot butts in the restroom at recess, having had "the works."

♠ ♠ ♠

At midterm my family relocated in Houston, due to the railroad transferring of my Dad. We were not familiar with the Houston area but did locate a suitable home on Nance Street in the fifth ward, this was the "Hells Kitchen" of the city. The area was inundated with guys who roamed the streets in wolf packs preying on any hapless individual they encountered. Fights, muggings, and hijackings were their forte.

When we moved there, I was a bull of a lad for my age, having attained a stature of six feet and weighing 180-pounds on my sixteenth birthday. It might be assumed that these attributes would or should insulate me against kids my age testing my macho appearance, but not so!

The first day at school I was put to "the test." During lunch period, a "hoodlum" had one of his cronies get on his hands and knees behind me, as he gave me a forceful shove backward, tumbling me like a ten pin. My head bounced off the hard ground and was buzzing like a bumble bee for a moment or two.

When I rose, I realized the reckoning with this "one" was now! I made a pretense of brushing the dirt off apparently ignoring him, but I was not. I was moving a little closer to him with my head down while brushing my knees. When the toes of his shoes came into sight I shot a left uppercut just below his ribs that caused him to lean forward involuntarily, and then I hung a good solid right hook just below his ear. He was down like a poleaxed cow. I stood over him trying to look as fierce as possible while waiting for him to arise. He did not choose to, but instead said, "I'll get even with you." That ended the episode for the time being.

During the next two years, I had several such encounters but was always able to hold my own, and was regarded as a fellow who could take care of himself in a brawl. The word got around that I was pretty tough to handle, so my problems diminished as my reputation as a street fighter grew.

Harry Benbow came down to visit me and to put me on to a job. I had dropped out of high school and had been working for a truck sales and service firm, but I was restless and unhappy. Therefore I was very receptive to the idea Harry presented to me.

He had also dropped out of school, and had been working in the oil field around Kilgore as a roughneck. We went back to that area to seek work on an oil rig. We got a room in a two story hotel in Kilgore that had been hastily constructed, as evidenced by the cracks in the walls. It was a real orange-crate building and harbored a gamut of humanity. One could hear conversation occurring in the next room, it certainly was not the Adolphus or Baker hotels in Dallas.

Two days after arriving, we met a "pore boy" operator whose quest was conning enough men to make up two crews, so he could work a location on which he had an option to drill. His offer, in lieu of wages, was room and board, and part interest in the well when and if we brought it in. Being a gambler at heart, and playing a hunch I accepted his deal as did Harry.

That afternoon the five of us forged our way into the piney woods about three miles west of Pistol Hill. We found what passed for a rig scattered in disarray over an acre of pine trees. Only one man in our gang had experience building a rig so he automatically became the foreman, we all pitched in to erect the derrick under his supervision.

♦ ♦ ♦

His name was Scat Henderson, a two-fisted, whiskey drinking, hard working fellow. We all liked him and as a result had the derrick up in ten days. The man we were all working for was a crafty, conniving character who had a lot of traits associated with coyotes. He did not have a truck, nor any money to rent one as he sold a piece of the "sky" to the farmer, who owned the land we were drilling on, for use of a team of mules and wagon when needed.

We erected a rotary drill, and the topic of discussion among the crew was usually concerning the true owner of the rig. We were all guessing when the real owner would come to lay claim on it.

We worked twelve hour shifts, and after two days we noticed the absence of any rock bits. We knew somewhere around eighteen hundred feet we would get into a harder formation and rock bits would become necessary. The boss took leave the third day of drilling, saying he would see us in a couple of days.

Our crew was eating in a boarding house run by Mrs. Gentry. She set a good table of solid food but nothing fancy. She stood at one end of the long table, with arms akimbo, surveying the many hands reaching for this and that while we carried on with a constant banter of frivolous conversation.

One morning I was spiking the butter rather generously on the hot biscuits when she pointed her finger at me like a 38 pistol and said, "Hugh, that butter cost me forty-five cents a pound."

"Yes, and it's worth every damn cent of it," I retorted, helping myself to another sizeable chunk.

She was a very pleasant sort of person who always maintained her composure in spite of the kidding and verbal jibes we directed at her. On this particular occasion, she lost her temper as a result of Harry's ensuing remark, "Mrs. Gentry, I hope no one yells whoa, as I'm swallowing a bite of this meat for fear it may stop and choke me."

This bit of teasing from Harry prompted her to ask, "When is that shifty boss of you all going to be back? He promised me some money for you guys eating here, but so far I have not received a cent." Her voice had a caustic tone.

Suddenly the raillery ceased and silence came down on us like a heavy blanket. There was one thing we feared more than all else . . . going hungry. If she did kick us away from the table, who'd feed us?

Scat tried to dissipate the tenuous position we were in by an attempt at bolstering her confidence in our boss. He pointing out that he was a man of his word who was held in high esteem, a person of unquestionable character and completely reliable. We thought that perhaps he was outlining the traits of Saint Paul, rather than our employer! At least it nullified some of the doubt existing in Mrs. Gentry, about the continuance of our eating there. She remarked, "Okay boys, but if he doesn't come across with money by Saturday, you can find somewhere else to eat."

This assured us of five more days of three meals a day. It also filled each of us with a determination to arrive at some concrete solution to the problem as soon as the boss put in his appearance. We had to have a showdown with him.

He appeared Wednesday morning, emerging from the piney woods like a swamp mist. The mist being formed by his steaming Model A Ford. This fellow had the conscience of a hyena—but the charm of a peacock, and his very being presented an amazing paradox. He was over six-feet, about 200-pounds of deceit, muscle, and agile brain. Even in the field he was always the very essence of sartorial splendor. This morning he came draped in a navy pin stripe suit, cowboy boots, very expensive ones—a Texas style, ten-gallon hat that shaded a craggy, rugged face showing tell tale creases that it had been lived in. His appearance brought about the same effect as the ring master delivering the first crack of his whip opening the circus.

This man was an enigma—he was unbelievable as he strode to the derrick floor to survey the activity, and greet us all with an amiable bellow. His smile exposed a broad expanse of even white teeth that would defang a diamondback rattler. But this morning I was committed to settling my status as regarded the immediate future, before he could overwhelm my intentions with his fatal persuasive line of bull.

"Hey, Hugh!" He yelled above the noise of the clanking machinery. "Go out to the car and bring those tri-cone bits." I gestured Harry to come with me. We found three rock bits on the floor of the car, causing Harry to comment, "Wonder where he stole these?" We got back to the derrick floor with the bits, then I bored right in on the subject of Mrs. Gentry's attitude regarding some money. He assured us that he would pay her today, naturally we believed him. Then Scat hit him with the bombshell.

"Boss, we're out of drill pipe, and unless we're going to abandon we've gotta have some, today for sure."

We were all watching the reaction at this bit of disturbing information, as we were all aware that he was "pore boying" this well.

The boss methodically lifted a pack of Lucky Strikes from his vest pocket, extracted one, poked it between his lips and turned a big smile on the crew. After striking a match with a sweeping stroke on the rear of his pant leg, lighting the cigarette, he inhaled deeply, then expelled the smoke from his nostrils, all the while smiling and thinking. The whole scenario was fascinating.

Here was a man head-to-head with a dilemma that would confound anyone else, but he was smiling as if we'd just brought in a gusher.

"Don't panic fellows, we'll have the drill pipe later today. I'll be back around five so you guys stay put," he stated in a matter-of-fact tone, then wheeled, heading for his car.

When he was out of hearing distance Roy said, "Ole Houdini will perform today by snatching drill pipe out of the air. Step right up folks and see this feat of magic. Lookee—Lookee."

The past two weeks had found me thinking constantly of an easier way of life than working like hell on a derrick floor. Besides I'd almost lost a finger in the chain tongs. That near accident accelerated my thinking greatly.

I had been going up and down the streets aimlessly, being jostled by the teeming human flotsam, as I made my way to different hotels, to observe what was transpiring. My observations had revealed that buying and selling leases was an easy life style, requiring no hard manual labor. So, I began to pay close attention to the activities of the "lease hounds." I had determined that if we brought in a well, I would gamble my proceeds in the leasing endeavor, hoping to hit it big. My observations were all conducted at night, the town of Kilgore was teeming with a plethora of humanity composed of lawyers, roughnecks, whores, pimps, bankers, and robbers. It was a veritable cauldron of activity spiced with fights, shooting and robberies.

This night Harry and I were trying to worm our way through the throng of humanity that clogged the board walk and filled the muddy street, with the hope we could get into the movie located in the center of town. Harry was walking on the inside to my left, as a lady of the night suddenly appeared beside Harry and clutched him by his arm. After two or three steps she asked, "Are you boys looking for a good time?" With an effected drawl Harry responded, "How much you want Honey, for that good time?"

"Five dollars."

"Hells Bells! I don't mean I want to buy it, I meant just to use it awhile." The repartee was terminated as quickly as it had begun.

"You're a cheap bastard," was her parting shot as she reversed directions and was lost in the crowd.

We eventually were in front of the theater and quickly decided that the line waiting for admission was too long to wait out, so we returned to the hotel.

Awaiting our arrival was "Houdini," the boss and the rest of our crew. Before I could ask, what's up? The boss spoke softly, "Boys, I'm sorry I did not get back when I said I would this afternoon, but I was taking care of business. I paid Mrs. Gentry up-to-date for your eats, and I've made arrangements for the drill pipe we need to bring this hole in."

I asked, "When do we get it?"

"Tonight. You fellows get in the car and we will go get it now. I've been waiting on you so let's get going."

We all piled into the Model A Ford and there were five minds in tandem on the thought—where in the hell were we going to get pipe at night?

We drove to the rig and as the headlights probed the dark we could see two teams of mules tied to a pine tree, about fifty feet from the rig. I thought maybe he is replacing us with mules, and had to chuckle as I expressed my thought to the others. We unloaded and stood around as Roy shot this query, "What's with the mules, Boss?"

"Well, I'll tell you. That rig Humble moved in over there last week saved our bacon. I had a talk with their field superintendent today and he told me they were not going to get started for another two weeks. So I made a deal with him to loan us twenty-five joints for no more than ten days, then we would return it before they need it. I had to grease his palm with some oil coupons to make everything okay—let's get going."

I had never been nearer a mule than when I was a kid shoveling manure for the rodeo, so I wasn't about to attempt to handle them. Each pair was hitched to a double tree with about twenty-five feet of logging chain attached. The boss untied one pair asking, "Who can handle mules?"

Roy silently reached for the reins, got the team in motion and headed for the Humble Oil location about a fourth of a mile distant. The boss untied the remaining pair and followed in the same direction. He was a ludicrous sight urging those mules through the dark woods, with that ten-gallon hat riding high on his head and dressed in a blue business suit.

We all had misgivings, that perhaps, we were accessories to perfidy or the outright theft of the drill pipe, but dismissed it from our minds as we were perfectly in accord with pilfering the pipe to finish the well. We simply didn't wish to be caught in the act of theft.

We made six round trips, dragging the pipe through the woods as the mules snorted and strained against the load behind them. Limbs from brush and small pines stung our faces and bodies as we continued the hairy adventure. It was a hell of a lot of work for both the mules and all of us.

"Hold it boys!"

We all froze as headlights near our rig were making a sweep of light as a car turned full circle, but drove away in the direction of town. We dumped the last string of pipe heaving a sigh of relief when we learned that it was Roy who had warned us.

The next morning we started using the borrowed drill pipe, and during the next three days made good depth.

About two in the afternoon, on the third day, we began to get odors of gas, and at four o'clock the hole started bubbling gas and traces of oil. It was then that we felt sure of a payoff for our hard work.

We all remained on the rig, even when the night crew came on, to see her come in. At six thirty she started blowing gas, rocks and debris about thirty-feet high with a rumbling like an empty stomach as the column of black gold shot over the foble board. She was in! We danced, jumped, flailed our arms, shouted cheers, obscenities and thanks as the shiny liquid cascaded down upon us. We were in the money, the elan of the group was boundless, having made it at last.

We choked the flow of oil with the Christmas tree, and congratulated ourselves on our good fortune. About nine o'clock the boss drove up, leaping from his car like a frog diving from a log. He ran to the derrick floor, face beaming with glee and satisfaction, hugging each of us and getting oil all over his clothing. He was a likeable scoundrel, as he stood there oily, but satisfied with the world.

"Okay fellows, in the morning we will have a settlement, a legal settlement of all that is due to you. You've worked hard and stuck with me, you'll be given the alternative of our original agreement, a share of the production, or a cash-out. The choice will be yours to make, so think it over tonight. We'll meet at First National Bank at nine o'clock. Good night and thanks for a job well done," with that he offered us a ride to the hotel, making two trips to do so.

On the way in, my mind kept remembering the night we transferred the pipe from Humble. My concern centered on the car that had turned around at the rig as we approached the area with the last of the pipe, I had a nagging fear that something bad would come out of that venture.

As we alighted from the car, at the hotel, I nodded to Harry to follow me. We walked away a few steps and I commented, "Harry, we 've been friends a long time, I'd like to give you some advice. As you know that Texas Ranger they sent in here to restore law and order, is still around and he's a tough, persistent cookie. He has the reputation of sniffing out lawbreakers, stepping on them like a bug. Now I've been thinking about that pipe. It could've been "Lone Wolf" Gonzaulles out snooping around that night at the rig. If you're not familiar with him, let me inform you. He is the most feared lawman in the Texas Rangers. If it was him, we'd better get a cash settlement in the morning and get the hell away from here."

"Okay that suits me. I'm ready to get the hell outa here for a change of scenery. Where are you going, back to Houston?"

"I'm going into leasing and try to run whatever we get from the well into some real big money. Want to join me?"

Harry studied the light over our hotel entrance as if it could provide him with an answer to my question, then replied, "Hugh, I think I'll go back home, at least for awhile. You know where to write me if you get on to something big. Let's turn in, so we can be alert and ready to bargain in the morning."

We were prepared the next morning to joust with "Houdini" for what we considered a fair settlement—to cash-out for our labor rather than accept a share of the production.

Mrs. Gentry was in a jovial mood at breakfast, greeting us with, "Come in, you two, the others are waiting for you just as one dog waits for another. If you millionaires make haste maybe you can at least get a biscuit before they eat everything in sight."

"By golly, Mrs. Gentry, that's something you seldom see," Harry snickered.

"What's that?" she asked, with her hands on her hips and her arms bent outwards, looking Harry straight in the eye.

He darted by her planting himself on the bench at the table before replying, "A horse tird in a garage."

We all laughed, that is, all but Mrs. Gentry. She was furious but amused at the same time. She eventually joined us in the laughter, dismissing the incident with a wave of her arm, and departing for the kitchen to bring in more food. She was a gem and we were all very fond of her.

Harry and I were the only ones leaving town as the rest of the crew had decided to remain in Kilgore. As we finished our breakfast we bade her good-bye, good luck and we both received a friendly hug in return.

A bright sun was searing everything that moved as we approached the bank at nine o'clock. The boss was awaiting our arrival, mopping his brow when he sighted us. His face was split with that genial smile which was his usual custom when greeting anyone. I suspected that smile had conned many a man to part with his money, and many a woman to discard any opposition to whatever he might have proposed. He was a rake, as well as a scoundrel, and this financial settlement was being considered with a great deal of determination on my part. I would bargain relentlessly for the amount Harry and I had agreed was a fair an equitable settlement for our portion of the proceeds. That figure was seven thousand each.

Before we started discussing the business at hand, on the board walk, the sheriff with another man, passed our group without much scrutiny—just passing a glance as they went by. The sheriff's companion was of medium height and dark complexioned. He wore a five-gallon Texas style hat pulled low over his brow. His two dark piercing eyes scanned our group in a fleeting second, but I sensed he had missed nothing with those hawk eyes. His left trouser leg was tucked inside a cowboy boot which had the outline of Texas embroidered in red thread on the side. The pistol he was wearing was a part of his movement, riding his hip as if it came into this life with him.

Cold fear chilled the nape of my neck as I realized we had just passed their scrutiny real fast and catch the next bus or train out—which ever came first! I heaved a sigh of relief as he and the sheriff were lost in the crowd and no longer in sight.

It was then I took my first thrust to start the bargaining.

"Boss, Harry and I are willing to forfeit any and all rights to any production of the well for seven thousand apiece."

He studied me without any emotion for fully one minute—it was vis"—a—vis—eyeball, then replied, "How do you want it, cash or check?"

He acquiesced so quickly that it required a great effort on my part to conceal my surprise. Damn! Maybe we sold-out too cheaply. He agreed so readily, it was too easy—had we been conned? This possibility raced through my mind. He had completely disarmed my plan of action—my determination to put up a tough bargain. Nevertheless, I felt I still carried the offense.

"Get us a cashiers check for $6,500 and $500 in cash. Okay?"

He turned toward the bank door saying over his shoulder, "Wait right here."

We stood sweating profusely in the hot sun awaiting his return. Harry sidled up to me asking, "Did we do the right thing, or did we get screwed?"

"If he doesn't return with the checks and cash, we can say we were screwed without benefit of a kiss, how's that?"

Almost ten minutes had elapsed, secretly I was wondering if the bank had a rear exit and he had left us holding the bag. Not so.

He emerged from the bank with that damn smile beaming, as I reminded myself that I never did trust a man that smiled too much. I always had the feeling the smile was like the warehouse cat's as he cuffed the mouse around, and I was the mouse.

"Here you are fellows, it's been my good fortune to have met-up with both of you. It's a pleasure to give you this. If you're not staying I'll say good-bye and good luck." He handed Harry and me each a cashier's check in the amount of sixty-five hundred dollars and ten fifty dollar bills.

I scrutinized the check quickly to ascertain it was valid, and recounted the ten fifties—my fears were allayed as all was in order. Harry and I shook hands and departed in the direction of the bus station.

The ticket seller informed me the bus to Houston was in and would load in five minutes. Harry had a two hour wait, so the next few minutes were used in the usual procedures as two friends part.

The four hour journey to Houston was spent with my thoughts presenting a kaleidoscopic pattern of things past, present and what I was planning to do in the future. It was difficult for a young man used to earning around twenty dollars a week, to direct his rationale and/or discretion properly while sitting on seven thousand dollars. That much money presented many possibilities as to its use, and my character being saturated with all the foibles that beset those of us that are subject to infirmities of character, enabled me to reach one decision before departing the bus in the Houston terminal.

I was going to purchase a prestige automobile to use as a tool to impress the subjects of my devious plans for the future. I hailed a cab, directing the driver to head south on Travis as there were several auto dealers on that street.

The cab had traveled about ten blocks as I scanned the passing scene. Suddenly, there it was! On the front of the dealers auto display was parked the answer to my boyhood dreams—the apex of automobiles! In my opinion it was my "golden fleece" and I knew that I would end my quest here and now, by buying it.

"Stop here driver," I barked.

My elation was so great I gave the cabbie a generous tip, the sum of one dollar. I hastened to the car lot, touching the gleaming white hood as lightly and tenderly as a pickpocket plying his trade. The white Cord Sport Phaeton had me completely entranced as I surveyed its elegance. Never had I seen red as exciting as the leather upholstery, nor chrome as brilliant as its adornments. The beautiful machine being inanimate, still was comparable to a sprinter in the starting blocks, poised, with muscles taut, ready to spring into action. The car was so perfect it was having a hypnotic effect on my senses when I was rudely returned to reality with, "How do you like it?"

The spell was broken, I was ready to deal, "Is it second hand?"

"Yes, but it's had excellent care, as you can see. You may know this car has front wheel drive, there were not too many of them made."

I came back, "How much?"

He pursed his lips, jammed both hands in his pockets, rocking back on his heels as if preparing to donate a thousand dollars to his favorite charity.

"Tell you what, we will let her go for three thousand, five hundred, and we won't call the police on you for stealing it."

I was surprised it was not higher, but exerted effort to conceal my surprise by strolling around the car slowly, then asked, "Anything wrong with it?"

"Hell no," he chortled, "I'd run her in the Indy 500 just as she sits. And I'll tell you something else, it's the only one like it in this whole cotton pickin' town. You can bet on that."

As I stood in the September sun considering the situation, my mind was wheeling, reviewing the good things this white front wheel drive Cord could make possible for me.

It would lend an air of success to my being. Then too, the rear seat would serve as an excellent "work bench" when I succeeded in persuading some female part with her virginity. This car would be my "Argo"—the means to embark upon my quest of fame and fortune.

"I will take it."

"Fine. Shall we go in the office and take care of the paperwork?" He asked as we directed our steps toward the dealers showroom. I was aware one must be at least twenty-one to consummate a legal purchase of an automobile in Texas, so I evaded that obstacle by calculating my date of birth two years earlier, as I was only nineteen. It worked.

The sales manager then asked, "Do you want us to arrange financing, or do you have a preference of a finance company?"

"I will pay cash," putting the cashiers check on his desk as he was trying unsuccessfully to conceal surprise at my reply. He gave the check a skeptical survey, checking every detail, then after a minute or two, he broke the silence by asking, "Do you object to me calling the bank in Kilgore? No offense intended, but do you realize we are involved for more than the car, as we will be giving you a check for three grand, in addition to a bill of sale on the Cord."

I replied, "Go right ahead, call the bank. No offense intended, but do you object to my calling your bank in reference to the check you'll be giving me?"

"Not at all. Here's the phone, the check will be on this bank," he pushed a business checkbook toward me, pointing to the bank's name.

The check was verified by the bank in Kilgore, and I produced identification. The dealer's check was also okay.

I wheedled a full tank of gas from them and planted myself in the luxurious driver's seat, scanning the beautiful dash punctuated with dials, meters and lights. I thought I was surely seeing a Jules Vern creation there before me.

♠ ♠ ♠

For a kid educated on the streets—nursed to manhood on borderline poverty—street fights on the daily menu, turning the switch to on and hearing the throaty roar of the powerful engine as it responded, was indeed a heady experience as I drove on the street.

I cruised a few blocks, but narrowly had a collision at an intersection due to my constant surveying of the car's interior as I gloated over its beauty. And it was mine!

I drove to the bank, cashed the dealer's check and as I returned to the car my mind was massed with a galaxy of thoughts. Phase one of my life's plan had become reality—this car, a stake of over three thousand dollars, plus indefatigable determination, would launch me toward the second phase of my obsession to become rich and powerful.

I made it to a men's clothiers just before closing. I emerged wearing a charcoal grey suit, new black shoes, a white shirt with french cuffs, and a maroon polka-dot tie. It was the first suit I had ever worn, my confidence soared as I viewed myself in the three way mirror.

Eating a steak at Kelley's across from the Rice Hotel was another of my boyhood dreams. Awaiting the order of their largest steak was indeed gratifying.

The patrons were all people of financial means and were frequent habitues of this dining place. Some were lined-up at the oyster bar, and a ribald group of oil men were gulping the oysters between insults, creating an atmosphere of camaraderie that only they possessed.

Scattered at random were couples at tables located in semi-darkness—the darkness being an ally to the probing hands checking-out the thighs of some of the female companions. The conversation was muted and my ears could pickup very little of the talk around me. I did intercept one bit of juicy repartee directly behind me, as the man seated there with a companion, got up to leave, saying, "Honey, here's the key. I'm in room 315, allow me ten minutes, then come-on over."

One of the group, at the oyster bar, evidently had been drinking for sometime, as he was very noisy and boisterous. He greeted a crony entering the door with, "Come in here, Bill. How's my short peckered friend?"

He was extending a hairy hand when Bill replied, "Sounds like your wife's been gossiping again."

They all guffawed, switching the conversation to oil wells, locations, dry holes and the usual terminology associated with the industry.

As I ate I made a vow to myself that soon I would become a part of all that surrounded me, and they would be greeting "Hugh" as he made his entry. The meal was great. I paid my check by accenting every gesture getting my roll of bills from my pocket and searching for one small enough to cover the tab. The cashier was blase about the size of my bankroll by not noticing it.

Just as I was passing the oyster bar the fellow who had greeted Bill stepped back, not seeing me, planting his heel directly on my right foot, and it hurt like hell. He turned quickly and apologized profusely for being so clumsy, then held out his hand saying, "I'm Joe Bob Miller."

I shook his hand noticing he had a good friendly grip. "I am Hugh McCulloch, it's a pleasure to meet you."

"You in the oil business?" he asked.

"I've been working on drilling rigs."

"Man, you ought to get where the money is, in leasing."

I was elated and said, "Strange you would say what I have planned to do for sometime."

"Where you headed to now?"

"Well," I paused, "I had really started out to Missouri City to see if they were still running the crap game as I feel lucky."

He laughed, "Hell Boy, I can tell you they are still running it because I lost six hundred to the bastards last night. I'd like to go and get it back. My car is parked a half block away, let's get going."

"Just a minute, Joe Bob, how about going in my car, it's right outside."

"Suits me," he replied and we headed for the door. When we reached my white Cord with the top down I said, "Here we are."

"What the Hell! You mean to tell me this is yours?"

"Yep, bought it this afternoon."

I told him about the well I'd worked on in Kilgore as we rolled out South Main to Missouri City. The motion of the car stirred a small breeze. It was very refreshing as the night was hot and humid. Joe Bob remarked he wished he had this sports car in lieu of his damn closed up Cadillac.

We reached the crap game in a few minutes, crowding-up to the table, like horses getting to the feed trough. I looked around at the fifteen or so players to see if I knew anyone there, I did not.

We played until four a.m. I was four thousand ahead, Joe Bob about fifteen hundred, when I suggested we quit while ahead.

On the way back Joe Bob said, "Kid, I like your style and I'm going to make you a proposition you can't turn down.

"Try me," I answered.

"It's this way. I'm a geologist, I work for a major oil company but I won't say which one. You say you want to get into the "lease hound" game. If you're as smart as I think you are, I can get you in, in a big way. First let me warn you if you do throw-in with me and ever get cold feet or talk too much, then we would both end-up in that "cross bar hotel" in Huntsville."

I needed no enlightenment about Huntsville, it being the location of the state's main prison, maximum security.

He continued, "We have been doing a lot of surveying and "shooting"—seismology around Conroe. I'm in a position to know where the hot locations are, and will be. Do you follow me?"

I thought to myself, here's a likeable, larcenous, character tailor made for a partner in any nefarious venture. He's established a rapport with me, during the past few minutes, that tells me he fits into my devious schemes like a carburetor for a car.

"Yes, I follow you. It's sounding like a perpetual grant from the Ford Foundation every minute you speak, so keep talking, Joe Boy."

"It will take some money, how much dough can you raise? I'll match what you have, then we'll split 50/50. How do you like that deal?"

"Say no more—count on me. I can cough up six grand. I sure hope that's enough, because your proposition is as interesting to me as a new comet to an astronomer."

"Okay Partner," he leaned over and shook my hand.

I was following his directions to his parked car, thinking over the words of the past few minutes. I thought, "Somebody up there likes me," to send this opportunity my way. The chance to get it made, or "made to get it," if we were detected!

His black Cadillac was parked at the curb, I pulled in behind it and stopped. We sat there a moment, then I could not wait any longer to fire the question.

"When do we start? What do I do? I'm green at this lease hound bit so you'll have to tutor me."

"There's nothing to it. All you do is go where I tell you, contact the owner of the land, drive as hard a bargain as possible, get the lease signed, then we or you rather, will peddle the lease at a higher price than we paid for it. If you're ready to go, meet me tomorrow morning at the courthouse in Conroe at eleven o'clock. We will go the bank and setup an account for your operation, then you'll hit the names and locations I give you. Here's a phone number, contact me everyday at five thirty p.m. and I will give you more prospects to run down. Oh yes, buy some khakis and boots as you'll be wading through mud, cow dung, dog shit, poison ivy, and hell knows what else in finding the owners you have to deal with. The success of the lease hound is dependent on getting there first, with the most! It's that simple, a lot of leg work, looking-up county records, then when you've got them cornered, you entice them with that motivator of all mankind, money! Another good weapon to have is a water pistol filled with ammonia, squirt it at the damn dogs that will be charging you. Now do you get the whole picture? Do you think you want to get into it?"

"I'll be there at eleven in the morning. Good night and thanks a million for offering me this start. You'll not regret taking me as a partner."

"See you in Conroe, partner!" I watched him drive away with the thought foremost in my mind, could I trust him?

Chaper Two
Reba And The Parrot Killer

I arrived in Conroe around six a.m., sleepy but happy as the Cord had performed in a magnificent manner. It was my first chance to let her out! I was proud of that car. Being the first time I had been in the business section, I found it necessary to circle the courthouse before locating an acceptable cafe, and parking directly in front.

I alighted from the Cord, stretching my arms above my head when I heard an interesting sound approaching me from the rear. The sound of a female walk, heels clicking lighting on the concrete walk. I turned to check her out. She surely associated my scrutiny with that of a judge at the county fair as he might stare intently, attempting to select the blue ribbon heifer.

Her smile telegraphed a message, and I turned one on that let her know she was attractive and very desirable. I almost leaped straight-up as I traversed the three steps to the sidewalk level to reach the door an instant ahead of this voluptuous, lovely specimen of femininity. Making an exaggerated bow, I opened the door with the utmost panache saying, "Good morning, Sunshine," she responded with the most delightful throaty chuckle, then followed with, "Do you know something? You're crazy, but I love it."

She entered the door with me forming an admiring entourage of one at her rear, while she walked to the back of the cafe. Her walk was something to behold. It was the emanation of graceful motion, as effortless as a bengal tiger bounding through the forest. The cheeks of her buttocks were alive as she walked, no vulgar swaying, just a fascinating undulation of the firm flesh. I must admit her appearance had filled my mind with a gamut of emotions plus some lurid mental scenes that were of a lascivious nature. She activated my juices as they had never been aroused. She was the one thing filling my thoughts as I sat at the counter awaiting her reappearance.

Picking-up a menu from the holder before me, I scanned it, really not seeing it, just holding it before me. My mind was centered on something more carnal than ham and eggs. My thoughts were centered on a close physical contact with her—a seduction! A lilting voice returned me to reality with, "Now Romeo, what will you have this nice morning?"

I gazed across the counter into the most arresting green eyes I had ever encountered, her impish smile made me tingle with pleasure as I admired the very sight of her. The honey-hued hair, sparkling green eyes and puckish smile had transformed me into a bumbling bumpkin. Momentarily I mumbled something garbled, but gathered my wits quickly assuming my urbane confident manner and asked, "What do you suggest, Sunshine?"

"I'd suggest you get your mind on the business at hand by giving me your order, Romeo. Incidentally is that your white car you are driving? It's a real beauty."

"Yes, it belongs to me and it has a vacant seat that you would add much elegance to by riding in it. When do we start?"

With that bit of kidding she smiled, turned and gave me a glass of water saying, "Here, this is almost all ice. Perhaps it will cool you off so you can give me your order."

"Okay, I'll have bacon, eggs, coffee and you for dessert." The order was given with what I hoped to be my most intriguing smile.

She returned in a few minutes with my food and another question, "Are you the lawyer for that fellow they call the Parrot Killer?"

"Honey, do I look like a lawyer? Who is this Parrot Killer?" She continued, "He's a young fellow about twenty, they're holding him in jail for murdering a woman, two nights ago. She was a fortune teller with the carnival that's here. They say this young man was the one that hacked her terribly with an axe. Talk about goofy people, some of the women are feeding him like he's royalty. I wouldn't get within a block of that jail. I thought you might be his lawyer, being dressed so nice, and driving that expensive automobile."

"Sounds like a horrible crime, but tell me, why do they call him the Parrot Killer?"

"The fortune teller worked in a tent with the carnival, she owned a beautiful parrot that sat on her shoulder as she plied her trade. When they discovered her dismembered body, the parrot was lying beside her torso, headless. So the news media has given him the sobriquet of the Parrot Killer."

"That seems to be placing more attention on him beheading the parrot, than the ghastly hacking of a human being like stovewood, don't you agree?"

Throughout this conversation I had been consuming my food, and as she attended other customers my eyes were on her constantly. The more I saw of her, the more entranced I became.

I suddenly realized I didn't know her name. Her smile was sincere, not a facade. The necessity of learning more about her involved facts like, marital status, name, and most important—if my efforts at being charming, disarming and available had succeeded in arousing any desire on her part to pursue the flirtation any further. I would soon establish my position, as soon as she returned to refill my cup with steaming coffee, by asking, "What time are you off work, do you have a big, bad, mean, husband, and what is your name?"

"I believe you're a lawyer from the way you ask questions," she laughed continuing, "I'm off at five, not married, however," she paused, "I don't make it a practice talking about personal subjects with strangers, but somehow you don't seem like a stranger.

If you're around at five we might go somewhere and continue getting acquainted, my name is Reba. What's your name?"

I arose to leave, pausing at the register to pay my check as she had moved to the register to accept payment. When she returned my change I gave her a two dollar tip, saying, "I will be here at five, and my name is Hugh McCulloch."

♠ ♠ ♠

There was a general store located in the same block. Their sign reminded me that some khaki clothes were in order which I purchased. I then sought a place to stay.

My attention centered on a hotel sign across the courthouse square and as I crossed the tree shaded area surrounding it, my appearance attracted much attention. The lawn was sprinkled with benches occupied by local nesters, drifters, and others just relaxing. Each surveyed me as I passed, nodding a silent salutation, but I could detect suspicion in several glances as I made my way to the Montgomery Hotel.

The clock on the First National Bank indicated nine a.m. as I entered the hotel lobby. Approaching the desk, the clerk, a woman who could portray a typical spinster in a Sherlock Holmes movie, was so engrossed in a book that my presence was not noticed. I peered to see the title, "The Grapes of Wrath."

I cleared my throat. She quickly closed the book and rose. "Oh! I didn't hear you, I am sorry." Her face flushed a cherry-red as she pushed the hotel registry to me.

"That's a potent book you're reading," I said.

"I was not reading it, only checking to see what author would write such trash."

I was feeling devilish, spearing her with the question, "If you were not reading it, then how do you know it's trash?" Her face was getting more crimson with each passing second as she snatched the register book from the desk, "You can have room 203. The rate is fifteen dollars per week. How long do you intend to be here?"

I laughed replying, "Indefinitely, but let's get back to the book. Did you find anything offensive about it?"

"I told you, I was not reading it."

"Come now, Priscilla, you know I can tell by your reaction you were reading it." I continued to puncture her prudish veneer for pure devilment.

"My name is not Priscilla, Mr.—, she paused as she glanced at the register, McCulloch, and for your information my name is Miss Maggie Lee Hawkins."

"Okay Miss Hawkins, if you do read the book will you promise to tell me if you liked the chapter relating Jodie's night in the hayloft with Lucy Bell?" With that parting shot, I picked-up the key and started for the stairs.

After changing to khakis, I left through the lobby heading for the courthouse lawn to kill time until Joe Bob would arrive, in approximately twenty minutes.

I stretched out on the grass beneath a huge gnarled oak tree, placed my hands under my head and watched the restless leaves above. I was feeling a warm glow of anticipation about my immediate future—the oil leasing with Joe Bob, and as usual my plans were made to use the present as a bridge for the future. The future that would bring me wealth and power!

The desire for financial power had become an obsession that could not be denied, my insatiable lust for money was the driving force behind my every act, my every thought. I would let nothing intervene or deter me from my goal. I would be recognized as an entity to be respected and catered to, by people seeking favors. Some day soon my name would be bandied about in the closed circles of the country club set and in the select, subdued atmosphere of the Petroleum Club.

As I lay there on the grass, I pictured myself sitting casually in the lobby of the Rice Hotel in Houston scanning the Wall Street Journal, and hearing the bell captain chanting "Call for Mr. McCulloch." My vision of this scene was so realistic, I could catch the scent of the expensive cigars. A sparrow terminated my reverie with his well placed droppings splattering on my forehead!

I was mopping the chalky white mess from my brow when Joe Bob drove his black Cadillac into a slot in front of the bank, and eased out from under the wheel. He saw me crossing the street to greet him, lifting a hand in recognition. As I approached him I was still mopping the sparrow's mess on my brow when he said, "Hey Kid, it's not that hot, you must be nervous." We shook hands and I related what had just occurred.

"Hot damn! Don't kid me Hugh. Tell me the truth. Did a bird really crap on you?"

"Hell, yes. That would be a weird tale to makeup now, wouldn't it?"

He chuckled, "Didn't you know that was a sign of good fortune ahead, when a bird craps on you. Was it a sparrow?"

"Of course it was a sparrow and he was a good shooter! He hit me right between the eyes!"

"Wonderful, you've heard the story about a sparrow saving Galileo's life, haven't you.

"They had the wood all piled around the stake and were leading him to the post when the bird flew over, letting go a white blob of crap that landed directly on his head. Man at that time was more superstitious than now, so the mob interpreted the bird droppings to be some sort of omen they hesitated to execute him for his abnormal beliefs at that time. Galileo must have thought it an omen too, as he recanted his teachings and was permitted to live."

I replied, "I know it was a sparrow as there were scores of them flitting around the trees. Let's get to the bank. I'm anxious to get going on my first million!"

We entered the bank, making our way to the first desk available. The chair was occupied by a pimply-faced fellow wearing a pained expression, as if his hemorrhoids were acting up. He asked in a squawky voice, "May I help you?"

Joe Bob answered, "We want to open an account." He nodded his gnome-like head in the direction of the desk across the lobby, as we introduced ourselves. We stated our reason for being there and sat down at his invitation.

I had often tried to guess just how long a banker practices that blank expression that all bankers project across the desk to clients. I've referred it as the "mackerel stare," as it is so very much like the expression in the eyes of one in a display case in a fish market. The way he was surveying us, one would think we had come to draw-out money with a pistol, rather than being there to deposit it.

"What kind of business are you gentlemen engaged in?" Joe Bob answered, "Leasing business, sir." After a little more explaining, we had transacted the whole operation in fifteen minutes, proving it's faster to get money into a bank, than to get it out.

Departing, Joe Bob suggested we have lunch. I was tempted to tell him about Reba, but declined lest he get the idea I had more play on my mind than work.

We selected another cafe. While eating, he gave me five names of landowners who were sitting on possible oil productions. This fact being established from seismograph results. He reviewed all he had told me the night before, repeating the phone number. Convinced I had it all straight, we walked to his car. As he was getting behind the wheel he said, "Remember Hugh, no one must ever know of my involvement in our business and if you should ever get the thought of revealing our association don't do it. What I told you last night about the strong and lasting retribution that would come down on you if you were ever that foolish. If I thought there was any possibility of that happening, we wouldn't be here now. I have confidence in your ability not to betray our trust. You're on your own now. Good luck, I know we'll make a lot of money. Call me tomorrow and everyday thereafter."

As he disappeared from view, I was suddenly hit with the realization that I was embarking upon a sea of responsibility—a journey that would end in success or failure—I was the captain of my fate.

♠ ♠ ♠

I located one of the landowners on the list that afternoon. His farm was about three miles east of Conroe, presenting no problem in finding it. As I drove up and parked beneath a large tree, a Doberman came bounding into the front yard and stopped, sitting on his muscular haunches as he appeared to be giving me a malevolent appraisal. I got out of the car, standing a few moments, trying to determine if he was friendly or aggressive, then walked normally toward him. He did not growl, bark, or make any movement as I drew nearer. I was beginning to view him with a bit of apprehension as I suddenly remembered I had not bought a water pistol as Joe Bob had recommended. With each step I took toward the brute, in a low plaintive manner, but could not tell if my attempts at making friends were getting a friendly reaction as he had no tail to wag. His eyes were boring into mine as unwavering and intently as staring at a portrait. He arose as I went about five feet from him still holding out my hand, snapping my fingers,

"Here boy." He was motionless until I reached a point equidistant from the porch, then he trotted over and fell beside me as I continued climbing the steps to the porch. As I knocked on the door he resumed his sitting stance and fastened his eyes on me once more.

I knocked very loudly the second time, then a lady appeared at the door peering at me through the screen with a slack-jawed expression, as if she was seeing a spirit—then asked, "How did you get on the porch?" I quickly turned my head to see if the steps were missing, or some other obstacle had been over looked, then answered, "Mrs. Henshaw, I just walked here from my car. Why do you ask?"

"My lord almighty man, that dog won't let anyone come on this porch." I glanced at the dog, "Well, he let me get up here, if he's that mean I surely hope he let's me leave in peace!" I tried to pass it off by stating, "You know the saying, Fools rush in, etc."

After stating my business, she told me where I could find her husband. He was about two miles down the road in a big metal barn, where a cockfight was in progress. She advanced the information that he raised game roosters to enter in fights as far away as Dallas. I thanked her, asking if she would object to keeping the Doberman in the house until I got into my car. This she did, making my breathing normal again.

The area around the barn was cluttered with vehicles: other pickups, trucks, model T Fords, various other cars, plus three wagons hitched to mules. I parked on the outer fringe, then entered the side door, or at least started to enter. I was confronted by a yokel as large as a Clydesdale horse, who inquired in a not too friendly tone, "Who the hell are you, and what do you want here?" The din coming from the crowd clustered around the pit was almost deafening, as they egged the bird to kill the other.

I'll never know what there was about this bastard who had intercepted me, to create such rage within, but the urge to knock him down surged through me like an electrical current. I shot a hard right to his jaw, followed by chopping down with my left on the bridge of his nose. He reeled back three or four steps shaking his big head while bellowing like a Hereford bull, trying to get his vision back into focus.

The crowd around the rooster pit, hearing the commotion, had suddenly silenced their ribald chatter and transferred their attention to me and the gorilla who was advancing on me. If I wanted to leave there on my own power I knew I had to get him quickly, before he could clear his head, so I bored into him with a flurry of well-placed punches that had him back pedaling to escape my onslaught. This was one time my experience from street fights in Houston was saving my ass. So far I had him completely off balance, half blinded, and reeling from the solid blows I'd been planting on his ugly face. I was the aggressor, taking the fight in angry fury. He finally tumbled backward into the recessed pit, falling on one of the roosters, thus ending two fights with one fall, as he was out cold.

The crowd collected around me firing questions, "How did it start? Why did you do it? Do you know you just whipped the toughest guy in the county? Where did you learn to fight like that?"

I was unmarked in anyway, considering myself very lucky to be standing. But a nagging question within me. Why did I lose control of my temper—my senses? Why did I resent the big fellow so much? He had triggered a fury within that had never erupted before, it had me puzzled. The pain in my right hand shifted my thoughts to its swelling, a result of landing a punch on the man's hard head.

The fracas had dissipated any desire to conduct business, so I left the barn—made my way to the car, drove into town arriving at four thirty.

♦ ♦ ♦

After shaving and changing clothes, my thoughts turned to lovely Reba, whose eyes had held much promise this morning, so I made my way to the city cafe to continue my conquest.

Seating myself at the counter, I looked around to locate her but she was not in sight. As I sat there appraising the damage to my right hand, which had swelled to a size equal to a small ham. I was thinking, plotting the best tactical path that would terminate in the seduction of this woman who had tantalized, and activated all the eroticism that nestled within this man-animal—me!

Should I adopt an attack of certitude—leaving no doubt in her mind I was confident of my success with her, or should I apply the old surefire tack employing jesting. Snowing her with flippant banter while conducting an insidious attack on her resistance, if any? Maybe a frontal assault of panache—flamboyance—or a dashing-type would be successful. I was probing for a strategy that would end in the bedroom, and I'm sure Napoleon had not been more intent in developing military tactics for Waterloo, than I employed at that moment to assure success for my love quest.

"Hello Hugh." The voice was like a carillon bell. It made my tailbone tingle, and raised the hair on my neck like an aroused tomcat. In fact, when in her presence my brain words had no correlation whatsoever. What I said never came out the way I intended. I had to get control of myself if I was going to impress her as a sophisticated man—a man that could be articulate—yet naive to the wiles of a woman. I desired to be warm, gentle and congenial so something might develop from this association. These thoughts raced through my mind as I replied," How's Reba?" I thought to myself what an asinine reply to her greeting. Get your brain in gear, Hugh, you're a dolt, a bumpkin—say something impressive, shift your thoughts to her rather than talking to yourself. Let yourself go!

"If you're feeling as well as you look, you must feel like a million. It is any wonder I have counted the minutes as I awaited five o'clock to enjoy your company. I am indeed fortunate and am here to fulfill any wish you may have—I am at your command, shall we go?"

She smiled, shook her head in a gesture of amusement at my gush of sycophancy, saying, "Lead on Romeo." We entered the car, she admired the interior and expressed her admiration by saying, "This is the most beautiful automobile I've ever seen. Do you mind circling the square, then we'll go to my place. I've planned a nice steak dinner for the two of us. You appear to be a man that would enjoy a home cooked meal for a change. Right?"

"Right. Incidentally where does the local bootlegger live?" She directed me and I purchased a quart of Gilbey's Gin. I left there with the hope it was Gilbey's and not the bathtub variety. Reba pointed out the route to her place, then leaned back against the plush upholstery with an expression of ecstasy. Letting the breeze blow her face, it moved her hair about, giving-off shimmerings of gold in the late afternoon sun.

Her home was a neat, well-maintained, frame structure and the white with black trim was very pleasing to the eye. The lawn was carefully trimmed, the whole picture reflected the abode of a person with character.

We entered a living room furnished in excellent taste with a fireplace, and a decor I rated as perfect. It was evident she was an immaculate housekeeper. This impressed me as I had tried to picture her environment—the whole room seemed to say, welcome.

Reba asked me if I wished to stay in the living room, listening to the radio, or playing records while she prepared the steaks but I wanted to be near her and I told her so.

We went into the kitchen where I plopped into a chair. I placed the gin on the table at the same time Reba produced a quart of ginger ale from the refrigerator, saying, "Please, make us a highball while I prepare dinner." Making the two high-balls laced with generous portions of gin, I toasted, "Here's to us, may our association be as bright as your eyes." I consumed three drinks as she performed at the stove, during which time she had two.

We dined on an exquisite steak about two inches thick, complemented with the best salad I had ever eaten. The effects of the drinks had made me more garrulous than was my usual self, I was really bordering on the "salty" as I related jokes I had in my repertoire—I was telling them and using them as a fencer feints and thrusts with the aim of determining how far I could expect to go on this night. She was getting big laughs at my tales, her laughter growing more relaxed as we sat downing one drink after another.

I was getting high, yet I had not convinced myself I would leave there successful in my conquest, as she had maintained an air of propriety during the period we were working on the bottle. Laughing and friendly, yes, but no indication that she would be agreeable to what I had in mind.

It was nine o'clock, the bottle was empty, I was generating my courage to the point of propositioning her when she said, "Let's go to bed." We arose, she latched the rear screen door saying, "Follow me."

She turned-off the lights and started for the bedroom, steering me by the elbow through the darkened house, saying, "I have some nosey neighbors."

There was a street light on the corner which cast a small bit of illumination into the bedroom, making it possible to dimly see each other.

I undressed very quickly, piling my clothes on a chair, shoes on top, then sat on the side of the bed as I awaited Reba's return. In a few moments, I could feel her presence, and smell the exotic scent she had applied to her body.

"Wow! That's a seductive essence you're wearing. What is it?" She gave a schoolgirl giggle while sliding around me on the bed answering, "Man Killer, by Reba Inc."

By now I could see this was not to be an ordinary jump in a bed, but an experience to linger long in my mind. She had me entangled in a snare of allure and desire already, so what would an hour or two in bed with this desirable woman do to me. I would soon know as I pulled her hot pulsating body hard against mine. The kiss began with the slightest brush of lips, a tantalizing touch indeed. Then her lips were against mine ever so lightly, but soon bearing down with burning passion as she rolled over on top of me, sparks were flying, she was creating an absolute electromagnetic sensation throughout my whole being as she flickered the tip of her tongue to mine. My mind was in a vortex of colors, reeling, and spinning. The inevitable instant was at hand, as I moved my buttocks into a position for action.

A crashing sound, coupled with the overhead light flashing on, produced a state of shock in me momentarily. I focused my eyes on a guy standing beside the bed with the upper half of a screen door hanging across his shoulders like a bandoleer. His eyes were glazed with ferocity as he pointed a huge, ugly pistol at my head. The silence was driving a wedge between reality and illusion, as I stared into the black maw of a pistol's muzzle. I feared any motion on my part might prompt him to squeeze the trigger. In a flash, I tumbled off Reba and was in a sitting position—scared as hell.

If my situation at the moment was not so precarious, I might have said something to him, but he was clutching a full house. I held the deuces, so I remained silent. Reba broke the cadence of his heavy breathing by uttering something she never finished. The intruder swung a meaty, hairy arm landing in a vicious slash across her face. She ended up between the wall and the bed—face down, bare rump and legs pointing upward. I glanced toward her to see the result of his blow, the picture was comparable to a French photo card, except for the serious possibilities that were prevalent at the moment.

Frankly, my feelings were of a desperate nature. What should I do? If he was going to shoot me I might as well go down fighting, there was nothing to lose, except my life. This thought was oscillating with the alternative of should I let him initiate the action, or should I?

His eyes were boring into me as if he were a starving hyena having the good fortune to stray upon a fallen zebra. They were as red as a branding iron and I could not deduce what he was planning, when he erased the uncertainty with, "Get the hell out of that bed!" I sprang to my feet with alacrity, planting them in a stance that would permit me to get foolish and try to disarm him, if necessary. There was a metronome swinging in my mind. Should I take defensive action or let him determine what would follow?

No one could possibly comprehend the total sum of my emotions. I was frightened—I was blinded with humiliation, standing there before him naked, as he leveled the pistol at my gut. I was wholly at the mercy of whatever whim he might generate in his frenzied mind, fermented with anger.

His face contorted gargoyle-like, as he dictated my next move, "Get the hell out of here before I blow your backbone into pieces. Don't ever come 'round here again. Move, you bastard, before I fix you for good."

His frame of mind, bulwarked with the pistol, encouraged me to get moving. As I picked up my clothing from the chair I glanced toward the bed. Reba was out cold, perhaps dead, as she had not moved since being struck. She was still in the inverted position with nothing visible, but her butt and legs.

I said, "Let me see about her before I go. I think you killed her."

"This is the last time I'm telling you to move, and I mean now!"

The click of the sear was deafening as he pulled the hammer back. With that I needed no further cause to depart, as I headed for the rear door barefoot, with my apparel tucked under my arm. I passed what was left of the screen door, going to the alley behind the house to get clothed. The walk toward the garage was made of crushed oyster shell, and was sheer torture as it stabbed my barefeet. I dressed behind the garage to the accompaniment of a curious, barking dog behind the fence next door. I took leave as soon as I had on my shoes, underwear and trousers. It was well that I did, as the barking of the dog had caused his master to light up the backyard to see what had aroused him. I slithered down the alley in the darkness to my car, leaving with reluctance as I was concerned about Reba's condition.

I may have been chicken for leaving but the character flourishing the pistol brought out the "chicken" in me to the extent of a hasty departure in the nude.

Driving to the hotel I mused the incredulous events of the past half hour. I had learned that a man naked during a confrontation, experiences a malaise very unpleasant. Without clothing you're a maladroit bungling fool. The feeling I imagine, could be likened to a stud horse after castration, or a eunuch booted from the harem by the Potentate. I never knew the attire contributed so much to the machismo of man. Without it, you feel like the fencer that has dropped his blade—the nun whose petticoat dropped while touring the thirteen stations—like the dude who paid the prostitute in advance, only to see her vanish in the dark.

I retired knowing sleep would not come as my mind was cluttered with three trains of concentration. What was Reba's condition? How could I inflict the greatest, most stringent ignominy upon the character that had degraded my stature with the aid of a pistol? Would I ever forget and overcome the humiliation he had forced upon me? I had to sate my desire for revenge as my dignity had been encroached upon, my pride trampled in the acidulous dust of despicable apparent cowardice. I surrendered to sleep consoling my troubled mind with the saying, "He who fights and runs away, lives to fight another day."

The morning found me reviewing the events of yesterday, along with feeling concern for Reba, as I shaved and dressed. The kaleidoscope of happenings passed in review through my mind, the incredulity of them was stunning.

In one day I had been challenged by a Doberman—engaged in a fist fight—had the brass ring of romance snatched from me by the antics of an irate lunatic brandishing a gun, who had caused me to react like a sniveling coward. What a day!

As I approached the city cafe, I was hoping to see Reba behind the counter, her usual ebullient self. I found a seat at the counter then surveyed the surroundings for her, with no success. A middle-aged woman was waddling up and down behind the counter serving the group of customers. She stopped in front of me smiling a sunny smile, ready to take my order. I was craning my neck to checkout every person in the place, to see if the gunslinger of last night was present. He was not.

I asked the waitress if Reba was working and was told she had called in reporting she was ill. My order was taken, then she asked me, "Are you a relative of Reba's?"

"No, just a friend." She departed, then my thoughts centered on the possibility that the crazed intruder of last night could have been Reba's husband. But, she told me she was not married and I believed her.

The waitress returned placing ham and eggs before me, then refilling my coffee cup asked, "Did I see you yesterday driving a big, white car?"

"Perhaps, I drive a white car. Why do you ask?" She cast a surreptitious glance along the counter, then replied in a subdued manner," I was leaving Cantrell's Dry Goods Store yesterday afternoon when you drove by, with Reba. Her ex-boyfriend was sitting on a bench beside the door with two worthless characters when you passed. I heard him say to them, "Who is that S.O.B. driving that fancy car?" One answered, "Stranger in town." I just thought I'd tell you as he is still crazy about her even though she ignores him, and has for over a year. He's what I call a nut—he's dangerous—he shot a man about two years ago because the man went on a date with Reba. The law didn't do a damn thing but try him and turn him loose, so I advise you to watch him pretty close."

"Did he kill the man?"

"No, he didn't die but was hospitalized for several months. Take my advice and keep him in front of you if your paths ever cross."

"Thanks a lot for warning me and I'll keep him in front of me if possible."

I left her a generous tip for the second hand information, she had no way of knowing I had already been convinced he was a nut, and dangerous! I then drove into the country to seek out Mr. Henshaw once more.

I found him sitting on the steps, the Doberman at his side as I got out of the car. I greeted him, then started walking his way, when he said in a loud voice," Wait 'till I put this dog in the house, he will chew you up!"

I continued walking, replying, "I don't think he will bother me as we are friends. Here boy, Here boy."

The Doberman came to me in a fast trot, taking up my pace along side me, as he had done yesterday. We reached the steps as Mr. Henshaw looked first at the dog, then at me. He was dumbfounded and speechless at the pacific action of the dog.

"Mr. Henshaw, I am here to make you an offer you cannot refuse. I want to lease your four hundred and forty acres for oil development. I'll give you a fair price and one eighth of the royalties. My name is Hugh McCulloch."

I was the very essence of brevity not wasting any time on small talk or nonsensical subjects e.g. weather, crops, etc.

"Say, Mr. McCulloch, ain't you the fellow that beat the tar out of that big bastard, Charlie Hooker, over at the cockfights yesterday?"

"Well, I had a fight with some guy over there. I don't know his name. I do know he was as big as a well-fed gorilla, but I don't know anything of his origin, or who sired him. He could of been a bastard alright."

Henshaw's voice rose an octave as he squealed like a Poland China pig being stepped on by his big sow mama. He was slapping his thighs, bent over with violent laughter, as tears streamed from his eyes. Regaining his composure he said, "Every man and woman in Montgomery County has waited for the time when someone would come along and kick his ass good and proper, and by gum, you did it, and a good job of it too. You should've seen that bastard when he finally come to in that cockpit. He had rooster crap all over his back and several feathers clinging to it, made him look like chicken shit. He mashed one bird deader than hell when he fell in there, but the fellow who owned the rooster said he would sacrifice a rooster any day to see the show you put on. Wait 'til I tell Ellie that you're the one who kicked ol' Charlie's ass. Ellie is my wife, she can't stand the sight of Hooker cause he tried to get fresh with her one day and she cussed him out. Come in the house and we'll have a shot of the best moonshine you ever smacked your lips on." We went in and he introduced me to Ellie, telling her I was the man who had interrupted the cockfight yesterday by knocking Hooker in the pit.

"I'd have given a hundred dollars to have seen that," she said. Mr. Henshaw opened a closed door and removed a half gallon jug of white corn whiskey, then nodded to me to follow as we made our way to the kitchen where he placed the jug on the table.

"Pull up a chair. Can I call you Hugh?"

"Yes, please do."

He called Ellie to come in and get us some ice and grape wine for a chaser. She quickly appeared with a gallon jug, placing it beside the whiskey. This man was showing me something about the drinking of corn whiskey by mixing it with wine. The thought occurred the combination would be a potent mixture. He poured about three ounces of booze into a glass, dropped in two ice cubes, then filled the glass with the reddest wine I had ever had seen, and pushed the concoction to me.

"Don't stir or shake it, Hugh, lest you ruin the pleasant experience of having it bite you slowly and painlessly." He guffawed and continued, "Take a couple or three of that, then we will discuss business and get that behind us first. Then we can enjoy as much of these spirits as you think you can handle."

"Suits me. May I call you Felix?" I was sipping the tantalizing elixir.

"You sure can, Boy. Something tells me that you and I are going to hit it off fine. Now what can you offer me for the lease you mentioned?"

"Tell you what, Felix, how does ten thousand sound to you?"

"I hate to tell you, Hugh, but there was a man here two days ago representing some oil company, Gulf, I think. He offered me twelve thousand for the lease, but I told him we'd have to think it over. He tried to high-pressure me into signing then, but I don't like to be bulldozed on anything so I told him I'd think on it. He left in a huff saying he'd return tomorrow morning for my answer. You may think it ridiculous, but somehow the fellow didn't set right with me because Hans, that's my Doberman, chased him back to his car on the run. I noticed the dog seemed to take to you, that makes me think you are an alright guy. You can't fool a dog as you can a man. Did you know that?"

My glass was nearly empty, but not my head as it seemed to be filled with a thousand bees—buzzing as they worked. It was a pleasant hum in my head and my muscles had become so relaxed, they were a flaccid mass. The mixture of whiskey and wine had resulted in my being in a state of complete relaxation—with the exception of my brain. It was very active, churning the realization that I was facing the dilemma of being dealt out with the first hand. The competitor had offered more than I had in the bank. I had concealed the shock waves of uncertainty coursing through me as I pondered my course.

"How about a refill, Felix? This recipe of yours makes me feel that all is well. It may even produce a state of euphoria that will make me very generous in my bargaining."

I failed to mention that the effects of the mixture had also saturated my usual caution, converting it to a state of reckless abandon, as evidenced by me blurting out, "I'll pay you and Ellie, fourteen thousand if we can do business today."

That statement after instant review on my part, sounded as if someone else had said it, not me! Knowing there was only twelve thousand in the bank did not deter me from pressing on. He sidetracked my thoughts by clearing his throat, then he called out, "Ellie, come in here."

She came to the door looking askance when Felix ordered her to sit down. She took a chair beside him as he continued, "Ellie, Hugh has offered us fourteen thousand for the lease. I think it's a good offer and I'm willing to sign for that, if you are too. What do you say?"

She pursed her lips for a moment, then said, "You're the boss, go ahead."

I produced the legal papers—explained them—and had the signatures in about ten minutes. As they were signing the documents, my mind was engaging the problem arising from my writing a check in the amount that exceeded available funds in the account. The drinks consumed, provided an insulation that shielded my conscience against any pangs of wrong doing and I proceeded to write a "hot" check in exchange for the signed lease.

The booze was talking to my mind saying, do not worry, you'll find a way to make up the deficit. From past experience, I had found that inner voice to be accurate even when embellished with alcohol. So, I dismissed the felony from my mind and made another drink.

While talking with Felix about fighting cocks, I suddenly was aware of the fact, I had to stick with him until three o'clock so he couldn't get to the bank that day with the check I had just given him. It was a matter of self preservation! It was now twelve, three more hours to go.

"Hugh, Ellie and me would like you to have lunch with us, what do you say?"

"It's nice of you to invite me, sure I'll stay and thank you for your hospitality."

As Ellie was preparing the meal, Felix and I consumed another drink. It was then I proposed a devious scheme to keep him from the bank by asking, "Any cockfights going on today?"

"Yeah. They are having one at Huntsville. Want to run up that way?"

"Sure do, if you'll tout me some birds to bet on as I feel lucky!"

We arrived in Huntsville around two, found the rooster fights were being held two miles east of town in some woods. Felix knew most of the spectators, as the usual ribald greetings were tossed about. As we worked our way to the pit, I passed within five feet of Charlie Hooker, who was observing the birds, intently, not seeing me. His face was swollen and purple as an aroused hemorrhoid, from the pounding yesterday. His hat was perched atop his stony head barely touching his hair in deference to his sore head.

Ten minutes after arriving I glanced around to observe Hooker, as I did not want any sneak attack. His eyes met mine then dropped as if he had looked upon some witch doctor's curse. It was then I knew I had nothing to fear from him, the beating had cowed him, discouraging any thoughts of revenge.

Felix and I bet several fights, winning some, losing some. At three, I suggested we start back. He was agreeable, arriving at the farm about four. I went in, thanking them for their hospitality, wishing them luck as I turned toward the door and left.

Ten minutes later I was parking in front of the city cafe. As I was going in to inquire about Reba, I met the waitress that served me, coming out the door.

"Have you heard anymore from Reba?"

"Yes, she called about one to tell us she would be in tomorrow. Incidentally, is your name Hugh?"

"Yes, that's my name, why?"

"She asked me to tell you that she is alright and hoped to see you tomorrow." I thanked her, entered the cafe for coffee, and looked patrons over. Perhaps the "door buster" might be there I thought, but he wasn't.

After having coffee, I made my way to the Metropole Hotel. The lobby was filled with oil people milling about like a bunch of spooked cattle. The hotel was the unofficial headquarters for those engaged in the frenzied, lucrative search for oil. I would get myself out of the uncertainty of having a check outstanding that was "hot."

My first target was to be the fellow, who had contacted Henshaw about the lease. After introducing myself to a fellow who seemed to be on speaking status with most of them collected there, I asked if he knew Sam Gaines. He pointed to a man reading a magazine. I interrupted his reading with, "Sam, I am Hugh McCulloch."

He peered up at me through thick lens glasses—not rising. He studied me for a half minute, his searching, methodical survey warned me at once, that this man might prove difficult to deal with. But that did not discourage me from getting-on with what I came to accomplish. Gaines had folded his arms in a gesture to indicate his readiness to learn why I had encountered him.

"Are you interested in the lease on Felix Henshaw's place?"

With my question he arose, surveyed me from head to foot, then replied, "Might be. Do you represent Henshaw?"

"In a way, yes, I have the lease. He told me you had made an offer and was to return tomorrow to negotiate some more. Is that right?"

"Yes, I was going back in the morning to see if I could get the old fart to budge. How in the hell did you get him to sell? I spent all day out there, but they couldn't make up their minds. No offense meant, but you must have held a pistol on them if you got the lease, that is a signed lease."

I unfolded the document from my shirt pocket in a slow-meditative manner, then folded the amount paid under the signatures holding it under his nose to read, making sure he could not see the lower figure.

He stared at it a full minute, then looked me directly in the eye, lying by retorting, "I wasn't too interested in it, but just for curiosity what did you have to pay the old goat?"

I laughed as I slowly folded the papers, putting them in my shirt pocket, as I purposefully turned my head in the direction of the door. I could afford to laugh as he had shown me his hole card by asking how much I paid. I had him literally by the testicles and could squeeze hard, make him wince as I hit with, "Sam, let's have a man to man agreement. I won't bullshit you and you grant me the same consideration. Okay? I know that you know there is oil there, so it's a question of who leaves here with the lease. You're a crook and so am I, so let's agree "that" to be shared knowledge. We both know that Gulf and others have shot so much around there the ground is like swiss cheese. The chickens have stopped laying due to the seismograph racket."

Then I shot from the hip—my desperation move. I continued, "I was tipped you had orders from Gulf to get that lease regardless, so you can have it for twenty-five thousand. Just give me a company check for that amount and I'll release it to you here and now."

I was once more getting the papers out of my pocket as I talked.

"I'll give you twenty-five—in a pig's ass, I will! You must think I just fell-off the turnip truck. You damn kids these days are a bunch of smart asses. Wait 'til you're dry behind the ears, and stepped in a few more piles of cow shit, then maybe you can con ol' Gaines, but not now, Sonny."

"Okay, okay! Keep your hemorrhoids puckered up. I know an independent driller who is interested. If he don't go, then I may contact you again, Sam."

With that I turned—started for the door. As I reached the sidewalk a hand clutched my right elbow. Without breaking stride or turning my head, I knew it was Gaines. He had been snared by the artifice of my being tipped about him having orders to get the lease, regardless. He held my arm tighter trying to restrain me in a dignified manner. So I stopped. He darted around to face me saying, "Come on back, I'll take your deal."

We went to his room where he produced release forms and wrote me a check for twenty-five thousand. I signed the release, giving him the papers. He snatched the lease from my hand letting his eagerness run rampant as he scanned the amount I had paid the Henshaw's. His enthusiasm was converted to dismay as he saw the figure of fourteen thousand. I felt he was entitled to one burst of vehemence, so felt no resentment when he burst out with, "You bastard you. You bastard you!"

I took my leave, content with a good days work, but reminding myself I must get that check on deposit the minute they opened the bank in the morning.

I drove by Reba's house and saw one car parked in the driveway and another one in the street. So having no knowledge of her situation, I thought it best to go on to the hotel, calling it a day.

As I parked in front of the cafe the next morning, Reba was looking out the window. She smiled and waved to me as I was mounting the three steps going up to the sidewalk. I sat at the counter but she nodded to me indicating that I sit at a table. Moving provided some privacy as to conversation. She brought me coffee and water, then said in a low tone, "Hugh, I owe you an apology."

I could see the results of the forearm blow she had received two nights before. Her right cheek was bruised, appearing to be very painful, but it did nothing to detract from her desirable appearance. In a low voice I said," Honey, who was that wild man? I surely hope I did not cause any serious trouble."

"He is a fellow I went out with a few times, but his pugnacious, jealous nature was more than I cared to endure, so I broke it off with him. He has interfered with my life several times since, but he will not interfere anymore as I have had him placed under a peace bond. I'll bring you some bacon and eggs, the owner is looking over this way."

As I sat in the car after breakfast, I suddenly remembered I had forgotten to call Joe Bob yesterday at five thirty. Perhaps he would overlook my negligence when he heard about the Henshaw deal, at least I hoped he would.

Nine o'clock found me waiting for the bank to open. As I entered, the young fellow at the front desk greeted me with a distressed expression occupying his face, a face that appeared to have erupted in a disarray of pimples since two days before. I made a mental note of the nameplate on his desk, as I wished to learn if he was the bank president's son. "Egbert Snaveley—1st Vice President.

The attractive woman teller greeted me with a cheery salutation that I gladly returned as I pushed the twenty-five thousand check to her for deposit. As she was performing the customary shuffling of paper to handle the deposit book replying, "Mr. Eustance Snaveley. His son's desk is near the door."

"I surmised as much and thank you."

I departed the bank bubbling with an inner drive to get much accomplished on this day, and all future days. The scenario of two nights ago had chastised me to the degree that work held precedence over play. The experience at Reba's had effected as great a change in my priorities and desires just, as if that Jack the Ripper had entered a monastery. My thoughts and goals for the present, did not include a woman, only getting the bank account up to one hundred thousand. That was my goal, and all my energies, and actions would be directed toward that goal. When that point was attained my plans would be shifted to bigger things—I was determined to enjoy success and fame at no cost. One way or another, I would succeed, even if I had to step-on anyone who got in my way and mash them like a bug.

Today I was slated to seek out a landowner, a widow of some means. At least that was the information I received from the prudish woman employed in the County Clerk's office. I asked where this widow lived and how to get there. The prune-faced clerk, her hair resembling a huge pone of bread, all the orgasms she had deprived herself—all the Victorian guidelines she had used in the past to keep philandering males from tainting her chastity and destroying her virginity—all the excuses she had regimented her life with—all these restrictions and self-denials had been successful in producing a woman completely devoid of femininity, but with a mouthful of medusan tongues that were being employed at the moment in the graceless art of denigrating a fellow human being, by erupting like Old Faithful in Yellowstone Park. She gushed forth a maelstrom of facts and data, garnished with venomous gossip regarding the woman I had inquired about.

"Do you associate with the likes of her? If so, you are one among many. She belies the scripture,' Many are called, but few are chosen,' she chooses them all just as long as they wear pants. Don't say I told you, but she is a wanton woman since her husband died and left her all that money. Course she was playing around before he died. She has seduced more men than a New Orleans prostitute and she's very blatant about it. You'll be lucky if she doesn't have you on the couch fifteen minutes after you arrive there. She's been involved in more divorces than any judge in Texas. Believe me, the women around here are talking of running her out of the county. So watch your step, as you seem like a nice man. I hope you don't let her ruin you."

I had to shut her off some way without being rude, besides I would need her assistance from time to time,

"Alright, Miss—"

"Carruthers, Annie May Carruthers."

"I won't call on that unscrupulous woman as I value my chastity as a man, and would not want to be guilty by reason of association. Can you direct me to Judson Carey? I will see him in place of the Widow Farrington."

She gave me directions to Carey's place in a glib manner, as if she were contributing to my soul's salvation by helping divert me from the widow.

I thanked her, left the courthouse, slid under the wheel of the Cord to find the Widow Farrington! Carey could wait.

A short distance from town, I sighted the name Farrington on a mailbox that set beside a circular driveway. Turning in, I could not suppress my admiration for the structure I was approaching. It was of native stone, a sprawling ranch-type, with a red tile roof. A four-car garage formed an appendage to one wing of the house. Two cars were visible, a Lincoln and a La Salle. The smell of money pervaded my nostrils serving to dampen my aim of getting a lease here, as money was not the prime motivator.

What the hell! If I didn't get the lease, I would have had the opportunity of exercising my ability as a con man and this was an attribute that needed constant honing to always be ready. With some trepidation, I stopped in front of the main entrance then made my way to the door. My uncertainty naturally was nourished by the graphic description of Mrs. Farrington as orated by Annie May Carruthers. I poked the bell button. Awaiting a response I will admit my curiosity was piqued. I was forming pictures in my mind as to her looks—how she would receive me—would I be seduced as certainly as Miss Carruthers had predicted.

"May I help you?' She was before me and I must say her voice was graced with a seductive timbre, the question was posed by a most attractive woman.

"Yes, please do, I wish to see Mrs. Farrington. I am Hugh McCulloch." She turned an impish smile on me, asking," And what would Mr. McCulloch wish to see Mrs. Farrington about? I am Mrs. Farrington."

"First, I wish to state this is the most appealing home I've seen. It's beautiful and the architecture is unique. Having expressed that, I am here to discuss the possibility of getting an option or lease, to drill for oil on your property. May I come in?"

"Please do," she replied, releasing the lock on the screen door, opening it permitted me to enter.

"If you care to, we can conduct this in the kitchen while enjoying a highball, okay?"

My optimism at meeting success soared with her congenial invite to the kitchen, coupled with the offer of a highball. We made our way to the rear of the mansion, passing expensive furnishings as my eyes bulged with admiration. As we entered the hall, I jammed my toe into some object on the floor, causing me to stumble. However, I regained my balance. Seeking the cause, I looked down into a baleful pair of eyes piercing me with a malevolent stare. They were the eyes of a gigantic Kodiak bear, a skin that completely covered the hall, scaring the hell out of me as I viewed the immensity of its size. I apologized for my clumsiness as she was showing amusement at my discomfort, then said, "I've intended removing that monstrosity for a year, before someone breaks their neck with their foot in its mouth. My husband killed that thing on Kodiak Island ten years ago, paying an exorbitant sum to have it preserved. But now that he's gone, the bear skin must go. Would you like to have it?"

"No thank you, Mrs. Farrington. Sorry, but I haven't a place for anything like that." We entered the light, attractive kitchen, pointing to a chair she said, "Have a seat, Mr. McCulloch, while I mix us a drink."

While she blended the ingredients, I sat there drumming my fingers on the table admiring my surroundings. A holstered 45 Colt automatic pistol caught my attention. It was hanging from a peg at the side of the rear door. I arose, walked over and examined the embossing on the holster. It was hand-crafted, reflecting the works of a true artisan, which really complemented the pistol it embraced. The gun displayed silver filigreed grips as well as being nickel-plated. The pistol was also a thing of beauty, as beautiful and deadly as a King Cobra. I asked, "Can you shoot this weapon?"

"I'm glad you asked. That gives me an opening to demonstrate my dexterity as an Annie Oakley when we conclude our business and our drink. Here you are, about to try a libation that is guaranteed to produce a panacea for any inhibitions you may be harboring. May all your children be born naked," she laughed, as she raised her glass in a gesture of a toast, and drank.

I raised my glass and drank. This was pure nectar. It had the fragrance of an exotic Pacific Island spice, my taste buds were awakened ever so gently as the silky liquid swirled over my tongue. Control of my thought patterns were becoming more difficult by the moment as I studied the woman sitting before me. She presented an attractive, alluring paradox, e.g. as per Annie May Carruthers description. It was axiomatic that tripping on the bear's head—followed by my mummy-like repartee, was presenting me as a maladroit yokel. If my visit here terminated with success, it would be by the luck of the Irish and nothing else, as my mind was flitting as a hummingbird from one flowery prospect to another. No deliberate concentration would come to me as I sat there in a somnolent fog.

"Mr. McCulloch, I have two hundred acres here and I have been told that it sets right on the Woodbine, whatever that is. I assume it has some bearing on oil, right?"

I gulped some more of the drink that had ignited the embers of eroticism within, trying to muse the hidden meaning of her statement.

"Yes, yes, that is right Mrs. Farrington. There is indication that this land could produce oil. That's why I am here."

I blurted the truth as my questionable sense of reason had convinced me this woman possessed the certitude to handle any sycophancy, flippant banter, or rhetoric that I might use in the attempt to lease her land. Her demeanor projected a silent warning that she could cope with any situation. As I studied her features my reasoning told me, it would be safer to pursue a wounded grizzly bear into a cave with one opening, than try to panegyric or influence her.

Eschewing any attempt at bargaining I said, "Mrs. Farrington, I will give fifteen thousand for the option to drill for oil on your two hundred twenty acres, plus one eighth royalty of any oil produced."

As she pondered the proposal, I drank the last of my highball, savoring every drop while considering my chances of selling the lease at a profit. She interrupted my reverie with, "That seems a fair offer. Do you have the necessary papers?" As I filled in the required information she asked, "Do you want to see me demonstrate my accuracy with the pistol before you leave?"

Pushing the papers to her, I responded with, "I certainly do." Having closed the deal, she arose, removed the weapon from its holster, then said, "Follow me."

We walked to the rear of the garage where she pointed out a regulation target situated about one hundred feet away, backed by bales of hay. Sliding the receiver back, she raised the pistol aiming it by gripping it with both hands, then fired seven shots in rapid fire order. My amazement at her assuredness in handling the weapon must have been evident as she said, "Go down there and see how I did Mr. McCulloch." Looking the target over, she had placed four in the bull's-eye and three in the ring. I called back, "That's some kind of shooting!"

She insisted I try the remaining two shots. I did and missing the target completely, probably shooting over the hay into the distance.

On the way to my car, I complimented her on the great marksmanship, and how well I liked her home. Then thanking her for the hospitality, I departed for town. While tooling the Cord along, my mind was considering the possibility that maybe I had paid her too much, finding it difficult, if not impossible to peddle the lease. I also was questioning my actions the past hour. It was my inaction that brought about my malaise as I reviewed what had just transpired. There I was with a very appealing widow whose peccadillos were known to me—yet I was a very sedate, dignified man who conducted business only. I had become an enigma to myself. Perhaps I was maturing while letting nothing get in the way of making money, or maybe my courage had liquefied after analysis of the widow. So what! There would be other days and other women!

At five thirty I placed a call to Joe Bob as directed. After two rings he answered.

"Joe Bob, this is Hugh. Hope you have overlooked my not calling yesterday, as events caused me to forget."

I rushed on in order to head-off any adverse comment from him regarding my neglect, "I made a pretty good deal yesterday." He interrupted, "When you didn't call I almost made a good deal too. I entertained the thought that maybe you had cleaned out the account and was bouncing some señorita on a bed in Mexico. Needless to say, I had conjured up some stringent, painful retribution to be meted out if and when I located you. I am very happy to hear from you as it has refuted all the evil I had believed lurked within you. Now tell me about the deal you made."

I related the details of the Henshaw transaction, also the deal with Mrs. Farrington. He was elated over my activities, complimenting me for my adapting so quickly to the basics of a successful "lease hound," but cautioned me about excessive elan that could sometime have dire consequences, e.g. paying too much for a lease—letting my enthusiasm become apparent to a prospective seller. These things were anathema to success in the leasing operation.

That night I succeeded in selling the Farrington lease for twenty-five thousand. I then retired to my room, stretched out on the bed, and looking at the ceiling reviewed the events of the past two months.

The realization we had netted twenty-one thousand on two deals had inflated my goals for the future, moreover the situation had impregnated my ambition to the point of obsession. The future was panning across my mind with mellifluent ease as the visions came into view, I was one of the most feared tycoons in the petroleum industry—living in a penthouse with several custom automobiles at my disposal—had my own airplane with a pilot subject to call twenty-four hours a day. Seductive women flocked to me like flies around an outhouse. I shucked them as the farmer shucks the corn. I'd have all types at my beck and call: blondes, brunettes, redheads, all with varied endowments and talents. I lay picturing myself surrounded with all these beauties—these were the things money would provide. Money was power and I was gripped with an insatiable lust for power! I was on my way as I lay there gazing upward.

♦ ♦ ♦

The next three months proved very lucrative to our operation. Our bank account having now reached the magic number of one hundred thousand dollars! That figure had been the Lorelei of my voyage to power and wealth. Now that it was reached she was beckoning me onward.

I was now in a position to launch the next phase of my quest for the Golden Fleece. I was conditioned mentally for the challenge ahead, and prepared financially to facilitate the ultimate action. I was going to Houston as it was the arena housing the gladiators and the lions. Houston was a giant with muscles coiled with the strength of oil—always ready to accept the challenge of any individual who was willing to chance the fires of failure, or the rich rewards of renown. She was a giant that could pulverize an individual as effectively as falling into an open hearth steel pot. Yet, with Lady Luck and ferocious determination, one could vault the pits of failure to the golden stair, then up, up, as far and as long as iron will was within to draw upon.

Life in the Texas State Hotel, the Rice and, the Petroleum Club was one giant never-ending poker game. The stakes were high, the pits are deep, as the game was played with lives and oil wells, and wildcatting, and transmission, and refining, and marketing.

This was where the siren call within my heart, that could not be silenced, bade me go. No heroin addict could describe the flaming desire, the unquenchable force that pulled me in to engage in combat in that arena of oil.

A twist of irony occurred last night in Conroe. Charlie Hooker, the man who had barred my entrance to the cockfight several weeks before, had gotten drunk. Succumbing to the eroticism the whiskey had aroused, he made his way to the widow Farrington's home. I did not learn if he went prompted by habit, or if it was a spur of the moment decision. The next morning the cafe was saturated with conversation regarding his death.

The summation of his last hour of life was related to me by Reba. Charlie had gone to the widow's home around midnight, most likely being driven by an amorous urge, had almost torn the front door from the frame by kicking it in a storm of anger stemming from her refusal to admit him. He returned to his car, remaining in it for about thirty minutes as he licked his wounds of rejection and crushed pride.

After renewing his courage he returned to the yard where he walked along the side of the house to Mrs. Farrington's bedroom window. He sliced the screen, then smashed the glass with his fist. He reached in, unlocking the window frame, then raised it, lifted his body up and was halfway over the window sill when all his drunken plans were obliterated. The widow had directed a .45 calibre slug between his eyes—taking off the rear half of his skull. The bullet exited his brain fragmented and spread over the lawn behind him. She had then slipped on a robe and driven to a nearby neighbor's home to remain the rest of the night.

After arriving there she telephoned the sheriff, relating the events of the past hour. "Do you think you killed him?" he asked.

"I did not examine the damage to him, Sheriff, but he didn't move after I fired the shot. I wish you would go out there and take him away."

After arriving in the driveway, the sheriff focused the spotlight down the side of the house moving the beam until it was on Charlie's rump and legs dangling from the window. A fleeting thought that what he saw looked like a sack of feed on a fence crossed his mind. He sauntered down the side of the house to Charlie and pulled and tugged on his hips until the body dropped from the window sill, striking the earth with a soggy thud.

"My God Almighty!" The sheriff was now talking to himself. "This is the deadest one I've seen in my twenty years as sheriff in Montgomery County!"

He left the body as it had tumbled from the window, then sped back to town where he roused the undertaker from a sound sleep, requesting him to go out with the coroner and pick up Charlie Hooker's remains.

The mortician asked in a somnolent tone, "Was she screwin' Charlie too?"

This is the way the happenings were told to me by Reba. I had finished my breakfast, but before arising from the table I told her that it had been very trying and difficult to keep my distance from her the past three months. Adding that it was only for her safety that I had not pursued her, lest the lover boy might beat her up again. She replied, "Sometimes I am tempted to shoot him out of my life. That is a terrible thing to say, but he has kept you and I apart, as well as making life miserable for me in other ways."

"Please convey this message to him for me, that somewhere, sometime we will meet when he will not be holding a pistol, and I will be fully dressed. Then I will proceed to make hamburger of his face as I pound him to a pulp for striking you. Will you tell him that?"

"Yes, and I would love to be a witness when it happens." I arose stating, "I am going to Houston now, I will either call you, or see you before too long. Okay?"

Reba was looking from the cafe window as I drove away thinking of what might have been between she and I, except for the interference of the jealous suitor, and my voracious, driving force that did not permit time for dallying.

Cruising along toward Houston my whole being was filled with anticipation of what was ahead for me. I found myself analyzing my capabilities, my infirmities of character, my habits, what I had done, and what I hadn't done. It was a bizarre feeling as though I was out of my body viewing it as a psychoanalyst. I questioned the fact that my feverish ambition had just about made a eunuch of me.

After the fiasco at Reba's house, being subjected to total humiliation by the maniac with the gun, I realized that business had advanced in my life's priorities. It superseded sex as if I plied myself with saltpeter. This was a quixotic sequence of thoughts that crowded my mind—thoughts that were revealing a new facet of my makeup as women always presented an irresistible lure. An appeal so powerful that I would put aside business in order to appease my desires for them. This change in me was deprecated by my recent shift of placing business ahead of all else, consoling myself with the reminder that money and power would produce anything I would desire—when I had reached my goal.

I conditioned my mind to the state that I would rather be envied than loved, and was prepared to devote my heart, mind, time, and energy to reach the pinnacle of success. In essence the change produced a physical machine eager to serve the machinations of an obsessive mind. A mind that equated the exercise of stepping on people as an integral plan to attain status. I was willing to act as a member of the wolf pack—the ones who finally climbed onto the peak after biting noses to establish identity on the way up. It mattered not to me that these tactics were unattractive—I viewed them simply as human manifestations. If one could probe the inner recesses of my mind, they would discover them totally void of anything related to a conscience. Look out Houston, I am moving in!

Chapter Three
On My Own

I parked in a lot near the business district, then walked to the Rice Hotel, had lunch in the dining room and while eating was working out a plan of action to get my half of the hundred thousand as quickly as possible. The plan being to go to Conroe with Joe Bob and close out the account.

I called him from the hotel lobby, on the second ring the familiar voice came on, "Hello, Joe Bob? Hugh here. I am calling from the Rice. It is imperative that we get together, can you meet me in the lobby?"

"What's the trouble, Hugh? Are you in some kind of jam?"

"No, no. There is nothing wrong, but I have to see you as I want to break-off our operation. I must go it alone from here on, I want to talk with you."

"I will be there in thirty minutes. I hope I can change your mind about getting out. I'll meet you in the lobby."

As he entered, I walked to meet him. We shook hands, then he snapped, "What's this crap about wanting to break up our little operation?"

"That's it, Joe Bob. Let's sit down over here." I pulled two over-stuffed chairs close, then we sat down facing each other.

"Joe Bob, I cannot find the words to express my appreciation of your taking me in as a partner. You have no way of knowing it, but you are responsible for getting me a start in life that I doubt anyone else would have given me. For your action, I will be forever in your debt, but right now I have to scratch the itching of my inner self. My heart and my mind tell me that I must change the course of my life and now is the time. When I reach a status of envy and repugnance coming at me from those around me, then I will be in a position to reward you for the confidence you placed in me to help me, get started."

"Started on what? What do you have in mind? Does it have to be undertaken alone? Come on, out with it. What's driving you?"

"Well, it's like this. I want to get into exploration, drilling as an independent. That's where the big money is, and to accomplish my goal, I must go where the money is."

"Listen to me, Hugh. I like you and know you to be ambitious and capable, so try to understand what I am telling you now. Wildcatting is as chancy and uncertain as you being Moses reincarnated. You cannot visualize the malaise that becomes a part of a wildcatter as he spuds in a location. It sleeps with him, walks with him, uneasiness and uncertainty is his constant companion. You'll find yourself praying for prescience, or anything to dissipate your vague fears of drilling a "duster." I refuse to resort to any artifice in order to discourage you, but damn it Hugh, those wolves will chew you up in the game, I wish you would get it out of your mind. Anyway, just how do you propose to become a tycoon with only fifty grand?"

"There must be a way, and I will find it."

"Okay Hugh, what are your plans for tonight? If you have nothing arranged and have a tuxedo, how would you like to be my guest and go dancing at the River Oaks Country Club? Ted Weem's Orchestra is playing. I can introduce you to some people who may be useful to you in the future. How about it?"

One word he had used prompted an immediate acceptance from me—USEFUL—my future involved using people. Using them as a tool, an extension for my energy, creativity, and devious nature. Yes, I would be glad to meet someone that might prove useful.

After agreeing to meet at the country club, we parted. I went immediately to a Sakowitz Store to buy a tux and maroon cummerbund, complete with all the accessories. Then I returned to the Rice where I registered as a guest.

As I showered and shaved, my thoughts played the possibilities ahead as the Maestro strokes the harp—producing a mellifluent state of mind. All was well with me and with the world. Tonight would find me stirred and mixed with the mainstream of high society. These habitues of River Oaks were mainliners. I might stumble into the honey pot tonight.

Nine o'clock found me parking the Cord in the club parking area, headed for the huge clubhouse, walking among the Cadillacs,

Lincolns, Rolls, Auburns, and other expensive cars on my way. The sight of these cars had charged me with an effervescent feeling as I anticipated the night ahead. I had turned Ted Weems on many times on the radio, but must admit seeing him in person gave me a tingle of excitement.

I was seeking Joe Bob as I entered the huge foyer of the clubhouse, hearing the sounds of the musicians warming up, along with a low babel of voices. I spotted him, appearing as stoical in the tuxedo, as the maitre d' at his podium in the Blue Room of the Roosevelt in New Orleans. Maybe I looked stoical too, but I certainly was under no spell of stoicism. I felt great, having a feeling of certitude, this night was mine! I should have been cringing under the spell of ludicrousness, this being the first time I had worn a tuxedo, but I felt at ease. This was my debut, my entre to the world of opportunity that had been twenty years in coming.

Joe Bob and I entered the lavish bar. The atmosphere was subdued, yet the patrons were engaged in bar talk, punctuated occasionally with raucous laughter. We threaded our way through a maze of tables all fully occupied. I was missing no detail as we coursed the route to the bar. The patrons paid scant attention to us, however one glamorous woman arrested my survey as we passed the table she shared with two men and another female. The woman's appearance aroused my aesthetic senses as our eyes met in passing. In a fleeting second her beauty had imprinted in my mind the lovely embellishments her presence emitted. She was wearing an evening gown that reeked haute couture, accented with accessories that complimented her striking physical features.

We had to stand as we sipped our highballs, giving me a vantage to study this woman in a thorough, yet unobtrusive manner. Once more our eyes met as she cast a glance my way, and once more a message was transmitted by that glance. She fanned the embers of a gamut of emotions within—curiosity, challenge, amusement, desire and intrigue. I was aware that she also was being churned by a degree of like emotions. This prompted me to ask Joe Bob, "Who's that woman to my right, the table with two couples? The one with the honey-hued hair, wearing the gold sequined gown." He casually turned, seemingly scanning the ceiling, then replied," She is Audrey Brent, considered one of the most attractive women in Houston society circles. Her old man is perhaps the wealthiest in the state of Texas."

I interrupted, "Hells Bells! Is she married?"

"No, I was referring to her father. As to her, she is in my opinion, the most desirable, most eligible female in these parts and must add, the most unattainable. She succeeds in fending-off sophisticated, urbane, dedicated scalp hunters with unfailing results, and has disposed of many since her debut. A friend of mine joined the legion a couple of years ago, but after several months of unflagging conquest, gave up the good fight. He told me that capturing her interest was as likely as the Pope becoming Master of a Blue Lodge. I did some work for her father a couple of years back and got to know him rather well. He has some dominant, affable and pleasant characteristics. He's a person who has reached the apex of success by way of diligence, acumen and with an established high degree of integrity. He was and is responsible for the development of several oil patches in the gulf coast area and owns perhaps fifty drilling rigs. If he's here tonight, I will introduce you to him."

"I would like that, but first I would like to meet his lovely daughter. Can you arrange that?"

"Listen carefully Hugh," he ordered more drinks, then continued, "That man sitting with her is also a person of stature. He is wealthy from his dealings in oil and I have heard he's in the pole position in the hectic race for Audrey's hand in marriage. All the widows and fortune hunters have been engaged in a frantic pursuit to snap the trap on him for several years since he became prominent, but he's outsmarted the pack. He remains quite possibly the most desired bachelor in Houston. Gossip has it that his position has now reversed. He has become the pursuer—of Audrey's favors. But the world is cluttered with hopeful analogies and beautiful, dubious things called possibilities, so he could become another casualty of Audrey's hummingbird ways. Who knows? Let's go in and look over the dance?"

We entered the Pavilion where the dance had been in progress for sometime and looked at the bobbing mass of humanity gyrating in unison to the music. I was happier than ever at being here in proximity with people who had it made, anxiously awaiting the meeting of both Audrey and her father, as he could possibly give me a step-up the ladder of success.

Joe Bob interrupted the lurid gossip of three semi-attractive women by introducing me to them. They were clustered near the circle of dancers and were awaiting an invitation to dance, as evidenced by their affected, gushy response to my introduction. My mind was diverted, however, as I was attempting a show of sophistication while pressing the hand of each as Joe Bob presented me to Mrs. Whitley, Mrs. Jacobs and Miss Marlene Shannon. The split state of mind was a result of a portion of my concentration still centered on Audrey Brent, and her father, and what they might contribute to my advancement.

After usual amenities, then listening to Joe Bob's graphic, exaggerated description of my status in the field of petroleum, I asked Marlene if she would like to dance. She smiled and nodded in the affirmative.

Excusing myself to the others, Marlene and I blended in with the eddy of dancers. She was a very good dancer, offering a sensuous, vibrant body that mated perfectly with mine. We were settled into perfect unison of movement, to the strains of "Stardust," as I wished I was holding Audrey this close. My desires ceased abruptly as the music had stopped suddenly, not finishing half of the chorus. The dancers were concerned at the sudden silence.

"I regret the interruption, ladies and gentlemen, please bear with us. I've just been informed of the loss of a very valuable diamond stickpin by one of our guests. Would all of you please step carefully to the wall nearest you, then begin directing a search of the floor for the pin, as you converge in the center of the ballroom. Please be careful before you step to avoid damaging the pin if you do discover it. Now everybody please begin the search moving toward the center. Thank you." Politely requested the orchestra director, Ted Weems.

All heads turned downward and the search for the pin began. I had covered about ten feet when a brilliant blue and white ray from the floor entered my vision. Instinct told me it was the lost pin, as I leaned forward and lifted it from the floor. "Did you find it?" Marlene asked in a stage whisper, as if I might desire to keep my find a secret. I squeezed her by the arm to follow—we made our way to the stage where I informed Ted Weems I had found the missing pin. Handing it to him I said, "Will you please finish "Stardust?"

He laughed then retorted, "I will do better than that. We will play it through just for you and your attractive companion." I thanked him, and turned to leave when he clutched my arm saying, "Hold it I have instructions to secure the finder's name and how they can be reached."

Producing a small pad from inside his jacket, he entered my name and place of residence, Rice Hotel. He then thanked me, informing me the owner would most likely contact me.

Announcing the pin had been found, the band flowed into the melodic strains of Stardust as Marlene and I finished our pleasant interlude. I returned her to her lady friends, then strolled outside to be alone, to struggle with my inner self. There was a probing, jabbing voice within, telling me what a fool I had been to surrender the huge diamond tie pin. For a minute or two I was holding a fortune within my grasping fingers in the form of diamonds. I could have easily acted, as if it were something else I had picked from the floor. The longer I entertained the thoughts emitting from the felonious sector of my brain, the more convincing they were.

I had flubbed the opportunity to elevate my financial status by returning it! I am certain it was of such size it could have been fenced for more than enough to lease or buy, a drilling rig. The chance at the "Golden Fleece" had slipped through my grasp!

I needed something to quench the anger resulting from my analysis of my fictitious act of honesty, so I went into the bar where I found an empty stool. Ordering a double bourbon, I directed a casual glance in the direction of the table where Audrey Brent was seated earlier. She and her three companions were still there.

I had consumed three doubles while casting glances periodically in the direction of my interests. Each time our eyes met I became more convinced that my presence had stirred some activity within her. It might be only curiosity, or maybe a desire to know me better. I was in perfect accord with either. Observing her, I concluded she could not be drinking alcoholic beverages the length of time she had been there. She was still as reserved, calm and assured as the cat in the cage with the parakeet.

The double bourbons I consumed were producing a state of musing and reverie, so I was responding by peering into the shot glass as if it could provide a picture of the future. Still staring Joe Bob slapped me on the back breaking the spell by asking, "Where in the hell have you been?"

He was not aware I was the finder of the tie pin, and surprised when I told him. He said, "Whom did it belong to?"

"Damned if I know. Weems seemed to be secretive about the owner. He did get my name and address, perhaps a reward will be forthcoming. Joe Bob do you think you could take me over to the table and introduce me to the Brent woman?"

"Hell no boy! You must be nuts to think we can barge over to that table and have me break into their camaraderie by introducing you as if you were the Prince of Wales. Those people live and abide by the accepted protocol of society, and the act you have suggested not only violates the normal accepted rules of courtesy, it invites what could develop into disaster! The man, with the lady I don't know, just happens to be a Golden Glove Champion. The one across from the Brent girl, her suitor, has established a reputation of kicking anyone's ass that presents a problem to him. So you won't get any introduction from me, as long as she's presently guarded so heavily. Forget for now you ever saw her, there will be other opportunities to meet her." He continued," Listen to me Hugh. These people you're mixing with tonight are held in restraint by customs that evidently you are not accustomed to. The men get the hots for the women just as you do. The women get aroused over the men. That is as it has been since we were created, but this cult resorts to discreet measures to accomplish their seductions. They use finesse—they screen their emotions by saying "yes" when they mean no, and no when they mean yes. This subterfuge serves as a balm to ease their conscience as well as to confuse the aggressor. Even if one of these women knew you would have her expensive Niemann-Marcus panties swinging from a door knob within the hour, she would still act the part of Whistler's Mother. What I am trying to tell you is that you cannot snort and stomp around like a Hereford bull chasing a "bulling" cow in the pasture. You have to let them think that you are sneaking-up on what you want, even though she might all the while be unzipping your fly. Got it? Be discreet. Even though they are all living the "Law of the Wolf," employing fang and claw, you'll notice they come on as sheep. That's enough lecture for tonight—remember, don't reveal your robust drive, just approach your target in a smooth manner."

"Joe Bob, can you get away to Conroe tomorrow morning? If you can, I'd like for us to withdraw our funds and divide it. We can go in my car. Can you meet me in the lobby at nine?"

"Yes, we can do as you suggest, however, I wish you'd continue our arrangement."

"No, my mind's made up, Joe Bob. I have to go for bigger things and I repeat, I'll always be in your debt for getting me started on what I must accomplish. I'll always be your friend and trust the feeling is mutual."

We walked together to the parking lot, then parted to meet the next morning.

♠ ♠ ♠

I peered from the window into a gray, cold morning—so cold the sparrows on the window sills were lined up, looking like dirty tennis balls. As I left the elevator in the lobby, I spotted Joe Bob settled in one of the huge leather chairs reading the morning edition. We had breakfast, then he suggested we go in his sedan in deference to the cold.

His car was parked in a loading zone outside the hotel, bearing a traffic ticket tucked under the windshield wiper. He made no comment as he removed the traffic ticket, cramming it into his shirt pocket.

We drove out North Main and after a few minutes I broke the silence with, "Joe Bob you must perform your civic duty by writing a memo to the Police Chief, pointing out the dedication to duty of his patrolman. Case in point, the citation in your pocket."

"In a pig's ass, I will. The bastard had damn little to do, to write me that ticket this early in the morning," he muttered.

As we were approaching the North Main tunnel, a car traveling a block ahead had captured my interest. It appeared to be a duplicate of my Cord. We were passing the car as we exited the tunnel when I exclaimed, "That son of a bitch!"

"Who's a son of a bitch?"

"The son of a bitch who sold me my car. He swore on his mother's grave that mine was the only one in Houston. That one's identical, and will you take note of its driver? Who the hell is he? You seem to know him."

"Not really, but he is none other than Bubba Hughes, the emperor of bootleggers in Houston."

I proposed we stop at the Lazy Susan and have a beer. The joint was occupied by the manager, the bartender and three customers, obviously oil field workers that had finished a night "tower" shift. They were washing the acrid odors that surround a drilling rig away with the illegal brew. Joe Bob and I continued past the booth where they were, to one in the rear.

The manager looked back at us seeing the two cold, dripping bottles before us, then returned to his station near the door. The three men in the booth were carrying on raucous conversation truncated with boisterous laughs. The noise of conversation suddenly stopped.

I glanced in the direction of the booth to see one of the men arise and weave his way back to us. I observed him closely as he made his unsteady way to where we sat, determining that trouble could arise from his presence. He reached our booth, then stopped. Looking down at me he growled, "I don't like your looks, fellow."

I was keeping close watch for any movement out of the corner of my eye, as I answered his interruption, "Why don't you go away, we don't want any trouble, okay?"

He stood there swaying as a sea oat on a beach dune, while leering at me with malevolence. I was determined to avoid any melee with him, if possible, by ignoring him.

The manager of the place noticed his action and made his way hurriedly to our booth. He gripped the trouble maker by the elbow, turned in, propelling him back to his booth and admonished him to stay away from us.

A few minutes passed as Joe Bob and I drank our brew while discussing the trouble seeker, when he was before me again saying," I still don't like your looks, pretty boy."

I said nothing in response, then he repeated his statement. He was beginning to prick my veneer of complacency. I was getting angry by contemplating knocking the hell out of him, when the manager once more escorted the pest back to the booth where his cronies were.

I suggested we leave. We passed the booth the drunks were in as we made our way to the door. Just after passing them, I was startled from being kicked in the ass with a heavy boot. The pain was intense.

My reaction was a result of both mental and physical coordination. In a sweeping motion while spinning on my toes, I grasped one of the cane-bottom chairs as my body revolved. I brought the chair up high—in a flash I was facing my tormentor and bringing the chair down atop his head and shoulders. The total action occurred in less than five seconds.

Chair pieces were scattered as if thrown to the wind, while the one that delivered the kick was down on his hands and knees wagging his head like a puppy. His right ear was swinging from his head like a pendulum with only skin keeping it from leaving his head, and bleeding profusely. Joe Bob tugged on my arm saying, "Let's get the hell out of here."

The manager was resting a sawed-off shotgun across his forearm in the direction of the booth where the two drinking companions were still seated. It had occurred to me that they too would join the fray, but after seeing the shotgun trained on them it was understandable why they had elected to remain neutral. I could not fault their good judgment.

As we went out the door, I heard the operator saying, "You asked for it, fella."

We took-off for Conroe, Joe Bob remained silent for several miles while studying me closely, then remarked, "Hugh, I have to admit that you are the most complicated person I've ever known."

"Will you please clarify that remark?"

"Well, when that bastard started his insulting tirade you could have stopped him cold by showing resentment, and using some rough language with him. But no, you sat there like a frightened boy scout that had failed his merit badge test. I can't figure you out. Were you sacred of him, or were you just luring him into that ungodly fury you unleashed?"

"I am guilty of neither. I didn't want to start the day on a discordant tone, so I chose to ignore his verbal jibes hoping he'd forget about not liking my looks."

"I will say this about you. When you get your temper out in sight, it's frightening to see. The fury in your eyes would've turned a crocodile into a docile lizard. I sure hope you never get mad at me. I honestly believe you'd have killed that man if he tried to continue fighting."

"Joe Bob, have you ever received a kick in the ass since you have been an adult, delivered by another adult? I can tell you, having just experienced that indignity, it's the most ignominious, degrading, humiliating experience that's ever befallen me, having that son of a bitch kick me in the ass as if I was some dumb jackass pulling a cart and had balked on him."

The experience had been more denigrating and humiliating to me than the night with the pistol, but I could not tell Joe Bob of that episode, lest I lose face with him.

Upon arriving in Conroe, we entered the bank where I asked the pimply-faced young Snaveley, sitting immobile behind his huge desk, "Who do we see to close out an account, and secure cashiers checks?"

He grunted some unintelligible response while nodding in the direction of the elderly Snaveley across the lobby.

We withdrew the funds—had fifty thousand dollar cashiers check made for each, then departed for Houston.

Chapter Four

The Family Brent: A Golden Goose

As I entered the lobby of the hotel, the clock above the desk clerk pointed to three thirty. Entering my room, I noticed a message form on the heavy plush carpet. It had been pushed under the door during my absence. The memo said to contact the desk clerk, which I immediately did, but was asked to wait a moment.

I was questioning the purpose of this request while waiting for the clerk to come back on the line.

"Mr. McCulloch, Justin Brent called for you, leaving a request that you return his call before four thirty if possible." Then he gave me the number. I asked, "Did he state the purpose of the call?"

"No sir, he did not."

Thanking him, my thoughts reverted to why a Justin Brent would be calling me, and who was he?

In a flash the name Brent was associated with the lovely Audrey Brent I had seen last night at the dance. Could it be possible the two were related? I dialed the number feeling like the new bride—knowing something would happen, but what, and how? A resonant voice came on, "Justin Brent here."

"Mr. Brent, this is Hugh McCulloch returning your call."

"It's a pleasure to talk to you Mr. McCulloch, my being in your debt."

"How's that? How could you owe me when I don't believe we've ever met?"

"May I call you Hugh?"

"Yes, you may."

"It's this way Hugh. The diamond stickpin you returned last night was mine. Words can't express my gratification at your apparent honesty by returning it. The monetary value of the pin is secondary to its intrinsic value. My father gave it to me ten years ago. My grandfather had given it to my dad as a graduation gift. So much about the pin, do you like to play poker?"

"I surely do, Mr. Brent."

"Hugh, would you accept an invitation to my home this evening for dinner? After dinner, three of my friends will be over for our weekly session of poker and I'd like you to sit-in on a friendly game. How about it?"

"I accept your invitation with gratitude. What time and how do I get there Mr. Brent."

He gave me the address and some directions.

"Fine, I will expect you for dinner at seven."

"Just a moment, Mr. Brent. Are you the father of the stunning, beautiful Audrey?"

"Oh boy! I am proud to answer, yes! It becomes apparent by the question that you've met her, and fallen prey to her overpowering charisma." He had a hearty laugh with his answer, then continued, "I must tell you that most men turn-up like a netted trout when seeing her, but she appears to be very interested in someone right now, we're awaiting an engagement announcement any day."

"I'll be looking forward to meeting you tonight at seven, good-bye."

Locating the address, I turned into the tree-lined driveway on time, thinking what a layout! The driveway was strung with hibiscus between the palms, a great distance before the lights of the mansion were visible. The driveway circled to my left, then beside me was an impressive, colonial-type home that shone, as white as fresh fallen snow, in the darkness. I stopped behind a Rolls Royce, then made my way across the spacious porch to face two large opulent doors that seemed to beckon—welcome!

I pushed the bell button and straightened my tie just as the butler opened the door saying, "You are Mr. McCulloch." The way he said the words, I could not determine if he was stating a fact, or asking a question.

"Yes, I am Mr. McCulloch."

He bowed slightly, then said, "Come this way, sir."

We passed through a huge living room where I caught the scent of hardwood smoke from a gigantic fireplace that occupied one wall of the living room. I thought, that fireplace can hold a half cord of wood. When we entered the library, it looked warm and inviting as if lived in. The walls were lined on three sides with bookshelves. The chandelier was emitting a soft glow on the entire scene. Pointing to one of the several huge chairs, the butler requested I be seated as Mr. Brent would be there momentarily.

I did not sit immediately but walked around surveying the hundreds of books on the shelves. There was every type of reading one would expect to find in any erudite person's library. Shakespeare, Cicero, Greek Mythology, Petroleum library, Thesaurus, etc. There was a green-felt covered game table, a standard size pool table, plus two leather covered divans. The many huge leather-covered chairs appeared to be demanding of attention, and were as austere as sentinels keeping watch over this room of comfort and peace.

I selected a chair and immediately visualized the surroundings as my own. I too would have a library comparable to this. But not at the moment, as my reverie was dissipated with the scent of sandalwood. It had to be the scent of a woman—my reasoning was on target as Audrey Brent had flowed into the room. She was standing beside me, smiling down at me, as I leaped to my feet.

She was totally devastating, dressed in a burnt orange evening gown, no accessories to detract from her natural beauty, only a black crucifix was comfortably nestled in the cleavage of her distracting breasts. As she looked at me, she did not hide any surprise of my presence by asking," I saw you at the dance last night with Joe Miller, didn't I?"

"You surely did see me and I must apologize for staring at you. I am Hugh McCulloch."

She offered her hand—a warm, tender hand that possessed strength and character, as we squeezed our palms together. Damn! What a woman!

"Dad asked me to keep you company until he could get-off the telephone. I am Audrey, and I wish to thank you for returning Dad's pin. He treasures it highly."

"I'm only too glad I found it, as it has given me the opportunity of meeting you, which I consider a heady experience. Please excuse me, I am a believer in the axiom 'Brevity is a great charm of eloquence' so when I say to you, that seeing you, is likened to the drama of viewing the Sistine Madonna, that is the essence of brevity and truth."

She laughed a hearty, sincere response to my attempt at eclat, then said, "I wish, really wish I didn't have the commitment to attend the Little Theater tonight."

"Why?"

"I'd like the opportunity to pursue this conversation as you're a funny man. You make me laugh. You cannot realize how refreshing your verbiage comes over, as compared to most guests who come here. I hope you enjoy your dinner and poker. There's the bell sounding the arrival of my escort, I must go. It's been pleasant conversing with you—maybe I'll see you again. Good evening."

I replied, "If it's my choice, we will meet again."

At that moment Justin Brent entered the library. As he approached me, face beaming, hand outstretched in welcome, my impression was one of awe. The man was almost gigantic, towering over six feet, with a tousled shock of straw-colored hair resembling the panache of some exotic bird. His face bore a cherubic air of genial innocence as he traversed the room with the graceful fluid motion of a jungle cat. He greeted me with, "It's indeed a treat, a perquisite to have you in my home, Hugh."

We shook hands, then he steered me to the cypress paneled wall that was bare of bookcases. The paneling was Alaskan cypress, punctured with worm holes. One could readily see this library was a result of meticulous planning with cost not being a factor. Pressing the button on the wall, an elaborate solid mahogany bar well-stocked with spirits and mixers pivoted as a lazy susan ten feet long, with six bar stools visible.

"Pick a seat Hugh, and name your preference."

Brent took a position behind the bar, assuming the stance of a bartender. "What'll you have, sir?"

I thought I would contribute to the charade by asking," Do you have any bootleg whiskey? If so, I'd like that with some branch water."

His face split into a boyish grin, then he reached his huge hand across the bar to shake mine, saying, "You're doggone right, I've got corn. You're my kind of man. I keep a supply for myself, as all who come here go for Scotch, Rye, or Bourbon. Some weirdos even ask for Gin."

He produced a full quart jar from the back of the bar, then set a glass gallon jug of water beside it. Coming around the end of the bar to join me he said, "You're the only person ever to ask for corn whiskey here. That indicates to me, you must be a young man with no fixations, or apocryphal tendencies and I like that. Before I forget, I want to give you a small gift—a gift expressing my gratitude to an honest man who recovered my stickpin."

He tendered a folded paper to me. I made no gesture at receiving it, instead making a deprecating gesture with my hands. His insistence that I take the paper was emphatic. Not wishing to offend, I accepted, knowing it was a check. I opened it to discover a check, payable to me, in the amount of twenty thousand dollars.

My astonishment spirited my voice away, as I could say nothing for several seconds. I was mute. A melange of thoughts crossed my mind—my felonious thoughts when finding the pin—should I accept the reward—do I refuse it? The power of self-aggrandizement prevailed. I needed this man. He was a rung on my ladder to wealth. I would refuse the reward as a ruse to overcome my ultimate purpose. By this act of refusal, I could establish an aura of integrity—a halo of honesty.

I proffered the check to him, after recovering my voice, by saying, "Mr. Brent, I can't accept any gratuity for returning the pin. Accepting it would be contrary to my rules of living. I've always maintained a posture of treating others, as I wish to be treated. I appreciate your gesture, but I can't accept it."

The butler appeared in the door and solemnly intoned, "Dinner is served."

"Come Hugh, we can discuss this later."

We sat at a huge dining table. We were served vichyssoise, pheasant marengo garnished with crayfish and fried eggs, truffles, asparagus spears, stuffed baked potatoes, then finished with baked alaska. The meal was exquisite and served with meticulous care. I savored every bite.

"Hugh, I want you to call me Justin, as all my friends do," he said, as we got up and returned to the library. He requested the butler setup the game table with five chairs, then we sat on the divan ostensibly awaiting the arrival of the others.

"My friends should be here anytime and I'm sure you'll enjoy the game. Incidentally I haven't inquired as to what business you engage in, do you mind my asking?"

"Not at all. I had a stint on a drilling rig, then about three months of being a lease hound, and have now decided to get into wildcat drilling. That's the story of my life."

The butler entered the library, followed by three prosperous appearing men, judging by the suits they were wearing. One could readily see the fabric had been draped on them, then tailored expertly.

Justin introduced me to them using first and last names, no misters. One of the men was slightly rotund, but exuded charisma immediately. He was Bob Manning.

Curtis Waring was a tall man with angular features creased with a constant smile. Curtis owned and operated an exclusive clothiers in downtown Houston. This, I learned later in the evening.

The other, a man about my size, was friendly, yet taciturn and reserved, Al Finney. They were all in their fifties, including Justin Brent. I had the feeling I was being viewed as a juvenile, but entered the conversation showing enough aplomb and assurance that I could handle the situation in an acceptable manner.

We had drinks with Justin. I was going for the corn whiskey, they imbibed Scotch on the rocks, with a twist. While we were enjoying our drink before starting the poker session, I was engaged in conversation with Al Finney. We were discussing Conroe when he interjected the case of the "Parrot Killer," after I had mentioned leaving there recently. During the interchange of ideas, I discovered Al Finney was the Police Commissioner, while Manning was the Fire Commissioner. What a gamut of personalities! Finishing our drinks Justin said, "Let's get started. I feel lucky."

I paused at the table before sitting, as I assumed they had specific locations around the table, and I would take the vacancy. Justin explained their usual rules for my benefit.

"Play nothing but stud—dealer changes with each pot—five dollar ante—five hundred dollar limit—one raise per card."

What the hell was I doing in this game? Five hundred buck limit! If I could have departed with any lame excuse, acceptable and credible, I would have made my exit before the seal was broken on the deck. But I was trapped, snared by my effected mein of prosperity. As regards to playing poker, I was in fast company. My only way out was to sit in a few hands. Justin was talking, "Incidentally Hugh, we do not buy chips. As the game progresses we use markers, then settle accounts at the end. Is that okay?"

"I understand."

Lady luck was with me as I won the deal and the first pot that amounted to twelve hundred dollars. My luck was then turning erratic—I would win a pot—lose three or four, then another. This pattern prevailed for about twenty hands then the decision to start kicking the pots weak cards occurred. The first victim of my audacious act was Justin. The third card dealt brought me a pair of tens up, Justin, queens up. He bet five hundred, the others dropped out, then I called and raised five hundred.

He was musing the possibility that I could be bluffing from the manner in which he was looking me in the eye. He called the raise, then I caught another ten and he a queen. He bet five hundred on the three queens—I called and raised five hundred. He studied my features for what seemed an hour, trying to detect some telltale sign that I did have four tens, then he pushed his cards face down to the center of the table. I raked in the pot adding it to the ample pile of chips before me.

That occurred once more before the session ended, their usual practice being to stop the play at midnight. At that time, I had won thirty seven hundred dollars.

We had another drink before Manning, Waring, and Finney announced they were calling it a night. I arose as they did with the intent of calling it a night also, when Justin cast a look that indicated he wished me to remain.

He escorted them to the door, returning to pour us another generous shot of corn whiskey. As we sipped the drink, Justin broke the silence with this comment, "Hugh, I'm convinced you bluffed me out of a couple of good pots tonight, and after playing poker with hundreds of mediocre, and scores of the best poker players around, I found your finesse refreshing. You can judge a man very well when seeing him under pressure and poker does compress one's will in a whipsaw effect causing the worst side of a man to break out into view. You're a cool operator—that brings up the subject of why I wanted you to remain."

During his monologue, I remained silent as I sipped the drink, but looked directly at him as he talked. He took a deep draft from his glass and smacked his lips saying, "Boy, that's really good whiskey, isn't it? I get it from a bootlegger, Bubba

Hughes. I've known him for several years and have confidence in what he tells me. He's the kingpin of bootleggers in Harris County. Ever hear of him?"

"Yes, he and I have identical automobiles."

"You've a Cord? Is it white like Bubba's?"

"Yes, they're exact duplicates, right down to the red upholstery. I discovered the duplication this morning as I passed him on North Main."

Justin remarked, "Hughes swears this corn whiskey to be aged in a charred hickory barrel for no less than a year. I find it superior to any so-called prescription whiskey."

"Hugh, you told me earlier you wanted in the wildcatting game. After observing you here tonight, I'm convinced you've got the qualifications necessary to become a successful wildcatter. You've self-confidence, you're a gambler as proven by your theft of two or more pots in that poker game, and you possess the facility of having people view you in a favorable manner. You establish rapport quickly with those you meet. These traits I've just pointed out may not make you a success. However, I've never known a successful wildcatter that didn't possess these characteristics. Now as to finances. How much capital do you have to invest in a venture?"

"I have fifty thousand available."

"That's good. Here's what we'll do if you are in accord. At this time, I've twenty rigs stacked. I also have a forty-five hundred acre lease near Hebronville that the option is nearing expiration. Just to motivate you to keep your head in the business, you can put twenty thousand for drilling expense, and miscellaneous. I'll move a rig down there on location as soon as you are ready to go. I know a driller that can smell oil above ground. He's punched many holes for me and is available. We'll have to pay him fifteen a day, but he's a good investment at any price. I'm willing to split any production down the middle with you. A fifty—fifty arrangement."

Damn! It was difficult to control my exuberance at an opportunity like that. What a deal. I realized he was being very generous with me, probably due to my returning the stickpin, but I seized the chance by saying, "Justin, you've made me a very generous proposition and I'll welcome the possibility of working with you. When do we start? I can go tomorrow, I've nothing to hold me here."

He asked, "Have you been to Hebronville?"

"No."

"Then I must point out to you that life there is a struggle. There's nothing there for amusement. No place to go, once you're there. It has the dubious distinction of being the rattlesnake capital of Texas. Most other areas find rattlesnakes hibernating in the winter months, but not so down there. They're on the move all year 'round. You won't believe this, but I was driving out of there to Houston one day last summer. The temperature was about a hundred ten degrees causing heat waves to rise from the pavement like wraiths of fog in a swamp. About three miles north of Hebronville I noticed a mesquite log up ahead several hundred feet. It was blocking my lane completely, but that was alright as it was a two-lane highway and no traffic at all. I crossed over into the left lane to avoid the log and as I passed it, it moved, as if alive!

I pulled over on the shoulder, walking back to see the thing that moved, and there was a diamond back rattlesnake at least eight inches in diameter and about ten feet long. He was so huge, I was fascinated as he wriggled his way across the highway, then disappeared in the mesquite. If a snake of that magnitude should ever strike a man rigor mortis would set in within a minute. You could be sure of death."

"If you wish to get started tomorrow come by my office around ten. I'm on the twenty-first floor of the Gulf Building. I think you should leave your car in my warehouse and take a company pickup down there. The trails will put a good car beyond repair in three months. The brush will remove the paint in less time than that. Let's have one more shot of that corn whiskey to cement our agreement."

We had reached the point of quaffing the mellow whiskey without water so we disposed of this round straight—no branch water.

I arose, thanked Justin for the enjoyable evening, the delicious dinner, then we shook hands.

As I went out the door, I turned to Justin and said, "It's my objective, from this moment on, to become the most successful wildcatter and developer in south Texas, thanks to my affiliation with you. See you at ten in your office. Good night."

I experienced difficulty finding sleep, as my mind was actively reviewing the events of the day. I had lucked out in what appeared to be the greatest opportunity of my life and I would capitalize on it. This was one venture that allowed no foul up on my part. I was dealing with a man who was honest and straight forward. It pained me to realize I must put aside any ideas of dallying with Audrey, lest he cast me aside as a soiled shirt, for sullying his daughter. Sleep finally came.

♠ ♠ ♠

I stepped from the elevator at five minutes to ten, discovering his office just in front of me. The clean khakis I was wearing were stiff from excessive starch resulting in a degree of self-consciousness. I opened the office door and was greeted with a cheery, "Good morning, may I help you? Coming from a comely middle-aged lady seated behind an expensive desk. I noticed an exquisite single red rose by the nameplate, Phyllis Reed, secretary.

"I'm Hugh McCulloch to see Mr. Brent, please."

"Mr. Brent is waiting for you."

She arose, then conducted me past three doors to the end of the hall. There she pressed a button located beside the door handle. The voice of Justin Brent came out a speaker above the door saying, "Come in, please."

As the door opened, Justin with a genial smile and outstretched hand said, "Welcome, Hugh."

I grasped his hands in a friendly shake, then said, "You'll have to excuse me Justin while I recover from the stark beauty and unique decor of your office. It's like walking into a different world."

Above the massive desk was the head of a young elephant with its trunk raised and ears flaring full width. It gave the effect of bursting from the wall, ready to do battle. The realism being so effective that I would not have been surprised to hear an ear splitting trumpet emit at any moment.

The ceiling was covered with a mural depicting some oil boom town—muddy streets—derricks towering above the board sidewalks—the street choked with trucks—wagons behind straining mules—plus a polyglot of humanity lining the sidewalks. The work was graphic and detailed, representing the result of some artist that possessed extraordinary talent.

The wall to my left displayed a massive, fearsome wild boar's head. The bristles on his neck jutting straight up, and tusks three inches long, gleaming white, capable of ripping an adversary into a submission of death.

Surveying the scene I was awe struck. Turning to my right, a snakeskin about twenty-four inches wide and spanning the length of two walls, making it at least thirty feet long, was beautiful in a peculiar way, being mottled with large dark markings, about a foot apart.

Looking above the door I had just entered, I gazed upon the majestic head of an African Oryx, his horns protruding back like two fencing swords.

While I was viewing these unusual trophies, Justin was observing me, as an artist when one stops and admires the seascape he is displaying with pride at the flea market.

"Justin, did you bring down all these trophies?"

"I surely did, Hugh. I shot the elephant in Kenya, the Oryx in Mozambique. The wild boar in Madagascar and the Anaconda in Bolivia. I used to hunt extensively, but have lost interest in recent years."

My sense was relaying a message. Justin, or anyone, who would display things like these in an office, had to be regarded with caution. I was convinced he was not one to accept any double dealing or anything less than total commitment on the part of any associate. I thought any individual capable of being surrounded constantly with things of such deadly nature would surely be an individual that would not countenance opposition. I believed him capable of destroying anyone obstructing his progress.

I made a mental note to regard him in business activities as a coiled rattlesnake. I would make no moves that smelled of ulterior motives—nothing that could be construed as a double-cross.

I liked the man, he impressed me with his genial manner and apparent integrity. I liked his mein of certitude—his personality. In no way was I questioning his solidity—it was my own character infirmities that were being analyzed. As success loomed ahead it was advantageous that I strive for prescience, diligence and acumen. These were imperative to my attaining great wealth. I ceased my musing by asking, "Justin, do you really feel that I have the know how to go to Herbonville and supervise the development of the lease there?"

"No problem Hugh, I've contacted the driller. He's ready to start and will meet you in front of the bank in Hebronville tomorrow morning at nine. He knows his business and is qualified to advise you on any problem or question that may arise. I didn't dwell on your experience while conversing with him. As far as he knows, you're an experienced "wildcatter." For awhile you just act the part of the old pro by observing and listening to the crew. You can do this in an effective manner. I am sure of that, or I'd never have made you the proposal."

"I can do that easily."

"Alright, take your car over to the warehouse and get one of our pickups. The address is on this card. But first we must go to the bank to open your operating account. Do you have the twenty thousand?"

"Yes, right here." I produced the fifty thousand cashier's check.

We left the entrance of the Gulf Building going across the street to the bank. Justin introduced me to a Mr. McNally, who in turn effected the opening of the drilling account, and a separate personal account with the remaining thirty thousand.

Justin and I parted at the corner, he wishing me success in Hebronville and informing me the drilling rig would be there awaiting the driller and I tomorrow morning.

"Hugh, just one moment. I forgot to tell you the driller's name is Clarence Ward. He's better known as Curly. You two will get along well. Also, I didn't mention the geologist. He'll meet you and Curly at the bank. I tried to have him in the office this morning to meet you, but he couldn't arrange it. The geologist will locate the drilling site for you. His name is Joe Bob Miller."

God almighty! I said to myself, what an unholy trinity, Joe Bob, Justin, and I. At this bit of information, I was overwhelmed with an eagerness to depart Justin's presence lest he detect my astonishment.

"You had better be on your way, Hugh. Good luck."

Arriving in Hebronville at five, the growling of my stomach awakened me to the fact that I had omitted lunch.

My first impression of the community was one of curiosity. Why would one live here by choice? The business section was the duplication of the typical western movie. All vestige of paint on the buildings was scoured by the blowing sand and scorched by the searing heat of the relentless sun. Looking down the central street in quest of a restaurant, the thought occurred when and if I did locate one, it would surely be the City Cafe. Every small town in Texas could point to one.

Hebronville boasted a City Cafe alright, that I entered in search of food and information. While eating, a small man wearing a huge, white hat entered and seated himself two stools to my left. He was weighted with two pearl handled revolvers tied down with leather thongs. The handles of the pistols jutted from hand tooled holsters supported by a wide belt that was joined with an enormous silver buckle adorned with the figure of a bucking horse. I caught him giving me the "who the hell are you" scrutiny, usually afforded to a stranger in town, so I ignored him.

As I was having my coffee and pie, I had determined the pistol wearer to be a lawman. One who presented a ludicrous sight—yet one that might possess a sadistic nature sated with the use of the pistols hugging his hips. They gave him a sense of power to offset his diminutive stature, as revealed by his rolling swagger when he entered.

I asked the man serving me where I could locate a place to live. He suggested I try the Adam's house one block west.

The lawman came closer, but remained standing with thumbs hooked in his belt, then said, "You're new in town."

"That's right."

"Well, I've been looking you over, as I'm the town Marshal, and it's my job to look everybody over that comes into town, you understand?"

"Yes, I understand."

He was shifting nervously from one pointed boot to the other, evidently irritated by my air of disdain and feckless attitude.

"What's your business here?"

I had begun to seethe inside and my neck was getting hotter by the second from this pimple of a man's interrogation. His arrogance infuriated me.

"I'm in the oil business."

"Ah Ha! That's just what I figgered. Let's get one thing understood here and now. I know you oil guys. You come into town with the idea of taking it over. Doing as you please.

Screwin' all the women and beatin' up all the men. But not here, Buddy Boy. I'm the law and I enforce it."

His face was livid and his hat was brushing my brow as he had moved closer and closer during his tirade. His breath smelled as rank as a sack of water moccasins. I was leaning back ever farther to avoid his breath of putrefaction. Gulping air for a new start he continued, "Ask Joe here if I take any crap off you oil men. He'll tell you that I'd rather pistol whip ya' than argue for a moment. I'll slap your ass in jail quicker than hell if you get out of line. Do you heah?"

"Yep, I hear."

I paid my check, then exited the place while the marshal ranted to Joe about me being a smart ass, as he could tell the way I acted.

The Adam's house appeared clean, so I made arrangements to room there.

♠ ♠ ♠

On my way to the cafe the next morning I saw three large oil field trucks loaded, parked at the end of the central street. The logo was Brent Exploration Corp., painted on the sides. This was our rig and I could not deny a feeling of elation, as I looked it over. I never doubted that my success was there before me on the three trucks, I knew it.

Making my way to the cafe I was considering what problem, if any, the injection of Joe Bob into my activities, would produce. If he should ever reveal the facts of our past associations to Brent, would it create a chasm of distrust for me? Joe Bob could not disclose this damaging information to Brent or anyone, as he would be vulnerable to criminal charges as a result. I need not harbor any concern about Joe Bob talking in the wrong places.

I got out of the truck in front of the city cafe, then saw a man loitering beside the door apparently awaiting someone. He was dressed in clean khakis, muscular, a freckled face and a duplicate of me in size. His head was adorned with a mat of tightly-curled brilliant red hair. This had to be the driller, Clarence "Curly" Ward.

He had observed my arrival in the Brent Company truck which resulted in him asking, "Are you Hugh McCulloch?"

"Yes, and you must be Clarence Ward."

We shook hands. He had a grip comparable to a vise, that indicated great physical strength. I liked the impression his meeting had given me, prompting me to say, "Just call me Hugh."

He laughed as he replied, "If you call me anything but Curly, or maybe a son-of-a-bitch, if I should happen to twist-off a drill stem, then I won't know who you're addressing. Just call me Curly."

We found the three truck drivers in the cafe trying to stave off sleep by drinking black coffee, and made ourselves known to them. One driver asked, "How far in the boondocks is this location?"

I answered, "Damned if I know, the geologist will meet us at nine in front of the bank to take us to the site."

Curly pointing to the front door and said, "There he is now."

Joe Bob made his way to the table, then pulled a chair beside me saying, "How's the wildest wildcatter in Texas?" Then extended his hand in greeting. He knew Curly, also the truck drivers, and cast some remark of recognition to each of them. He then turned to Curly and said, "This Hugh McCulloch here has brought in more 'dusters' than any blue norther ever did. But I'll tell you this, he's a man foursquare, and will fight a circle saw bare knuckles. I've known him a long time and you can rely on what he says. You're safe betting your ass and all its fixtures on anything he tells you."

"Curly, where are the rig builders?"

"They should be here at anytime, Mr. Miller."

A truck and pickup were pulling into the curb as we reached the sidewalk. Curly waved to them in recognition. In both vehicles I saw a total of six men and realized these were the rig builders.

Joe Bob suggested he leave his car there and ride with me as we were heading for some rugged country. Rugged it was. We traversed nine miles of mesquite trees so thick they gave passage of the vehicles grudgingly by gouging paint, and giving-up limbs with screeching agony. Negotiating the trees and brush was a veritable obstacle course, requiring constant physical effort in maneuvering the zigzag, erratic growth.

After thirty minutes I asked, "Joe Bob, do you know where we're going?"

"Keep up the good work. We're only one mile from our first site."

Fifteen minutes later, looking intently ahead, he said, "Here we are, right here. Stop!" I stopped then said, "I want to thank you for the buildup you gave me to Curly Ward. I hope he believed at least half of what you said. Incidentally how can you be sure this is the location, and how in the hell did you come directly to it?"

"See that piece of yellow cloth tied to the mesquite tree there on the right?"

"Yes, but how did you pinpoint the location?"

"You didn't notice the small red pieces of cloth on the trees coming out? I've this forty-five hundred acres all laid out with drilling sites, indicated with yellow cloth as you can see. Simple, isn't it?"

Two of the rig builders had produced axes and were awaiting clearance instructions from Joe Bob. He designated the area to be cleared, then he asked me to drive him back to town.

As we started Joe Bob was silent while looking at me in the same manner he did after I had broke the chair on the drunk's head. Fully five minutes had elapsed when he began talking, "There's something I must tell you, but I sure as hell want you to maintain a level head, and don't go snorting and charging into this information like a hereford bull. Audrey Brent called me last night after she'd left you in the library at her home. She plied me with questions concerning you. They were woman questions. I mean those generated by romantic inclinations on the part of the questioner."

"Be more specific. What did she ask?" It required an inner effort to effect banality in my voice.

"Damn it, Hugh. She wanted to know how long I'd known you. What business you were in. Had you been married. Questions all women ask when a spark has been struck. This Audrey worked on me like a skilled surgeon, probing with a razor sharp scalpel to lance a boil. She even inquired as to your fiscal weight. When they venture into the area of finances during an interrogation, you can be certain that you must've delivered the equivalent of an amoret at the least."

"What answers did you give?"

"Hell Hugh, are you practicing law? I'm not on the witness stand. I answered the first with a lie. I told her I'd known you for four years. That you were an oil developer and had never been married. About your financial status, I might've blown it up a little too much, but that won't hurt your cause. Do not screw her up, as she's a golden egg in anybody's nest. She's interested in you to the extent of giving me the number of her private phone to deliver to you, with a request you call her when possible. Here's the number written on this card."

He leaned over depositing the card in my shirt pocket. "I really think you struck high C on her romance scale to create such interest in her for you to call. Remember what I told you about finesse. If you attempt an iconoclastic siege be prepared for defeat. Her armor is composed of a potpourri of female wiles and snares that have resulted in ignominious defeats for many suitors. Men who fancied themselves as artisans in the intrigue of romance, imaginary nonpareils. I'm sure a rough cut gem of your class would be no match for her, if you make the wrong approach. So much for the lecture. What's the deal you have with Brent?"

I related the arrangement that we were working on and Joe Bob expressed surprise that a man of Justin Brent's position in finance would consider a partner, and that I was indeed fortunate to be in the catbird seat.

We parked beside Joe Bob's car and told him about yesterday's exchange between me and the town marshal. He cautioned me to skirt any confrontation with the little piss ant, as he had a reputation to uphold, shooting an offender on the slightest provocation. In fact, he boasted of eliminating twelve Mexicans and three Americanos during his ten year tenure as marshal. This bit of information did not surprise me as I had calculated his eagerness to resort to the power the pistol afforded him. I would avoid him if possible.

Joe Bob instructed me to call him when we had drilled to a fifteen hundred foot depth. He wished to be there to evaluate the core samples at that depth. He then departed to Houston.

Chapter Five

Hebronville—A Texas Armpit

While in the restaurant, a sign on the wall caught my attention. The sign indicated a public dance would be held, starting at nine, above the Old Rialto Theater. The cafe owner informed me that the location was one block east, and added," A single man can usually find whatever he is seeking as there are more woman than men there. You ask Cotton here, he pointed to a big blonde man sitting near me.

"I've never heard your name, I'm Joe Childs, and this big bastard here is Cotton Burns."

"I'm Hugh McCulloch."

Cotton asked, "You goin' to the dance tonight?"

"I don't have anything in mind, I might go to check out the town people. Do you know where we can buy some whiskey?"

"Hell yes, if you want to go, we'll get us a quart of moonshine and go up there and bump crotches with some of those innocent females."

"Let's go. We'll get the whiskey first."

Cotton directed me to a house at the edge of town where I bought a quart of white corn. It went down fairly easy without a chaser. We hit the jar several times and were in a state of euphoria as we climbed the stairs to the dance at nine fifteen.

The musicians were dedicated in their efforts at volume and successful too, as the din was ear-splitting, but not melodic. The wall was lined with benches occupied by about fifteen women. Several men were standing beside the dance floor observing the acrobatic antics of some of the dancers, while electing to watch rather than select one of the females from the bench and join the jumping, sliding, shaking couples on the floor.

I asked a nice looking brunette, if she would care to dance. She responded with alacrity, and we wheeled into the energetic twosomes crowding the floor. This young lady was very genteel and reserved, yet amiable and friendly. While dancing I introduced myself and learned her name was Alice Thompson. We sparred with the usual questions and answers that prevail in this situation, making a reasonably good dancing pair.

Cotton and I had made several trips to the car to partake of the booze. Its effects had produced a state of good feeling for our fellowmen.

I had danced with the Thompson girl several times and felt sure she regarded me as someone she would like to know better. The feeling if true, was mutual. At the moment, she was dancing with another while I observed things from the stag line.

A jarring, shattering explosion wracked my whole being. I was flying backward, my eyes viewing the ceiling through a hazy film—then I struck the floor on my back, and blackness engulfed me. I could hear voices near, but could see no one. The voices became intelligible and slowly my vision began to return. First I saw the glow of the overhead light then I was staring into a pair of eyes saturated with hostility. Above these eyes, a white-brimmed hat. At that moment I realized I was flat on my back, peering glassy-eyed upward into the ugly face of the town marshal leaning over me.

He reached down, grasped me by the arm while growling, "Get your ass up off the floor, I'm taking you to jail."

I was trying to rise on my rubbery legs as he was lifting my shoulders, an arm under each. When I reached an upright position he started to propel me toward the stairway saying," Let's go! Let's go!"

My head had cleared somewhat and I realized that someone had approached me from the rear, delivering a devastating uppercut to my chin. My jaw felt like it was fractured and I could feel with my tongue that I'd chipped a front tooth.

I balked, pushing back on my heels, then asked, "Why're you taking me to jail? What's the charge?"

"Fighting in a public place, you bastard. I told you I enforced the law here. But you're a smart ass and have to learn the hard way, let's go."

We had reached the stairs when a feminine voice behind interrupted, "Just a minute there Vail Dennis, you little toad of a man, you aren't taking this man anywhere. If you persist on locking him up, then I'll personally appear before the judge and relate what occurred here tonight. I saw the entire episode. You and that sorry specimen, Cotton Burns, are working a dirty, underhanded racket. I'm aware of the whole deal. Cotton Burns doesn't have guts enough to face a man so he hits him from behind. Then you, you little cockroach, arrest the victim for fighting—fine them—then you and Cotton divide the fine. If you take this man in, then I'll be there tomorrow morning and I promise you, the true story of what has been taking place between you and Cotton Burns, will become common knowledge all the way to Austin.

"How would you like a Texas Ranger to relieve you of your big pistols? You had best release him now. He has violated no law."

Marshal Dennis turned to me shaking from anger and retorted, "I'll get you sooner or later. You're free to go or stay." With that he departed quickly after knocking me down.

After thanking Alice Thompson for her intervention in my behalf, I left the dance to go to my room. I needed the rest. Also, the seat of my trousers had been ripped open from hitting the floor with such force, needless to say I was feeling humiliated.

♦ ♦ ♦

The following morning found me painfully sore from bouncing off the floor and my jaw was swollen and blue from the unexpected blow. I was filled with a driving urge to seek out Cotton Burns and pound him into hamburger. This was a vow made to myself as I entered the City Cafe hoping to find him there.

Joe, the restaurateur, greeted me with this statement, "If you're looking for Cotton Burns you're too late. I understand he boarded the five a.m. bus to Laredo, headed for who knows where. That was a dirty trick he pulled on you and confidentially, I believe Vail Dennis is in hot water too. Maybe some good will come from it all, even though it was tough on you. We'll wait and see."

The rig builders erected the drilling tower very quickly, then Curly took over the operation and our first effort at developing this large tract was underway. Four days before Christmas I had been on the drilling site around two in the afternoon. While getting into a pickup truck, misfortune struck.

I had one foot on the running board when a hot, searing stab of pain hit me just below my left knee, causing me to reel backward. It was so unreal—I could not imagine the source of it. I lifted my trouser led and discovered two punctures below my knee, oozing a drop of blood. One of the drilling crew had observed my actions, then ran to me asking, "What happened?" He looked at my leg exclaiming in an excited manner, "You've been hit by a rattlesnake."

He looked under the truck for the snake, but could not locate him at first glance as the rattler had squirmed his way up into the undercarriage of the vehicle. In the ensuing minutes, I had tied my handkerchief around my leg as a tourniquet, while the crew had secured a rake, dislodging the snake and killing it. Curly instructed a crew member to drive me into Hebronville immediately.

The doctor sent me on to Laredo where I was hospitalized for five days. During my hospital confinement I received an unexpected gift.

Christmas Day, at six p.m., I had a visitor, Audrey Brent. Appearing in the door of my room, she paused, smiling. A smile as radiant and endearing as that of a sleeping baby graced her pretty face, as she made her way to my side. I made a mental note to dub her 'Sunshine'. The essence of sandalwood, teased my sense of smell as she stood beside my bed. The fragrance titillated my male glands and stirred excitement within. This is one hell of a woman—completely devoid of any fallacious manner or illusive words. She greeted me with a sonorous, though frivolous, "How did a big, virile man like you, get disabled by a little snake? However, I'm glad to see you regardless of the circumstance."

She placed her hand in mine as I was considering a worthy response to her appearance, and greeting. She was awaiting some word from me as my silence was skirting stupidity, then I let go with, "Audrey, your presence has restored my belief in Santa Claus. Last night I sent out a silent request for him to bring me something of beauty, that would also bring comfort, and be of inestimable value. Look what he sent! You. You with the beauty of the vibrant stars of the desert night. Your presence is as comforting as the billowy depths of a feather bed on a frigid winter's night. Your being here will instill upon the pages of my memory, an everlasting reminder that today someone thought enough of me to come and hold my hand. This memory I'll treasure forever. Thank you for coming, Sunshine."

"Hugh, when I first met you I told you that you made me laugh, remember? With that flow of persiflage just emitted, I don't know whether to laugh or call you a fraud. I'll say this, I liked every word of it. Now about you calling me 'Sunshine", I consider that the greatest compliment ever bestowed on me, and believe me, I've been the target of experts in the practice of sycophancy. None can equal you in saying what a woman likes to hear, even though she may not believe it. When are you getting out of here?"

"The doctor is releasing me tomorrow."

"Good. I'll stay over tonight in Laredo and be here when you're released. Would you like that?"

"I'll look forward to what tomorrow and you bring."

"Dad asked me to bring you back to Houston as the driller can handle things at Hebronville. He wants to discuss some business with you, then our pilot will fly you back down. I must go now, I'm staying with some friends of the family. I'll come for you in the morning. Good night."

"Good night, Sunshine, it was so nice of you to come."

She left the room, but her presence remained in the tantalizing, erotic form of the essence of sandalwood. The delightful fragrance favored me by putting me into an exhilarating state, followed by a trance of eroticism, then somnolence, then sleep.

I was resolved to adopt the role of a listener as we made the drive to Houston, my goal being to learn everything possible about this bewitching woman that had exuded such exotic allure. This woman, so entrancing with her air of freshness, who had captivated me when our first glance had arced into an arcane situation shared by the two of us.

When she talked I was as inert as a beached whale, just as silent lest I dispel the magic of the moment. With a few probing questions I had extracted a volume of knowledge regarding her way of life, her criteria of conduct, morals, and most satisfying, she revealed her stance on the lack of importance of chastity to the woman of today.

Audrey was the first woman ever to conduct a conversation composed of such delicate subject matter as morals, promiscuity, chastity, decorum while eating with me. She stated her views in a way that dissipated any traces of doubt that I may have had regarding her sincerity, deceit, or meaningless rhetoric.

I thought, if my analysis of her character borders on the panegyrical, then so be it. She deserved it. I would be as hard to shake as a loan shark collector. What a specimen!

We arrived at the Brent home around six p.m. where we found Justin crouched over a golf ball poised to stroke it with a putter, hoping to see it drop into the cup about twenty feet away in an expanse of lush green grass. Hearing the car, he straightened up, then walked toward us saying, "I see this daughter of mine is developing good taste in her men, for a change. How's the snake bite, Hugh? Come on in, we'll have a few shots of that good corn whiskey you like so well, before dinner."

We shook hands as we mounted the steps, then proceeded to the library where Justin conducted the ritual of opening the wall bearing the bar on the reverse side.

"Dad, do you mind if I have a highball or two with you, as I have time on my hands?"

"No honey. Anything I have to say to Hugh can bear your presence, so pick a stool and give the bartender your order. But please, no fancy concoctions. Keep it simple like Scotch and water or Bourbon on the rocks."

Audrey had informed me on the way back from Hebronville, about the loss of her mother ten years ago, and how Justin had been both mother and father to her ever since. As he mixed her drink and produced the bootleg whiskey, I was studying this man before me in a different light. My previous observation was void of the knowledge he had been so close to Audrey as she grew to an adult woman.

Arranging the drinks on the bar, Justin came around to sit with Audrey and me saying, "Do you play golf, Hugh?"

"No, I've never had the inclination to play the game, nor the time. Why do you ask?"

"That's right. If you haven't any desire to play the game, perhaps it's a waste of time considering the time required. I don't play very often due to a dwindling of interest. Audrey and I've discussed the action necessary to get you accepted into the Country Club, provided you've the desire to become a member. That's why I asked her to bring you back so we could assess your views on the subjetc. Audrey made the suggestion, pointing out it could provide the important contacts so essential to a young man venturing into oil exploration. I concur with her thinking and will advance the idea by sponsoring your membership. We'd like you to have various reasons, we think it would open future doors for you—right now there's a paucity of enterprising young members. Too many old goats getting long in the tooth, cluttering up the clubhouse and reliving heroic deeds of the past—some of the spurious tales are fantasies rather than deeds. We need some new blood—young members to combat the flatulence their presence has provided for so many years.

"If you desire membership, consider it accomplished, as my sponsoring you is tantamount to acceptance. I'll pay the membership fee as a token of appreciation of your past act."

I answered, "I'd consider it a privilege to be admitted."

"Now that's settled. How are you making out in Hebronville?"

"I'm finding it just as you predicated, not much of a town. But, if we bring in some producers I could care less if it were a microcosm of Little America—ice garnished with penguins. If you haven't detected it, let me tell you, I'm a man swept along with an insatiable ambition to vault to the top rung of the ladder of success. Neither hot nor cold, rattlesnakes, or man-made obstacles will detract me from my goal."

By now I was standing, emphasizing my words with gestures, the protagonist, an Elmer Gantry. Audrey was looking at me in a quizzical manner. Justin was expressing curiosity, I think, at my deluge, my gush of animated desires, when I realized I was no longer conversing, but preaching.

Justin found my performance amusing and rewarded my rhetoric with a hearty laugh, then said, "Hugh, by God you have to be the devil's advocate. Any young man as charged with ambition and panache, as boils within you is sure as hell destined for the top. The brass ring. I cannot express the anticipation with which I await your entry into the arena, where you'll tangle with the grizzlies, the cobras, the tigers, and the skunks too. Excuse old Dad's language, Audrey, but this Hugh is the gladiator capable of kicking asses over the moon of any damn fool stupid enough to get in his way. I'll do all possible to give you a leg-up I want to watch the show as it progresses. Yes sir, you're my man,"

I was still steaming with oratory and continued, "Justin and Audrey, a year from today I'll have an office downtown just like yours, except for the difference in adornments on the walls.

Casting a surreptitious glance to Audrey I continued, "I may be fortunate enough to have a portrait of a beautiful woman to grace the wall behind my desk. A portrait of Audrey."

There . . . I had said it. The gauntlet had been dropped. The challenge disclosed.

Audrey demonstrated her eclat—her savoir faire by replying as her cheeks tinged slightly, "I consider it a mellifluent compliment that you would wish my portrait in your office. I thank you."

Then showing me an impish smile, she added, "I think your office will reflect your good taste in decor."

During the drive to Houston I had been constantly fighting the audacious urge to elicit some expression from her regarding the man in her company at the club dance. I wanted to know if he was a prospective groom or an object of amusement, but I could not mobilize the courage to present the question to her. Joe Bob's advice about propriety had shackled my normal certitude by causing me to weigh my words and acts, effecting a transition in my tactics. His warning and description had transformed me from a 'snorting bull', to a timid sneak, lest I ask the wrong question.

As we were dining, I resolved to determine, at the first opportunity, my status in Audrey's stable of suitors, regardless of propriety, protocol or any other standard she was accustomed. This woman had stirred a vortex of novel and alien emotions within me. Emotions that had been in a state of lethargy during my life. I had never been aware of their existence before her eyes first met mine, and by God, I was committed to get into her life, or get her out of mine. The turbulence of uncertainty was clawing at my insides as if I were filled with giant sea crabs, scratching, clawing, pinching to escape.

After dinner, a meal that was an epicurean delight, we retired to the library where Justin made us a drink. As I sipped mine, I was musing various stratagems that would provide me with the information I sorely needed to get peace of mind, when Audrey suggested we go for a drive.

I looked askance toward Justin. "You two get out and go. When I was your age I wouldn't be sitting here with an old goat like me."

"Justin, was there any other business you wished to discuss with me?"

"Nothing else Hugh. I'll put you up for membership in the Country Club tomorrow, and then the Petroleum Club. When you get to Hebronville tell old Curly Ward that I said he'd better bring something out of that hole, and I don't mean salt water. If he fails, you and I'll stuff him in it to cap it off! He'll get a kick out of that. Audrey, you can drive Hugh out to the plane at ten in the morning. I'll call McDonald, he's my pilot. I'll have him there to fly you down. You'll stay here tonight before you leave. Now you kids get out of here. Good night."

Audrey got up and I followed, then as we started out the door Justin said, "Hugh, don't worry about a thing. That tract at Hebronville is going to produce enough to sate a great deal of that burning ambition of yours. If we shouldn't happen to get it there, remember there's a lot of dirt in Texas. I repeat, the prospects of seeing you in action when you attain the status of oil potentate, is something worth waiting for. So don't permit your drive and ambition to wane. You're my gladiator! Hot Damn! I can hardly wait. Get the hell out of here you two!"

Audrey insisted on driving, suggesting we go to Galveston. The night was fairly cool, not cold, this being one of the mild winter nights in south Texas. We had been riding for about ten minutes in silence, when Audrey said, "Hugh, I'm sure you're cognizant of dad's liking for you as he's a very expressive person. Frankly, I've never known him to share a rapport with anyone comparable to what he shares with you. I'm very happy he's found someone to associate with in a condition of camaraderie as he has with you. You're someone with whom he can relax, and conduct man-to-man talk.

"This business arrangement he offered you came as a surprise to me. He's always been more or less reticent to have any ties with anyone. He appears to get a vicarious effect from the prospects that you offer. I suspect he's always wanted a son to share life with, even though he loves me very much. He says I filled some of the void that occurred with the loss of my mother, you must realize we're very close."

"Yes, one can see you're very dear to him. As to him accepting me, perhaps my finding his pin contributed to any rapport that exists. Regardless of the success of the Hebronville venture, I'll always hold him in esteem for giving me this opportunity in the oil business. Then too, there's another facet of the whole picture I have to know, and I trust you'll provide the answer."

This was the moment of truth. I realized I was treading on thin ice, but reason and custom be damned, as a driving urge within me forced me to ask, "What was the man's name you were sitting with in the bar, the night of the dance when I first saw you?"

"Why do you ask?" her voice carried a flippant tone.

"Okay Judge. I'll rephrase the question. Do your dulcet words lull him into an ecstatic state as they do me?"

"Come on, Hugh. Out with it. You want to ask if he's the object of my affection. Right? The answer is no! He'd like to be, and he's trying to leave the impression around that we're practically engaged. I've been refuting that illusion for a year as a result of his making the implication to everyone. Now I'll answer your question. His name is Jack Cook."

"On a scale of two—he and I—where do I rate?"

I was plunging now. This was romantic brinkmanship.

She drove a little faster. The only sound was the throaty hum of the powerful Rolls Royce engine, and the whisper of the tires caressing the pavement. Silence prevailed for fully five minutes, during which time the invisible golden wire of communication was conducting silent messages between us—that line of communication that exists between two human souls with vibrations in perfect orchestration. When the two hearts are as one. I knew the thoughts coursing her mind. She knew the motivation of my question.

"One." She had broken the heavy silence. Her answer brought a surge of ecstacy to me—no surprise—I had known what her answer would be, but can offer no practical reason as to how I knew. I remained silent for a few moments savoring the feeling of equanimity, and the cessation of the inner pain that uncertainty had produced.

Now that she had answered my question, I settled back against the plush upholstery of the Rolls, pondering the issue of what my response should be. Audrey continued, "Hugh, why did you choose to ignore my request that you call me? I gave the number to Mr. Miller, I assume he gave it to you, so why didn't you call?"

"It's this way. I'd been told Jack Cook was leading the pack in the race for your charms, and I had the feeling you'd requested I call as a way of extending me courtesy due to my association with Justin."

"Let me paint you a true picture of what exists between Jack Cook and I. He attended high school with me, we were in the same class. He's persisted in dating me since my junior year. He's never believed I'd have an interest in anyone but him. I dated others and without any encouragement on my part, he's been successful in creating the belief among our friends, that eventually he and I would marry.

"I deliberately waited before enrolling in college until he'd decided on the school he would attend, in order to select a college in a different city. He called to tell me he'd been accepted to matriculate at L.S.U. in the School of Petroleum Engineering located at Baton Rouge, Louisiana. Then I applied for Hockaday at Dallas and was accepted. Damned if he didn't withdraw from L.S.U. and attend S.M.U. in Dallas, offering the excuse he just had to be near me.

"I'm relating this to you in the hope you can comprehend our actual relationship. After college he went into Petroleum and became quite successful. This success and the activities in which he was involved brought about contact with Dad on numerous operations. During the time since then, he's conducted himself in a manner that implied to others I was his property. Nothing could be farther from the truth. As of this moment I belong to no man, and that includes you.

"However," she followed up quickly, "I did give you a sincere answer to your question. Frankly I find you most refreshing, your candor intrigues me and excuse my candor when I say I believe you to be a diamond in the rough. Dad has been impressed with your apparent honesty, as I have. He and I were discussing you one night recently and he described your makeup perfectly. He sees you as the epitome of a vanishing type of true 'wildcatter'. We agreed you were a sort of cavalier in the oil drilling business. We both see in you the ambition necessary to survive in such a highly competitive enterprise. You appear to have a great degree of determination and the imaginative soul of an artist, plus the verve of a nobleman. You're self-sufficient, but also vain. That won't hinder you in the years ahead. I too, have the utmost confidence in your ability to succeed in whatever you do. I'm not being facetious when I tell you that should you desire to capture me, that success won't evade you." She continued, "Enough about you for the moment. Permit me to expand on the association between Jack Cook and I, a bit more. He's made a veritable crusade of his efforts at getting me to share sex with him. You can't believe the tenacity that obsesses him. He's resorted to every conceivable strategy employed since Adam and Eve started mankind on the quest for sex. Don't underestimate the charm Jack Cook can muster when he desires. There were several times, during the past three years, that I questioned the perseverance of my resistance to his onslaught of romantic attempts. There were times when his artful maneuvers almost succeeded, but you can believe me when I tell you he's never realized his goal of getting me between the sheets."

"You've cleared the issue that has plagued me since the first time I saw you. That being how deeply entrenched Jack Cook was in your life. Now that you've erased the belief you were engaged to Cook, I can proceed with the knowledge we share a degree of respect and admiration, and I'm sure both will increase as time goes by."

"I'm certain of it, too," she replied as she turned the car around and asked if I cared to drive back.

I didn't make an issue, but this was my first experience at driving a Rolls Royce. However, it gave me a pleasant hour to savor. We conversed at length about varied subjects and I found her erudite and very knowledgeable on subjects alien to most women. During the conversation, she asked me when and how I chipped my tooth. I thought it was unwise to reveal it was the result of a brawl, so I skirted her question by telling a lie. A roughneck on the rig had been applying pressure on a nut with a spud wrench. The wrench slipped out of his hand, bounced and struck me in the mouth, chipping my tooth."

We then turned into the drive finding the house dark. She remarked as we were entering the door, "I suppose Dad was tired tonight."

Audrey pointed out the bedroom I would occupy, then placed her arms on my shoulders, as our eyes met in a silent message of understanding. Sliding her arms ever so gently around my neck, while pressing her exciting body lightly against mine, our lips softly touched like the brush of a master painter's touch to his canvas. I was exerting restraint at not snatching her warm, voluptuous body and pressing it hard against mine, when she squeezed my neck with entwined arms. Not a hard firm hug, but bordering on it. She was now shifting her dainty feet to match the contour of her body to mine. A sudden, ludicrous thought penetrated the allure and thrill of the moment. The thought of Joe Bob Miller's counsel of not charging in like a snorting bull.

She chased my review right out of my mind by bringing her lips to mine once more, with the compound effect of tenderness and desire.

Damn it, this woman had me boxed in a dilemma. Should I pull her into me and kiss her, while telegraphing the cauldron of lust that shrieked for release rolling within me, and accept what followed, or should I let her determine when the detour sign would appear? By God, my mind was made up. If a seduction occurred now, or in the future, it would be Audrey who set the stage. Not I. I had too much going, to chance being viewed as an insouciant bohemian in her eyes. She was too near the heart that pumped life blood to nourish my ambition, Justin.

It is canny how thoughts composed of logic, sound reasoning, and practicality can appear in certain situations as asinine and ill-advised. Yet they appear at the most inopportune times and result in frenetic action—sometime disaster, in the mind that harbors them. This time I would be the seducee if it went that far, she would be the seductress.

"Good night, Hugh," then she touched her forefinger on my lips, as if to hold me back from my pursuit. The way she said, "good night," left no idea she was toying with me. She meant good night.

Chapter Six
Falling In Love

The company pilot controlled the tri-motor plane as deftly as the puppeteer animates the marionette, and placed it as gingerly and tenderly on the dusty runway as the ornithologist would lightly handle an egg of an extinct dodo bird. Hebronville's airport was identified as a fifty yard slash in the mesquite and cactus, with a half mile runway. It's only attempt at sophistry was an orange colored windsock situated at one end of the cleared runway. McDonald, the pilot did not deplane but was taxiing for his takeoff as I made my way into town. The quarter mile walk was spent with me reviewing the conversation and events of yesterday, and last night, plus the possible effects resulting from the fascinating, emotion charged interlude Audrey and I shared.

The following five weeks were devoted to learning the technical aspects of oil well drilling by remaining on the derrick floor ten to twelve hours a day. I would call Audrey each night, and each call resulted in a closer relationship as we expressed our inner feelings.

I was anticipating our next meeting, as I observed the activity of the drilling crew. There was an element of excitement this morning. Curly Ward had declared today would bring in a producer.

At two-thirty the hiss of rising gas, mud, water and green crude began to rise around the well head. Curly shouted, "Douse your smoking! No more smoking!"

A faint rumble, then the column of green-black oil was spouting from the top of the well head valve assembly. Higher and higher the dark finger of crude gushed, showering rocks and oil over the entire operation. At that moment I was impervious to all that surrounded me. My imagination was rampant. The sound of the escaping oil and gas was as soothing as a woodwind section delivering Ludwig Mendelssohn's, 'Spring Song'.

The column of crude had mesmerized me, as I saw it all as a liquid stair to acclaim the realization of my life's dreams. The odor I smelled was as tantalizing as the essence of a seductive perfume. My mind would no longer be tormented with the torturous itch that excessive ambition creates. This column of black gold, that had brought a state of trance, would be a soothing balm to that itch. Curly was turning the valve stem wheel to stem the flow, as we all observed the column of crude receding ever lower until the valve had reached closed position. We crowded around the pressure valve to see what we had. The needle indicated eleven hundred pounds per square inch. It was then we realized we had brought in a quality producer.

I leaped from the derrick floor racing for the pickup, pumped up with enthusiasm, feeling the need to share it with Justin and Audrey I removed some mesquite trees on my reckless drive to town, heading for the first telephone. The truck withstood the onslaught of brush better than I, as I was trembling with the intoxicating thrill of having my first oil well.

I was soon placing a collect call to Justin's office. His secretary, Phyllis Reed, intercepted the call, the operator giving her my name, she replied, "Just one moment, please," Justin's well-trained modulated voice came on, "Hello Hugh, glad you could call. What can I do for you?"

"She came in, Justin! About thirty minutes ago!" My voice was quaking from excitement.

"That's just great. Boy, that's wonderful news, I'm sure you're as thrilled as I was when my first well came in. Did you check the well head pressure?"

"Sure did. Eleven hundred pounds."

"Damn, that's a beauty! Well Hugh, you're on your way. I want you to know you won't travel alone. I'll be beside you when and if you need me. I know Audrey would be thrilled with a call from you when we hang up. She's home and very anxious to hear any news about the well."

"I'll call her."

"Incidentally, the winds of success can dissipate the embers of ambition if permitted to languish too long. When do you want to start another location?"

"Tomorrow."

"Fine. I admire your vitality and drive. I'll have Miller down there in the morning to locate our next hole. Bear in mind, you're the major demo of the activity, so don't hesitate in asserting yourself. I'm always receptive to any suggestions you offer. I'll relieve you of the concern of marketing our production. There's no need of you being delayed with that phase of our agreement. For a while, just be concerned with mastering the exploration and production, then you can come in here and learn this end of the business.

"Oh yes! I have before me a written acceptance of your application for membership in both the Petroleum and the Country Club. They came in the morning mail. Congratulations! How would you like to come up Friday afternoon to spend the weekend with us? By then you'll have everything on the next location. Be at the airstrip at four thirty Friday and McDonald will be there to pick you up. Okay? I'll let you go now. Call Audrey! Looking forward to seeing you Friday, Hugh. Good Bye."

I had Audrey on the phone a few minutes later, she expressed sincere surprise at my calling so early in the day, saying, "This is the nicest thing that has happened so far today, hearing your voice."

"I've some marvelous news, Audrey. The well came in this afternoon and it's a good one too."

"Wonderful! I'm so happy for you, Hugh. You can't be more thrilled than I. When are you coming to Houston, now that you're an oil baron?"

"I've just talked to your Dad. He asked me to come Friday for the weekend. I certainly hope you can keep sometime open for me while I'm there, if you can arrange it. He's sending the plane down to pick me up. In the meantime, I'm planning to busy myself with the next location, while I anticipate sharing many hours with you."

She laughed in that manner of a Maestro stroking an arpeggio on a concert harp, then said, "I believe I can allot you approximately sixty hours during your stay here. Will that be enough?"

With some quick calculation I concluded sixty hours would have to entail some all night company, as usual she had confounded my thinking by injecting ambiguity. That in turn, resulted in her emerging as an enigma. But a lovely one.

"If you can't spare seventy hours, then I'll compromise with sixty. Anything to keep you from the clutches of the villain, Jack Cook."

"You must possess E.S.P., Hugh. He's called me every night since you were here. Each night his questions become a little more pointed and personal. Last night he asked me if I was serious about another as he'd been turned down so constantly. I almost told him I was engaged, as somehow he's become dull and lackluster. I really can't find any valid reason to accept his company. I hope you don't object to being used as a shield against his relentless declarations of ardor."

"Object! My dear, I consider it a privilege to serve you as a buffer against any prospective suitor. I've been toying with the thought of hoping to become a permanent buffer—a shield against any ambitious seeker of your attention."

"Who knows? You may just qualify. I'll be looking forward to seeing you Friday. Good-bye for now."

From that moment on, I launched a mental as well as physical attack on the work ahead. The development of the forty-five hundred acre tract.

♦ ♦ ♦

Joe Bob arrived the next morning, proceeding to locate the next site of our search for oil. While there, he confided in me his opinion of the one hundred drilling sites the tract provided in accordance with well spacing laws. He had produced a roll of white satin ribbon, one inch wide.

"Hugh, I told you the red cloth indicated the routes to the sites. The yellow, the drilling site. In case you're interested in this white ribbon, I'll explain. It's reasonable that a geologist being human, succumbs to the ever present human element. There were forty-nine of these hundred sites that, in my opinion, would most likely be producers. The other forty-eight remaining are scattered to hell and back, so I'm willing to devote the time necessary today, placing the white ribbon with the yellow, so you can ascertain in advance your next move. I sincerely hope my sixth sense is accurate. I want you to succeed in this operation. When you've exhausted the most favorable locations, you can exploit the remainder. There's no need of you mentioning my predictions to Justin. We'll let him believe the action was yours. If I'm right, it should impress him that you possess some prescience in your endeavor. That should please your future father-in-law."

He was laughing and throwing up his arms, in a gesture of defense, following his last statement, "If you can get lucky and eliminate Jack Cook."

Joe Bob departed for Houston after we had marked the most promising sites. I entered the cafe to find Joe Childs, the owner, beckoning me to the rear table. As I was pulling out the chair, he was beside me in a state of excitement, with animated expression saying, "Have you heard about Vail Dennis?" He was spouting the words in a gush, "The little bastard has finally got his bacon burned. He was charged today with malfeasance of duty and accepting bribes. The County Commissioners offered him an alternative, if he would resign as Marshal and get the hell out of town, they wouldn't pursue the charges. He accepted the out—departing on the three thirty bus toting two suitcases. That little piss ant looked as undressed without his two guns, as a maiden with a wind lifted skirt without any panties."

"Good riddance as far as I'm concerned, but I'm waiting for the return of Cotton Burns. Bring me the veal cutlets, please."

The eight months had been busy ones, but productive too, as we had brought in twenty-eight producing wells on the tract. Justin had moved in three more rigs.

Overseeing four rigs and getting into Houston on weekends to see Audrey, kept every minute occupied. We had worked thirty-five of the sites Joe Bob had considered most likely to produce, the results being phenomenal. Twenty-eight producers and only seven dusters.

Justin had bordered on being a sycophant by heaping praise on me to all who would listen. He voiced his opinion that I was the best damn wildcatter in Texas, to the Country Club set as well as the members of the Petroleum Club. It is axiomatic that this iconoclastic verbiage, on the part of Justin, had made my name synonymous with success stories. Those tales making the rounds of the Petroleum Club set, and by November of 1933 I was being panegyrized in the local newspapers as the up and coming young lion of the Industry.

The gossip had me marrying Audrey soon. This bit of journalistic foreknowledge appeared in the society column of the two daily newspapers intermixed with a potpourri of coming events. It was pure conjecture on the part of the writer, but as I read it, the urge to hatch the egg of reality prompted me to pick up the phone and call Audrey.

Hearing her sweet voice I commenced, "Hello Honey, have you read the society column in the Post and the Chronicle?"

"Yes, I'm amused at the writer's comments about you and me. Where did you get the basis for such rhetoric?"

"I realize my question to you should be presented in an atmosphere of captivating allure. A starry night to augment the bewitching strains of the violins as I squeeze your hand in a gesture of unspoken love. But what I'm really trying to get around to, involves four little words and right now is the time for a quid pro quo proposal. I'll give you me in exchange for you. Will you marry me?"

Stark naked silence for a full minute. Audrey then answered, her words spongy with tears of happiness, "I've been your woman since first our eyes met, so all you've to do is suggest the date. You've never told me you loved me until this moment, even though it comes out as a non sequitur—it's better than hearing you say those three little words."

"I'd like Joe Bob Miller to be best man for our wedding. I'll call him, then we can set a date on his availability. I'll get back to you to finalize the great event. Perhaps I should come up today and extend the courtesy to your Dad for his daughter in marriage. If he voices any opposition, we'll proceed without his sanction, provided you're in accord. Would you go through with it should he object?"

"You silly man, I'd marry you if it resulted in him ostracizing both of us, but he'll be very pleased to have you in our family. He looks upon you as a son. I can hardly wait to see you, so please come as soon as possible. I love you."

The remainder of the day was very taxing mentally, as my brain provided constant eruptions of thought. Thoughts that entailed myriads of possibilities. I had planned a hedonistic lifestyle when finances would permit. I now had the money necessary to fulfill all those fantasies of lust, greed and power that had infiltrated my very soul, always screaming within to be released with fulfillment. These infirmities of my character were viewed with disdain by the normal segment of society—yet these desires had fueled the zealous, unserving ambition that had made my present status possible.

Would marriage alter my evaluation of these goals? If marriage failed to quench the allure of beautiful women, then what? Would the turmoil of deprivation of all that had obsessed me fulminate in divorce? If I had permitted the many impassioned interludes with Audrey to result in ardent gratification of our physical desires, would the desire of marriage be lessened—or nourished?

My mind was honeycombed with desire confronted with obstacles. Possibilities challenged by eventualities. Decisions emasculated with indecision. A vortex of confused thinking finally entered a state of calm. From all this emerged the desire to marry Audrey.

While driving to Houston, time permitted me the opportunity to scour and cleanse my mind of the confusion and indecision that had prevailed all afternoon. With Audrey as my wife, I would be more acceptable to society, thus making her an asset. In addition, I was certain it was love that drew me to her.

She responded to the doorbell by throwing the door open, offering me that lovable disarming smile, then she made an exaggerated bow saying, "Welcome home, my conquering hero," placing her expressive, comforting arms around my neck. The exciting smell of the whole woman she was, engulfed me, then the meeting of our lips ignited the male desires that flamed with each embrace. Her welcome had generated such a state of ambition within me, it prompted me to blurt, "Is Justin here?" Closing the door, she took my hand leading me to the library saying, "He's expecting you."

As we entered, Justin arose and made his way to me as he exclaimed, "Damned if it isn't the best wildcatter in Texas," shaking my hand vigorously as he steered me to the wall containing the bar, he continued, "I've been waiting your return to share my corn whiskey. I find it more tasty when you're sharing it with me. You're looking fine, Hugh."

As the wall revolved to reveal the bar, my mind was active with alternative approaches as to how my request for permission to marry Audrey would be phrased. I had the feeling Audrey had not mentioned my proposal of marriage, and I'd be the one to surprise Justin. But when? How?

He set the whiskey and water on the bar, then came around to sit beside me. Sliding onto the barstool he surprised me by saying, "Hugh, I compliment you for the terrific success you've had in developing the Hebronville operation. Your unstinting efforts, good judgment and dedication haven't gone unnoticed."

He was sipping his drink while looking in the glass giving the appearance of reading his words from the ice floating in the drink.

Turning to me, our eyes met and he continued, "Your success prompts me to give you a surprise. You now know enough about the business to operate as an individual, and for your sake, I suggest you open an office in Houston. By operating as an individual you'll erase any doubt that may exist that you're dependent on me, or influenced by me. By doing this you can make your own decisions and act in the manner you choose. I'll add, you'll be successful. I'm sure of that. What do you think?"

I looked him directly in the eye and replied, "Justin, I think your suggestion is one of merit. Your confidence in my ability is matched only by my own. Also, I'll toss you a surprise. Audrey and I wish to marry . . . with your approval, of course."

Justin's features reflected no surprise at my bombshell. He surveyed me head to toes. "Do you imply if I should object to your proposal, you'd let my objections keep you two from getting married?"

"No disrespect, Justin, but hell no. Your not liking the idea won't stop us."

He emitted a trumpet of laughter as he was slapping his thighs with glee. After catching his breath he shouted, "Audrey, this is one hell of a man you've picked. His answer proves that brevity is a great charm of eloquence, and it bears out what I've believed. He's as venturesome and bold as a long-tailed cat in a room full of rocking chairs. You kids have my blessings, and I consider it a privilege to call you son. Let us drink to the joust of two strong-willed lovers entering the arena of marriage."

With that bit of raillery he poured drinks with the flair of a man flooded with gaiety and happiness, then raised his glass in the gesture of a toast. Audrey and I raised our glasses as he recited in a sonorous tone, "Here's to the two I love best, may the years bring joy all the while, as the two of you are put to the test and each year brings joy with a child."

Audrey laughed, then said, "Dad, can we skip a year every now and then?"

I quickly responded, "I'll drink to that."

Justin asked if we had set a date. "No, not yet. We want Joe Bob Miller to act as best man and I haven't discussed it with him. We'll do that now." I went to the phone and called Joe Bob.

"Miller here."

"Joe Bob, this is Hugh."

"I know, the man who never drills a duster. Are you in town?"

"Yes I'm at Justin Brent's. Joe Bob will you serve as best man at Audrey's and my wedding, two weeks from today?"

"You're damned right I can. Boy! I don't know what you have but it sure as hell must be concealed. You weren't given a rat's chance in a dogfight, to succeed in getting Audrey. At least not in my judgment. She was and is, so far out of your class that her consenting to marry you, is a greater miracle than Perseus decapitating Medusa. But congratulations anyway, you've proven to me that the mountain can come to Mohammed."

"I'll get in touch with you later Joe Bob. Thanks a lot."

The ceremony was performed in Saint Paul's Methodist Church—bridesmaids, matron of honor and all the accoutrements of a high society affair.

Immediately after the wedding we flew to Monterrey, Mexico for a week of honeymooning. The week was a memorable series of blissful interludes with each experience binding our togetherness closer and closer.

As the plane was touching down in Houston a week later, I looked at Audrey and asked, "Here we are Honey, back to reality. Do you feel as I, that we've just experienced a week in another world—a week in Eden?"

"Yes dear, this past week has fused my whole being with you. I feel we two are an entity. One that can never be two again. You've become a part of me and the crucible of life can never separate us, physically perhaps, but never the memories of this first week as Mrs. Hugh McCulloch. Memories being the treasure and guardian of all things."

Upon our return to Houston, the first week was spent locating suitable office space, and reaching a decision of rejecting Justin's plea to live with him in the family home. He was very dejected when we informed him we'd leased an apartment in the Plaza Hotel. A feeling of guilt stabbed within as I observed how Justin's disappointment was revealed so painfully in his facial expression. He must have been given precognition of things in the future. Since the death of his wife, he and Audrey had been very close, so he probably visualized the loneliness of the big home which would result from the vacuum created by Audrey moving out.

As I watched Justin being racked in the throes of despair, at losing the companionship of someone dear to him, as a result of me, I had the wish he would curse me for robbing him. If he would only strike me, or curse me, it would provide some surcease for the torment of quilt that prevailed within me. If I could offer some form of apology for taking her away that did not reek of flatulence what would I say? I said nothing.

"I know it's better for you to be alone. You can best get acclimated to marriage without the presence of others. You'll enjoy living at the Plaza, it's not far from here—you can drop in on me anytime. This home will always be your home, remember that."

He somehow created a smile of geniality, with these words, even though I knew a painful sword of reality had pierced his heart.

Justin presented me a portrait of Audrey to enhance my office wall. The portrait was the essence of reality. The artist had captured her likeness in perfect detail—it was so realistic that after hanging it on the wall, I could feel her eyes looking over my shoulder as I sat at my desk. It gave me the illusion of her presence.

Justin provided me the benefit of knowledge gleaned frm his many years in the Petroleum Industry, thus preventing me making many errors. As a result, my activities had been successful to the extent of my attaining the sobriquet of 'Lucky Bastard' among the Oil Colony when 1935 arrived.

Chapter Seven
Violence And Betrayal

The past two years had indeed been lucky for me as wealth produced more wealth, that in turn projected me into the higher echelons of competition. I was now in the arena of the gladiators that Justin had referred to in the past.

Audrey and I had purchased a sprawling ranch-type home in the River Oaks section, settling into the usual melange of activity that wealth seems to make necessary. Like lolling around the Country Club, chasing golf balls and spending hundreds of hours at worthless cocktail parties while telling and listening to sagas of sexual exploits—some true—some imagined.

The past year had unearthed two undesirable flaws in my character, in addition to the existing ones. These being a fetish for automobiles, and an advanced use of alcohol for a crutch to make me more acceptable, I thought.

I had enlarged the garage to house five cars, then stocked the spaces with two expensive Roadsters, two sport Phaetons and one Limousine. I had a paint shop added to the garage for the purpose of changing the colors of the autos frequently. This practice provided nourishment for the gossipers and eventually was carried in the society column of the local newspaper. It provided the gentry, the pastime of guessing what color would appear next as I drove to the office each morning, always following the same route, South Main to the business district. Weather permitting, I always drove with the top down to provide an unobstructed view of myself, to the curious onlookers, as I tooled along South Main. The attention I was getting served to inflate my ego, as I recalled my days in the fifth ward in comparison.

My conduct around the Country Club was fast becoming the subject of the members conversation while sipping highballs. It concerned my most recent boorish behavior e.g.; the last dance at the Club found me drunk before the dance had hardly begun. Following my usual routine I had become boisterous. Then came a period of resentment generated by my imagination, that the ones around me were discussing my lack of culture, where upon I would become belligerent and aggressive. I would violate every de rigueur accepted by my peers. This unsavory behavior had resulted in three brawls during the past year, with each encounter resulting in embarrassment for Audrey and my reimbursing the Club for damage to furniture, etc. As a result of my actions, the members had begun to view me as the protagonist of all the things they could discard and feel no loss. I was finding it more difficult to engage in conversation with either men or women. If they did get trapped in my company their brain became very active at summoning excuses to depart.

Justin had never mentioned my escapades occurring at the Club, choosing to remain silent, probably hoping I would change my attitude and habits. Audrey had never mentioned my efforts at browbeating those in my presence while I was under the influence, but she had decided on an apparent effort at reproaching me for my reprehensible conduct. Doing this by suggestion, we declined all invitations to social functions because, 'they were nothing but a waste of time.'

She didn't deceive me with this statement as she had always enjoyed social gatherings. Her state of malaise was the result of my conduct, and my false pride flamed into rebellion at her suggestion.

"Like hell we will. We'll attend any and all affairs we receive an invitation to, and furthermore, don't expect me to ever, and I mean ever, take any crap from any pompous, narcissistic bastard stuffed into a moth eaten tuxedo. They're no higher up the pole than we, so we'll go anytime, anywhere we like."

I was playing cards, a few weeks before Christmas, with three oil men in the quiet confines of the Petroleum Club, imbibing ample shots of whiskey as the game progressed. I was experiencing feelings of grandeur and well-being stemming from the sale of several producing wells to Gulf Oil the day before, for the sum of two and a half million dollars. Regarding the size of bets, I was playing my cards with reckless abandon, and was matching wits with one of the three players. Two of them were apparently playing for pastime, as their betting was conservative, but the other was plunging and kicking bets and raises as if this tactic would give me a faint heart and force me to fold. Not so.

I grew more aggressive as the cards fell, expressing my bravado with larger and larger bets. This was a no limit game. Lady Luck was with me to an uncanny degree. Everytime the 'plunger' would get a good hand, I would have a better one resulting in my raking in unbelievable pots. Some as much as one hundred thousand.

At this point, Justin came into the Club and seeing the game in progress pulled up a chair to observe. We invited him to join the game, but he declined.

An hour after Justin's arrival I made a cursory assessment of the chips accumulated in front of me, determining there was about four hundred thousand in the stack.

The next hand my chief opponent opened as if it would be the greatest hand ever dealt. Feeling reckless I called and raised one hundred grand. When the last card fell, he gave a surreptitious glance as he cautiously raised the corner of the card to peek at his fate. When we had bet and raised the moment of truth had come. This guy was as tough as a warehouse rat. He nonchalantly turned up queens over jacks as a benign smile formed slowly, disarming his stern visage. His cupped hands were reaching for the pot—the gesture of preparing to embrace the pile of chips when I rolled my cards over revealing kings over tens, the most regal full house I had ever held.

"God damn it, where did you get those cards? Not from the deal, you cheat."

A chilling rage engulfed me as I quietly pulled the huge pile of chips to me. I calmly stacked them with exaggerated care, then got up, walked around the table to my accuser and delivered a terrific uppercut to the point of his chin.

He lifted from the chair, then started his backward tumble with the whites of his eyes showing. The whole scene seemed to be occurring in slow motion. He continued his backward fall, out cold, falling across a game table that surrendered his weight with a splintering crash.

This was crazy. As he finally cradled in the crushed pile of wood, the thought flashed through my mind—another damn table to pay for! The dealer converted my chips to seven hundred and forty thousand, placing it in a briefcase for my convenience, then handed it to me. I turned to say something to Justin. He had departed at some point during the malee, leaving me to sort out my composure alone.

The maitre d' of the Club made his way to where I was standing, as I studied the inert form of the man crammed between the sections of the wrecked game table. I had begun to fear the blow had killed him as he remained motionless for at least five minutes. The maitre d' was now crouching beside the fallen man, rolling his head side-to-side and slapping him lightly. The fellow fluttered his eyelids, then raised himself on one elbow, scanning the surroundings with a confused expression. At this point, I was given the nod to leave the Club.

I reached the bank a few minutes before closing, in order to deposit my winnings, then started for my office.

♠ ♠ ♠

I had hired a very attractive receptionist shortly after opening my office. She had proven to be very efficient as well as comely. With the passing of time, she had provided me much pleasure. Not physical pleasure, but erotic situations between she and I that my imagination created.

When I told Audrey I had been fortunate in getting the services of a very efficient receptionist, her womanly instincts arose to the occasion by asking, "What does she look like? How old is she? What is her name?" These questions were posed in rapid fire order, I answering, "Her hair is dark brown, green eyes, lovely complexion, about five foot three, around one hundred ten pounds, and I'm compelled to comment the weight is distributed perfectly. She states on her application she is an old lady of twenty-eight. Her name is Barbara M. Hunter."

"Well, I must say you've all the vital statistics at your command. Tell me, what does the M. stand for?"

"You won't believe this Audrey, but I asked her the same question. It's her mother's maiden name, Mann. Isn't that an unusual name for a girl?"

"Maybe no! Not having seen her I can't say with certainty, but the alacrity you demonstrated while reciting her vital description, I'd guess she could dispense with the Barbara. Are you certain she was employed for her qualifications alone? I must get down to your office and see the results of this tour de force you seem to have accomplished."

Her eyes were glowing as twin beacons from jealousy. A jealousy that surprised me what with her ingrained aplomb and sophistry. I did not think her capable of the passion of jealousy until this moment, but her words had hoisted the red flag of caution in me—making a mental note to confine my bedroom cowboy antics with Barbara to my imagination.

But the best laid plans of mice and men, do not always emerge according to reason or common sense. As I entered the office Barbara was standing on a chair straightening a picture that was slightly askew in the outer office. The picture had always fascinated me but this explained why I had elected to hang it on the wall in the waiting area. The picture being the one of the dogs dressed as humans playing poker.

Barbara turned to see me open the door and greeted me airily with, "Hi Mr. McCulloch, you didn't expect to see me going to the dogs did you? I've intended to straighten this up for days."

My eyes were taking in every detail of her standing in the chair. The elevation afforded me a tantalizing glimpse of her thighs and curvaceous legs and ankles. She was wearing a brown skirt that undulated with mesmerizing movements of the solid white flesh beneath. As I momentarily observed the sensuous view of her attractive hair—shoulders that had the bearing of nobility—the small of her back beckoned to be hugged—and her thighs and buttocks all combined to arouse such a hot lewd desire in me, that all self-control vanished.

I closed the door, crossed the office to her standing in the chair, then reached out both arms as a gesture of assisting her down, placed a hand on each side of her waist, then lifted her as I pushed the chair with my foot bringing her willing body hard against mine. As we embraced we joined in a brash, brazen, tempestuous kiss.

The kiss was imparting pure lurid passion between two, who had dared to test self-control. For my part, I was in a man's state of eroticism. Suddenly I had become the man on a white horse, eager to cut corners—ravenous—full of conviction that this travesty of good conduct must terminate, here and now with fulfillment. I pulled her harder and harder against me, as she was hunching her pelvis hard against my male organs—up and down—up and down—by now I was so hard a bobcat could not have scratched it, Barbara was riding it with her up and down motion. I could stand no more delay. I broke the spell when I pulled away to lock the door.

When I turned from locking the door, Barbara was seated at her desk looking like the efficient receptionist she was. Her face flushed as a September sunset. Her tranquil manner had to be affected as no normal being could quench the inferno of lust that quickly and effectively. I reached for her hand saying, "Come on Barbara, we can't stop now."

"We can, and I have," she replied as she lifted some papers from the desk and began sorting them.

"Damn it, why?"

"You had better leave me to my work for now, Mr. McCulloch."

I went out the door as my mind reeled from abject disappointment at having been deprived of sexual fulfillment. She had brought me to a state of intense, erotic desire with the kisses we had shared, and now that I had felt her warm erotic body against mine, then being denied, had put me into a frenzy. I could hardly think rational as I awaited the elevator.

Reaching the street the urge to get drunk filled my thoughts as I went for my car. It did not concern me that the past year, had found me seeking solace and intrigue with alcohol. This action had resulted in my being embroiled in numerous brawls, and the defendant in three costly lawsuits involving settlements which were sizeable. With each peccadillo the breach of closeness with Audrey had widened to the extent we now had separate bedrooms, and an air of awkwardness prevailed when we were together. This situation existing between she and I, served as a goad to hit the bottle, and hit it I did, getting inebriated almost nightly.

This night found me ensconced in the Chinese Duck nightclub throwing my weight around with my usual boorish conduct, telling everyone within hearing distance how tough I was—voicing my criticism of the service in a ribald manner—throwing tips around in a way defying common sense and creating commotion that disrupted the floor show.

After being admonished by the burly, oversized bouncer on two occasions, coupled with advice to quiet down, I leaped to my feet throwing a chair at him.

My aim was off as the chair struck the piano player by mistake, causing him to tumble off the piano bench unconscious. The bouncer charged me rumbling through the tables like a wounded rhino, while bellowing some threats of busting my ass, breaking my neck, then his fury made his words unintelligible.

As he reached for my neck, someone to my rear struck me on the head, producing total blackness.

♦ ♦ ♦

I regained my faculties on the door of the police paddy wagon enroute to the city jail. When the van arrived at the jail, the rear doors were thrown open by two husky policemen. Each grabbed a foot, then drug me from the vehicle permitting my head to bounce on the step, then striking the pavement. They were not affording me any care to avoid bruises and were quite rough as they hustled me inside to the drunk tank.

The next morning when appearing before the judge, the bailiff intoned the charges, "Drunk and disorderly, assault with a deadly weapon, and disturbing the peace."

I questioned the judge regarding the assault charge and was informed the piano player was hospitalized in serious condition.

"Could I plead guilty to the drunk and disturbing the peace, while contacting my attorney about the assault charge?"

The judge fined me on the two charges. He commented on the adverse publicity that had preceded my appearance before him by saying, "From the accounts, I'm surprised you haven't been before me several times. You may go now. Next case."

I felt unclean, shaky with the hangover and uncertain whether I should go home or to a hotel. I went home. As I turned into the driveway, the question of what Audrey's attitude toward me would be, prevailed. She was getting the morning paper from the porch as I approached. She spoke, "You certainly look like hell."

"Yes, and I feel like hell, having spent the night in jail."

I entered the house, went first to my room, showered and shaved. After dressing and starting toward the door she stated, "You're a genuine celebrity according to the morning Post."

"Is that right? How do they present that view?"

Her eyes were flashing as she retorted, "By giving a blow by blow account of your trying to wreck the Chinese Duck, and almost killing a musician in the process. That's how they present it. I repeat, I'm growing weary of your unsavory conduct as it reflects on Dad as well as me, I've had about as much as I can tolerate."

"Okay! Okay! I consider myself chastised, and I'm sorry," I then went hurriedly out the door.

With the turn of events my drive to the office was spent in concentration. I could sense that Audrey had reached the flash point regarding my escapades, and was on the verge of resorting to at least separation, if not divorce. I was certain Justin had become disenchanted with me due to my drunken sprees and absences from home, as evidenced by his avoiding me during the past several months. If he wanted it that way, it was satisfactory with me. He had regarded me coolly, and with disdain yesterday when he came into the Petroleum Club. He would sure as hell be chagrined with me at what happened in the nightclub. My domestic situation was being eroded by lack of communication between Audrey, Justin and me, so it was up to me to effect the change, or reap the results.

Barbara greeted my entrance with her usual honeyed tone, "Good morning, Mr. McCulloch."

"Hello Barbara, did you sleep well last night?"

Her green eyes probed my face searching for some motive behind my unique question, finding nothing revealing, she said, "Why ask me that question?"

"Because I was not blessed with sleep due to the exhilarating interlude of yesterday. I was so uptight with excitement, and disappointment, sleep would not come. You left me in one hell of a state. In fact the effects of your denial prompted me to get pretty drunk in an effort to anesthetize my male glands that had been aroused as never before. But it was as exciting as being shot from a cannon while it lasted."

"The mail is on your desk." She swiveled her chair and resumed typing.

After sitting, I picked up the morning mail stacked neatly before me. The stack was topped with an envelope bearing the return of River Oaks Country Club.

I opened the envelope, extracted the folded page, unfolded it and read:

Dear Mr. McCulloch:

Due to your atrocious behavior while attending past events staged in the Clubhouse, the Directors have taken the following action;

1. You will upon receipt of this notice, please return your membership card for revocation.

2. This action also revokes all privileges bestowed upon you as a bona fide member of the Club.

3. Please remit the sum of four hundred fifty dollars to cover the cost of replacing the tables and chairs destroyed during your recent assault, directed at several of our members.

Harley Simmons
Chairman of the Board

My anger arose after reading this notice of ejection, then subsided as I consoled my punctured pride with the belief I did not need the association of those "stuffed shirts" any longer. I had enjoyed a tremendous success, coupled with luck. Several of my ventures had placed me in the category of millionaire and there was more in the making.

I called Joe Bob primarily to learn if he could recommend a good criminal lawyer. He was elated I had called as he had some news for me. He had met the femme fatale and had proposed marriage, she accepting. He wished me for his best man. I said I would be happy to return the favor.

He then expressed the opinion my reputation was becoming a household word, "Stinky." He added, "What are you trying to prove, Hugh? You've everything you were scrambling for, and now you have the reputation of an undesirable ass due to your drinking and wrecking places wherever you go. What's the trouble, Hugh?"

"No trouble, Joe Bob. It's just the fact when I drink, I get argumentative, and when I'm in that mood, there is always someone challenging me and a fight ensues. I've been trying to knock-off the booze, but so far no luck. Can you put me on to a good criminal lawyer?"

"Yes, I can. From what I read in the papers you're in need of one after putting that musician in the hospital. I have it from a good source, he plans to hang you by your thumbs in a lawsuit. I hope it all turns out well for you. I'll call you when we set the date of our wedding."

He gave me the lawyer's name and address, then hung up.

After making an appointment with the Attorney and calling my drilling Superintendent in Beaumont, I found myself reviewing my marriage.

As I gazed out the window at the blue sky, my mind strayed upon a detour that had never been apparent before. How would my life be without Audrey? I did love her in my own peculiar way, but lately her cool demeanor had unveiled a facet of uncertainty in me which had not been existent before. A life untrammeled with domestic ties and not having to restrain my true self in order to present a blissful marriage, crossed my mind. The overwhelming burst of animal desire that had cracked the shell of propriety, as I'd held Barbara close, was taunting my baser instincts. The rogue in me was overcoming any immunity that marriage had created, I resolved the musing by buzzing for Barbara.

She flowed into my office with feminine flair, bringing with her a steno pad, the sweet redolence of honeysuckle that aroused my already active erotic senses to a higher level, and asked in a dulcet tone,

"Did you ring, Mr. McCulloch?"

She was standing before me, her green eyes expressing the inquisitive nature of a child, yet glowing with vitality and sophistication. She was indeed disturbing to look at and remain sedate while viewing her femininity.

I yanked the lanyard of restraint and fired, "Would you like to dine with me this evening?" By God! I had fired my shot with one bold bolt, awaiting the result.

Barbara pursed her beautiful lips in a gesture of effort at making a decision, then smiled saying,

"Why not? Dining out with you should be kindergarten stuff compared to what transpired yesterday. I think I'd enjoy it very much. What time will you pick me up?"

Her quick acceptance of the invitation had telegraphed a message. With her manner of phrasing her words, and the twinkle of anticipation glowing in those green eyes, she had revealed the promise of something that had eluded me yesterday. Something that at the moment was giving me an erection—it was conveniently hidden under the desk.

"Does seven o'clock suit you?"

"I'll be ready. Did you want any dictation now, or any other reason for calling me in?"

"No Barbara, that's all."

She left for the outer office as I leered at the thought provoking cheeks of her well dressed buttocks. As the door closed behind her I muttered, "what a walk—what a body—what a night coming up. Wow!"

I left the office around two. As I reached the outer door, Barbara halted me. "Did you consult your wife about taking me to dinner?"

I turned to her exhibiting my smile reserved for use on the opposite sex, then asked, "Are you kidding me?"

She gave a throaty chuckle, then restored, "I'll see you at seven."

As I approached my car the thought occurred that a color other than the fire red would be less conspicuous, especially when escorting women other than my wife. This being the first time I had employed the car as a tool to engage in philandering. I did make a mental note to change the color to a more unobtrusive hue.

Entering my home to change my apparel, I found a note from Audrey informing me she was playing bridge and would be home around six. This pleased me as it meant I could avoid any questioning of when I would return. As I started for the car, once more the color of it caused me to consider leaving it—using a white one instead. Pausing a moment, I opted for the red one, as the weather was cool and the closed car would be more comfortable.

I purchased a pint and a fifth of Jack Daniels sour mash whiskey, then dropped into the Sans Souci bar to while away the time, disposing of the pint. The Sans Souci was one watering hole in Houston that had never been subjected to my furniture moving antics while drunk. Some how the subdued atmosphere it presented had always had the effect of quieting my usual obnoxious behavior, as a result of this unique conduct the owner of the bar still welcomed my presence.

The following three hours was an exercise in futility as it was spent with me consuming the pint as I probed every avenue of the future. Reviewing incidents of the past year while considering my undesirable reputation as a result of those incidents, my resentment began to build, an eruption would surely follow. I was mad—mad—at the world. I reviewed my days of violence in the fifth ward—everyday experiencing some uncouth episode. Then my conscience would sear me because of the neglect of my parents. I had not been in their presence since I had left home to work in the oil fields, five years ago. Having attained wealth beyond belief, and all the material things wealth makes possible, I was sitting here alone, letting hate fill me with the bile of discontent. Hate for the snobs who refused to accept me as their social peer.

My relationship with Audrey had been lacking the intimacy and warmth I had desired. We could never reach that condition which occurs when two people can be themselves in a risk free environment—when there is no moral or value judgment—no right or wrong—or approval or disapproval. If we had found this desired environment, then we could have known ourselves, through knowing each other. By knowing ourselves maybe I would not be sitting here contemplating the feminine rewards of another woman.

The Jack Daniels had its desired effect—I was now the cavalier spurring his charger to the woman he desired. I was convinced the whiskey had transformed me into a sensitive, soft spoken, polite nobleman, this conclusion being reached as I drove to pick up Barbara for what I was certain would be a night to remember.

She answered the bell, greeting me with a radiant smile saying, "Here's my errant knight right on time."

She was so divesting in black. I could give no response for several seconds as I was stunned by the beauty of her cameo face with the contrast of the black evening gown. This woman was a superb specimen of femininity, presenting such allure and desirability as to cause me the momentary loss of my senses.

"You're positively stunning Barbara."

She closed the door, grasping my elbow and on the way to the car I asked, "Would you please clarify your greeting to me? The adjective, errant?"

"Don't play dumb with me, Hugh. You know very well an errant knight was one in search of adventure–not a knight assigned to guarding the castle, but a wanderer."

"Well, I guess you have me tagged accurately, as I hope tonight will find me jousting with the adventure of romance and excitement."

She laughed saying, "Lead on Galahad. Where are we going?"

"How does the Rice Hotel Empire Room sound? Then we'll go to the roof for some dancing to the romantic music of Freddie Martin. Okay?"

"Marvelous."

We left the car with the valet, then made our way to the Empire Room. As the maitre d' was wending his way to our table, I was scanning the patrons to determine if any were familiar. We were seated at a table near the string orchestra playing dinner music, I thought surely I would see someone I knew, but I did not.

We enjoyed an excellent dinner that was preceded by two highballs I had concocted from the fifth of whiskey I was brown bagging, due to the state law.

After dinner, we went to the Rice Roof Garden to dance, what an experience it was! The Martin band delivered danceable music—music that produced exhilarating effects when two warm vibrant bodies swayed as one to the melodic, syrupy tones of the orchestra.

Between dances Barbara and I were imbibing highballs with regularity. Around eleven thirty we were soaring on that magic carpet structured of whiskey and erased inhibitions, enjoying every minute of its magical ride, when I suggested we depart.

Due to so many messages being related to and fro between us during the past hour, I was certain the evening had been a positive harbinger of things to come. The silent conversations which occurred when we squeezed hands, the telltale glances that a willing female can read so accurately—those vibrations that flow between two healthy bodies of opposite sex when pressed closely undulating to the rhythmic beat of music for romance. These things when honed and embellished with alcohol took on alluring, compelling dimensions.

It was this allure that controlled my hands as I turned into a Motel on South Main, not expecting any resistance from Barbara, and getting none. After signing the register and paying in advance, we parked. Then entered the room.

As I was locking the door, Barbara said, "Okay you ruttish moose, now we'll learn if you're for real."

As I turned she was standing in a chair, the black evening gown was dropping from her white shoulders into a heap around her feet. I was fascinated as I watched her unfasten her bra as two beautiful breasts seemed to leap out and up! Her eyes were aglow with enticement and promise, as she fastened her gaze on my look of bewilderment. Raising one foot, she kicked her shoe off in my direction, then raised the other foot kicking the shoe off with distance enough for me to catch it in midair. In spite of the enormous amount of alcohol I had consumed, my reasoning told me this was no burlesque I was observing, but a real portrayal of a guileless woman, letting her hair down.

I was enraptured by her actions as I stood there motionless holding her shoe in my hand. She was now stepping out of her panties giving me a full frontal view of everything that was Barbara. She turned to the side affording me another devastating facet of her body. This could not be real. It was as if I was observing the unveiling of a white marble statue at some art museum as she continued turning. After a full turn she said teasingly, "Do you make a practice of going to bed fully clothed?"

With that, I undressed quicker than anyone who has ever had the misfortune of standing in a fire ant hill. My socks being last off, I stood saying, "My turn now," as I hopped up in another chair and struck the familiar Charles Atlas pose, hands clasped, flexing my biceps, then turned slowly full circle. I was feeling devilish. Why not? Here with me were all the ingredients to put me in a messianic frame of mind. Hell! Wars had been structured on these same ingredients. Empires had changed power, and fallen into the dust of history because of, or due to, woman. Women who could in no way be comparable to the one standing before me in the chair.

"Come Junior, you've been staring at the display for quite a while. Do you not think you should come in and get your candy, rather than stand looking?"

I walked over to where she was standing in the chair, reached my arms around her thighs, then tilted her over my shoulder, her butt up, head and shoulders cascading down my back, I walked over, tossing her on the bed, not roughly, but lovingly.

"Turn off the light!"

While switching off the light a ludicrous question flitted across my mind. Why do I stumble into chairs, doors, tables, etc. when attempting to navigate ten feet of a darkened room in search of a match, yet can chart an unerring course to a bed where a woman awaits me?

Sliding into the bed beside her, my hand in the stygian darkness went directly to her right breast. With my forefinger, I brushed her nipple lightly, it reacted almost to the size of a pacifier, which, incidentally was used for that purpose a few minutes later.

The following hour can best be described as an astral projection as the experience proved a non sequitur of anything worldly. I came back to reality as a plastic man. I was ductile, I was spent, I knew I had been had as never before. I lay there in the darkness with every nerve, every sense of feel enveloped in a total state of lethargy. I did not care if I never left this room.

Barbara was beside me, sleeping on my arm. She was breathing to the sound of the night birds wings as they cleave the air passing near.

I looked at the luminous dial of my watch, one thirty a.m.

Awakening Barbara, we dressed, then went to the car. Three blocks away a traffic light halted me. I sat watching the red as I reviewed the night, Barbara had not spoken a word since I had awakened her. I inquired,

"Are you sleepy?"

"No, just contented."

I glanced in the rear view mirror, very startled to see a form on the back seat! Turning quickly as I muttered, "What the hell," I was looking into the semi darkness to assuage my imagination.

It was not imagination, it was Audrey. She was sitting with arms folded viewing us quietly, as a judge while determining the degree of sentence to mete out. The silence was a cacophony of unnerving eventualities racing through my brain.

Barbara had now turned, exclaiming, "Oh, my God!"

The car behind me was blasting its horn as the light turned from green to red. Audrey's presence had cast me into a quandary as I quickly pulled over to the curb to sort out my thoughts.

Audrey's silence was maddening, prompting me to ask, "What are you doing here?" The words tumbled out, my question was asinine. I was being subjected to a whirlwind of thoughts, but none merited being put into words. Sitting there awaiting some action or word from Audrey, a tide of anger at being caught in this escapade engulfed me. Suddenly Barbara had been stripped of her intrigue and Audrey had emerged in a mantle portraying a tour de force that threatened my present and future.

In a quiet controlled voice Audrey asked, "Please drive me back to your love nest. I'll leave you to carry on from there. In answer to your question of what I'm doing here, the answer will come from my attorney as I'll start divorce action tomorrow. I didn't spy on you tonight. I had determined that your actions of the past year had to involve another woman, so tonight when you failed to come home, or call, I felt the need to get out, drive and think. I admit when passing motels, I was looking at the cars parked in the areas with the thought I might find yours somewhere. Sure enough, the red caught my attention, so I drove in to check the license plate to learn if it really was one of yours. It was. You hadn't locked the car so I got in and awaited your return."

We had now reached the motel when I said to Audrey, "We'll discuss this tomorrow."

She opened the door, alighting as she retorted, "There is no tomorrow for our marriage." She then slammed the door and went to her car.

Turning the car, I started for Barbara's apartment, as the trauma of the situation occupied my thoughts. By the time we arrived at Barbara's, I had succeeded in placating my inner guilt with the nebulous carrot of convincing myself I did not need Audrey. If divorce was her course of action, then so be it!

After bidding Barbara good night, while returning to the car, I felt the need of some booze to calm the stormy waters of unrest. Under the driver's seat I located the pint placed there for an occasion like this, and proceeded to down two gulps of generous quantity before starting the engine. The booze activated my insulation against feelings of defeat and loss, as I drove to one of the leading apartment hotels located on South Main.

The late hour, two thirty a.m., didn't concern me as I entered the lobby. The night clerk greeted me with that lack of enthusiasm all night clerks show the public by asking, "How can I help you?"

"Do you have a suite available?"

"Well—yes we do. It's one of our most expensive. Perhaps you could return tomorrow and discuss the arrangements with our executive manager."

While making this reply, he was evaluating me by studying my tousled black, curly hair, and bloodshot brown eyes. At the moment, I was no example of sartorial excellence and did not give a damn about his assessment of me. His attitude was that of considering the business closed with his suggestion I return tomorrow.

This dismissal of me reeked of condescension, that in turn aroused my Irish temper as I came back at him, "Damn it, do you have a suite or not? I don't give a tinker's damn if it is your most expensive. You've said you had the vacancy so get moving and produce the key and register, or lease agreement, as I'm moving in now. I'll have my belongings brought in tomorrow."

"This suite has a rate of four hundred per month, in advance." He stressed the advance.

"Give me the goddamned register to sign. Do you want a check or cash? I'm tired, sleepy and provoked by your delaying tactics."

With that outburst, he promptly placed a huge registry before me and peered intently as I signed my name. His features expressed an apocryphal impression as he read aloud, "Hugh McCulloch. Are you the oil man McCulloch?"

"Yes, I'm in the oil business."

"We're glad to have you Mr. McCulloch. Here's the key. You can take care of the lease agreement tomorrow or when it is convenient. I hope you rest well. Good night."

In the elevator, on the way to the fifteenth floor, the thought occurred to me how the power of money controlled peoples thinking and/or actions as evidenced by the clerks change in attitude upon learning my identity.

Chapter Eight

Off To Mexico

I arose at ten, then drove to my home planning to have some attempt at dialogue with Audrey concerning the events of last night. There being very little material available to me in any effort at reconciliation. She had caught me in the act of infidelity, making my only defense nolo contendere.

She was not in the house, having left a note stating she was emphatic in her belief that I regarded our marriage as a game, a charade, as proven by my act of last night. The note continued by explaining her absence was due to the fact she did not wish to discuss the nasty situation, any contact with me would come from her attorney. She then described me as a sadist gifted with the undesirable trait of shredding her integrity in a rapacious manner—accusing me of doubting her intelligence—abusing her feelings—and violating my own self-respect, due to her trusting me and the casual manner in which I betrayed that trust. She wished me retribution for casting Justin and her into the untenable position of having to confront the fact our marriage was a gigantic mistake. She then ended the note with the coup de grace . . . "You can not make a silk purse from a sow's ear."

If I harbored any illusions of reconciliation, the apothegm of the sow's ear dispersed them with finality. I gathered my clothing and other necessary items, then placed them in the Cord, all the while pondering the question of should I write a note in response. Deciding any note on my part would be obsequious, I did write one sentence below her writing—a quote from Cicero. . . " Memory is the treasure and guardian of all things." Hugh.

Entering the lobby of the hotel, my first act was requesting to speak with the executive manager about a lease.

"Just a moment, please."

As he disappeared into an office behind the desk, I turned to survey the people sitting in the lobby. Three women, one man was reading the Wall Street Journal. The man's countenance leaped into my memory.

He was the poker player guilty of accusing me of cheating in the game at the Petroleum Club. The man I had dispatched to the confines of a shattered gaming table with a hard right to the jaw. Letting my gaze rest on him, while making sure of his identity, he had raised his eyes from the Journal to mine, then dropped them quickly. I knew he recognized me, but I had no fear of him desiring a resumption of the fray.

The manager came to the desk beaming a smile of welcome, reaching his hand across to shake my hand he said, "Mr. McCulloch, it's indeed a pleasure to have you as a resident of our establishment. Won't you come into my office."

We completed the lease paper and as I passed the lobby, the poker player had departed. After transferring my possessions to the suite, I went to my office.

As I entered, Barbara greeted me in a cordial manner comparable to the way a sister would acknowledge a brother. Closing the door to my private office, I sat down at my desk and sorted out the morning mail stacked neatly before me.

Opening a correspondence from the Petroleum Club and reading its contents, I learned effective of this date my participation as a member would no longer be desired. The rejection was succinct and had the ring of finality. I could not deny my disappointment—for a few minutes I gulped the acidulous taste of self-analysis. It was a bitter prognosis of terminal agromania. Luckily the pangs of being summarily ousted did not linger, and a few minutes of reverie bolstered my egotism to holding myself in esteem. To hell with the Petroleum Club and its array of acerbic members. I had found very few of them that could accept my luck at the tables.

With a few exceptions, all had viewed my good fortune with skepticism coupled with an air of deja vu. I did not need them—they did not need me.

An envelope on the stack bearing an official seal captured my attention. Lifting it from the stack, I gave the seal close scrutiny to learn it was the official seal of the Government of Mexico. This discovery roused my curiosity prompting the immediate opening of its contents. The correspondence was from the office of Government Operations, Mexico City.

Dear Mr. McCulloch:

This will inform you of my desire to meet you for the purpose of exploring possible correlation of your oil exploration technology, with my Government's enormous petroleum reserves. I've followed your illustrious career the past few years, which have produced success in your field. Permit me the liberty of revealing my knowledge of your so-called escapades. Escapades there, Señor, but seen as triumphs here! I'll be most gratified if you elect to meet with me. Please contact me at the address of this letterhead.

With anticipation I await a favorable contact.

Sincerely yours,
Saturnino Cedillo
Minister of Minerals

This proposal would have been enticing another time. At the moment I was very involved. First, in developing a new area of production west of Corpus Christi, Texas—I was awaiting the summons to stand in the box at "Old Bailey," to face the charge of assault on a piano player, a pending divorce, lawsuits charging me with malicious lease agreements and the major complication of possessing a brain at this time, active at convincing me I should be the protagonist in attacking the potpourri of asinine standards of society.

No, at this time my mind was in a maladroit state, I was mad at the world. I had to find some escape for a few days.

The image of Andy Jackson astride his charger flitted across my vision. Jackson Square of course. I would fly over to New Orleans for a few days and try to escape the defamation I had produced.

Going into the outer office, I paused at Barbara's desk, interrupting her typing with, "Barbara, I'll be out of the city for a few days, but will keep in contact with you. Keep things on an even keel while I'm away."

"Yes, sir."

"I must tell you something before I leave. My purpose in telling you is, a pledge to one's self should be made known to another, this adds to the determination of the one making the pledge. I vow here and now I'll never be guilty of any clandestine activity with an employee, regardless of their irresistible charm and/or any encouragement on the part of the employee.

I'm sorry my weakness placed you in the embarrassing situation of last night. Please accept my apology. It'll never happen again."

"No apology is merited. I contributed equally to the disastrous finish of an evening I'll remember forever. I don't blame you. Have a nice trip wherever you're going."

I parked the car in the airport garage and boarded the tri-motor plane for the crescent city of New Orleans. After a two and a half hour flight, we touched down, taxied to the hangar where I called a cab.

♠ ♠ ♠

After checking into the Roosevelt Hotel I laid across the bed on my back staring at the plain white ceiling. I was in a pensive mood while reviewing the facts of life. Concerning myself with only the facts that had influenced and contributed to my present status. After more than an hour of reverie, I had consoled my battered ego to the extent of believing there was nothing weird or bizarre about my behavior. It all being the fruits of provocation by others.

I dressed, entered the down elevator feeling the ebullient, erudite man of the world and ready for anything. Entering the Sazarac Bar I ordered a Ramos Fizz, the house specialty, then seated myself at an empty table affording a vantage point of the entire room. As I savored the drink, a state of total equanimity spread throughout my body and mind. I was considering the prerequisite that money provided the buxom breasted brunette displaying a tantalizing expanse of white thigh, gracing the table adjoining mine. The dulcet music being rendered by the string ensemble was a realization that this was a far cry from Nance Street in the fifth ward of Houston.

The brunette was in the company of a man and an auburn haired, well-endowed woman. Both females appeared to be near thirty and near frustration from boredom. As I sat there musing my capabilities of perhaps erasing their boredom, my stomach growled the usual signal, I was hungry. Heeding the pangs of hunger, I arose to depart for Antoine's.

A sudden tour de force steered me to the women's table. As I reached the brunette I paused, leaned close to her ear and said in a stage whisper, "I'll perform here tonight at nine," then continued on my way out the door.

The maitre d' greeted me solemnly as I entered Antoine's, guiding me to a table near the path used by the waiters making their way to the kitchen, indicating I sit there.

"I'll not be seated here. I detest dining to the accompaniment of kitchen noises, so please locate another table."

He found a suitable table where I looked the menu over, ordering Pompano En Papillote. Thirty minutes later, the waiter appeared pushing a serving cart containing my order. Picking up the cooking bag, he tossed the Pompano from it onto my plate, placing the other dishes in their proper places on the table, he turned to leave when I halted him by asking, "Will you please bring me some Tabasco sauce for the Pompano?"

"One moment, Monsieur."

He sought out the head waiter, conducting an animated conversation with him, embellished with waving of arms and shaking of heads. The head waiter made his way to my table saying, "Monsieur, you do not wish sauce for the Papillote as the chef has seasoned it fit for the gods, any addition to it would be a desecration."

I looked down at the Pompano, then raised my eyes to the head waiter and said, "I don't give a damn if this dish suits you, the waiter, or the damn chef, I'm paying for it. I want some Tabasco sauce, pronto."

The waiter brought the Tabasco muttering faintly, "Chacun a songout."

"Hows that? What did you say?"

"I said Monsieur, every man to his own taste,"

The dinner was exquisite, topped off with a frozen creme dessert. As I made my way from Antoine's I decided to roam the Vieux Carr'e, the French Quarter, in search of whatever it might present.

I entered Pat O'Briens to see what form of entertainment was offered. A woman with hair tinted a fire red was performing on the piano, singing risque songs while the teeming polyglot of humanity contributed a wall of discord as they accompanied her renditions. Elbowing my way to the bar was in itself an accomplishment. I drank two house specials, Hurricanes, while observing the maelstrom of activity surrounding me. With the last swallow of the second drink, I realized now was the time to depart as the effects of the drinks had produced a state of double vision and I was on the verge of being drunk. Forcing my way through the mob to the sidewalk, I had the misfortune of walking between two ferocious females engaged in a genuine combat.

One held a shoe in her hand swinging it downward in an attempt to scalp her adversary with its needle like heel just as I walked into the fray. The heel grazed my right cheek from ear to chin producing a bloody four inch slash. As I turned to avoid another blow from the shoe, the other combatant was in the process of delivering a vicious kick to her attacker, a kick that I received solidly in my crotch directly on my testicles. The instant pain blinded me as I staggered from between the two and sat on the curb, rocking to and fro holding my testicles. The two women were now on the sidewalk behind me kicking, pulling hair, rolling over and over, grunting and squealing. A large crowd had gathered to watch as they tumbled around cursing each other.

"Knock it off, Betty! Stop it! Now!" The policeman had been attracted by the commotion, and was pulling the one he had addressed as Betty away from her clawing, cursing opponent.

I was hurting so painfully, the action of the police held no interest. I did not even turn to witness the cessation of the battle. He hustled them down the sidewalk where they disappeared into the throng lining the walk.

After sitting several minutes, the pain had subsided somewhat so I arose and walked to my hotel. I found sleep easing me, due to the uncommon experience of being kicked. The pain lingered as I grew restless, wishing I had bought a newspaper on the way up.

I noticed a book on the night table beside the bed. I picked it up to learn it was a Gideon Bible, then flipped it open carelessly. It had opened on the Book of Proverbs. My eyes were directed to chapter seventeen, verse twenty-two, "A cheerful heart is a good medicine, but a downcast spirit dries up the bones."

Slamming the book closed, I thought what the hell was I reading that for, this book was for weak people. People who needed synthetic words of advice to carry on. However, the words, a cheerful heart is a good medicine, caught on a snag in my thoughts and remained. It was being reviewed when sleep came.

The next morning I awoke thinking of how I attracted trouble as a magnet attracts metal. Everywhere trouble and violence seemed my constant companion. The episode of the evening before was returned with stark realism and clarity as I looked at the damage the woman's kick had produced. My sac was a deep purple and sore as hell to touch.

After breakfast I placed a call to Barbara.

"Good morning, McCulloch Enterprises."

"Hello, Barbara. What's the good word?"

"Hugh, I've some alarming news. Curly Ward called a few minutes ago from Corpus Christi to tell you Clarkwood, number two well had blown out, caught fire and was cratering. He thought you should get there as soon as possible. There's nothing else of importance and I am sorry to have this bad news for you. I hope you've had some peace of mind before having this tossed at you."

"Thank you, Barbara. I'll leave immediately. Will let you know how things turn out down there. Any word from Audrey?"

"No."

"Okay, Good-bye for now."

After deplaning in Corpus Christi, I hired a cab to drive me to Clarkwood, arriving there around two p.m. I had seen the smoke from the airport, a distance of about ten miles. She was surely in full bloom as the flames became visible three miles from the location. The driver could get no closer than a quarter mile of the fire due to the intense heat. I paid him, then walked quickly to where the crew was standing, watching the holocaust.

Curly approached me with a somber expression and I could sense what he was going to say.

"Hugh, we lost two men. They didn't have a chance. I'm sorry."

"Do not blame yourself, Curly. It's a turn of fate."

We watched the steel derrick now tilted about fifteen degrees. The base of it was a cherry red, from the terrific heat the gas and oil was producing, as the flames were rising about two hundred feet above the crater. Curly broke the silence, "Hugh, I suggest we contact Jimbo Hooks in Houston to get him down here with the hope he may be able to snuff the fire. He has had good results on well fires, it's worth a try. I'm acquainted with the wives of both men we lost, so maybe I should be the one to tell them. Do you agree?"

"Yes, please do. You drive to the nearest telephone and try to get Hooks here as soon as possible. I'll remain here until you contact the men's wives. Are they in the area?"

"Yes both are living in the same apartment house in Corpus. I'll call on them in person."

"Damn the luck, I don't envy your mission, Curly, but go ahead. I'll see them tomorrow and do what I can. Get going now."

The fire was attracting hordes of sightseers, clogging the highway. The acrid odor of burning oil filled the air for miles around, while the generated heat was scorching all vegetation in a radius of a quarter mile.

As I sat on the ground watching the raging inferno, I was struck with the realization of how costly man's quest for money could be. I pondered the question what the two men were thinking when entering the fiery maw of death, when they realized there was no escape, no tomorrow!

As my morbid thoughts occupied my mind, the energy of the heat was sapping the strength from the steel derrick. The cratering had progressed, and now the derrick was beginning its death knell as it began to meld with the flaming pit. It was slowly changing its configurations sliding into the oily hell hole as the steel legs warped like warm taffy. Five minutes later the cauldron had gobbled a twenty-five thousand dollar meal of steel and iron, created two widows and its fury still unabated while roaring for more.

Curly returned as the shadows of dusk were penciling the countryside, fighting a futile battle against the glare of the flames. He came up beside me, stood staring into the inferno without saying a word. After a pause I asked, "Did you get Hooks?"

Looking at his watch, he replied, "They should be here by nine."

"Curly, it takes courage to do what you've just done. I admire you for doing a very unpleasant task."

Curly remained silent for three or four minutes, then turned looking to the west where the sun had retired for the night. It was a gesture of seeming to turn his back on something despised, the flaming well.

"Yes Hugh, perhaps I had some courage when I left here, but the tears of Charlie's wife and twelve-year-old daughter drowned what courage I had—the tears of Frenchy's wife washed it out to the sea of ended dreams and bitter tomorrows. I'm drained."

The tears were glistening on his leathery cheeks, highlighted by the flames behind him. They were little emeralds of compassion created by a tough, two-fisted specimen of a man whose heart had been reached from his duties of the past hour.

The Hooks crew were unsuccessful in their efforts at quenching the blaze by the usual method of employing explosives, due to the width of the cratered hole. They returned to Houston the next morning.

Hooks suggested before leaving, we should let it burn a couple of weeks, then perhaps the crater would deepen. That coupled with the burning crude might lower the level of oil making the explosive method effective. Three weeks later, he was successful in stifling the flames.

♦ ♦ ♦

In the meantime I had returned to Houston to be met with a shower of problems. The assault charge was settled out of court at a considerable expense to me, as were the two pending lawsuits pertaining to my devious, unethical, as well as unlawful action in siphoning two excellent leases from two major oil companies. My reputation had unfortunately preceded me to the court room where I was hung by my thumbs, fiscally, by a judge who did not countenance ravenous people resorting to cutting corners. He gave me a five hundred dollar lecture on ethical conduct, then levied a five thousand dollar fine on each count, for my questionable conduct.

Three down, one to go—the divorce.

A week later found me entering the gates of Rice Stadium to see the last home game of the season. They were pitted against Arkansas on this sunny, cool, Saturday afternoon. I was anticipating a pleasant three hours of good football. To add to the pleasure, I had a pint of Jack Daniels nestled in my inner coat pocket.

I had consumed over half of the bottle by halftime. The warm glow of the whiskey and Rice leading fourteen to three had put me at peace with myself and my surroundings for the first time in many months, as I made my way down to the men's room.

On my return, as I came out the tunnel entrance I noticed three men, apparently companions, approaching the tunnel. Where had I seen the one wearing the brown sweater? One more step, then recognition came as a blinding flash!

He was the son of a bitch guilty of depriving me of what I had believed would have been a memorable experience, a night with Reba! The humiliation of that night engulfed me producing a towering inner rage.

"Pardon me, are you from Conroe?"

"Yes I am, but I don't believe I know you."

I had shifted my feet slightly as he was making a mental effort to place me in his memory. I was making a pretense of scratching my forehead as I smiled at him like a long lost friend. I brought the edge of my right hand down with cruel slashing ferocity striking the bridge of his nose. I felt the bone and cartilage crunch under the hammer like blow, as his nose spattered blood like an over ripe tomato. He actually bellowed from the pain as he made a heroic effort to see his antagonist by shaking his head and taking mincing steps in a half circle. I followed his turn, then planted my feet and delivered the coup de grace—a hard right just below his right ear, followed with a sledge hammer left to his solar plexus. The wing left his mouth sounding somewhat like the snort of a horse, as he was crumpling slowly downward, crimson blood cascading from his wounds. Down to his knees, arms hanging as lifeless as a mishandled doll, he tilted slowly forward until his forehead was resting on the asphalt.

It was only at that moment I considered the possibility of interference from his companions. I fully expected one or both to take up the fray in retaliation. They were looking down at their fallen companion expressing shock and disbelief at what they were witnessing.

If it weren't for the blood spattered on the asphalt and the gun wielding—this beaten companion could have been viewed as some sinful Moroccan that had been reading his Koran and was seeking solace and forgiveness from Allah! His short, fat companion inquired rather meekly, "What did you do that for? He didn't even know you."

"Yes, he knew me several years ago. When he comes to his senses, tell him I said the smashed nose was in memory of what he did to Reba. I want him to let her see his African style nose. Tell him if he'll do that, then he'll know who I am."

I pushed my way through the crowd surrounding the fallen warrior, thinking how he did not present the formidable foe as he had on the night he made me walk barefoot on the crushed oyster shell. The thought made me furious once more.

I returned elbowing my way through the throng of onlookers to the fallen man still on his knees, forehead down. Walking to his rear, I planted my right foot on his ass and shoved him forward to a prone position. Then turning, made my way back to my seat to watch the second half.

The sage who remarked, "That evil all within us lurks," surely expressed my emotions of the moment. I should've been nagged with alarm that the guy might be dead, as he had not moved in five minutes. Rather I had the emotion of a coal miner, who had just paid up the company store. I actually felt cleansed within as if I had been purged with a powerful laxative. The laxative being redeeming a pledge made to myself, that somewhere, sometime, I would repay that character for humiliating me, and striking Reba the cruel blow. I felt exhilarated as I watched the second half.

Bemoaning the final score, Arkansas twenty-seven and Rice seventeen, while making my way to the car, I realized I had been fortunate to have sated my hatred by beating a man into insensibility, and leaving the scene without being escorted to jail. Maybe my fate with the minions of the law was changing in my favor.

♠ ♠ ♠

I had been avoiding Audrey since her filing for divorce and had found the life of a benedict pale in comparison to the hedonistic style of life that found me bed hopping nightly—I was a stud for any appealing female and was servicing the easy ones twice.

I had no cause to regret moving into the apartment hotel as it provided a nice bar and club right off the lobby, with music for dancing nightly. This place offered some mystic attraction for women as they surged in night after night, singles, doubles, triples and sometimes four or five in a group. The atmosphere was seductive, the hunting, productive.

It always puzzled me, why professional ladies of the night did not enter the confines. It finally dawned on me, the attractive habitues were doing it for fun—the pros could not compete with romance being indulged for the fun of it. I can't say enough about the quality, the appeal, the allure of the females gathered here nightly. It was non pareil U.S. prime—the best array of meat in Houston.

I had enjoyed apartment living for six weeks, most every night found me in the bar guzzling drinks to unwind my taut nerves stretched from the days business activities.

The past month provided my first financial disaster since entering the exploration-drilling phase of petroleum. Having secured an option to drill an extension tract adjacent to the old Spindletop field near Beaumont, I had three dusters to date.

This venture involved the investment of a considerable sum and I had entered the area based on a recommendation from Joe Bob Miller.

Failure in an undertaking was a new, undesirable experience and for the first time had brought about the mental inventory occupying my mind at present. The past year I had purchased several pieces of real estate in Houston as an investment.

One of the acquisitions being a ten acre plot located on South Main, bought for the sum of three hundred thousand dollars cash. The transaction, being of a natural distress sale, had placed it in the cash category and a bargain on any basis.

Even though my name was bandied about when conversation involved prominent people, I was regarded by my peers as an unprincipled rapacious corner cutter. One who vacillated from lawful to unlawful business ethics, and the one most hoped to see ground into the dust of failure. This dubious opinion of the citizenry, regarding me, had never penetrated my protective armor of self-confidence and an egoist manner. Success had always been my companion, with the exception of the past few weeks. These set backs were part of the gamble making them have precedence over my reputation.

This assessment of my reputation had been related to me by numerous wives, and bedroom playmates of the petroleum hierachy. These bits of information were passed on to me in intimate surroundings, i.e. hotel and motel rooms when the informants were being anxious to prove their opinion of me that did not correspond to that of their husbands or sugar daddy's.

My accountant had advised me numerous times to diversify—suggesting petroleum transmission—real property—hotel—

constitutional food, in order to hedge against any decline in my present business. These suggestions were now being reviewed and given consideration on the heels of my malfunction of judgement in the Beaumont operation. Maybe I should extend to a new field.

Friday night found me in the hotel club trying to cope with the inner Hugh McCulloch. This practice was becoming more often than ever before. I would find my mind in a quandary—dichotomy of reasoning. At times, I felt a need of the comfort of Audrey, then the bohemian life would erase the need and malaise would take over, bringing me the feeling of being stretched on the rack. Tonight was one of those times.

I had consumed several doubles to anesthetize the inner quarrel, when I became cognizant of the charms of the female vocalist. Funny, I had never before noticed her enticing figure. I was sure the Jack Daniels was not producing a fantasy, as her bouncing breasts held me in awe. She had a better than average delivery in song, and a body to match. When she tapered-off the last note of "Mood Indigo," she sat down at a table near the piano.

I moved in on her at once by pulling out a chair saying,

"I'm Hugh McCulloch," as I sat across the table from her.

She smiled saying, "Please leave."

"Come now, I have just arrived and you ask me to leave, why?"

She was casting anxious glances toward the club entrance as I awaited her answer. Shaking her head with emphasis, she replied, "Because I'm married and expecting the most jealous husband in the world, any minute. Please go."

"He's coming now!" she nodded toward the entrance.

I was not about to hop up and scurry away like a wharf rat, in fact I never looked in the direction she had indicated, I remained seated. Shortly I felt a tap on my shoulder, then, "Up and away buster! You're in my way, and this is my wife."

I glanced up into a pair of porcine eyes set in a gargantuan head atop the biggest body I had seen in a long time. His size was accented by the brown shaggy sweater he was wearing. The hair on the sweater was a full inch long, giving him the appearance of a full-sized angry gorilla.

I thought of rising quickly butting his chin with my head and maybe picking up some advantage of surprise to offset his size. I stood, pushed my chair back, then replied, "My name's not buster, "all the while looking in his gimlet eyes.

This monolith before me towered over my six feet two, by at least four inches, and was twice as ugly. I was thinking, "Damn it to hell, here it goes again. Trouble!"

"Your name is anything I call you, Sonny."

This was a brazen, fearless bastard I was facing and if he had left me any out, I would have gladly departed, but he had closed the door on any honorable escape when saying my name was anything he chose it to be.

He reached for my coat lapels with the intent of shaking me like a cat with a mouse. When he did, I realized the situation had passed the point of no retreat. I threw my right arm upward knocking his arm aside, then pivoted, hooking my left fist into his stomach with every ounce of my one hundred eight five pounds behind. Expecting him to bend forward from the blow giving me the opportunity to deliver an uppercut to his chin with my right.

My punch to his stomach landed on muscles that felt like a whalebone corset and numbed my fist. He was standing there laughing at the surprised expression on my face. When he did not wince at receiving my best punch, he laughed in derision. I experienced the same feeling of desperation the captain of the Titanic must have had as that famous ship slipped beneath the waves of the North Atlantic.

He threw a straight right at me that sounded a menacing whistle as it passed my right ear, barely ticking it, due to my evasive move of my head. This guy was a genuine head hunter and I felt like the selected pygmy. It was then I made the decision to resort to anything, to escape with my life. Backing quickly, I picked up a chair to use as a cudgel, hoping to expose his brain. He charged me, I swung the chair in a vicious arc bringing it down across his head and shoulder. It disintegrated leaving only one of its legs in my right hand, he was still on his feet, slowed down slightly, but still coming.

I drummed a tattoo on his head with the chair leg as he was pummeling me with rights and lefts. I was now backed against the piano facing the moment of truth. I brought the chair leg down across the back of his neck will all my strength. This stopped him momentarily, I then circled the piano and toppled it over on his feet and legs causing him to fall, pinned beneath the weight of the instrument.

I got the hell out of there to my car and drove away to bless Saint Christopher for saving my ass with the piano. When I returned to the hotel around two a.m., the lobby was empty. The night clerk was reading a pulp magazine and did not notice me until I was pressing the elevator button.

He spoke, but made no mention of the fracas. I went to my apartment, undressed, filled the tub with steaming hot water, got into it hoping to soak away some soreness that had already set in.

♠ ♠ ♠

My phone rang at seven thirty a.m. It was the executive manager, "Mr. McCulloch, will you please stop by my office on your way out?"

"Yes, I will"

"Fine. Thank you."

I interrupted the day clerk working on a report, when asking to see the manager, "Just one moment Mr. McCulloch."

He entered the office behind the desk, then reappeared saying, "Go right in."

I entered the office certain the request had some relation to last nights brawl.

"Have a seat, Mr. McCulloch. I'm sure you have an idea of why I asked you to drop in. Do you?"

"Yes, it probably concerns the fight in the club."

"Right, Mr. McCulloch, when you applied for residency in our hotel, your acceptance received careful consideration by me. In fact, I exercised care to the extent of consulting the owners whether to accept you or not. I must admit one of them is a director of the River Oaks Country Club. He advanced strong objections, stemming from your conduct around the club, eventually resulting in your being asked to resign your membership.

"The other owner had heard of your reputation as a brawler and troublemaker, and he had reservations about your application also. But the two of them, after lengthy discussion arrived at the decision to accept you, advising me to go ahead with the lease. May I be perfectly frank with you, Mr. McCulloch?"

"Certainly."

"Well, I had ideas of my own about taking you in, as I too had been alerted to your quick temper. Excuse my candor, but you've a notorious reputation throughout south Texas, so notorious I felt we had a land mine on our hands since you moved in. A land mine subject to explosion at anytime and from the damage evident in our club you must've exploded last night! I haven't any choice but to ask you to vacate today, and settle an account of four hundred dollars damage."

This man sitting before me, taking the liberty of detailing my faults had at last triggered my hot button, my reputation.

"Now you listen to me, you misguided lackey. I don't need you or anyone to point out my shortcomings. You've been given the privilege of expression and I demand the same accord. As far as I know you may squat to piss, or you may wear lace on your shorts—I don't give a damn for your opinion of me and care less of what your superiors think. I'll move out today gladly, and I want you to inform the owners I'll build a hotel two blocks south of here, that'll make yours a flop house in comparison. Be sure you convey my words to them. Now what is the total amount of alleged damages plus any other charges?"

I hastily made a check for the amount, handed it to him remarking, "Remember, I'll build two blocks south! Pass the message."

♠ ♠ ♠

Monday morning I found Barbara as cheerful as always as I entered the office. This girl was a gem when considering her qualifications and I was lucky to have her even though she had been the catalyst of the divorce coming up.

Going into my private office, I asked Barbara to get my banker, Mr. McMillan on the phone.

Seating myself at my desk, the buzzer sounded indicating the telephone call was ready.

"Hello, Mr. McMillan, I need the name of someone in a position of authority to sanction or approve financing of a project that will entail a figure somewhere around four million. Is there someone you can direct me to? Also, I'll need an architectural firm to work with. Any suggestions?"

"Yes, I can highly recommend a Mr. Stan Hawley, associated with Prudential Insurance Mortgage loan division and the firm of Smythe-Giddings-Turcotte Architects. I can arrange a meeting in my office if you would like me to be present."

"I would appreciate your cooperation and presence Mr. McMillan."

"Good, I'll get back to you as to when we can set the meeting."

Two days later we all met in McMillan's office, seated in a casual arrangement occupying huge leather chairs spaced at intervals.

The formalities of introduction had been brief, then Mr. McMillan plunged into the purpose of the meeting by saying, "Gentlemen, Hugh McCulloch has asked me to recommend people in your business, that's why you're here. He hasn't informed me of what he has in mind so I'll let Hugh take it from here."

"Gentlemen as you may or may not know, I'm primarily in oil exploration and drilling. A few months back my accountant suggested I diversify. I own ten acres on South Main across from the Rice Institute campus. I want to build a modern hotel on the site, or at least I think I do. I've in mind an eye-popping modern structure. As we know the Texas State Hotel was the last one built in the area and I feel Houston deserves a new, modern one. A show place. You gentleman must enjoy great prestige in your chosen fields, having been selected by Mr. McMillan. I know absolutely nothing about architecture and even less about financing. So now the ball is yours. "Having had my say, I leaned back into the luxurious chair awaiting some action.

Smythe spoke first, asking, "Hugh how large a structure are you visualizing?"

"I've in mind something around twenty to twenty-five stories. Can you shoot a dollar figure off the top of your head?"

"From what I've heard of you, Hugh, I've the feeling you're going for a structure that would seem to shout, 'Hugh McCulloch" when viewed. Am I right?"

I could not restrain a smile from his candid reference to me, but replied, "Yes, that's putting it very well."

"Okay. You own the land. We're looking at construction and furbishing. That would put us in the ball park of eight to ten million, based on conventional furnishings. You can let your wishes soar, furnishing it in the decor of a Harem, or Geisha House and hoist the cost to twelve million."

I turned to Hawley, asking, "By building this hotel on property owned by me, clear of encumbrance, what basis or should I ask what percentage of the project will Prudential throw in?"

"I would say seventy percent mortgage if we hold the outlay to ten million or under. Over that we would go on fifty percent. Now that's just off the top of my head. Don't hold me to it."

"Damn it, tell me something concrete, I'm not just horsing around, I'm going to build a damn hotel!"

"All right, the figures I gave you are based on present levels of involvement. How long before you intend to start?"

"Just as soon as Smythe can show me some pictures."

"Do you contemplate any problems on your end of financing?" asked Hawley.

"Hell no, I can lay mine on the table now, today." I continued.

"It's your ball Smythe. Be damn sure you include my penthouse topping it off. So get going on your plans. If you want a retainer, name it. I hope you'll do your best to get this hotel completed as soon as possible. I need a place to sleep!"

Having terminated the business for the day, we arose shaking hands all around, then headed for the elevator.

In sixty days, I had the entire project solidified and a marriage dissolved.

The construction contract was awarded, I turned up the initial spade of dirt starting the projetc. Reporters and photographers were present, giving it front page exposure. One article read:

"Mr. McCulloch possesses the facility of taking a bad situation and making it immediately worse. Proof of the pudding lies in the fact that he, being barred from every hotel in the area, has encouraged him to build one of his own, "Ejection Proof."

"There are three talents that abound in Hugh McCulloch. He is the best one man wrecking crew around, when inebriated. He could dally away a night in a convent, if he so desired. He is diligent and successful in the quest of wealth. When one says this, they have said it all, but things do happen when he appears."

I had been the recipient of this type of publicity so many times in the past, that when people recognized me on the street they were viewing me as some type of freak. Their stares at times disturbed me, but what could I expect when the news stories pictured me as a Frankenstein Monster.

The drilling west of Corpus Christi was proving to be one of my best ventures, having brought in thirty-five producers during the past eight months. The result of ten rigs operating in the area and all of them mine.

The hotel was progressing nicely as the steel workers were nearing the "topping out" stage.

So far 1937 had been a very good year financially.

Chapter Nine

No Love Lost In The Past

On a cool November day, I was looking out the office window when the decision to visit my parents came into my mind. I drove out to the fifth ward, cruising slowly along the street recalling events of the past. The neighborhood had not changed much in seven years. I drove by the school I had attended, recalling fights I had been involved in. The most noticeable change was the numerous beer joints that had opened since beer had been legalized.

I arrived in front of our house, then entered the fenced in yard. As I closed the gate my Mother appeared in the doorway, peering through the screen. Halfway to the porch steps she had recognized me, with outsretched arms she met me on the top step.

She did not say a word vocally, but the tears coursing her cheeks told me a story. A story of a Mother's love for a son that had neglected her by an absence of seven years. She put her arms around my neck saying softly, "I've prayed every day, every night, for your return. Now you're here. Thank you God for sending him."

For the first time in my life the tears of regret were welling up in my eyes and trickling down my cheeks as I held her close. My neglect of her was thrusting spears of pain through my brain. It was then I knew retribution for staying away so long. I held her at arms length asking, "Are you all right? How is Dad?"

"Fine Son, your Dad is working every day. We've missed you. Dad is always saying he can't understand a man being so busy that he can't find time to visit his parents. However, we've read about you numerous times in the papers. Do you really get into all the brawls they say you do?"

"Yes Mom, and I've been in a few brushes with the law. That's one reason I've stayed away so long, I knew you'd be upset by some of the reports. Enough of that.

"If you and Dad will select a home that appeals to you, anywhere—I'll buy it as a token of my love for the two of you. I don't care where it is or what the cost. Find one you like, call me at my office, it will be yours free and clear. Here's my card. I'd like for Dad to start looking right away. Please call me as often as you like."

I kissed her cheek still damp from tears of joy, then made my way toward the car. As I reached the gate, I turned saying, "If you or Dad ever need anything, please call me."

She had come to the edge of the porch. As I turned the corner I looked back to see her wave to me—a gesture of love.

Three blocks from my old home I noticed a beer parlor of some repute and quickly decided to stop for a cold beer. Perhaps after seven years I might see an old school buddy and review some nostalgia with someone I knew.

The essence of stale beer prevailed as I made my way to the bar where I placed my right foot on the rail, eyeing a gallon jar of pickled eggs setting before me. A hulk of a man behind the bar was peering at me, probably thinking I was an alcohol tax board investigator out to catch him in some violation.

"What'll it be?"

"Two of those pickled eggs and a Pabst, please."

As he forked the two eggs from the jar, I was adjusting my vision to the semi-darkness and scanning the booths for a familiar face. In one near the entrance were three men downing beer while trading insults. A booth near the rear contained a man and a woman exploring the advantages of privacy.

After munching the eggs washed down with beer, I asked the curious bartender the location of the men's room. He replied grudgingly, "To the rear on the right," still eyeing me with suspicion.

Entering the restroom my nostrils were breathing in the malodor of marijuana being smoked by an occupant of the enclosed toilet. The pungent smoke arising above the enclosure emitted an odor similar to burning cow dung.

The occupant of the stall opened the door as I turned to exit the room, giving me the chance to sate my curiosity at seeing the reefer smoker. He appeared vaguely familiar—someone I had seen in the past. He was combing his hair looking in the mirror on the wall and giving me scrutiny. He turned saying, "Where have I known you?"

Recognition came at the moment. We had attended school together and he was the individual who had pushed me backward over his crony who was on hands and knees. It had resulted in my taking a painful tumble, striking my head on the hard ground. I had released my fury by felling him with two blows. He had not elected to rise as I stood over him, but had promised to get even with me. I was looking him in the eye as I reviewed the incident after eight years. He had grown somewhat and was now heavier than I, presenting a menacing possibility. We were in a facing down confrontation. I would not take my eyes from his gaze as he was making a mental effort at placing me in his memory. His eyes were luminous with restrained hate pumped-up by the effects of the marijuana as he asked, "Is your name Hugh—?"

"Yes, that's my name. We were in school together. I'm the one you pushed over your friend, giving me one hell of a tumble . . . you bastard! You sneaked a lucky punch on me that day, but now let's see how sneaky you are."

He had damn near melted my courage with his glare of ferocity, changing the color of his eyes from brown to the gleaming saffron like those of a bengal tiger. I was fascinated by the show of intense hate his features were revealing. His upper lip was curled in a manner baring his teeth in an animal-like snarl as his eyes had now become slits. He was advancing on me in a shuffling sinuous glide, slavering as saliva coursed his chin, dripping to the floor. His arms at his side was presenting a mind-boggling scene—it was bewildering. The realization that I was on a collision course with peril hit me with sudden impact. I reacted by assuming a fighting stance never taking my eyes from his. I heard a metallic click. A darting glance to his hands revealed the source of the click. His right hand was now holding a gleaming three inch blade being pointed at my stomach as he glided toward me. The point of the knife was swaying as a metronome.

I backed several steps, hurriedly removing my coat and quickly wrapping it around my left forearm. He was stalking me in a relentless animal-like way as I swiftly stepped to his left, throwing up my coat wrapped arm as a defense from the knife. He flicked the blade upward burying it in the coat. At the same time I felt a burning sensation, but retaliated with a hammer blow on the nape of his neck. Moving quickly around him I fended off another vicious slash, but the blade had reached flesh. Again I delayed death with a horrible punishing blow to his kidney. At this point, I could feel the warm blood filling the palm of my left hand, but he was showing the effects of the devastating blows by slowing his movement—his grimaced face was now chalky from pain, but he came on. He seemed to be drawing energy and motivation to kill from the source of hate that filled him.

I was convinced only a force majeure would see us leave this stinking restroom. The elements of finality were prevalent. I did not want to kill my adversary—damn it to hell! Why had no one felt the need to use the toilet! This entire critical episode had been so silent—so deadly. How I wanted to break it off before it progressed to the point of death!

This time he threw his arm in a forward thrust, aiming the point of the knife at my abdomen. Once more my left arm deflected the thrust, but again the blade had penetrated my coat and entered the flesh. It was no longer a light gray pinstripe, my blood had tinted it to a lavender blob of shredded fabric.

A gamble on my part was imperative—I threw my left arm in a feint toward his chin hoping he would slash at my arm. He did. I lifted my weight propelling an uppercut to his chin that should have decapitated him, but did not. Instead he crumpled slowly to his knees as the knife slipped reluctantly from his grasp and clattered in unison with the thump of his head as he tilted forward face down, still on his knees. I tilted him sideways straightening his legs, leaving him lying on his back.

I unwrapped what had been a tailor made coat from my bleeding arm, then tossed the soggy blood soaked tatters into a refuse can in the corner. My next act would be finding a doctor.

As I was leaving the restroom, I had to step over my foe and noticed his eyelids move slightly. This pleased me as I did not want any involvement with the police. I stopped at the bar on my way out holding my left arm down out of sight. I then told the bartender quietly, "There's a man in the restroom who attacked me with a knife. Perhaps you'd better see what you can do for him."

I hurriedly made my exit, driving to Herman Hospital emergency room where an intern laced up my wounds using fifty-eight sutures. I'd convinced him I'd been involved in an auto accident. As he was performing the final cleanup of my arm he remarked, "Are you certain these cuts are the only injuries you received?"

"Yes, I was really fortunate to escape as well as I did." A truthful statement for sure.

Chapter Ten
Big Plans With Cedillo

I went to the Rice Hotel seeking the privacy of my room. I needed solitude to lick the wounds of confusion filling my mind, plus surrendering to total exhaustion. Entering my room, my first act was pouring a half glass of Jack Daniels whiskey. Drinking it quickly, I fell across the bed face down. After thirty minutes of mental self-castigation, I was startled at hearing Audrey call my name. I turned quickly on my back then sat up to answer, questioning her presence. I gazed around the room for the source of her voice, then got up and looked into the bathroom. It was empty. I scurried to the door opening it to admit her, she wasn't there—looking down the hall I found it to be a lonely tunnel. After closing the door, I consumed another big shot of whiskey to quiet the unrest clawing within, then sought the bed once more.

The silence of the room was exerting a powerful influence on my mind as it brought a deluge of self-pity. I was casting mental jabs into the past—reviewing my life with Audrey—the insensitive manner in which I had dealt with Justin—my constant inner conflict with my defiant temper—the unpleasant results my temper had produced. All these unsavory situations passing in ugly review were pressing their undesirable companionship upon me as the loneliness of the room hammered my ego.

This was a novel state to me. For the first time in my life, my dormant conscience was erupting within. Hugh McCulloch, the inflexible entrepreneur was being subjected to the inner scarification that ordinary people experience from wrongdoing. Perhaps another drink would give my troubled mind surcease. I lifted the bottle from the dresser, then returned to the bed placing the whiskey on the night table. Pouring a glass half full, then drinking it in gulps, I sat on the side of the bed to recover my breath. After several minutes of mental inventory I found myself lacking in the balances of life. Here I was, a person of ample wealth and power, sitting alone in a hotel room lamenting. I was rejected by my peers and seeking solace from a bottle. I had to get out of this room now! Dressing quickly I rode the elevator down to the lobby.

I entered the dining room seating myself in a booth offering a view of the street. I was looking at the flow of traffic but not really seeing it, as my mind was questioning the occurrences of the past half hour. Did I judge myself as a victim of circumstance created by others—or did I harbor an inner subconscious desire of defeatism? Surely my conscience was the projection force revealing my many unsavory facets of character. Was my greed justified? My manipulation of people was the accepted norm for survival in the jungle of business—or was it? The divorce was launched by Audrey, not me. My rationale for these ugly pangs of remorse was the essence of frailty and did nothing to give me assurance of righteousness!

"Would you care to order now, Mr. McCulloch?" The waitress had interrupted my reverie.

I welcomed the sound of a human voice as it brought me back to reality. Her question had rescued me from the dank cavern of true self-analysis.

"Hello, Thelma. I'm hungry so please recommend something that's good for a guy returning from a long trip where there was no one but himself."

"Have you been out of town, Mr. McCulloch?"

"Yes and no—even though it was a long trip," I replied.

She gave me a questioning look, then said, "The cordon bleu is excellent. The split pea au amigre would be an exquisite starter followed by our chef's special salad nicoise." She awaited my response with pencil poised above the guest check.

"Sounds good to me and thanks for getting me out of a dilemma."

Awaiting my meal, the decision to explore the possibilities of the Mexico offer was made. I needed to get out of Houston at intervals as new surroundings would give me a chance to listen to my inner self. I was being subjected to an unprecedented experience that involved matter and spirit, while an internal voice urged me to encourage and accept the self-appraisal. Ac-

voice urged me to encourage and accept the self-appraisal. Acceptance was not easy, anything bordering on the occult or metaphysics dismayed me.

After consuming the sumptuous dinner, I walked to my office reviewing the letter from the Mexican official regarding oil exploration. I checked the letter head discovering, to my satisfaction, the telephone number of a residence. Glancing at my watch, I decided to call Señor Saturnino Cedillo in Mexico City—the tender of the offer to work with me in his position of Minister of Interior Resources.

Leaning back into the depths of the comfortable office chair for five minutes of concentration regarding what I was prepared to accept or decline, I lifted the receiver placing the call. After several minutes of interchange between American and Mexican operators, the connection was made, a sonorous voice came through,

"Señor Cedillo's hacienda."

"Señor Hugh McCulloch. No hablo espanol. Por favor Señor Cedillo."

"Si Señor, uno momento por favor."

The seconds ticked by as anticipation of what would follow snared my thoughts.

"Hello Mr. McCulloch. This is Saturnino Cedillo. I've been awaiting a response from you. You've made me very happy by the courtesy of this call."

His voice came over as authoritative, yet gentle. I had a mental picture forming of a corpulent man with cigar between lips adorned with a handle bar moustache. He continued, "Have you given thought to the offer of my government? If you have, what's your decision?"

"Yes, Señor Cedillo I've given it thorough consideration. This call is made to set up a meeting with you. I'm prepared to move on your proposal. However, I wish to meet with you as soon as possible to discuss the overall operations and cement details. I can fly down to Mexico or meet you in Houston, or the place of your choice."

A few moments pause then, "Mr. McCulloch, can you meet me in Monterrey next Monday, the twelfth. I'll arrange a room for you at the Ambassador Hotel. We'll meet in the lobby at six p.m., if this arrangement meets with your approval."

"That'll be excellent."

"Tell me Mr. McCulloch, are you as macho with señoritas as the stories I've heard make you? Don't answer that question! You can demonstrate in person in Monterrey."

"Señor Cedillo," I replied, "One question deserves another. May I ask where you mastered the English language so beautifully?"

"Ha! Yes, you may ask, your efficient professors at Northwestern University transformed me into a Mexican-American and after five years awarded me a Masters of Journalism."

I gulped, then said, "The professors must be proud of the results of their efforts with student Cedillo."

Chuckling, he replied, "You're too kind Mr. McCulloch. six p.m., Monday the 12th, Ambassador Hotel in Monterrey."

"Right. It's been a pleasure conversing with you."

My thoughts were employed in an attempt at composing a mental picture of Cedillo as the conversation ended. The scope of his proposal was of concern also. Having heard many times the Mexicans were tough to bargain with, I would learn on Monday just how difficult it would be.

I called Jim Harris, the pilot, to arrange the Monday flight to Monterrey. He informed me his tri-motor plane was being overhauled but he would fly me down in a Ryan monoplane. We agreed take-off time would be at one o'clock.

After placing the receiver on its cradle, my thoughts reverted to Audrey. I wanted to talk with her, but my hand refused to lift the receiver. It was as if some psychic force had stopped my motion, or perhaps my inherent stubborn trait had prevailed. Whatever, I swiveled my chair to view her portrait still adorning the wall behind me. I studied her expressive eyes intently, hoping it would prompt me to follow through with my first impulse and call her.

For several minutes I gazed into her eyes, all the while recalling how sedate and genteel she had remained during the depressing procedure of the divorce. She had asked for nothing and would not accept anything of material worth in her plea. I had, as a last resort, insisted she at least accept our River Oaks home. This offer was also rejected. Looking at her portrait in the stifling silence of the office, the desire to be needed by someone at last penetrated my facade of independence—two large tears were gently forming and beginning their downward course—a hot, damp, poignant remainder—no man is an island. I got up, stepped closer to the portrait and looked directly into her eyes. I said, "You're one hell of a woman."

Locking the office door a quote came to me, "The happiest time in any man's life is when he's in red hot pursuit of a dollar with a reasonable prospect of overtaking it." This bit of conjecture certainly was not applicable to me at the moment. I retired this night thinking of Audrey and what might have been.

♠ ♠ ♠

The music coming from the radio on my way to the airport on Monday, was interrupted for a short news summary. The second item stated a prominent oil man was confined to Methodist Hospital with a serious heart attack. The victim was Justin Brent. He had suffered the attack Sunday and was admitted to the hospital at eight thirty in the evening.

The disturbing news provided a devastating effect to my immediate plans. Now was the time when Audrey needed someone. Someone to share the lonely vigil of waiting. Waiting for something she was powerless to seletc. Pangs of remorse shut out reality as I reviewed the last time I had seen Justin.

Driving into a service station to call Audrey, I questioned the reception my call might receive. The attendant pointed to a phone on the desk. I checked with the nurses station on the floor where Justin was confined and asked to speak with Mr. Brent's daughter, stating Mr. Brent was my father-in-law.

A few minutes passed, then the voice I had longed to hear, "Hello Hugh. You heard about Dad?"

"Yes, I'm on my way to the airport. I'm flying to Mexico. I had the radio on and heard about Justin on a newscast. Listen Audrey, there's nothing as important right now as my assisting you and Justin anyway that I can. Tell me, what can I do?"

"Hugh, there isn't anything you or anyone else can do, he's in God's hands. How long do you intend to stay in Mexico?"

"Audrey, I may not go to Mexico if any good could come from my presence there with you. Perhaps my trip will last two or three days at the most. I repeat your needs or Justin's takes precedence over all else. Can I help by being there?"

"No Hugh," she continued, "Dad is sedated now and the doctors report his condition as stable. I'm happy you called, what's more your call reveals you do have compassion—something I thought you didn't possess. Why not call when you return, then you may be permitted to visit him if you wish."

"I'll do that. Until then, keep your hopes in a positive vein. Justin will come through this in good shape. Good-bye for now."

Damn it. If she had only indicated a desire for my moral support, I would have foregone the trip to Mexico. Her attitude was difficult to analyze, even though her voice had a ring of sincerity. Especially as she referred to my having compassion.

The plane was near a hangar with Harris leaning against the fuselage awaiting my arrival. Wheeling the car into the hangar, I emerged as he was cranking the engine. As I stepped into the cabin door the motor caught. I closed the door. Jim turned, smiled at me and asked, "Are you ready Mr. McCulloch?"

"Let her go," I replied.

Two minutes later we were airborne, the altitude offering a placid view of cattle grazing on a carpet of green. Jim had now settled into the pilot's seat for our three hour flight. A few minutes of silence, then he broke into my thoughts that involved Justin's condition with, "How do you like the way this Ryan flies?"

"So far, no complaints if you'll set her down in Monterrey on two wheels.

"Okay, by the way, this Ryan can be bought at a bargain now. It's practically new, only three hundred hours on it and a new engine. Anytime you wanted to go anywhere you could be assured of not only the plane, but of me piloting you."

"Sounds practical. When we return I'll be in a position to give you an answer. If this trip develops into the conclusion I'm expecting, I'd surely be interested in following your suggestion."

We touched down at four fifteen p.m. and parked the plane by following hand directions of a fellow who put on the appearance of authority, as evidenced by his exaggerated motions and khaki uniform. A decrepit building served as the terminal.

As we climbed from the plane, we were confronted by three uniformed gents. Two were slick-faced kids carrying antiquated rifles at their side. Their posture appeared more as hunters roving the woods in search of a squirrel, rather than soldiers. The other member of the trio was wearing a garrison cap perched atop a thick mass of black hair that continued downward covering his face in a thorny mask. His moustache was as long as a colt's tail and just as dirty.

They were an interesting trio to behold as my eyes darted from the hairy one's glittering black eyes, to the array of medals covering his chest. If he had earned all that mass of decorations, then surely he was enjoying eternal life.

Stopping in front of us, the one with the medals, brought his stance to that of a military greeting, "Buenos dias. Who is Señor McCulloch?" His question was in cadence with his right hand slapping the leather which partially covered the biggest pistol I had ever seen.

"I'm McCulloch," nodding to Jim, I said, "My pilot, Jim Harris."

"I'm Colonel Carranza. Minister Cedillo granted me the privilege of escorting you to the hotel."

He barked a command in Spanish to the two soldiers. They darted forward and snatched our luggage, then we started the trek to the terminal. Passing through its shady confines, we emerged to find an aged Studebaker touring car bearing the seal of the Mexican eagle on its door. Mounted on the front fender a miniature flag of Mexico was hanging limp from its staff.

The Colonel graciously permitted us to be seated in the rear seat then sat beside me. The soldier slammed the door then joined the driver in front.

Considering the activities of the past five minutes our position was debatable. Were we under military surveillance, or being given a royal welcome? We would know soon enough.

The driver stomped the accelerator—the motor responded trumpeting a mighty frightening roar. The Colonel tapped him on the shoulder signaling him to take off. The vintage auto was instantly a juggernaut barreling onto the highway spewing gravel and debris in its wake, as the tires squealed in agony.

"God Almighty!" Jim said as he slumped in the seat in an effort to avoid seeing the apparent disaster certain to occur. We were weaving in and out of the mass of objects moving on the highway. We passed beneath a load of huge pipe being hauled by a mammoth truck and then the kid driving avoided a burro cart loaded with mesquite limbs. I was rigid with apprehension, as well as mesmerized. The driver had not touched the brake pedal since leaving the airport.

The conglomeration of objects moving on wheels seemed to be interconnected with some mysterious means of communication coming from within our vehicle. The density of vehicles didn't matter as they parted to give us passage. So far we had found openings, it was a hair-raising experience, and a memorable one.

The driver skidded the long vintage auto into the street-leveled garage of the hotel, where Jim and I unloaded—gratefully and gladly.

The desk clerk gave us a cordial greeting, then asked if we had reservations. He jumped with alacrity to the key when I gave my name. His face beaming with a smile of sincere welcome as he said, "Señor McCulloch, everything has been arranged for your stay with us. We hope it'll be an enjoyable experience for you."

"I'm sure it will be. You must have a room for my pilot, Mr. Harris."

"Yes, yes. We have a room for him," he said as he produced another key.

On the way up, we agreed Jim was on his own until my business was transacted. I went down to the lobby at five thirty to have a few minutes of retrospect before meeting Cedillo and eased into a huge leather chair to relax. The lobby and adjacent areas were blessed with dozens of birdcages, occupied with canaries and tropical singing birds. As I sat oblivious to the activity of people around me, my thoughts were drawn to Audrey. While we were here on our honeymoon, we had listened to the singing of the birds while sitting on the sofa to my right. I glanced at the surroundings, visualizing we two were there now. A stab of remorse pained me, filling me with a desire to make amends for my atrocious conduct and utter lack of consideration. When I returned to Houston I would try to establish a rapport with her, to convince her of my regret.

"Mr. McCulloch, please come to the desk."

This request roused me from deep thought. I arose, and made my way across the lobby to the desk. As I neared it, I observed a tall striking man watching me approach. A quick survey revealed him to be over six feet tall with steel gray wavy hair. His clothes were well tailored and he appeared to be of Mexican descent.

I said to the new desk clerk," I'm Hugh McCulloch."

He beamed," Mr. McCulloch, this is Minister of Minerals, Señor Cedillo."

We shook hands as he gave me the second best disarming smile I had ever seen. The best being the one "Houdini" delivered.

"Mr. McCulloch, it's indeed a pleasure to finally meet you. Welcome to our country."

He was still pumping my right hand as he placed his left hand on my shoulder. I liked his direct gaze. His eyes were a wedgewood blue, sparkling with vitality and sincerity as he spoke.

He continued, "It is amazing. You look very much like the mental picture I had formed of you. "

"Señor Cedillo, please excuse my candor when I tell you I had you pictured mentally, as short, rather fat, and around sixty-years-old."

"Ah ha! You're not the first person to tell me that. Come let us go into the dining room."

We walked to the entrance where Cedillo's appearance produced an eruption of activity. The head waiter was bowing and nodding, at the same time setting several waiters into motion. He led us to an alcove off the main room where the table was adorned with pure white cloth and napkins—crystal glass—sparkling silverware reflecting the tiny flames of two candles grasped by ornate candelabra.

The service provided and the attention showered upon us was indicative of the respect Cedillo received. He was being observed closely by me as I tried to ascertain his response to the red carpet treatment. He was gracious, cordial, yet aloof with those who served us. I was liking what I saw of this man as the dinner progressed. Surely his conversation was what one would expect of a government official. He was articulate and exuded sincerity when speaking.

We had just begun a gastronomical attack directed at the ten entrees covering the table when Cedillo asked, "Mr. McCulloch, do you object to my addressing you on a first name basis? And please call me Juan. It's my middle name—you'll find it comes out easier than Saturnino. Okay?"

"Yes, I prefer you calling me Hugh."

"Hugh, it's most important you and I leave this table with each having a clear understanding of the result of our meeting. Agreed?"

"Agreed."

"Well Hugh, you must realize this conversation must remain forever confidential. You'll be surprised when I divulge the answer to the question in your mind. Why did I single you out for the venture I'm about to propose to you. We have a common bond, that of a mutual friend, Joe Bob Miller."

My evident surprise had halted him momentarily. He beamed the disarming smile. The smile showed his added dimension of amusement.

"I knew that bit of information would rock your composure. Miller has done some clandestine service for me for which he was rewarded generously. He learned I was seeking a man to carry through and recommended you. This explains my contacting you."

He methodically removed a silver cigar case from his jacket pocket, flicked it open offering me one of the long slim cigars it contained. During this act, his piercing blue eyes were boring mine—bombarding them with a questioning gaze. I selected a cigar, he picked one, then passed it under his nostrils savoring the fragrance saying, "These are pure Havana Coronas—you'll enjoy them."

"Juan, you must've sworn Miller to secrecy as he has never mentioned this to me."

"Yes, and for a primitive reason—that being self-survival. If Presidente Cardenas should ever learn of his activities, he'd be assassinated as would I—you too, if you were my partner."

He was so matter of fact in coolly predicting our fate, a cold surge tingled my body. This gentlemen before me was a highly respected caudillo, a government official—to me, an enigma. His words delivered the possibility of a death knell. Was I in the presence of a Scandinavian troll? His predictions had quenched my appetite, but was producing the sweet, tangy essence of money. If his proposal presented the consequences of finality his words had expressed, the monetary rewards must off set the element of danger. So far this proposition reeked of mystique, adventure and lucrative reward. I was anxious to hear him out as I had begun to realize he was uncovering something dirty, chancy, and with possibly the means of recouping my recent investments. He leaned forward lighting my cigar, then his—he took a deep draft, still gazing at me, then expelled the smoke from his nostrils. I was fascinated as my attention centered on the two wisps of smoke curling upward. I saw them as the magicians cover being lifted to reveal the mystery to come. My mind was straying into a bizarre path as I observed the smoke as an omen, then came back to reality as he said, "Shall I continue?"

"Yes, yes by all means!"

"As you know a major oil company was successful in opening substantial production in the Tampico area. My position in government afforded me the torment of being subjected to temptation. The temptation coming from the well spring of human element that lurks within. I'm referring to the element of clawing, clutching greed. I comprised my greed through some unlawful manipulation of federal land grants, resulting in my ownership of a twenty-five thousand acre tract adjacent to the producing area of a major U.S. company. This purchase forced them to hop the tract as they extended development westward. My land is legally and dully recorded as belonging to a fictitious dummy corporation, but I'm the sole owner. You may be assured I've screwed the cover hiding true ownership down tight.

"My proposition will necessitate your casting off any cloak of integrity you may be wearing, donning one woven of the fragile, gossamer threads of deceit, larceny, and pockets stuffed with danger. The danger being the remote possibility of the government uncovering facts regarding true ownership of the tract and the structure of the association between you and me. Should that happen, we'd face the firing squad."

He paused, then puffed on his cigar, as possible results wheeled in my mind if I should align my activities with his—then have his unlawful operation exposed. He had made clear our lot would be the firing squad. He was obviously awaiting a response from me when I said, "You've presented an interesting challenge, but there's one thing you haven't covered, the financial structure. I'm with you thus far."

"Fine! I was just getting to that," he replied while brushing a cigar ash from the lapel of his coat.

I squirmed with anticipation, anxiously awaiting his proposal.

He leveled his gaze directly into my eyes, as I was thinking this man before me was the essence of self-assurance, fear being alien to him.

"Hugh, I must stress the fact this proposal in no way includes the government. I deliberately gave you the impression in my correspondence you would be working under the sanction of the Resources branch of the Mexican government to snag your interest. The proposal I'm making tonight is a clandestine operation. Certainly my government is to be excluded from any profits that may be realized for obvious reasons.

"You'll provide the equipment necessary to produce the oil, the drilling rigs etc., and supervise all operations. We'll share the cost of drilling, as well as the profits netted. Split equally. To enhance the offer, if you're interested, I can provide government permits for pipeline construction, as well as refinery buildings. We may as well avail ourselves to this additional revenue, don't you agree?"

"I surely do agree. Let's review this deal. I'll supply the drilling rigs necessary to exploit the existing tract of twenty-five thousand acres as you and I share the cost. If we do enter the transmission and refining phase, we share equal cost and net equal profits. A fifty-fifty split on everything. Right?"

"You have it. Do we go as partners?" He asked as he held his right hand across the table to grip mine in a gesture of cementing the agreement. I grasped his hand in mine saying, "Shake, partner. When do we start?"

"As soon as you get your equipment down here. In the interim I'll secure the necessary government approval, while you, if you wish, have your attorney draw up the papers for my signature. However, I'm a man of my word. I'd prefer not signing an agreement, as a signed instrument would be a sword of Damocles over my head in the event it was ever discovered.

"I can understand your concern of a legal instrument in existence, so I'm willing to proceed on a gentleman's agreement."

His face beamed as he smiled and said, "I knew you were my kind of man. We'll garner mucho dinero—much money."

"I'll fly to Corpus Christi tomorrow morning where I have six rigs available. I'll start preparing them for shipment to Tampico. Right now I can't predict the date of arrival, it's dependent on an available ship coming south that has deck space to stack the rigs. But you get on with the paperwork and send it to my office in Houston. With your influence speeding the permits, etc., it's quite possible we can spud in our first hole in three weeks from today. How's that?"

"Great! You'll have all the papers necessary to proceed within five days."

He snapped his fingers summoning a waiter who appeared quickly.

"A bottle of Chivas Regal, please," turning to me he continued, "We'll drink a toast to our success."

The waiter set the tray containing the whiskey, two shot glasses and ice before us. Cedillo methodically twisted the cap from the bottle, then poured the amber liquid. Raising our glasses in a toast he said, "Salud and bueno suerte, amigo. Good luck friend!"

After drinking our toast we arose to leave. Cedillo lifted the bottle of whiskey, then passed it to me saying, "Take the bottle, you may find it useful later!"

He escorted me to the elevator commenting, "You'll receive all authorizations needed soon. I'll meet you in Tampico. Good night."

On my way to my room, I found myself questioning the wisdom of my agreement with Cedillo. This had to be a smooth running association, lest we both depart this life. Hell! I'd go ahead and not look back!

I opened the door into total darkness. My nostrils were tantalized with the pungent odor of honeysuckle. It was indeed pleasant. I felt along the wall until I found the light switch. The source of the sweet fragrance was a vase of fresh honeysuckle on the desk. Leaning down to smell them I heard a hiss-ssssst. My first thought was a snake in the room, but dismissed it as being ridiculous. I was pouring a generous shot of the whiskey when I heard the hiss again. Damn it! What could it be? As I turned to check the clothes closet for a wayward snake my eyes fell on one of the prettiest faces I had ever seen. She was Spanish, smiling, and revealing pearly white teeth. This beautiful señorita was propped up on three pillows in my bed, the covers barely covering her navel. Two buxom breasts were taunting me as were her eyes. She crooked her forefinger summoning me over. I wasn't hard to move, as I made my way to the bed asking, "Who are you?"

Still smiling she answered, "Señor Cedillo."

"Hells bells! You don't look like a señor to me!"

"Señor Cedillo," she was still taunting me with her tempting smile. She pointed to the whiskey across the room, then pointed to herself. I surmised she wanted a shot of the Regal. I poured some in another glass, then walked back to the bed offering it to her. She sipped and giggled as she surveyed me with her big jersey eyes.

Reaching down, I yanked the covers away which revealed a beautiful female body, the color of bourbon whiskey. My eyes sucked up the exciting form before me, presenting the most appealing canape I had ever seen. She made no effort to draw the covers over her body as she coolly-eyed the contents of her glass. As I stood there like an impotent dullard, she began whistling, "My shawl," in a low captivating tone.

"Who are you? Who let you in?"

"Señor Cedillo."

"No speakee English—Americano?"

"Señor Cedillo!"

"Okay. Señor Cedillo, you're about to have a bed fellow. Do you understand?"

"Si, Señor Cedillo."

The finding of something like this would be fantastic on a palm sprinkled island, but almost unbelievable discovering it gracing a hotel bed.

Feeling devilish I reached down plucking at one of her pubic hairs lightly, she rolled quickly to her belly revealing the cheeks of her buttocks. They appeared as two oversized cameos and just as alluring, only more so.

"Well little Miss Señor Cedillo, the time has arrived to quit horsing around. From this moment on we'll begin to establish a communication that does not recognize language barriers. Will you like that?"

"Si! Señor Cedillo."

I undressed quickly—turned off the light, then slid beneath the covers.

Thirty minutes later as I laid on my back reviewing the day and the evening with sated pleasure, the thought occurred I should write Cedillo complimenting his selection of a bed mate for me.

♦ ♦ ♦

The morning light seeping through the drapes, coupled with the sound of a noisy sparrow chirping his warning to any unwary worm, awakened me. I turned over tossing my arm to embrace the warm brown body, but found only emptiness. She had left in the quiet of the night.

I called Jim's room, receiving a prompt response.

"Jim, meet me in the dining room in about half an hour."

"Right, I'll be there."

While preparing to depart, my mind was cluttered with a gamut of possibilities pertaining to the events of the past twenty-four hours. The ultimate being, if we were exposed in our business operation, the dire consequences that would befall Cedillo and me, would be fatal. And the enchanting interlude where two strangers had exchanged lurid passions with emotions veiled as love should not be forgotten.

When reaching the door I noticed a white card on the carpet. Picking it up I found instructions from the hotel manager detailing how I could contact the Colonel for transportation back to the airport. Upon reading it I shuddered, recalling the hazardous ride of yesterday. I made a decision to hire a taxi. If the tin soldier driver had made an attempt to return to the airport yesterday, it was likely a Requiem mass was scheduled for him tomorrow!

Harris was waiting for me in the lobby, wearing a schoolboy grin as I approached him.

"Jim, you're in good spirits this morning."

"You're damn right I am. How about you?"

"Let's have breakfast, then get flying for Houston."

The head waiter escorted us to a table where we sat looking over the dining room before placing our order. After ordering Jim asked, "Did you find anything unusual in your room last night?"

"In a way, yes. When I came in someone had placed a vase of fresh honeysuckle in my room. Why do you ask?"

"Hell! McCulloch, that's par for the course down here, there's always fresh flowers in the room. There was a vase of honeysuckle brought to my room too, and a few minutes later a slight tapping on my door. When I opened it, the prettiest piece of Mexican cheesecake I ever saw slid under my arm into the room. She came ready to papa. She dropped her dress before I'd closed the door."

He stopped while lighting a cigarette, then leaned back in his chair to observe my reaction to his statement.

After a moments pause I asked, "Could she speak English?"

"She spoke pretty fair English, but believe me when I say her actions were more impressive than her command of English. She had the moves of a waterbug, Wow! I knew I'd been for a ride before dropping-off to sleep."

"Mmmmm, that's interesting. Did she play house with you for fun or money?"

"I offered her money, but she refused. She waved me away, drawing her forefinger across her throat, while informing me

Señor Cedillo would kill her if she accepted money from me. What do you think of that?"

"I think Señor Cedillo is a gracious host and exercises excellent choice."

Jim chuckled, then said, "I believe she knocked on the wrong door, thought I was you, but you can't blame me for not kicking her across the hall can you?"

"No! I understand."

After a delicious breakfast we checked out, the clerk informing us everything was taken care of by Minister Cedillo. Reaching the street we found four taxis parked at the curb awaiting fares. The driver of the first cab in line leaped out relieving us of our bags, tossing them into the front seat. His strength and dexterity amazed me as I considered his stature. He was a diminutive fellow, less then five feet, slender as a pipe cleaner, and wearing an old garrison cap that shaded a thin handlebar moustache at least ten inches long.

"Where to, where to?" he asked.

"The aeroporte," I replied, then followed him around to the street side of the taxi to satisfy my curiosity of how he would see over the dashboard of the vehicle to drive.

I saw a wooden box about a foot high, crowned with a small leather cushion. This started the bell of alarm clanging in me. Damn, why did we have to get this pygmy.

Jim and I entered the rear prepared to settle down, each carrying some apprehension within. As I closed the door, not yet settled in the seat, the vehicle shot forward with breathtaking acceleration forcing its way into the grudging line of traffic. The abrupt maneuver set the stage for a rear-end collision involving two cars behind us. Jim and I looked back to the sound of crumpling metal, then quickly put our attention on our driver where it should be, or should it?

He was hunched over the wheel swaying his body as a palm frond whipped in a Tahitian gale. As I sat stupefied, trying to focus my vision on the passing scene, I was aware he had become wedded with the wheel. The undulation of his body was producing a hypnotic effect that was soon erased.

A truck loaded with cartons suddenly appeared in our path from an alley on the right. Jim and I threw ourselves on the floor instantly, bumping heads as we awaited the crunch of metal again. The little taxi jockey thrust the nose of the cab to our left, crossing the lane of oncoming traffic, then bored into a shady alley accelerating as he executed the strategy. I raised my head to see what he had resorted to, to avoid disaster as he traversed the alley to the next street forging his way into another stream of traffic.

I tapped his back in an effort to indicate he should slow down. He responded by swiveling his head to face me, but keeping his dangerous speed asking, "You want faster?"

"Hell no! Slow down, keep your eyes on the road."

"Okee, okee," he replied, turning his head back to the business of driving as he gradually picked up speed. A mile from the airport, as I was thanking my maker for letting us survive thus far, the inevitable happened. A mestizo driving a herd of goats attempted to challenge our driver for the right of way, driving the goats across the road in our path. The midget driver met the challenge with an effort at beating the lead animals by cutting to the left hoping to out race them, but to no avail. We experienced several dull thuds as we skidded in the gravel resulting in the cab changing directions twice before coming to a stop in the ditch. The cabby restarted the motor, crossed the road to our proper lane and continued toward the airport. Jim and I cast a quick look behind to see several of the shaggy goats littering the road, their broken bodies appearing as bundles of dirty rags. Turning to enter the airport drive, we noticed the cab's radiator spewing a jet of steam ten feet high. When we stopped in front of the nondescript terminal, I gave a sigh of relief at leaving the taxi alive.

Passing the front of the cab we discovered the cause of the heated engine. An unfortunate goat had been decapitated as the horns had penetrated the radiator, snatching the head from the body. The glassy eyes were staring upward, as if imploring for release. The sight was gruesome—sending a surge of repulsion through me as I moved to the side to pay the driver. He was muttering,

"Condenado cabeza cabron," as I paid him, not waiting for any change.

We were taxied to the runway when I saw the "wheel crazy" midget standing on his driving box, pouring water from a glass jug into the breathing, steamy radiator. I thought, "you little tird, you've scared the hell out of more people than any Bishop or Cardinal alive."Jim had put the plane in cruising altitude and settled for the flight to Houston when I said,

"Jim, my trip down here was successful. After thinking over your suggestion, I'll consider buying this plane. My operation in the Tampico area will entail frequent flights making a plane essential. The next four or five days will give me an accurate guide, so meanwhile you be thinking of what your services as a full time pilot are worth to you. Also get the information on the cost of the plane. I'll let you know as soon as I get the papers solidifying the Tampico enterprise."

"Okay. Mr. McCulloch. Call me when you're ready."

Chapter Eleven
Off To Tampico

We parked at the Houston airport, then I drove to my office. Barbara gave me a happy greeting saying, "It's nice to have you back. You've a list of incoming calls on your desk. One from Audrey—she called to tell you Justin was greatly improved and his condition reclassified from critical to serious."

"Did she request I call her?"

"No, on the contrary, she said that was her purpose in calling you, to erase the need of you calling her."

"Thank you, Barbara."

Seating myself at my desk, I was hoping my true feelings of disappointment from Audrey's call had been concealed from Barbara. My thinking today, on the Tampico venture, was more positive, thus prompting me to contact Curly Ward in Corpus Christi to inform him of my plans should Cedillo come through on his promise.

I was in luck, as Barbara had Curly on the line in a few minutes. His familiar voice sounded refreshing.

"Hi, Hugh. What's going on?"

"I've something to drop on you Curly. How would you like the land of enchiladas and tequila, for a change?"

"Mexico?"

"Yes, Tampico."

"Hell, Hugh, I don't know. You spring that on me after I've spent all my spare time in setting up a stable of willing females around here."

"Crap, a sensible woman wouldn't give you a second look, besides Mexico can supply an ample portion of hot food and warm señoritas. I intend moving six rigs down there, leaving

Elliott to push the four we leave here. I'll make it worth your while for making the shift. Have you ever worked down there?"

"No."

"Then don't knock it. You'll probably apply for citizenship after trying the señoritas and searing your stomach with chili con carne."

"How soon do we travel?"

"As of now, we could start moving as early as next week, however, I can give you something more definite in four or five days. You call me every day starting the day after tomorrow, as it could break any time."

"The move is timed well. I had figured relocating two rigs during the coming week. This way we can stack them instead."

"Good. Call me Thursday the fifteenth."

Then I called Lykes Lines. Their agent informed me he had a freighter scheduled to sail for Merida and Trinidad on Sunday the 25th, and would have room for the rigs on deck. I agreed to verify the shipment, hopefully before the end of the week.

All of Wednesday was exhausted in checking out the hotel construction where I was pleasantly surprised with the progress to date. Encountering Smythe, the architect, on the project was good fortune as it gave me the answer to some questions regarding my pride and joy. Smythe's answers were encouraging as he predicted we could open June first, without any cost overrun, provided we escaped any unfortunate labor strikes.

We rode the elevator to the penthouse where Smythe resorted to detailed explanation of his suggestions at the interior decor. As we entered the huge master bedroom, he mentioned the panoramic view of Houston's skyline that the glassed in north and west walls permitted. We halted in the center of the room, both surveying the scene when he said, "Hugh, will you permit me to exercise my expertise, such as it is, in decorating this room?"

I pondered the question a few moments then replied, "Why not? I know nothing about decorating—I'm willing to give you a free hand. At least until you stray into some far out scheme too wild for this old country boy."

He laughed, then retorted, "Country boy! That has to be the classic misnomer of the decade. Let me install a mirrored ceiling and east wall, with a mural decorating the south wall. What do you think of that?"

I paused forming a mental picture of the suggestion then said, "I like that, let's do it!"

"You hang with me Hugh. I've planned this penthouse from the day you turned the first spade of soil. When I complete it, I guarantee the atmosphere it presents, will advance any schemes you're pursuing, whether it be conventional business—erasing the bedroom boredom from a willing female—or just seeking rest and seclusion. I've worked out color combinations for the various rooms with a qualified psychologist, an expert in the field of human moods, desires and actions. The electrical contractor will work with us on the installation of rheostat controls, permitting color changes to the specific effect you desire.

"You can produce surroundings conducive to business, pleasure, relaxation, and last, but no means least, seduction! When I'm through with this penthouse, you can assume the air of a potentate when guests are present."

I interrupted him, "Hold it! Say no more. You've convinced me of your ingenuity and I'm looking forward to moving in. Shall we go?"

After checking my office Thursday morning my thoughts strayed to Justin Brent and Audrey. I made the decision to visit Justin, and possibly see Audrey with the hope a reconciliation could result if I could present my cause in a subdued manner.

The drive to the hospital was spent formulating words into sentences to be employed when talking to Justin. My chances of ever rekindling the flame of love within Audrey would surely be enhanced if Justin could be converted to the validity of my remorse of past conduct. I would display my battered ego—my contrition for abusing the dignity of the Brent name, and pray for arousing some degree of empathy within Justin, then proceed with the crusade of regaining respect from Audrey.

Entering the Methodist Hospital, I learned Justin was in room 518. The nurses station was situated near the elevator, making it possible for the nurse behind the desk to intercept me as I stepped out. She inquired, "What is your name sir? Whom do you wish to see?"

"I want to visit Mr. Brent. I'm Hugh McCulloch."

"One moment please," she answered as she arose and made her way to Justin's room.

Shifting nervously, awaiting her return, a sudden surge of fear of denial engulfed me. Would my sincerity impress Justin?"

The nurse returned saying, "Mr. Brent refuses to see you. I'm sorry."

"Tell me please, has his daughter been here this morning?"

She reacted with a look of disdain and stony silence prompting me to retreat to the elevator door. I had certainly fouled my nest, and Justin was determined I lay in it.

Driving to the office the thought occurred I should check on my home while in the area. Stopping in the driveway, I sat gazing at the attractive house that had never become a home. A flood of memories coursed my mind as I recalled the morning I had driven in to find Audrey gathering the morning papers, following my night in jail. In her pink robe she had presented the picture of purity of heart, and sterile mind, as she observed my approach. I was reeking with the distinctive odor of jail—the combination of urine and lysol. I was a sorry spectacle as remorse gnawed my conscience, and that created an eruption of self-pity, giving me the excuse of hurting her feelings.

The recall was so vivid, I opened the car door and rushed toward her, my arms outstretched. Reaching the porch steps, her smile ceased to exist. The smile luring me on had receded into nothingness—she had vanished leaving me with the realization I was alone, a victim of my hyperactive senses tormented with longing.

I looked around to learn if anyone had witnessed my futile act of reaching for something nonexistent. Seeing no one, I sat on the porch steps while trying to bring my senses back to reality. My conscience was waging a tremendous conflict with reality, giving ground in a miserly, grudging manner. The imagined scene required several minutes of reflection to erase, then I made my way to the car and drove to my office. While en route, I was giving thought to selling the house for the first time since my divorce.

Barbara greeted me with, "Mr. McCulloch, Mr. Cedillo called to inform you he's now in Houston at the Texas State Hotel. He requested you call him as soon as possible. You also have more calls to return on your desk."

"Please call Mr. Cedillo at once Barbara."

"Hello Juan! What brings you to Houston? I've just returned to my office, so sorry I was out when you called."

"Hugh, I flew up this morning. I've some important business to discuss. Can you come right over?"

"I'll be there in ten minutes Juan. I hope nothing has gone wrong with our plans."

"Not at all. Everything is worked out. That's why I'm here."

"Fine. I'm on my way."

"Barbara, I'll be out two or three hours with Cedillo."

I made a hasty exit for the two block walk.

Cedillo greeted me with kind words and the offer of a highball. He was the essence of sartorial splendor, wearing a chocolate brown tweed suit over a canary yellow silk shirt accented with an avocado four in hand tie. This attractive ensemble topped by his curly silver hair adorned a classic head. This man mixing our highballs presented a striking presence accented with the feline movements of a jungle cat, and I was glad we were on the same team. He would surely be one hell of an adversary. He interrupted my appraisal of him by asking, "Well Hugh, did you like your roommate while in Monterrey? I trust you found my selection to your liking," his eyes were twinkling like the waters of a sun drenched bay as he tendered our drinks.

"The language barrier posed no problem, and I must say your selection could in no way be faulted. Do you suppose she would consider relocating in Tampico?"

"Ah Ha!" he was now beaming that disarming smile, "She will abide any request of mine, so that would be no problem. I've bought the necessary permits for our operation."

He turned and opened a bag on the bed. Lifting a brown envelope bearing the official seal of Mexico from it, he handed the envelope to me saying, "With the documents contained within, you'll find everything needed to begin activities immediately. I'm anxious to start, that being my reason for flying up this morning. When can you get moving?"

"I'll have the drilling rigs there no later than the twenty-seventh. A freighter can load them in Corpus Christi on the twenty-fifth. Okay?"

"Fine, will you be there the twenty-seventh?"

"Yes, I'll be there to find office space and living quarters."

"I don't know how large a place you want, but there's a nice hacienda available on the western fringe of Tampico. It's the home of a prominent caudillo Raul Hernandez. He recently relocated in Mexico, D.F. accepting a government appointment in the Department of Agriculture. If you wish I'll contact him upon my return and request he lease it to you. It's completely furnished, I'm sure you'll enjoy living there as I've found it to my liking on several occasions."

"It sounds attractive to me. Please see what you can do."

"Hugh, as you go through the permits etc., you'll note they are issued to McCulloch Enterprises. I filed your applications after we met in Monterrey, then expedited the issuance. Everything is taken care of and I must start back as soon as possible. Can you take me to the airport?"

"Yes partner, my privilege. Do you have only one bag?"

"That's all."

"Close it and we'll be on our way." As I got up I glanced toward the bag, discovering it was empty.

Cedillo must've detected my surprise as he said, "I cannot afford any slip ups, that's why the empty bag. I left Mexico, my destination Tampico, to be gone overnight so a bag was necessary to augment the deception. There are many prying eyes in my country, some peering from heads capable of selling their mother in order to establish that fleeting, elusive element of being needed by our Presidente. I believe in your country you say I'm walking a tight rope. Right?"

"That's what we say."

Picking up his bag from the bed I said, "Do you mind a two block walk? We'll drop by my office on the way to the car."

"Lead on, I'd enjoy a stroll in your city."

As we made our way to the office, Cedillo's appearance prompted several females to unknowingly turn their heads while passing, in order to learn if they had impressed him. He rewarded them with his ingratiating smile as he glided by, followed by an impish wink to me. This man knew how to make a woman's day a happy one.

We entered the office with Juan preceding me as Barbara glanced up form her work, then seeing Cedillo, her face flushed like the rising sun as she said, "How do you do."

Cedillo moved to her as she arose, took her right hand as he gave a beautiful, diplomatic bow, and lightly planted his lips to the back of her hand. He raised his stately frame gazing into her excited green eyes. Never taking his eyes from Barbara's, he said to me, "Hugh, if this living Madonna is married, someone must be shot, her husband or me. The decision is hers."

I was so engrossed by this scene, I didn't respond for a few seconds. I was observing a maestro deftly extracting feminine resistance from a strong willed woman under the anesthetic of allure. It was an educational episode for me, as compared to my semi-polished assaults when trying to "rough in" a susceptible female. Casanova was a bumbling dolt when compared to the focal character in this scene unfolding before me. I came out of my state of hypnosis at last.

"Barbara Hunter, may I present Minister Juan Cedillo, my partner in the Mexico enterprise."

"A pleasure indeed," replied Barbara. "So this is the gentleman you described as gallant, as well as impressive."

Her eyes were dynamic green lights while bouncing tiny shafts twinkling with animation directed at Cedillo. They were vis a vis, eyes telegraphing a message words could not convey. Both were oblivious of my presence until I severed the romantic bridge by saying, "Barbara, I'm driving Juan to the airport. I'll return around three o'clock."

My words served as the vehicle bringing her back to the mundane word of reality, as she regained her usual aplomb and seated herself behind the desk once more.

"Shall we go, Juan," I asked.

"I'm ready," he replied, failing to hide his reluctance at leaving the source of the cauldron of desire burning within.

Turning once more to Barbara he asked what kind of automobile she owned.

"I don't have a car, but I'm saving to buy one. Why do you ask?"

The devilish smile creased his face as he replied, "I must tell you I'm gifted with precognition, that is why I asked the question. I was standing here visualizing you cruising the Reforma in Mexico City with a gentle breeze fondling your brown tresses. You're driving an Auburn Speedster—top down."

"I like your vision, who knows it may become reality. It's been a pleasure meeting you Mr. Cedillo—may we meet again?"

"We shall. Let's go Hugh."

En route to the airport Cedillo asked if I was married. After telling him I was divorced he volunteered the information regarding the death of his wife two years before, then asked if Barbara was married.

"No, she's single."

"Would I be an interloper if I pursued her? I mean to ask, is there any romantic interest between you and Barbara. If so, then I'd sooner lose my potency than come between you two."

"Nothing exists between us, Juan," I replied, thinking I was skirting the edge of deception with that answer, reviewing the night in the motel. "Moreover, as far as I know she is not entangled with any man. That should leave the way open for any advances you might care to pursue."

"Mi flechazo! Bless the Virgin Mary," he was pounding his fist on his thigh.

"What did you say?"

"I said, "My love at first sight, what a woman!" He was bubbling with enthusiasm, and was still in a state of animation as we parked at the airport.

We walked to the side of the hangar where a bright red and black Pitcairn mail wing plane was parked. The official seal of Mexico was emblazoned on the fuselage and a pair of riding boots protruded from under the wing. The boots being worn by a sleeping figure who was not aware of our approach.

Cedillo kicked the sole of one boot lightly as he barked some words in Spanish. The sleeping man scrambled quickly from beneath the plane rubbing his eyes, and smiling.

We shook hands. Cedillo wished me luck and promised to see me in Tampico on the twenty-seventh.

The plane was airborne after a short take-off run to disappear moments later headed toward Mexico.

Driving to the office the realization of Cedillo's position in governing my future emerged. For the first time in my life, another person could guide my activities and determine my future. I was questioning the sagacity of my commitment when entering the office.

"Mr. McCulloch, Curly Ward called fifteen minutes ago saying he'd be at Johnstone Testers for at least another hour. Do you wish to return the call now?"

"Yes, Barbara."

I took the call in my office, telling Curly everything was set for the Mexican venture.

"Hold the line Curly and I'll verify shipment date from Corpus Christi."

"Okay, Hugh."

"Barbara, please get the Lykes Steamship agent for me."

The Lykes agent informed me their ship could load a day earlier than previously scheduled. The freighter could enter Corpus Christi channel Friday the twenty-third, and dock Saturday morning the twenty-fourth. He continued, "Anything other than the six rigs?"

"Yes, two pickup trucks."

"Okay. Have it all on pier two, space four, ready to load by ten a.m., and we'll have it in Tampico Sunday afternoon the twenty-fifth."

"It'll be there and thank you."

I opened the line to Curly giving him all details and adding, "Buddy, go to the Ford dealer in Corpus Christi—purchase two half ton pickups to be shipped along with the rigs on the S.S. Tillie Lykes. Have the truck dealer call my office if he wants verification of the purchase. I'll be down the first part of the week. Do you have Elliott squared away to take over there?"

"Sure have. He said he wished it was him going to Mexico in my place, as his youth would lend more prestige and social standing among the females. Said he could establish better public relations than an old goat like me, especially among the señoritas in the vicinity. Can you imagine that "boll weevil" questioning my potency?"

"Okay. See you next week."

Beaking-off with Curly, I placed a call to Jim Harris to inquire about the plane he had recommended I purchase. We agreed to meet at the airport the next day at ten o'clock. Then I asked, "Jim, could we hop down to Tampico tomorrow and stay overnight. I want to discuss hiring you as my full-time pilot."

"That's swell, Mr. McCulloch. I'll see you tomorrow."

As I parked, I could see Jim had rolled the monoplane out and was checking the control cables. As I approached, my shoes crunching on the crushed oyster shell apron, caught his attention.

"Well, Mr. McCulloch, she's ready to fly."

"Jim, from this moment on, I want you to address me as Hugh. No more Mr. McCulloch, please. Did you get a concrete price on the plane, and have you determined what your service as my full-time pilot is worth to you?"

"I'm willing to be in your employ twenty-four hours a day for seven hundred per month. You can buy this plane for nine thousand."

"That is a good deal on both counts. I'll buy the plane and will pay you one thousand per month, plus your expenses when we're out of the city, starting today."

"Hugh, that is more than generous, and for your generosity I'll fly you low and slow at all times making nothing other than three point landings. If you've about fifteen minutes we can take care of the purchase of the plane, then be on our way to Tampico."

"Okay!"

Jim led the way to an office in one of the hangars where we found a tall, lean man reading the morning paper, his skin the color of blackstrap molasses, burned from the Texas sun.

Jim interrupted his reading with, "Hawk, meet Hugh McCulloch, the man I mentioned in connection with the sale of the Ryan. Hugh, "Hawk" Bird."

As I shook the man's hand I was preoccupied with the sight of his nose—one resembling the snout of an aardvark, the bridge curving in an arc comparable to that of a peregrine falcon. This fellow received an instant appraisal, one that told me he was a bird of prey. His remarks attested my judgment.

"Mr. McCulloch, that Ryan I have is an absolute steal at the price I'm asking. I bought it from an oil rich lady. She became a widow about four months ago and since has spent her time in Hawaii dallying with the beach boys. I'll sell you the Ryan for eleven thousand, but only because I think you'll maintain it in a proper manner. How about it?"

I glanced at Jim to find his reaction to the jacked up price. His face was reflecting astonishment as he interjected, "Hawk, you quoted a price of nine thousand, I brought Mr. McCulloch here on the basis of that figure. Now you ask eleven thousand, what's the idea?"

I had decided "Hawk" was capable of pilfering change from the tooth fairy, and found him more reptilian as he squirmed out of his self-made entrapment by retorting, "Okay. I'll let it go for ten thousand."

I produced a checkbook from my jacket pocket, then said, "Mr. Bird, I'll write a check for nine thousand, take it or leave it."

Hawk cast his flinty brown eyes in my direction, studied me for a few seconds—then reading the ring of finality in my words he slithered from his hole of deception by saying, "All right, it's yours."

When we departed for Tampico I had a temporary bill of sale for the plane, and a gentleman's agreement between Jim and I.

Four and a half hours later we could see the palm studded beach below, and to the right, the city. We circled the outer perimeter seeking the airstrip indicated on the map. We located a tattered windsock flapping in a gentle breeze, then turned into the wind for the landing. The runway had been paved with asphalt, but the ravages of time had eroded it. The cracks permitted weeds and other vegetation to seek sun and moisture by rising from between the crevices to spank the landing gear. We touched down and taxied toward what appeared to be a hangar.

As we stopped in front of the hangar Jim cut the engine asking, "How do you like your plane, Boss?"

"Fine, I believe it's a good one."

Chapter Twelve
Colonel Rivera At Your Service

Stepping from the plane we were facing two khaki clad officials, one bearing the air of seniority greeted us in perfect English, "Good afternoon gentlemen. We are customs officers. I regret the intrusion, but we must search your plane for unlawful arms, or ammunition. May we enter?"

"Yes, go right ahead. We're here on business and have nothing to declare or hide."

"May I have your names please, and your business?"

After telling him our names and the nature of our business a pleasant change occurred in his mien as he said, "You're the gentlemen Minister Cedillo alerted us about. Come to my office—you must have a drink with me."

We entered the terminal, then were seated on a divan as our inquisitor produced three glasses and a quart of Rotterdam gin from a desk drawer. Handing each of us a glass he poured generous shots all around. These movements were carried out with exaggerated, grandiose body action, while a friendly smile creased his brown face. Holding out his glass to tip ours, producing a click of hospitality he said, "Salud." We in turn answered the same.

The three of us downed the fiery liquid with a gulp. The customs officer smilingly drawing his sleeve across his lips after smacking them, showed pleasure, while I was gasping for air suppressing a grimace to avoid offending our host.

"May I see the bottle, please?"

"Bueno! You like it," he said holding the bottle out to me, I scanned the label to learn it to be one eighty proof, then I understood my difficulty in breathing. I graciously handed it back to him saying, "We'll get back to this later. Right now we must attend to business. Can you direct us to the Raul Hernandez hacienda? Señor Cedillo told me it might be possible to lease it."

"Yes, Mr. McCulloch I'll drive you there, and anywhere else. Shall we go?"

A black Buick sedan was near the entrance to the terminal, where our host opened the rear door for our entry.

"By the way, what's your name and title?" I asked before entering the car.

He popped his heels together, pulled himself erect, then said, "I'm sorry I didn't introduce myself. I'm Colonel Rivera, in charge of customs in this area."

Driving west through town, I observed several buildings bearing signs indicating they housed activities of various oil companies. Seeing them prompted me to ask the Colonel if he was familiar with the area where the twenty-five thousand acres were situated.

He assured me he did know the exact location. He turned from the thoroughfare and entered a shallow arroyo where the road led to a sprawling ranch-type, natural stone house, surrounded by large palm trees.

We parked at the front entrance. My gaze was fastened upon the structure before me as it presented a picture of tranquility, shadowed from the waving palms. The front entrance drew my attention as I walked to the steps of the porch. The entrance being two hand-carved doors embellished by ornate brass handles. As I studied the doors Colonel Rivera spoke, "This hacienda is harboring the spirits of many noted people of the past. The original wing was built in 1845, by Benito Juarez, a caudillo of moderate power at the time. An aborted ambush occurred in the large main room around 1850, resulting in the deaths of six men and one woman. The woman being the mistress of the local alcalde, who fortunately was not present at the time.

"Juarez later moved to Mexico City, leaving the place vacant until Ferdinand Maximilian arrived in 1863 from Austria. He came seeking enlistments for an army to rout Juarez. He had the hacienda repaired and made livable as a place to conceal his conquests with the opposite sex. Including Carlotta, who lived here for several months before moving to Mexico City.

"From 1867 to the turn of the century, this place was occupied by various revolutionaries, bandits, and officials. Anyone who rose to the top of the pecking order and desired the hacienda, would kick the occupants out and move in. Those beautiful mahogany doors are pocked and scarred on the inner side, having received many stray bullets.

"Yes, this place has contributed much to local history and myths. The story is told of a Colonel in the federal army, who lived here around 1910, killing and burning his wife in the huge fireplace of the main room, as a result of discovering her having sex with their large male wolfhound."

I interrupted his enlightening discourse with, "Damn, the Colonel was cuckolded by a dog? What a diversion!"

"That is the story. If you want to go inside I have the key."

"Hell yes, I wouldn't miss the chance to see the arena of life this place holds. I want to look it over and lease it, that is if the spirits and ghosts permit me." A boyish drive for adventure and intrigue had engulfed me as we entered the huge main room. Stopping to survey the mammoth room my imagination took over.

I stood visualizing a scene likened to Dantes Inferno. I was hearing a babel of voices—conversing—cursing—shouting in languages alien to me. The cacophony punctuated by the hellish roar of gunfire. The Colonel noticed my apparent transfixation returning me to reality by asking, "Is there something wrong?"

"No. No. Let's see the rest of it."

We traversed the whole structure, as I marveled at the arrangement and furnishings. Entering the master bedroom Rivera remarked as he pointed to the gigantic bed with posts reaching to the ceiling and supporting a scarlet canopy, "Mr. McCulloch, that real cama is much too large for sleeping alone, are you married?"

"No."

"Caruba! You can have a left side señorita and a right side señorita, and still have room to maneuver," he chortled.

Jim said gleefully, "Hugh, that bed is a real work bench, isn't it?"

"Colonel, can you reach Mr. Hernandez by telephone? I want to lease it."

"Oh yes, we can call him from the customs office."

Talking later with Mr. Hernandez I found the rent, twelve hundred dollars, payable by the year, very reasonable and made arrangements to mail a check the next day. I cradled the receiver, then looked at the Colonel saying, "It's all set. Thank you for your time."

"My pleasure," he turned, lifted the quart of gin when I blurted out, "Colonel, do you have anything with which to cut that gin? My stomach is acting up and I cannot take it straight."

"How would you like some cold beer? If you'll stay the night we'll drive out to the El Mundo. Maybe you could find something there more to your liking."

Jim asked, "How about it Hugh?"

"We might as well begin getting acquainted. Colonel, what hotel do you recommend?"

"It would please me very much if you would be guests in my home."

Knowing he would be offended if we declined his hospitality, we accepted with thanks, then went to the car.

The Colonel drove to a point about ten miles west of Tampico where we turned off the main road headed for the portal of a ten foot high adobe wall. The sun was casting long shadows as we drove through the opening. We were inside a compound composed of one large adobe structure and about thirty smaller ones forming a circle to the rear.

Parking, we entered the swinging doors of the large adobe building. Coming in from the sunlight to the shadowy recess, our vision was impaired for several seconds. After getting our eyes adjusted to the interior, we found we were in a saloon boasting a bar about 40 feet long. There were twenty or so chickens huddled on the bar with feathers fluffed, settled for the night. Colonel Rivera began brushing his arm along the bar rousting them from their somnolent state, this creating a bedlam of squawks and flapping of wings. Feathers were floating like falling snow as the chickens hit the floor while running for the rear door.

The Colonel was spewing Spanish in a strident tone of voice while slapping at the fowls, as they exited the rear opening. Becoming airborne, they looked like flying wild turkeys. Several dogs added barks, wails and whines to the orchestration of racket. When the last chicken had departed the Colonel began brushing feathers from his clothing, while calling in a loud voice, "Carlos, Carlos! Get your ass out here."

A sleepy eyed man dressed in white canvas jacket and pants, emerged from a door behind the bar. He was rubbing his eyes in an effort to awaken when he recognized Rivera.

"Colonel Rivera!" then a torrent of Spanish gushed, filling the air with what was apparently a warm greeting for all of us. The Colonel translating the animated dialogue by telling us Carlos was indeed happy to have us visit his humble establishment and anything we wanted was on the house, including a well-cooked barbecued goat.

We sat at a table as Carlos served us cold beer. Walking to the rear he removed a battered, brass cornet hanging beside the opening. I was expecting a cornet solo from him when he faced the rear door, but placing the horn to his lips he blasted out a facsimile of a military bugler sounding charge.

He returned the corroded horn to its hanging peg, seated himself at our table rubbing his hands in a gesture of anticipation. The blasts of the horn were producing lonesome wails by several dogs outside as well as curiosity within Jim and me. We were trying to guess his motive in delivering the bugle call when the answer came in the person of two señoritas entering, smiling and swishing their ample skirts.

They were followed by two raven-haired beauties—then two more and two more. They were entering in pairs—no two wearing the same apparel. Some showing more brown skin from scanty attire than any bordello or burlesque ever dared reveal. Entering, they each beamed a smile in our direction, then seated themselves in chairs lining the wall, each providing a flash glance of their bottoms while crossing their legs. When the promenade of femininity had settled, they resembled a shelf of dolls in a toy store.

Jim squealed, "Hot damn, look at that Hugh! There's enough here for a Roman orgy, and I've always dreamed of wriggling my toes in an expanse of beautiful breasts. I think my dream has come true. Damn and double damn!"

Jim's effervescence could not be suppressed as he stalked around the table, waving his arms like a wrestler awaiting a fallen opponent to arise and resume the scuffle.

Colonel Rivera spoke, "Carlos tells me you're free to take any, or as many of them as you wish to the buildings in the rear. He says my guests are his guests. The cerveza is gratis, as are the señoritas."

Jim walked to the row of the giggling females, scanning every inch of each one when passing. He resembled a duty bound lieutenant inspecting the ranks, hoping to find an unpolished boot.

I interrupted his inspection by saying, "Jim, remember the possibility of getting something you don't want."

He paused, then returned to the table. While pulling the cane bottomed chair aside, he snorted, "You sure are a kill-joy, Hugh. But you're right. I could probably get everything except good health from that covey of quail." With that he sat down to resume his beer drinking while smiling at the girls between sips.

Rivera asked, "You don't want the company of a señorita, Mr. McCulloch?"

"No, no. But thanks anyway. Perhaps another time."

We thanked Carlos for his hospitality, then drove to Rivera's house for the night.

At the airport the next morning, we bid the Colonel good-bye after telling him to look for us on the twenty-fifth.

I drove to my office upon arriving home. Being Saturday afternoon, I found it closed. I also found a notation on my desk from Barbara, informing me of a weekend trip to Mexico City—the guest of Cedillo. He had flown to Houston and would return with her Monday morning.

This note created a stab of jealousy, in spite of my avowal never to engage in personal relations with an employee. I had not been successful in erasing the memory of the night Barbara had ignited an inferno of lust within me, then quelled it with placid, gratifying surrender to my desire. She capitulated in a Madonna-like manner, leaving a void of any cheapness or promiscuity, only the impression of two souls weary from swimming the tides of struggle, deceit, and survival that mortals are subjected to in this world. The souls were given a brief, though beautiful respite from reality, then returned to the searching glare of everyday living. This interlude etched in my memory was now pumping a bitter taste—the taste of jealousy. I left the office concentrating on the results that night had produced.

♠ ♠ ♠

Entering the office Monday morning, my mind was still engaged in reviewing the results of my getting caught with Barbara. She greeted me, "Good morning, Mr. McCulloch."

Her cheeks were flushed—her green eyes dancing as a leaf riding a March wind—I was thinking, as I observed her, of how devastating an aroused woman can be. She was pumped up with titillation sired by Cedillo's charm.

"How was Mexico City?" I knew I would receive slight satisfaction probing her with this question before she could mention Cedillo.

"This was my first visit to Mexico City and it was absolutely fascinating. I'm eager to return."

Silently I thought, I'll bet you are falling under the irresistible charm of Cedillo. As I groped for some response to her answer, out it came, "What was more fascinating—your company, or the City?"

She studied me five or ten seconds, then said, "Mr. McCulloch, does that question bear a tint of green, or am I reading it wrong?"

Damn it all, why did our Creator bestow upon women the ability to read minds and ignore words, while at the same time he forces mortal man to rely on sight and sound. My silence lingered as I mused the proper answer to her prognosis of me. If I protested any trace of jealousy, she would tag me as a liar. If I admitted being uncomfortable with her association of Cedillo I would emerge as a rustic clod, so what the hell, "Yes, you might say I'm concerned over the chance I stand to lose a damn good secretary. You may have confused my concern with jealousy."

She eyed me in a puckish manner, then replied with exaggerated disappointment, "Your reply tells me that I'm safe in my position here, but it did prick my ego. Such is life!" She flipped a page of the appointment ledger, then said in a cursory manner, "Juan, Mr. Cedillo is at the Texas State Hotel and would like to see you before returning."

"Get him on the phone, please."

Cedillo wanted to learn if I could meet him in Tampico Thursday, the twenty-second. He wanted to familiarize me with procedures required by the Mexican government and introduce me to several individuals in the area, who could expedite our activities.

I agreed to meet him as suggested, and added I would be happy to drive him to the airport. He declined the offer telling me he might call the next morning as he was staying over night, but giving no explanation.

I bid him good-bye, then swiveled my chair to face Audrey's portrait. Her eyes seemed to reflect reapproval of me and all that I had been in the past. As I studied her face the element of reproach appeared to vanish, to be replaced by a look of compassion and understanding. The portrait evoked a gamut of emotions each time I studied it, always creating a melange of possible actions on my part to effect a reconciliation. The reasoning would always surface to plague me with questions—did I love her—or was I wrestling with an illusion brought about from my shattered ego? An ego tortured by her rejection—the divorce. Each time I gazed into her eyes the desire to hold her close arose with growing intensity and this morning the desire was flaming—I must talk to her.

I dialed her home. Her captivating voice answered, "The Brent residence." I could not speak for several seconds. I was swallowing my panic, producing a trembling falsetto I squeaked, "Audrey, Hugh here. I called about Justin, how's he progressing?"

"Where are you calling from? We must have a poor connection, you do not sound like yourself. Dad is doing great. He'll be released next week if all goes well. How are you?"

"Okay. I guess. I can't get over wanting you. I know now, I'll never be the same without you. I need you!"

"Just one moment, let me get the violin, this must have a musical background. No, Hugh, you don't need me. The little boy in you might think so, but the man, "Hugh," only needs the pursuit of money to keep the adrenalin flowing. I honestly believe you think you need me, but you're under a spell of deception. You're beguiled by being in love with love—not me. Have you visited Dad since he's been hospitalized?" She had dismissed my thrust at reconciliation by parrying me with this question.

"Yes, I went, but Justin refused to see me."

"Can you blame him? He's been shocked by your conduct. Not so much at your escapades, but more by the casual manner in which you violated his implicit trust in you. He does feel responsible for bringing you along too fast. He thought you were of sound character when he first met you, but quick success fractured that cocoon of integrity, releasing a butterfly. A butterfly using the breeze to travel from petal to petal, never having to exert the energy to use its wings. He believes his assisting you in your start at wildcatting was responsible for your missing the polishing of your rough facets. The polishing coming from life as it tosses one success to failure—failure to success." There was a pause.

"I'm telling you the thoughts he's expressed to me, they're not my thoughts. I'm sorry, but those are his feelings."

"All right Audrey. He's right. I did let both of you down, but I want to make amends. Is that asking too much?"

"Let's let it rest for right now. Maybe the winds of change will effect you, only time will tell. I'll say this without explanation, so please don't ask. You did give me something I'll always thank you for. I must go now, but please call again sometime."

The receiver clicked leaving me in more of a dilemma then when I called. I sat reviewing our conversation, recalling how I had begged her to give me another chance, only to have my plea denied. Between her apparent disdain, and Justin's disappointment with me, I was light years away from effecting any renewal of association with the two of them.

What had she concealed with her remark I had given her something she would always thank me for. Most likely she was referring to insulation against any future involvement with a man. My mind was cluttered with the debris of unanswered questions—questions about her—questions about myself—life being a path strewn with questions, the answers having to be grubbed out and never coming easy.

Around eight o'clock I entered Kelley's Steak House for dinner. I wanted to be alone and gather my thoughts in order to plot my course for the future. The rebuff from Audrey had triggered an intense self-analysis and I needed a quiet spot to lick my wounds.

The head waiter directed me to a remote shadowy corner, handed me a menu, then departed. I reviewed my first visit to this restaurant, recalling the electric thrill that day had brought me. I had bought my first automobile, fulfilling a desire that had prodded me since childhood. I was wearing my first suit. My enthusiasm was boundless as it motivated ambition that recognized no end. I was another Faustus eager to barter my soul to Mephistopheles for riches and power.

Six years later I had gained the riches and power, but was saturated with self-pity and eating alone. My youthful naivete had escaped the knowledge that whatever makes a man a slave, will also diminish his worth. Money and power was my quest—it was my master—I was the slave. Tonight, mounted on the precarious perch wealth provides, I was hounded with unhappiness.

The waiter interrupted my thoughts with, "Are you ready to order, sir?"

"What do you recommend?"

"The pheasant with oyster dressing, wild rice and liver pate is very pleasing."

"I'll have it. Thank you."

While awaiting my dinner I made a decision to seek a psychiatrist—if the morrow found me morose and melancholy.

After dining I purchased a fifth of Chivas Regal, went to my hotel suite and proceeded to drown out the fiery pangs of remorse.

Chapter Thirteen
An Auburn For Barbara

I was awakened by a commotion in the hall, glancing at my watch, it was nine fifteen.

I reached the office at ten to find Barbara more animated and effervescent than ever as she acknowledged my appearance by saying, "Good morning, I hope you feel as wonderful as I do this beautiful day."

"I'll admit your greeting has elated my mood, preparing me for living this day. Anything new?"

As I asked the question my thoughts centered on the irony of love. The evident, unquestionable aura emitted by a woman experiencing a new love—yet that love could depart her being, in such an insidious, silent manner, she would not be aware of its quiet, progressive death. It could disappear from total love to total emptiness and be as fading as the life span of man, which is entered with each individual clawing, reaching for everything in sight, but the span glides silently to the end when once more the clawing and clutching is all that remains. The inherent desire to hang on a bit longer persists until the span is ended. She interrupted my rumination, "I'm glad to contribute my bit to making this a lovely day for you. By the way, Juan just called to ask if you could meet him here at ten thirty."

"Surely. I'll go over my mail in the interim."

A few minutes later, Juan arrived coming through the door smiling as usual, crossing the room to shake my hand. This man was an interesting specimen. He hadn't said a word, yet his catlike, graceful movement when walking and his disarming smile presented an effusive charisma that demanded attention.

"Good to see you, Hugh," his sonorous voice filled with sincerity.

"Likewise, Juan. What brings you out this early?"

"Hugh, I'm facing a dilemma. I want your advice."

I looked at him to determine if he was serious or just toying with levity, then replied,

"Let me have it, but I must tell you my own dilemmas usually end up in the mental file of problems to be solved tomorrow."

"Come with me." He was showing me a facet of his makeup never revealed before. He appeared nervous as if overcome by indecision. This produced curiosity in me, and I must say, a certain degree of satisfaction to learn his armor of calm poise could be shaken—by what, remained to be seen. As we passed Barbara's desk, I asked Cedillo how long we would be out. He answered, "About fifteen minutes."

I nodded to Barbara, then Juan. We made our way to the street level walking a half block when Juan halted. He pointed to a gleaming new Auburn Speedster parked at the curb saying, "Hugh, do you think Barbara will accept that as a gift, with no strings attached?"

I stood admiring the sheer beauty of the vehicle. Parked at the curb, it gave the illusion it was flying while motionless. The eye-catching yellow, with black leather interior combined to make it a thing of irresistible pleasure to behold! I was thinking this car was a towering monument exemplifying the ingenuity of man when Juan broke into my thoughts, saying, "Well, why don't you answer me?"

"Pardon me, Juan. I was admiring the vehicle. If you get her to accept it I'll be surprised."

"Why?"

He was boring into my core with his persistent question—he awaited an answer.

"Barbara's a woman steeped with self-reliance and I think you'll have to do a selling job to get her to accept it." My answer came out as lame words. They needed bolstering with reasoning, but I couldn't supply it at the moment. Juan was leveling a visual examination of me, seemingly to detect a face of jealousy as evidenced by his probing question of, "Hugh, are you sure you were truthful when I asked if there was any romantic entanglement between you and Barbara? Like I said, I wouldn't do anything to divide you two, if anything did exist."

"Hell no. There's absolutely nothing. If you can get her to accept the car, more power to you. Let us go back to the office so you can spring it on her." Juan walked silently beside me.

As we entered the elevator I broke the silence by saying, "It's a wonderful, generous gift by any standard, and I hope she'll accept it."

As we approached the door, Cedillo clutched my elbow, halting me be saying, "I hope she accepts it. I must confess to you, Hugh, I'm truly in love for the second time in my life. I didn't think I was capable of loving again after I lost my wife."

His confession sounded the imminent possibility of my losing a good secretary, as well as the source of an unforgettable interlude in my life. I dismissed the lingering memory of the warmth of her body as it cascaded over my shoulders when I carried her across the room to the bed on that memorable night.

"Juan, there is an old saying, love and trouble is found by both seeking and avoidance. So I suppose we all are victims of our fate," I said opening the office door.

Barbara told me Curly had called and would be at Johnstone Testers for another hour. He wanted to talk with me about crews for the rigs in Mexico.

"Juan, will we have any problems recruiting workers for the drilling? Are rig builders available around Tampico?"

"No problem getting rig builders. If you can bring one experienced man for each rig we operate, you can fill the crew with native workers. Some of them have much experience and the others can learn."

"That is okay. If we have the equipment unloaded the twenty-fifth, could we begin operations the twenty-seventh?"

"Yes, we'll use the twenty-sixth getting around to all the minor details necessary for starting."

I knew he was anxious to learn his fate on the gift for Barbara, so I helped the action by saying, "Juan, why don't you and Barbara step out for coffee while I make the call to Corpus Christi?"

Barbara arose from her desk—they went out the door, she was clutching Cedillo's arm.

Watching the door close, I was gripped with a feeling of loss. I was losing more than a secretary. I was seeing the curtain being drawn, obscuring the woman who had been the catalyst responsible for wedding fantasy with reality within me. It had not left me since that night, and now I knew the memory of the experience with Barbara would forever be my companion.

I soon had Curly on the phone. He wanted to know when he should be in Tampico.

"Curly can you recruit five of our men from the Corpus Christi field to go to Mexico?"

"That'll be easy as more than five have asked me if I could arrange a transfer for them, too. How and when will we go?"

"Tell them there is a five dollar a day bonus in it. I'll make it right for all those who go down there. Everyone should be at the airport Monday morning. Jim Harris will fly down. You'll be leaving at eight a.m. Don't forget to buy the trucks. Call me if you need anything."

I stepped into the front office to see Juan smiling as if he had turned up four aces for a huge pot. Barbara was seated at her desk staring intently at the window. The silence was so oppressive it was noisy and this prompted me to withhold any question regarding the automobile. I halted, observing Cedillo, then Barbara. He was still beaming his likable smile, but remaining silent. I noticed he was no longer plagued with nervousness and appeared to have the situation under control.

If they chose to avoid any mention of the gift, I would refrain from asking anything about how it was received or rejected.

"Juan, are you going to Mexico today?"

"Yes, but Barbara has something she wants to say. Right, Barbara?" She turned her head slowly to look at me then asked,

"What do you think of it, Mr. McCulloch?"

"I think it's a beauty."

"I don't mean what do you think of the car, I mean what do you think of the gesture. Is it proper?"

My brain shifted quickly for the right answer, "That's what I was referring to, the gesture. I think it's wonderful that Juan knows you are worthy of such an offering."

As I made this statement, I could visualize the future when a replacement for Barbara would become necessary. The thought gave me a pang of hurt, realizing she would eventually leave. Cedillo was a jungle tiger stalking his prey—Barbara was the prey and certain to succumb to his fatal charm. I had no right to question his conquest of her, but damn it, he could have a million women in Mexico. Yet here they were, two souls needing to swim the rushing rapids of life in search of love and apparently find it. Fate could not be handicapped. The proof was here before me. Out of three billion people roaming the planet and these two came together like iron filing to a magnet. Perhaps it was meant to be, a force majeure.

Barbara said, "Juan, I'll accept the gift of the Auburn on the conditions I outlined earlier. It's very gracious of you to offer it—I thank you very much!"

She walked over to Cedillo, he arose awaiting her, she gave him a maternal kiss on the cheek, then went back to her desk, turned to face Juan and said, "I hope you never regret this morning."

His eyes were penetrating as he told her, "I won't regret any moment in your presence, ever. Hugh, can you take me to the airport now?"

Bidding Cedillo good-bye, he reminded me to meet him in Tampico on Thursday.

♠ ♠ ♠

Driving back to the office I could not chase thoughts out of my mind—thoughts concerning conditions Barbara had outlined with acceptance of the car. As I entered the office, I told myself I would never know, in spite of my curiosity.

Barbara hit me with a statement as the door closed.

"Hugh, I wish I could be certain I haven't compromised myself by accepting the car. Can you understand my concern?"

For a few moments, I studied her features trying to ascertain if the question had a sincere motive. Deciding she wanted some comment from me I answered.

"Barbara, no one remains in a state of indecision after submitting to compromise. You alone know the facts of your past experience with Cedillo, and you'll determine what transpires in the future. The word, compromise, means different things to each of us. Therefore, no one can answer your question except you. I think any woman under the circumstances would've accepted the automobile, if that consoles your doubt. Okay?

"Now, you and I must discuss the immediate future. I'm flying to Tampico tomorrow afternoon and will be absent from the office for an indefinite period. I'll contact you daily and will try to be in Houston each Friday thereafter. Any matter that requires my presence can be set up for Fridays. It's likely I'll not return for a couple of weeks in order to get things started down there. Are there any questions?"

"Yes, one. Can you take me to dinner this evening?" she smiled, held up three fingers, then said, "Purely platonic I assure you, on girl scouts honor!"

Now I was embroiled in a dilemma. Should I decline the suggestion using my vow to never mix business with pleasure as an excuse, or take her to dinner and wage war with my erotic desire for the entire evening. Vows and words being a product of the mind, do nothing to snuff out biological urges and desires that pop up from the physical-like toadstools in the night.

She interrupted my inner struggle with, "Alright, if it's that hard for you to decide, it must present a problem. I understand."

"No, no. I was trying to decide what time I could pick you up. Is eight satisfactory?"

"It's a date. Now, if you haven't any objections, I want us to go in my car tonight. I'd like you to show me some things about it that Juan didn't explain."

"That's fine with me."

I went into my private office to take care of some business that had accumulated, discovering a second proposal from the government of Venezuela to develop their petroleum resources. This being the second feeler from them, I reasoned it merited a response. I rang for Barbara, dictating a letter to Señor Raymundo Alvarez, one of the signatories of the inquiry. I outlined several reasons for having to decline the proposal at this time, but left the matter open for future consideration. Dismissing Barbara, I called Jim Harris, making arrangements to take off for Tampico the next day at noon.

The phone rang, it was Mr. McMillan, my banker, "Mr. McCulloch, I'm calling to get authorization for more construction funds. Smythe, the architect, contacted me yesterday about more money. He requested another million for matching funds with the insurance company in order to proceed with the hotel. Do you want me to okay it and transfer the money from your account?"

"Yes, please do. I'm driving out to see how things are progressing within the hour, also I'm starting the first well in Tampico next week."

"Good! I wish you huge success down there. I'm sure you'll make a lot of money. Incidentally would you consider a fourth interest in the laying of a pipeline from Conroe to Houston? I've two associates in the proposed venture, neither of them in petroleum. I mentioned you as the fourth member. Are you interested?"

"Thank you for asking, but I must pass. The activity in Mexico will most likely present the opportunity of pipelines and perhaps refining also. I'd better swing loose to snatch the opportunity when it arises. I do wish you and your associates the best."

"If you find the need of additional finances down there, you know where you can get them. Good luck—good-bye."

That night Barbara greeted me in a subdued manner. She was not her usual effervescent self as we walked to her car where I asked, "Why are you so quiet? Is there something troubling you?"

"If you've no objections I'd like to dine in the Empire Room again." Her deliberate evasion of answering my question gave me cause to drop the subjetc. She would probably reveal the basis for her mood later.

As we reached her Auburn, I adopted a facade of levity with, "Miss Hunter, you now have the service of a mechanical engineer, capable and ready to answer any questions you might pose regarding the operation of this marvel before us."

Her several queries pertaining to hood release, signal buttons, etc. were answered as I demonstrated how to perform various needs in the car's operation.

While dining, Barbara opened a wide avenue of possible questions by saying, "Hugh, do you know why I wanted to come back here to dine?"

Pursing my lips while considering the proper answer. Barbara was studying my face with a quizzical expression awaiting a response.

"Suppose you tell me why we came here," I countered.

"Because here was the beginning of a night that enriched my life in several ways. A night that provided me the unforgettable experience of my first view of the complexities life thrusts upon us when a man and woman set out to explore the inner desires. I'll never understand my total abandon of the pristine side. It had always served as a buffer until that night when it receded and submission filled the vacancy. I submitted to what followed with the innocence of a cherub, never questioning the morality of our actions. My mind told me it was the natural thing to do." She stopped as if she was searching for courage to continue.

I became embroiled in a melange of thoughts. Was she signaling a desire to repeat the experience of that night? If so, why should I hesitate to encourage such an exotic interlude? Let my vow to keep business and pleasure separated be damned. My ego prevailed by prompting me to ask, "Do I understand your words right? You're willing to have a repeat experience?"

"No Hugh," she said continuing to eat her sherbet. Her answer sounded a connotation of sincere rejection to my question and I pursued it no further.

"Hugh, Juan has proposed marriage." She fixed her eyes directly on mine to gauge my surprise. She found no surprise to gauge, as her statement evoked no astonishment from me. I had interpreted the telltale signs accurately.

"Congratulations."

"For what? I've not accepted his proposal. There are many things to be considered before I decide."

"Like what? Any available woman would make a speedy decision on a proposal from Cedillo. He oozes charm—is wealthy—a prototype of sartorial excellence—handsome and courteous. Shall I continue?"

"You omitted two very important considerations. Do I really love him and more important, does he love me?" she stated in a factual tone of voice. "All men are afflicted with the lack of ability to place things of value in this life, in their proper sequence of importance. You just proved the point I'm making by omitting any mention of love."

"Hell Barbara—anyone can see both of you enter a state of animation when together. Marry him. That's my advice, if you love him."

"Damn Hugh, you make it appear as sudden and imperative as a shotgun affair. I have to convince myself I'd adapt to living in Mexico as well as accept Catholicism."

I broke in, "If you don't know you love him, then take the time to sort out your mind, as well, as your heart. Just give me enough time to get a replacement for you, okay?"

She sat silently gazing across the dining room, her face showing a feeling of being hurt. After a full minute or more she reached across the table taking my hand in hers. She squeezed it tightly as I felt the quivering fingers around mine. She turned her gaze back to me revealing a tear coursing each cheek as she spoke in a modulated tone, "This is why I gave you the answer to your question about us having a repeat experience. My heart taunts me with yes, while my mind restrains me with, no. I'd like to believe your words of the past few minutes came from your head and not your heart. Now if you're ready, I wish to go home. This has been a touching, memorable interlude for me, and one I'll recall with bittersweet emotion as long as I live. Shall we go?"

As we stopped at Barbara's home, she turned to me saying, "Good night, it's been wonderful talking my situation over with you. I'm depressed somewhat by your nonchalant attitude toward the prospects of my marriage to Juan, but that's life."

"One minute please," I grasped her hand in mine and continued, "I too will remember our two nights together. You must try to understand why I appear nonchalant over the prospects of your marriage, while my insides roil with the effects of losing you. Yes, I'll lose more than a secretary when and if you go. I'll lose a part of me as well. I cannot honestly try to discourage you, I have no right to impede your association with Juan or anyone else. Besides I hope to remarry Audrey someday. This is why I tried to receive your statement coolly, and without objection. Can you understand my logic?" With that confession I slid out of the car, then walked with Barbara to her door where we exchanged our good nights in a cordial, yet restrained manner.

As I drove to the hotel, I was thinking of how elusive peace of mind had become since I had acquired wealth. I could grasp the material things, then manipulate them at will with ample success. But reviewing the past six years revealed a sobering fact. I had not enjoyed boundless enthusiasm since bringing in my first well. From that day on, the pursuit of money and power had become an inferno dwelling within, that could not share the inner me with life's intrinsic rewards. Tonight I faced the stark reality of reaping the painful reward of loneliness for my neglect. Neglect of nurturing the things I wanted so very much yet I did not have a woman to share the dark of night with me. A woman by my side because that was where she wanted to be—not because of my wanting her there.

Chapter Fourteen
Getting The Teams Together

The morning found me anticipating the flight to Tampico and I entered the office bearing a changed attitude toward Barbara. I was feeling admiration for her, due to her refusal of going to bed with me. She had exhibited more sound judgment by her action than I had, by offering to resume the affair. She smiled asking, "Aren't you happy?"

I paused studying her smile, then replied, "Should I be? About what?"

"Happy that we enjoyed a pleasant evening in a platonic manner."

"Barbara, have you ever considered mental telepathy as an avocation?" Not awaiting an answer, I continued, "You should consider it and I'll recommend you. The manner in which you probe my thoughts borders on the occult. Yes, it's best the way it is and I'm happy. Okay?"

After dealing with office matters, it was time to start for the airport. Stopping at Barbara's desk I asked, "Any message for Juan?"

She stopped typing, swiveling her chair to face me. She studied my eyes several moments, then said in a quiet, sincere voice.

"Yes, tell him I miss him."

"Is that all?"

"Yes, that's enough."

I stood silent considering the impact of her succinct yet golden words. They conveyed visions of a bridal gown—the essence of orange blossoms—the presence of babies—a mansion in Mexico, and the finale of a glorious physical relationship between two people being pulled apart like warm taffy. She and I, from this day on, could reach for a warm memory of what had been. I had to get out now, before emotion dissipated my feigned self-control.

"I'll contact you each day, take care."

Jim was checking out the plane as I approached. His back being to me, he was not aware of my presence until I asked, "Will it fly?"

He turned, laughing, retorting, "Damn tootin'."

"I'm ready when you are, Jim. Today marks the beginning of a project that can make or break me. If all goes well you'll be rewarded for your services. I must point out they'll entail more than just being a pilot before this venture closes. I'm looking forward to whatever comes and I hope you share my anticipation," I said placing my bags in the plane.

The Wright Whirlwind engine responded with staccato barks, belching white smoke, then smoothed out to a powerful roar as Jim nosed it down the runway, then opened it up. Five minutes later, reaching cruising altitude, Jim turned to me and asked, "Now Hugh, tell me what I can look forward to in addition to being your pilot?" He was smiling while awaiting my reply.

"For starters, I'll expect you to be more or less a sounding board to whom I can voice my opinions and ideas. At times you'll serve as my courier. You may even get involved in violence by reason of association. Anything can happen in the oil fields. The added setting of Mexico offers the ingredients of intrigue, consternation, maybe even danger at times. We are in alien surroundings and anything is possible. If uncertainty of planning the future any further than today chills you, now is the time to get the hell out. However, I hope you stay with me."

"Sounds interesting. Yipee! Mexico, here we come!" He shouted with a show of high spirits.

At four thirty we were circling the airport to head into the breeze for landing. Tampico awaited us eight hundred feet below when Jim aligned the plane's nose with the east-west runway and began our descent. As the wheels thumped their greeting, I could see Colonel Rivera walking toward the parking apron to welcome our return.

As we climbed from the plane Rivera greeted us with a smile. "Welcome back to Tampico, Mr. McCulloch—Mr. Harris," he said while shaking our hands energetically. "Come, let us celebrate your arrival with a drink."

As we started for the terminal, I was considering a valid excuse to avoid any more of the Rotterdam gin if he offered it. But we had tequila instead and after downing it Colonel Rivera asked, "Mr. McCulloch, do you wish to have the bags taken to your hacienda? Here are the keys."

"Thank you, Jim and I'll move in today. Juan Cedillo will arrive tomorrow. He wishes to check my permits, etc. before we begin operations. Do you know where I might rent a car or truck for a few days?"

"That will not be necessary as Minister Cedillo has directed me to provide you with transportation as long as you wish. Courtesy of the Government of Mexico, with a chauffeur."

I was suddenly recalling the two terrifying rides we experienced in Monterrey. Jim cast a woeful glance in my direction, I knew we were of the same opinion regarding an unknown driver. I had no intention of permitting some wheel crazy individual the chance to expose us to another hair raising ride.

"You don't have to provide a driver, Colonel. Jim and I can do the driving, if you've no objection."

"Come outside, I'll show you to your transportation!"

The Colonel headed for the front of the building as we trailed behind. He stopped in front of a long, black vehicle with the top down, then pointed saying, "There it is. A good one too."

I moved to the side of Rivera to see the make of automobile we were being offered. It was a 1928 Studebaker touring car, fully 18 feet in length. The fenders had more dimples than a fat girl's chorus line. The dimples resulting from many contacts with Mexico City taxis, no doubt.

"The key is in it, and it's all yours." The Colonel had hooked his thumbs on his ornate leather belt as he looked at me trying to assess my reaction, "How do you like it?"

I climbed in under the wheel and pressed the starter as I turned the ignition key. A subdued rumble came from under the hood. I tromped the accelerator. The straight eight engine responded with a snorting, trumpeting sound like that of a herd of rogue elephants rumbling through the African veldt. I glanced to the rear where a huge cloud of dust was rising from beneath the car, churned up by the exhaust pipe. It was evident the Studebaker had no muffler. I turned off the engine, then got out while saying, "One thing is sure. That car won't sneak up on anyone."

Rivera guffawed while leaning forward slapping his thighs, "That's a good one, Mr. McCulloch. I like your humor."

"Get your bags Jim, and we'll go to the McCulloch hacienda."

I thanked the Colonel for his courtesy while Jim was tossing our bags in the rear seat. We stopped for two quarts of tequila and two dozen lemons on the way.

We arrived at the rambling house as a lingering dusk was slowly fading from gray to the dark of night. The tall palms surrounding the structure appeared as spokes in a huge wheel, the house being the hub.

When Jim stopped the motor, silence rolled over us like an enveloping fog gliding in from the sea. I spoke, "Listen to that, Jim."

"What? I hear nothing," he responded.

"That's what I mean! Have you ever listened to silence?"

I could sense his motion of turning his head my way, most likely to learn what prompted my quixotic question. At that moment, the intriguing wail of a roaming coyote floated across a sea of black that remained after the exodus of dusk. The palm leaves offered their soothing rustle to the sounds of night, but not to be upstaged by the coyote. After a few moments, I opened the door saying, "Jim, turn the car and direct the headlights on the front door while I open it and see what kind of lighting we can discover."

I mounted the porch as Jim positioned the light beams on the double doors. Placing the heavy key on the lock, then turning it I found the spirit of adventure had possessed me. The back of my neck had suddenly become chilled as the ponderous door swung slowly inward. Instantly I reviewed my mental impressions of all the people who had entered this portal in the past. I must have paused longer than I realized as Jim sang out, "Any problems, Hugh?"

"No, just one more minute." I was feeling along the wall for the switch, then flipped it. The huge chandelier shot cascades of light throughout the large room. The illumination was a welcome sight as it erased the possibility of spending a night in darkness, surrounded by ghosts of the past.

Jim set the bags in the center of the room, then opened a small briefcase extracting a flashlight saying, "We might need this to explore our surroundings."

We made our way to the kitchen in an effort to locate some glasses, and to learn what other necessities were available. We were pleasantly surprised to find a kitchen equipped with contemporary gadgets that included a barbecue pit seasoned from much use.

The dining table was made of solid oak planking, finished to a glistening surface. Ten high backed oak chairs upholstered with calf skin completed the set. The chairs seemed to beckon our company. I obliged by asking Jim to get the tequila and lemons, then drew a chair back and sat down.

After mixing and pouring two generous portions, I raised mine. Then we touched glasses and downed the fiery, white liquid causing us to grasp for breath. We followed with lemon juice and a taste of salt. This procedure was repeated numerous times before we found it necessary to open the second bottle.

During the interim, we had discussed varied subjects. I found Jim to be knowledgeable and articulate in the realm of the occult. He injected the subject into our conversation by asking me if I felt any presence in the house other than ourselves. The tequila had most likely provided him the audacity needed to ask the question, bolstering my courage enough to answer in the affirmative.

When I admitted I had felt the presence of many, since we entered the house, he responded by revealing he suspected as much.

"The day we went through this house you stopped in the big room as Rivera was talking, you seemed to be in a trance. Tell me, what did you see, or hear?" He was awaiting an answer.

"Hell Jim, if I told you what I saw or was thinking, you'd fly back to Houston tonight!"

"Try me," he was bubbling with anticipation awaiting my reply.

I poured another shot—swished it around the glass, then gulped it down. I fixed a steady gaze on Jim's eyes and asked, "Did you see or hear anything that day?"

"Yes, I did."

"Alright Jim, we'll put the subject to an acid test. I reached in my jacket pocket, removing a note pad. Tearing two sheets from it, I handed one to Jim saying, "You write down your impressions and I'll do the same. We'll fold them, then exchange and see what we have."

After jotting my impression of hearing many voices upon entering the large room, I folded the paper handing it to Jim. He, in turn, gave me what he had written. Reading it I realized some unknown element of mysticism had entered our mental process.

He had written about seeing many human forms crowding the room. Some with features revealing happiness and integrity—others with faces lined and etched, showing the result of a vile, vicious lifestyle. I glanced at Jim to see his reaction, then exclaimed, "I'll be damned." He had made the same exclamation in perfect unison, as if we had rehearsed the thing! Still looking at his comments I continued, "This is weird. There can be no logical explanation except perhaps two overactive imaginations."

"Not so," Jim replied, continuing, "It's apparent you're gifted with the psychic ability referred to as audile cognition, while I've a degree of pre and post cognition. This explains my seeing the spirits while you heard their presence."

"Come off it, Jim."

"Listen to me, Hugh. The world is filled with spirits of people. People of another age—another century. These are the spirits of people whose physical vehicle, the body, underwent the decomposition of the molecules that animate our bodies resulting in what we know as death. The spirits of those individuals in numerous instances, have refused to accept the finality of the death of their bodies and elected to remain on this planet in spirit form, in lieu of transition to the spirit realm. If they had chosen not to remain and ascended to the higher plane, at some future period they could've returned in another human body, to live a better life. As you know, Hugh, life is but a school for the soul. This acceptance is known as reincarnation. That's my lecture for tonight—let's go to bed." I quickly and quietly agreed.

I slept in the vast canopied bed, Jim occupied one of the five guest rooms. After donning my pajamas and turning off the light, I found the giant bed very conducive to sleep. The spirits did not delay my slumber.

♠ ♠ ♠

The morning came quickly and I greeted it with an unwelcome hangover. While shaving, then preparing to go into town for breakfast, I found myself growing fond of the old house, considering the thought of buying it if Hernandez was willing to sell. I also made a mental note to engage a cook for the hacienda.

In the El Fiambrera located on the main thoroughfare of Tampico, we ordered Mexican style eggs, Huevos Rancheros.

After eating we drove to the airport to await Cedillo's arrival. The Colonel was already on duty.

"Ah—Good morning Mr. McCulloch—Mr. Harris. Did you sleep well? I hope the—how do you say it—spirits, did not keep you awake." He was showing his white teeth with a sardonic smile, as if awaiting a response to his show of levity.

I answered, "No, as you can see we weren't destroyed by evil spirits and we did sleep well. Why do you ask?"

He cast an affected, furtive glance around the office, then replied in a stage whisper, "They say there are spirits there. Lots of respected people have taken an oath to the Virgin of Guadalupe that they've seen them."

Jim shifted his gaze from Rivera to me, hoping to catch my reaction to this bit of local mystical lore. I decided to let his statement pass without comment, however I did sneak a sly wink at Jim.

At that moment the sound of a plane's engine drifted into the office. A bright red and black plane was circling to line up with the runway for landing. Colonel Rivera spoke, "That's Minister Cedillo!"

We walked to the plane as it rolled slowly onto the apron, then stopped. Cedillo was flashing the smile that had devastated Barbara and no doubt countless other females, as he climbed down.

Holding out his hand, he gave me an impressive welcome. As I shook his hand he wrapped his left arm around my neck in a friendly hug saying, "How's my compadre?"

"Just fine, Juan. I want you to meet my pilot and consort, Jim Harris."

Juan gave Jim the same effulgent welcome he had bestowed me, and I could see the glow of admiration in Jim's eyes as they shook hands. We started for the terminal with Jim and Rivera trailing.

Juan said in a low voice, "Your pilot hasn't any idea of the extent of our association, has he?"

"No, that'll never be revealed to anyone by me."

"I should've known. Did Rivera provide you with transportation?"

"Yes, as you'll soon see, and hear! Do you plan to stay overnight?"

"Yes, I'll return to Mexico City when we get everything in order, and to your satisfaction—not before."

"Excellent! You'll be my guest tonight at my newly acquired hacienda, the Hernandez house."

Cedillo chuckled upon seeing the Studebaker, then remarked, "Hugh, this car has carried me many miles in Mexico City."

He stopped at the front of the car, pointing to a small hole in the hood said, "That hole was intended to be in me, and would've been except for some very evasive driving on the part of my aide. I had just spoken to the engineering graduates at the university in Mexico City. When I returned to the car we found it was surrounded by a sea of humanity. They were protesting the tobacco tax imposed by Cardenas in 1936, and were giving vent to their anger by attacking anything bearing the government seal. There were several thousand in the mob and it required the efforts of a platoon of soldiers to open a way to our car. As we inched forward, actually pushing the demonstrators aside, they retaliated by hurling stones and bottles at us. To avoid being seriously injured, my driver bored into the crowd, knocking some of them down, as we made our escape. One wild-eyed devil leveled an automatic pistol at us, firing at will. The driver swerved to run him down and did hit him after he had fired several shots. Then we were out of the crowd speeding for our lives. This explains all the dents. It was a frightening experience and one I don't care to endure again. If this Studebaker had stalled that morning, it would've been destroyed and burned. I wouldn't be here now. I have an affinity for this vehicle."

He patted the radiator as if it were a puppy, then continued, "I want to introduce you to a man who can help in locating rig builders, truckers and crewmen. He's the Superintendent for Gulf Oil, "Tri-cone" Becker. His real name is Ralph Becker. Drive down main street for three blocks, Gulf has their field office there."

I saw the Gulf sign perched atop a corrugated metal building and drove to the shady side and parked. As I placed my hand on the door to alight, Juan clutched my arm, saying in a low voice, "What does Barbara think of her Auburn?"

"She's thrilled about it and she should be!"

"I'm glad to hear that, as she gave me the impression she was hesitant about accepting it."

We entered the office, a burly man dressed in khaki with a Stetson hat pulled down over his face, was sleeping with his feet parked on a battered desk. A large red dog next to him laid with his shaggy tail drooping down the end of the desk, limpid as a broken rope. The dog sensed our presence, swung his tail upward, whining a welcome. Cedillo patted him on the head saying, "Good boy—good boy."

The somnolent man pushed his hat on top of his head, then fastened his sleepy puffed eyes on us. Recognizing Cedillo, he shot straight upward to a standing position, saying in a croaky voice, "Minister Cedillo! Good to see you!"

He darted around the desk to shake hands, as he passed the red dog he swung his arm, brushing him from the desk barking, "Get the hell out of my way, Pluto. Beat it."

After pumping Cedillo's hand several times, he turned to me saying, "Ralph Becker."

I shook his hand saying, "Hugh McCulloch."

"Hell, you must be the feller that has the tract west of us."

Cedillo broke in, "Yes, Mr. McCulloch has the adjoining tract. He wanted to meet you."

I spoke, "Ralph—"

Becker interrupted me with, "Call me "Tri-cone," hardly anyone knows me as Ralph."

Okay Tri-cone. I've six rigs coming Sunday. Can you put me onto some rigbuilders and some trucks to haul the rigs?"

"You bet your ass I can. Sunday, huh—"

He was now walking toward the telephone. Picking up the receiver he got the operator, chanting several numbers in Spanish. After a few moments Becker yelled, "Ernesto, you lazy bastard, get your ass down here and give your wife a little rest. A man is here that needs truckers and rigbuilders. No, not manana, now! He wants to talk to you, now. Okay."

Becker dropped the receiver, then turned to me with, "He'll be here in ten minutes."

Cedillo was smiling as a result of the play on words we had heard and I was toying with the question of asking Becker the source of his sobriquet, "Tri-cone."

"Who tagged you Tri-cone, and why?"

Becker stretched to his full height of six feet plus, grinned at me while ruffling his sandy hair as he tossed his hat on the desk saying, "Sit down while we're waiting for Ernesto and I'll tell you how I got the nickname. It was during the wildcatting before the Kilgore field was brought in. I'd been hired by a man in Houston to follow Dad Joiner around to snoop on his locations, then we'd get as close to him as possible and drill. This was, in fact, a compliment to Joiner and his ability to sniff oil above ground. Anyway, my man ran out of money just as we entered hard formation. I was not about to walk away from that hole with dust in my pockets, so I visited a wildcat location one night located a half mile from ours. Being a major oil company's location, I was sure they had an ample supply of all types of drill bits. They hadn't started yet so I snuck into the equipment like a fox entering a henhouse. Groping around in the darkness I tripped over a box of tri-cone rock bits. I could smell cigarette smoke in the night air, so I figured someone was keeping watch. I leaned down to heft the box to my shoulder and found out it was heavy as hell. After two strenuous attempts, I managed to hoist it up there, and started my half mile trek back. That damn box of bits was so heavy, it was driving my feet a half foot into the soft ground with every step. Just before collapse I reached our location, then dropped the damn thing, falling on my face from exhaustion. I heard footsteps approaching, but I was too tired to move. A flashlight's beam probed the dark, but centered on the derrick. Then all was quiet. I had it made.

"Later I walked over to the derrick floor stretching completely out and spent physically, I dozed off. I was awakened by someone shaking me, while shining a light in my face. I roused up realizing I was being hustled to my feet by two lawmen. They escorted me to the Kilgore jail where I sweated it for three days. On the fourth morning, I was brought before a judge and charged with stealing equipment, namely one box of tri-cone bits. The box of bits was setting on the floor in front of the judge's bench. The charge was read, I entered my plea of 'not guilty'. During the legal procedure, the judge requested the big, muscular bailiff to lift the box to ascertain if I had in fact carried the bits to where they were found.

"The bailiff bent down, grunting and straining while attempting to lift the box. The judge was observing this intently. After four attempts the bailiff said, "Judge, I can't get it off the floor."

The judge at once announced, "Case dismissed."

"I asked the judge if the bits were declared not stolen and if I was free to leave. He said, "Yes, to both questions," where upon he left the courtroom.

"I bent down, found strength beyond normal, raised the box to my shoulder, walking out of the courtroom amid applause and laughter. That's how I got the nickname Tri-cone."

He leaned back with hands behind his head, then cast a boyish grin on us. Becker's eyes were dancing as he said, "Our man has arrived."

I turned to see a wizened, dehydrated looking fellow just entering the door. Surely this diminutive specimen was not a rig builder. He looked more like a strand of beef jerky than someone capable of bearing under the rigors of rig building. He was not over five feet six in height. Maybe he had heavy duty trucks.

"Mr. McCulloch, meet Ernesto Roel."

I stood shaking hands with the little squirt. He had a grip like a giant clam and actually exerted pain in my hand. What a surprise! Becker introduced Ernesto to Cedillo, then we got down to the business at hand.

"Ernesto, I've six rigs coming in here this weekend, can you haul them off the dock to their location?"

"Yes."

"Fine. Tri-cone tells me you've a crew of rig builders. Will you be available next week?"

"Yes."

"Are you and your crew fast?"

"Yes."

I turned to Becker saying, "Does he understand what I'm saying?"

"You're damn right he does. He's a little short on size, on words too, but he delivers the goods. You can bet on him. He gets around in a derrick better than a tomcat in a tree full of wild canaries."

"Alright, Ernesto, be prepared to roll Sunday. Be at the docks around noon, and I'll meet you there. The rigs are coming in on the Tillie Lykes and will be put on the dock. Do you understand?"

"Yes."

"Want some advance money?"

"No," he grinned at each of us, saying, "Sunday." He left the office as quietly as he had entered.

"Come Hugh, I want to show you the location."

Jim was half asleep in the rear seat as Juan and I approached. He sat up saying, "I think I'll like this climate."

We rode fifteen miles west of Tampico to an area of rolling hills where Cedillo pointed to the left of the road saying, "Mr. McCulloch you're now looking at your twenty-five thousand acre tract. The drilling rights reach from that lone tree—westward to a survey marker. Drive on, I'll show you."

We drove west until Cedillo halted me with, "There is the west boundary."

He was pointing to a white post rising about three feet above the ground.

"Concrete posts like the one there mark the border of the tract. They're spaced one fourth of a mile apart. You'll have no problem with delineation of the tract. I wish you many producers and a speedy start. Do you have any questions?"

"Yes. If I do get production soon, would there be any delay in my laying a pipeline to Tampico based on the permits I have?"

"None at all. You have permits for both pipeline and refinery construction, if you elect to utilize your options."

"That is great. I'll call my geologist today, in hopes he can be here by Monday."

Driving back to Tampico, Cedillo was very quiet. I was certain he was thinking of Barbara, and possibly our coalition, so I used the time reviewing what I should accomplish that day.

As we entered the business district, Juan glanced at his watch suggesting we have lunch at the El Fiambrerea.

As we sat down, Jim continued on to the men's room while Cedillo remarked, "Hugh, you won't have to call Joe Miller. I've asked him to fly down Sunday as I knew you'd want him to suggest site locations. He'll be in around eleven a.m. Perhaps you can meet him at the airport."

"I certainly will, thank you Juan. Sometime today I must try for telephone installation at the house, and an office if we can locate a suitable space. I need a cook and housekeeper too."

"After lunch I'll show you a building recently vacated that will make us a good office. Do not worry about getting telephone service, that isn't any problem."

We dined, then drove to the building Juan had mentioned for our office. It was situated about a half block from Becker. Deciding it was satisfactory, we drove to the owner's store, and fifteen minutes later came out with a year lease.

Colonel Rivera was very helpful in my employing, Alicia Sandoval, as a cook and housekeeper. She was a comely woman, who spoke good English and she agreed to live-in with weekends off unless I needed her for a special occasion. She was available immediately and the Colonel assured me she was an excellent cook.

Cedillo used his influence in getting both telephones installed that afternoon. I bought furniture for the office, then secured a supply of groceries and meats for the house, plus an ample supply of spirits and mixers, then called it a day. I drove Juan to the airport and used Friday and Saturday for setting up my office. Jim was out with Ernesto rounding up crews for the rigs.

Chapter Fifteen
Tying Up The Loose Ends

I met Joe Bob on Sunday, then drove to observe the unloading of the equipment. He asked about Audrey, then realizing we were no longer married he hurriedly changed the subject to drilling locations. As we approached the piers we could see a ship maneuvering to dock.

The Lykes freighter tied up in Tampico around eleven a.m. and started unloading immediately. The two pickup trucks came off first and I noticed they bore the firm's name on the doors. Curly had done his work well. All was unloaded and the freighter was backing down from the pier at three p.m. underway for Merida.

We decided to wait till early morning to get the rigs on location.

"Okay, Ernesto? That's good, we'll start at six."

Joe Bob and I drove to the tract. He pointed out forty-two drilling sites, while I drove a stake to mark each location. The sun was dropping below the horizon as we started for the house. It was then I reopened the subject of Audrey.

"Joe, don't think I was ducking behind a hubris shield when you asked earlier about Audrey. You know me better than anyone and I'm not foolish enough to point the finger of blame at anyone, or anything, except myself. I was the sole cause in the failure of our marriage. As you've remarked so many times in the past—I'm a crude, arrogant, bellicose, insensitive bastard, and I must add, an unhappy one since I've been alone."

"Do you talk to her often?"

"Hell no! I wish I could. When I've talked with her the chill of her voice has brought me to the brink of despair realizing what I lost while bargaining my soul for money and power. Justin refused to see me when I visited the hospital—Audrey never answered the phone, moreover my thinking is all screwed up as a result of our last conversation. She asked me to call again, 'sometime'."

"That's encouraging, isn't it?"

"Yes and no. The word 'sometime' was a pyrrhic victory for me as it bore the connotation of an indefinite time in the distant future, something like infinity. You know what I mean. The invitation was there, yet it wasn't. I don't know who said it, but I'll quote an astute observation that goes like this, 'money and time are the heaviest burdens in life, and the unhappiest of all mortals are those who have more of either than they know how to use.' He should've added, the burden of a misused love."

We turned into the drive and Joe Bob chuckled saying, "Boy, you always land on your feet. How did you find a house like this?"

"Cedillo put me on to it. I really like it." Jim had a lively blaze going in the huge fireplace, giving off a welcome warmth. I could hear pans clinking in the kitchen, the sounds floating into the large room were garnished with a tantalizing aroma of food. Jim greeted us as he walked in, "Hello, I'm Jim Harris."

He and Joe Bob were shaking hands as I asked, "What's that delicious smell coming from the kitchen?"

"That, my friend, is the essence of Chiles Rellenos. Alicia told me so!"

Joe Bob was standing in the center of the main room, with his eyes sweeping the surroundings he said, "I'll bet if these walls could talk they'd have some stories to tell."

I answered, "No doubt they would," catching a sly grin on Jim's face I continued, "There are some lurid tales involving this house so don't be alarmed at anything you see or hear tonight."

It required effort to keep a straight face as Joe Bob studied my features to detect any trace of humor. At that time Alicia rang a small silver bell announcing dinner.

Because he had to take off for Corpus Christi at four a.m., Jim retired early after dinner. This left Joe Bob and I sitting at the dining table with a quart of tequila in front of us. After three of four shots of the tequila, Joe Bob surrendered to his curiosity by asking, "What's the deal between you and Cedillo?"

I bounced his question around mentally before answering, "It's a fifty-fifty operation." Then related the possibility of a pipeline and perhaps the construction of a refinery later.

"Hugh, have you considered the effect, if any, of President Cardenas' request of congress to pass laws permitting expropriation of all things considered to be of public utility? He made the request November of last year, and naturally considers petroleum and natural gas as being in the category."

"Yes, Cedillo and I discussed the reaches of the Cardenas proposal, however Juan is convinced his position of Minister could be used as a buttress against seizure. In the event it did come about, Cedillo would defend me automatically as he protected his own financial flank. He's very sure of his influence in thwarting any expropriation. I believe him to be capable of resolving any situation that might arise. He's a potent force. He's persuasive and could influence a Catholic priest to officiate the rites of a Mormon marrying his fifth wife!

"I'm not concerned about our venture going sour. Did you get married?"

"No. The woman I was expecting to marry discarded our hopes when an old forgotten love emerged from the distant past. He succeeded in convincing her his station in life offered her more security than mine could give her, and damned if she didn't cast me aside like a stocking full of runners! Believe me, I was lucky to learn her character before marriage and a child or two."

"I'm sorry to hear that."

"Don't be. It was best it happened that way. Let's go to bed, I was up late last night at a party."

After seeing Joe Bob off I drove to the pier to observe the progress of moving the rigs. I found Ernesto and five brown natives busily engaged in loading two long wheel base trucks. Ernesto saw me and came over asking. "Can you spot the locations to unload about nine o'clock?"

"Yes, Ernesto I'll be there."

He turned, trotted back to the activity of loading where he vaulted his diminutive brown body up on the truck with the agility of a cat.

While having breakfast in a cafe, I looked at my watch noting it was eight thirty. If Jim had taken off for Corpus Christi as planned at four a.m., he was probably with Curly and the men preparing for the return flight.

Turning off the road onto the tract there was one loaded truck awaiting the arrival of the other. Following a hunch, I directed the driver to a marked location some distance from the boundary marker. I walked past two stakes, then pointed to the next one.

"There!"

The second truck was approaching, giving off the musical sound of metal clanking accompanied by the roar of an engine reaching for more power to roll the ponderous load. Walking around the trucks and checking the equipment they hauled, I became convinced Ernesto knew what it was all about. He walked to the stake—looked down—gave the sign of the cross and returned saying, "You'll find much oil here!"

They started unloading after I instructed Ernesto to concentrate on getting one rig assembled for drilling before taking the remainder from the dock. A few minutes later, a pair of machines appeared on the scene operated by natives. Ernesto had secured their services for digging the slush pit; there wasn't any time lost in getting started.

As I left for Tampico I glanced back to see a beehive of activity around the drilling site. I was thrilled as I realized we were at last starting this venture. A venture offering all the facets of a wildcatter's dream—wealth—accomplishment—intrigue—and the possibility of failure!

Becker was in his office and greeted me with friendly enthusiasm. "Well—I see you're getting ready to roll this morning. What can I do to help you?"

"Tri-cone, I would appreciate some information regarding fuel for the boilers and water."

"No problem. You'll find a two inch water line running along the western border of our tract. You may tie into it anywhere you choose. A quarter of a mile in from the west border you'll find a three inch line carrying oil. I'll go out there with you if you wish, but the shut off valves for both lines can be located easily, so go right ahead and tie into them. This'll be between you and me, right?"

"Right. I do appreciate your help in launching my operation, if there's anything I can do in return, just let me know."

I then drove to National Pipe and Supply to order the pipe where I found a redheaded, freckled face man in his early twenties standing in the door.

"What can I do for you, sir?" His eyes sparkled like crystal as he surveyed me.

"I need two thousand feet of two inch galvanized pipe and two thousand feet of two inch black with fittings. Four reducers from four to three. Can you make a delivery today or tomorrow on location? It's about fifteen miles west, adjoining the Gulf Oil tract."

"Sure can. Who's it for?"

"Bill it to Hugh McCulloch."

"You work for McCulloch? Tell me something, is he the hellion the newspapers paint him to be? I've heard he sleeps with a different woman every night, then gives them a new automobile the next morning as a going away present. He must be a regular Arabian stallion from what I hear. My brother said he saw McCulloch whip three guys once in a nightclub in Houston, then stacked the furniture for good measure." He paused to get his breath, then wrote up the billing pushing it towards me to sign.

Signing it, I returned the paper saying to him, "McCulloch's not Superman!"

He glanced at the billing to read my name, his face turning crimson, giving the effect of vanishing freckles as he stammered, "I'm sorry, I didn't know who you were. Gee, I'm sorry."

It was a humorous situation for me and I replied, "That's all right, even though I'm not exactly as the papers see me. Incidentally my superintendent is named Ward. He's authorized to make any purchase, please take care of him."

"Right! We'll get this order out there today. We're glad to welcome you to Tampico, and hope you bring in many gushers."

As I drove away he was leaning against the door frame observing me as a big grin split his freckled face, while I was thinking how ironic my reputation had preceded me to Mexico.

♠ ♠ ♠

Jim flew in around one p.m. bringing the group from Corpus Christi. I had spent the last half hour in Colonel Rivera's office being subjected to his narration of how he attained the rank of Colonel. He cited some gory details of why and how he was elevated to the rank. Some of the events were credible, then he continued by summing up all the reasons he should've been promoted to General. I found the latter incredible but sympathized with his missing out on advancement. I was pleased when

Jim's landing released me from the Colonel's monologue, and I hastened out to greet Curly and the men.

We drove to the restaurant where Jim asked me if Ernesto had moved the equipment as planned.

"Yes, he predicts he'll start building the first rig today. The guy really moves fast. He's promised to have eight or ten men in action this afternoon. There are two new pickups on the dock. I want you to take over one and Curly the other.

"Curly, you and Jim get the men over to the El Gringo Hotel after lunch and get them settled in their rooms. I've made arrangements for you there. If any of you wish to seek other lodging, that's your privilege, so feel free to relocate if you find a better place. You'll probably have two or three days before we get started so try your best to avoid the local jail. I appreciate your coming here and hope you get acclimated quickly. Let's go!

"Curly, I want you to ride out to the tract with me after you get the men settled. Jim will show you to our office, I'll wait for you there."

While awaiting their arrival, my mind had strayed, I found the present activity routine but visualized the future when I could see producing wells by the score dotting our tract. The arrival of Jim and Curly halted my mental projections.

♦ ♦ ♦

Six weeks later in January of 1938, my visions of producing wells had become a reality. We had four wells flowing an average of twenty thousand barrels per day, and six rigs running twenty-four hours a day in search of more of the black gold.

Cedillo and I were forced into laying a pipeline sooner than planned. We built a twenty-four inch line to Tampico in a period of three weeks. At one time during construction, we had one hundred workers laboring around the clock to expedite the completion date. The terminal being the Mata Redonda refinery at Tampico. This refinery had a capacity of twenty-five thousand barrels per day and boasted the most modern cracking unit in Mexico.

On January 20th, the operator notified me they could process no more than the present daily production. We had invested a million dollars in the emergency construction of the pipeline and now faced the dilemma of disposing of future increased production. The only practical solution was the erection of a refinery, but this was a costly alternative.

I placed a call to Mexico City to arrange a meeting with Cedillo. Having his private number, Juan answered, "Minister Cedillo."

I didn't know if anyone else might over hear our conversation, so assuming an impersonal tone of voice I replied, "Minister Cedillo, this is Hugh McCulloch. I'm encountering some obstacles with my oil business that only you can remove. It's imperative I talk with you at once. I can leave for Mexico City within the hour if you can see me today."

"Yes, we can meet today. What time do you expect to arrive?"

"I can be there at 5:00 p.m."

"I'll meet you at the airport. I'm sure we can overcome your problems when we meet. Good-bye."

Juan met us, then escorted us to a new limousine parked near the runway where a uniformed driver stood motionless as we approached. Upon our arrival he moved quickly to open the door, then stepped back smartly permitting us to enter the plush confines of the vehicle. We settled into the comfortable suede upholstery as the driver tooled the car onto the busy street. Juan leaned forward, closed the sliding glass divider between the driver and passenger space, then smiled saying, "Well, Hugh you must have something dramatic to spring on me but wait until we get to my place. On the way you can see many interesting sights. I'll even serve us a drink now."

He pushed a button located on the rear of the front seat—the panel opened silently revealing a miniature bar stocked with crystal decanters, labelled denoting their contents.

"Here, let's enjoy a cognac," he produced the silver cigar case passing it to Jim, then to me, "While I prepare the drinks."

The traffic was a fascinating movement of orderly confusion as the assorted vehicles darted in and out, most of them spewing a plume of smoke from their exhaust. The driver of our car was performing maneuvers a water bug would envy, yet his dexterity allayed any feeling of impending disaster. He was a maestro of the wheel as he weaved and passed slower traffic.

We traversed the Paseo de la Reforma, then entered Chapultepec Park for a short distance where the driver turned into a meandering tree-shaded drive. After about two hundred yards, we came upon a ten foot high iron fence. At this point two soldiers darted from a sentry box located inside the fenced area, slid the locking bar, then each leaned against the ponderous weight of the two filigreed iron gates. When the opening permitted, the chauffeur thrust the limousine deeper into the forest of tropical vegetation that grew to the edge of the drive. We had driven a full minute when a towering gray castle came into view. The structure was four stories high, presenting a formidable picture nestled in its wooded surroundings. Formidable yes, but beautiful in its awesome strength and durability. The drive formed a complete circle around the main building. Cedillo opened the glass panel and directed the driver to the game room entrance. He circled to the rear of the palace stopping before a canopied door.

Stepping out of the car, I stood drinking in the exotic beauty of our surroundings. The main house looked the same from both rear and front. A pond located between the castle and the multi-car garage at the rear drew my attention as a resident frog croaked his welcome. About a dozen pink flamingos expressed boredom by tucking their heads beneath their wings—one foot poised as if another step posed too much of a strain. As I watched, a musical offering was composed of a myriad of bird calls; each feathered performer puffed with confidence as though his song was the best on the bill.

I was entranced—gone were the problems of the morning—gone were the pungent, unique odors of the oil field —gone were the complexities of an unrequited love. At this moment my being was a vacuum, except for the euphoria generated by the surroundings. Surely I'd been projected into another world. The spell was broken when Juan spoke, "Do you feel alright, Hugh?"

"Fine! Fine! This has been the most peaceful moment of my life, and I suppose the beauty of it overwhelmed me. Excuse my curiosity when I ask, how old is the castle?"

"It was started in 1790, and completed in 1796. It was built during the reign of Charles IV, who was the king of Spain at that time. King Charles was my great, great-grandfather, my mother descended from the House of Bourbon." He laughed, then continued, "One might say I'm the true hybrid—my great-grandmother deviated from the path of royalty by marrying a basque ship's captain, who met death from the trigger fingers of a firing squad. He was found guilty of transporting materials of war to be used in the cause of installing Maxmillian as

Emperor of Mexico. It might interest you to know he was confined a prisoner for several days in the house you've leased in Tampico. In fact, it was there he faced the firing squad. So much for my family tree, let us go in."

Entering the game room I discovered the elegance of furnishings to be impressive as well as practical, with the exception of the wall to wall floor covering—solid white fur. Cedillo informed us the fur was polar bear.

We had a few highballs, then Juan asked Jim if he would like a game of pool. Jim answered, "Yes, I would. I've been admiring the beautiful table."

Juan summoned the butler and after a few words in Spanish, he removed a cue stick from the rack, then smiled and nodded to Jim indicating he select a stick. They had the game progressing when Juan suggested we go to his study for our discussion.

We rode an elevator to the second floor. Pressing a button, the door rolled silently into the wall revealing a view of a large room. We entered through a beautiful hand carved mahogany door. Juan indicated for me to go in. As I stepped into the room I faced a wall of leather bound books, filling shelves reaching from the floor to the ceiling. A thought flitted through my mind, "This is why he's so damned smart!"

Juan waved me to a massive leather chair, then rolled a duplicate one to a position facing me. "Now, Hugh, what's the problem?"

I summarized our projected production for the immediate future, then covered the problem of having nowhere to send it due to the refinery operating at maximum capacity. Thereby refusing any increase of oil we might want to put into line. "Do you have a solution?" asked Juan.

"I see two alternatives. We can extend the pipeline to the water front, install facilities for tanker loading, or build a refinery near the water front with loading docks. Whatever we do, we must move quickly."

"What do you recommend?"

"I suggest we secure land adjacent to our waterway property, award the contract for refinery construction—erect holding tanks at the refinery site—extend the pipeline to the holding tanks—build emergency dirt retaining dams for above ground storage until the holding tanks are ready, then pump the dirt tank oil into the pipeline."

"What kind of outlay are we facing?"

"Well, I've checked the cost of the Mata Redonda. It was built six years ago at a cost of five million, so I feel sure we could put a new plant with a Kellog cracking unit in operation for no more than six million. How does that sound?"

"Go, man go. We have no other choice. I can secure the land for us at my cost under the congressional magnet program for new industries."

My elation at Juan's concurrence of the suggestion, moved me to decline his invitation to remain overnight. I wanted to get back to Tampico for an early start the next morning. Jim flew me to Houston the next morning where I entered my office at eleven thirty to find Barbara very cheerful, gushing with questions about Tampico. After dispensing with the greeting and questions, I entered my private office with work on my mind. I called banker McMillan.

"Hello Hugh. How are things in Mexico? Good to hear from you."

"Everything is going better than anticipated Mr. McMillan, have you been near the hotel lately?"

"Yes, I was there yesterday—caught the architect, Smythe. He says several floors are ready for furnishing. You should contact him, I sensed he had his hand out for more finances."

"Speaking of finances I'll need some assistance in building a refinery at Tampico. Are you receptive to the project?"

"How receptive?"

"The area of one million."

"Why not? You know your business."

"Can you quote me a ball park figure of my cash reserve?"

"Yes I can. After conversing with Smythe, I came back to the bank and reviewed your status. Slightly over five million."

"Okay Mr. McMillian. Will you please set up a construction account of three million including the million I'm floating. This'll leave me three million in a liquid state to handle the hotel and miscellaneous. In the next few days there'll be an additional three million added to the construction account. Please handle it for me. I'd be obliged."

"Consider it done. Don't forget, contact Smythe."

Smythe requested permission to furbish my penthouse which I granted, at the same time admonishing him to avoid furniture bearing any remote resemblance to Early American or

Contemporary Italian. I bore an aversion to both. He followed by requesting I make a half million available for continued progress of the hotel. Having dealt with Smythe my actions were directed to the refinery.

Placing a call to Norfolk, Virginia to the construction firm of Rhome and Hester, specializing in chemical plants, power plants and refineries, I found myself connected with Hester. After identifying myself he interrupted me by saying, "Well, well Mr. Hugh McCulloch. I hope you've written your autobiography and calling to offer me a copy. I've often wondered if our paths would ever cross. What can I do for you?"

"I need a refinery at Tampico, are you interested?"

"You caught us at a good time Mr. McCulloch, we have just buttoned up a chemical plant at Texas City and are available."

"Good. Here it is. I need a thirty thousand barrel capacity facility with Kellog cracking unit."

"When do you want it?"

"I need it last month, but didn't know it, so sixty days from now will have to do. I'll give it to you at cost plus and I don't care how many men you put on it. Just have them jumping around the clock—seven days per week and put it on the line sixty days from starting date."

"Hell McCulloch, you could buy an ocean liner for what the overtime will run and sail away across the deep blue to some remote island and forget the rat race!"

"I don't give a damn about the overtime, just get it on the line in sixty days!"

"You've a deal. Cost plus ten. Okay?"

"Okay."

"We'll have our engineer there Monday, the 27th. He'll fly in from Houston. Meet him about noon and we'll build you a refinery."

"I'll be there. If you wish you can verify my financial capability by contacting Mr. McMillan, President of First Chemical National Bank in Houston."

"Don't need to, my secretary has checked you out with Dun and Bradstreet as we were talking. Looking forward to meeting you.

The ensuing call to Cedillo resulted in him agreeing to fly to Tampico the next morning when we would select the site for the refinery. The call also resulted in my composure being rocked when he asked if I could attend his wedding on Saturday, the 25th.

"It'll be a privilege," knowing I was losing a secretary made it difficult to sound casual as I asked, "Who's the lucky woman?"

"The ceremony will be held in the Metropolitan Cathedral here, at two thirty. I hope you'll forgive me for proselyting your secretary, who's honoring me with her eternal presence as my bride. Your pilot, Harris is also invited. If you tell me what time you'll arrive I'll have a car and driver awaiting your arrival at the airport."

"Congratulations, Juan. I regret losing Barbara, but I'm pleased you found each other, and the union will surely prove to be a happy one. I offer my blessing to both of you."

"I set up the refinery construction account here today with Chemical National Bank with a three million dollar credit line."

"That's good. I'll have an equal amount transferred from a London bank within the week to the account. We'll discuss it tomorrow. I should arrive in Tampico around eleven, see you then."

I walked to the outer office to congratulate Barbara, where I found her concentrating on a stack of statements. Without raising her head she asked, "How are things in Mexico?"

Moving around to face her I replied, "It seems a great event is scheduled for Saturday." Watching her reaction I followed up with, "Congratulations."

"He told you, didn't he? I was waiting for you to finish on the telephone then I intended to break the news, it's just as well. I feel guilty about leaving on such short notice, however a good friend who's an experienced secretary and receptionist, has agreed to leave her present employment to take my place. This of course will depend on your acceptance of her. I can call her now and have her come over for the interview, if you like."

"Call her, please."

The replacement arrived fifteen minutes later. After introductions she related her qualifications in an articulate, appealing manner as I studied her physical attributes.

Her name was Lydia Evans, she was about twenty-five. Her raven hair was coiffured in a style accenting the striking features of her face and especially her eyes, the color of blue glacial ice, exuded an effervescent warmth. She was pretty as a fantasy, dressed in a three piece knit suit, the color of ripe bananas. I was impressed with the casual, though methodical, manner in which she projected her assault. If I had possessed any mental requirements of what a secretary should offer, her five minute iconoclastic siege would have prevailed. I was sold on her in every way. I hired her on the spot.

Barbara would tutor her the balance of the week on my office procedure. I thanked her for coming and expressed my loss from Barbara's impending marriage, but stated my good fortune in finding a suitable replacement.

In the confine of my private office a review of Lydia occupied my thoughts. After recalling our dialogue of the past ten minutes, I was convinced she would prove to be a real find. She was all business as well as all woman, and would be an asset to me.

After completing business that required my presence, I made preparations for my return to Tampico. As I was leaving I stopped at Barbara's desk saying, "Barbara, if you ever need me, let it be known and I'll be there. I wish you much happiness for the years that lie ahead and I'm certain you'll like living in Mexico. Teach Lydia all you can. I'll see you at the wedding."

She arose from her desk holding both hands out to me palms down, as I grasped her hands in mine. She pulled me ever nearer, her eyes studying mine for something, searching for an unspoken word in my gaze. She must have received some message as she then placed both arms on my shoulders and planted a kiss softly on my lips. The kiss was sensitive as it produced a quizzical state within me. I was on the verge of pulling her body against mine when she backed quickly from me, her gaze holding fast to mine as she smiled and said, "Good luck, Hugh. Memories are the reward of living. See you Saturday!"

At the moment I was sure my countenance reflected the portrait of a long suffering Griselda, so I exited the office quickly.

♠ ♠ ♠

We arrived at Tampico late that afternoon where I found Ward anxiously awaiting my return. As we entered the office, Curly came around the desk saying, "God damn it, Hugh. With your permission I'm prepared to kick the ass if any labor official who shows up around our rigs in the future."

"Hold on Curly! What has aroused you now?"

"It's these damn crazy union rules. Today I was on the rig, Simpson is pushing, when some officious asshole rode up in a government car, then proceeded to talk down to me like I was a four year old. He reads the rules governing the ratio of foreigners to nationals to me while ignoring my pointing out I was not a member of the crew. But had stopped by in my supervisory duties. It really burned my ass having him give me a lecture on a subject which I'm well versed."

"Curly, I'm building an addition to our pipeline and a refinery in Tampico. Both start as soon as possible, therefore we'll eschew any and all confrontations with any piss ant connected with the government. In fact, we'll present an obsequious front on any discussion that may arise, at least until we get the refinery in operation."

"Hugh, I'll do whatever you say. Tell me what kind of front will we present? That word you used."

"Curly, in essence the word obsequious means we will kiss their ass if we have to in order to get enough workers to see this through. That's the way it'll have to be. Learn to live with it, Curly!"

"You can count on me! I won't do anything that might jeopardize our operations."

The past several weeks had resulted in my presence becoming known in the Tampico area. This sudden recognition having spawned from my employing a great number of workers in the construction of the pipeline, as well as hiring crews to operate the drilling rigs. As I drove to the office each morning, more and more of the inhabitants would wave—some would sound a greeting in Spanish. While others would offer a friendly smile. I had questioned Becker about my sudden rise to acclaim with the local gender; he, in turn, pointed out the fact that I had established a favorable rapport with my policy of paying a peso a day over the union scale. Besides, the Mexican people as a whole admired a hedonist, or at least anyone whose reputation was garnished with sagas of conquests of females. The workers were clamoring for a spot with Señor McCulloch.

While driving to the office this morning, several of the friendly natives called out "El Patron." This salutation bore the badge of respect, thus providing me a feeling of being needed and accepted. They were an appealing race, with the appeal of a Spanish puppy and I was liking it more each day.

I drove to the airport to ask Rivera to accompany me on my survey of prospective sites for the refinery, hoping to benefit from his knowledge of the area. After the usual acknowledgments I offered to return the car, then remarked Cedillo was arriving in the morning.

"You keep the car. Minister Cedillo instructed me to see that you had transportation for an unlimited time."

Rivera lifted one foot and began rubbing the dust from his shoe in an up and down motion on the back of his leg. After shining the toe, he switched, then polished the other shoe with the same motion on the back of his other leg. I found this both amusing and puzzling as he had always appeared spotless in his military greens, yet here he was shining his shoes on his trousers. He detected my smile saying, "Gotta have my shoes shining for Minister Cedillo."

"You may be shining them too soon, Señor. I'm hoping you can show me around the waterfront area this morning. I'm searching for a suitable spot to build a refinery. Will you go?"
"Yes, yes its my pleasure, shall we start now? We'll take the government car. I know a vacant area located on the Panuco river. I don't know the owner of the property, it could belong to the government."

While driving to the waterfront I pointed out my need for property affording water deep enough for tankers to load. Rivera responded, "This place is situated on the river."

"That is well and good, but how deep is it?"

"The river has been dredged to accommodate ships drawing up to twenty-five feet of draft. It's been dredged to a point about five miles inland."

"The hell you say! I wasn't aware the port was that extensive."

At the south tip of the town, we had passed the last of the docks and warehouses, when Rivera turned into a dirt lane leading to the river. The area was dense with reeds and palmetto that formed a solid wall of vegetation capsulizing the narrow lane we were following. Riviera stopped as we neared the river. "We'll park here."

I walked to the bank of the river and looked south where the narrow road followed the contour of the meandering stream, then disappeared around a bend in the river a half mile down.

Turning to Rivera I asked, "Is there any more industry from this point south?"

"No, the last warehouse we passed was the end of industry."

This is exactly what I want. Let's go back and find the owners of this property."

We drove back to the airport awaiting the arrival of Cedillo. The plane thumped the runway twenty minutes later. Exiting, Juan stretched his body as he beamed his devilish smile at me asking, "How is Mr. McCulloch this beautiful morning?" Holding out his hand in greeting, I shook it thinking he was a lot like a disturbed magnum of champagne, minus the cork! He was more effervescent than ever, probably induced by the wellspring of love. Whatever the source of his ebullience did not matter as his radiant appearance overwhelmed any presence near. When this man appeared he presented a force as demanding of attention as the changing of the guard at Buckingham Palace, and as colorful! This morning his apollo-like frame was draped in an exceptional navy blue pin stripe suit. His shirt made of shantung silk, was faint coral color, enhanced by a navy pin dot necktie. The silver mane adorning his head stood out in pleasing contrast to his clothing as we made our way to the car.

Cedillo was holding a small package in his hand as we entered the car. Rivera was driving and retraced our route to the prospective site of the refinery. After we were under way Juan handed me the package saying, "These are for you."

I removed the wrapping from the carton to reveal a box of Havana Coronas.

"This is thoughtful of you, Juan. Thank you very much."

"You seem to enjoy them and I've an unending supply, so I'll keep you in cigars."

When we arrived at the river site Cedillo stated, "This is suitable for your needs, is it?"

"Yes, it'll be an excellent site."

"That's good, This is government owned land and is available to you. How many hectares will you need?"

"Hectares! What's that?"

Cedillo chuckled, then answered, "A hectare is two and one half acres."

Calculating quickly I said," Twenty hectares."

Juan followed up with, "To be safe, I'll file a magnet claim for you for forty hectares—one hundred acres. Shall I make it ten acres river frontage and ten deep?"

"Great. That would provide for future expansion."

We drove back to the airport where Juan and I transferred to the car I had been using, then motored to the cafe where we selected an isolated table in a corner. After we had ordered, I sensed Cedillo wanted to say something, but was delaying while he gazed out the window. In a few moments he shifted his eyes to mine asking, "Hugh, I must ask you, are you certain you do not harbor any ill feeling toward me about marrying Barbara?"

"Absolutely! I think fate has been kind to both of you by bringing this marriage about. You'll be wonderful for her and she'll bring you much comfort, affection and honor. It has to be the perfect union—it will be. Jim and I'll fly in at noon. We are looking forward to a beautiful occurrence!"

"My car will be there for you."

I started telling him of my conversation with contractor Hester—how the advance engineers would arrive Monday to plot the refinery, and how we must immediately begin the construction of the extension of the pipeline and storage tanks. Then I opened a narrative of my thinking on the subject of our present producing wells, and wells of the future.

"Juan, we should sink around a half million in a reinjection system for our drilling tract. An oil well can be as powerful as a tropical storm or as dainty as the petals of african violets. If a well is permitted to flow too slowly or too fast you're opening the way for the entry of salt water —the death of oil wells. If we install gas reinjection, we can regulate the flow of wells and more important, extend the period of flow for an indefinite time, and avoid putting the wells on the pump. I've seen wells turn to salt water overnight due to choking them down or letting them flow freely too long. I'm suggesting we make the investment in gas reinjection.

"Hugh, as I told you in the beginning, you're the major domo. If you think we need the system, then install it. I'm with you on anything you suggest."

After seeing Cedillo off, I contacted the contractor who had built the pipeline. He was a prominent Mestizo having attained his financial position as a result of supplying labor supervision of projects for the petroleum industry. He assured me of the availability of tank builders, then we arranged a meeting. After our consultation he was eager to handle both, the tank building and pipeline construction, beginning the next day. This arrangement was to my liking as it permitted me the freedom of movement between Tampico and Houston.

Thursday morning the site of the refinery was teeming with workers fighting the morass of palmetto and reeds in their efforts to clear the area. There were mules straining into creaking harnesses hitched to fresnos and slips. Mexicans cursing the mules in Spanish, while a galaxy of birds swirled overhead protecting eviction from their nests with threatening swoops at the heads of workers. Their shrill calls were a cacophony of dissent at progress. Ten bulldozers were snorting and bellowing as they gouged the carpet of growth from its roots. I counted a hundred workers sweating and cursing their way through the morning all awaiting the signal for lunch—a time for tortillas and frijoles.

Friday afternoon the tank builders began erecting three, twenty-two thousand barrel storage tanks on the refinery site. The crew laying the pipeline numbered over fifty and they were now within a half mile of the storage tanks. Things were progressing swiftly—the workmen were giving their best efforts having been told it was a seven day work week, this meaning overtime pay. The pipeline contractor had been instructed to tie into the tanks as soon as possible and I was eagerly awaiting the arrival of the engineers from Rhome and Hester on Monday.

In the meanwhile I had a wedding to attend on the morrow in Mexico City so I drove out to the tract to locate Jim. He and Curly had become bosom friends since we had started this enterprise. Curly was teaching Jim the nuts and bolts of well drilling, as well as the technical aspects. Curly had informed me Jim was capable of supervising a rig anytime.

As I parked the car, both fellows came down from the derrick floor to meet me. Ten feet from where I was waiting Jim yelled out, "Hey Hugh, when are we going to the El Mundo? I've been telling Curly about it and you're looking at two guys ready to go."

"We're flying to Mexico City early tomorrow morning. I'm turning in early tonight. There's nothing to stop you from going to the El Mundo, if you wish."

Jim turned to Curly saying, "You fellers go ahead, just follow the road as I told you. I'll turn in early too, I don't like to fly with a hangover."

♠ ♠ ♠

We landed on time and while taxiing to the parking apron I could see Cedillo's driver standing beside the long black limousine awaiting our deplaning. The chauffeur drove us to the Alameda Hotel where Cedillo had engaged a suite of rooms to accommodate the participants and guests of the wedding. We went up to the fifth floor where we were welcomed by Señor Hector Alvarez, whom I learned was to serve as Juan's bestman.

A long table in the center of the room was laden with a fabulous array of gourmet foods, consisting of every conceivable hors d'oeuvres plus exotic entrees. Alvarez insisted we partake of whatever appealed to us, then pointed out the bar set up in the adjoining room where two bartenders were busily concocting drinks. He led us to a gentleman standing quietly at the end of the table surveying the twenty or more men enjoying the perquisites provided by our host.

Alvarez introduced this quiet man whose name was Pepe Garcia. Mr. Garcia addressed us in precise English saying, "Gentleman, I'm sure you must be ready for food and it will be my pleasure to identify the various dishes for you—as some are unique, especially to a North American.

We followed him as he made his way the length of the table pointing out and identifying epicurean adventures in dining, such as iguana en truffles, Madagascan boar with chestnuts, roasted cape buffalo, creamed rattlesnake, smoked sturgeon, baked testicles of young bulls, casserole of turtle eyes from the Comoros Islands, chateaubriand, cordon bleu, filet mignon and Alaskan salmon steak. "Take your choice, gentlemen." Jim and I selected the filet, salmon steak and stuffed shrimp, then sat in two huge chairs against the wall with a low coffee table upon which we set heaping plates. The food was exquisite and the chocolate mousse delectable! Pepe Garcia approached saying, "Señor Cedillo is graciously requesting the presence of Mr. McCulloch."

Entering an adjoining room, I found Juan pacing the floor, his brow furrowed from intense concentration.

"Sit down Hugh. Thank you for coming and giving me moral support for my wedding. Damn! The time draws near and my heart is filled with love for Barbara, but I find my usual aplomb escaping me by the moment. My mind being stuffed with possibilities of my not measuring up to the life ahead. Can you understand my state of confusion?"

He was looking at me as if hoping I could offer an instant panacea for his evident state of attrition.

"Juan your reaction is perfectly normal. All prospective grooms suffer a malaise and self-inflicted cross examination as their wedding draws near. Calm yourself and think of the wonderful future—a life with Barbara!"

He stopped pivoted quickly to face me, then blurted out, "I'm impotent!" He was a picture of dejection while I studied his impassive features as he awaited some response from me. The seconds ticked by as my thoughts centered on his surprising revelation. I thought, so this is his achilles heel, impotence! A fleeting picture of Barbara responding to my lovemaking with a veracious abandon—how would she receive Juan in their fulfillment of the act of mating, or rather the lack of it?

"Are you sure the condition is permanent?"

He turned looking out the window avoiding my gaze, then continued with his back to me. "Yes, after failing to respond to any excitation of the offerings of several females, my concern drove me to seek first, medical evaluation of the condition, then I followed up with' many hours on the psychiatrist's couch. I haven't experienced a satisfactory interlude with a woman since the death of my wife. The prognosis of all I've consulted is practically identical, they advanced the same ray of hope. Perhaps when I met the right woman my ability to perform might return. Each of those consulted invariably tossed in the term, "might return" and I'm in a state of confusion. Should I tell Barbara, or proceed with the marriage and hope for the best? If I should prove impotent with Barbara, then I'm guilty of a crime that might prove impossible to sell to my conscience. Please, Hugh give me some advice—what shall I do?"

Damn it, his agitated state presented a pitiful sight. Here was a man before me that had influenced my life, my demeanor, by appearing the prototype of all a man could aspire to, yet he stood before me now stripped of the infallibility that confidence and sophistication affords, and the scene was depressing. The inexorable pull of pity within me forced me to offer some advice that gave me a feeling of employing deceit, but I said, "Juan, everything will be alright. Any problem that might arise will be solved by the love and understanding of Barbara. Let's have a toast to the happy future for the two of you!"

He poured two generous shots of whiskey, we then raised our glasses and Juan's face once again was embellished by his captivating smile.

"Hugh, your presence here at this moment is an invaluable buttress for my sagging spirits and may God bless you in this life and all future lives. Your friendship is inestimable, may you always be near."

The wedding was enhanced with a fluidity and beauty serving to give the conviction that it was meant to be, and was right and proper.

During the ceremony while my eyes were scanning those in attendance, I discovered several attractive women scattered among the guests, busily dabbing away tears with crisp white handkerchiefs, I sensed some were tears of loss. Loss of an eligible Spanish stallion, Cedillo, who at the moment was being placed out of their reach by the holy bonds of matrimony! Little did they know that perhaps their loss was not as great as imagined!

The bride and groom boarded a plane for Rio De Janeiro, and we took off five minutes later for Tampico.

The end of February found me entangled in so many operations, in varied states of completion, my head was swirling with problems. These problems being presented by the refinery rearing from the banks of the Panuco river, construction of waterfront docks, installation of a gas reinjection system in the oil field, and final touches being added to the hotel in Houston.

The out flow of finances were staggering and I had thrown in all my cash reserve plus two million borrowed from my bank. Juan had never expressed any words that would indicate financial stress on his part and never questioned any expenditure suggested by me.

The problems confronting me at this time were involving the Labor Union of the Mexican workers on one hand, and rumblings of rumors the President of Mexico was pressing the

Congress to vote him carte blanche powers over all utilities in the nation, including expropriation of all foreign owned industry. The thrust of this request stemming from the innate doctrine or belief that all foreign interests were raping the Mexican resources. These rumors bore the ingredients of planned disaster for me and the oil companies operating in Mexico. I had sought the assurance of Cedillo on several occasions this would never happen and each time he soothed my jittery nerves by pointing out the government lacked the personnel who possessed the expertise to operate the petroleum industry, and this knowledge would cause restraint of expropriation. His words bore logic—this logic providing me surcease from worry.

The opening of my hotel was scheduled for April 15th. I'd make certain the hotel would open with much fanfare from saturated advertising. The firm employed had inserted notices of the gala date in all principal cities. Arrangements were made to fly five movie stars from Hollywood to add pizazz for the spectacular occasion. Just thinking of the notoriety the opening would provide me, served to nourish the vile juices of revenge coursing my veins. My rancid rancor for the press had never been dormant since they had literally ridden me out of Houston on the ignominious rump of a questionable reputation. A reputation riding on a character punctured with traits and foibles that invited critical comment. The press had not muted any of my escapades but had chosen to enlarge on them. This practice had contributed to the erosion of Audrey's respect for me, and right or wrong, it was my insatiable desire to wreak vengeance from a triumphant return to the scene of my defeat. A contest had been opened to the public for submitting proposed names for the hotel. It resulted in my selecting, from the thousands of entries the name, "Capri." The person submitting the winning name was rewarded a five hundred dollar check. The "Hotel Capri" would serve as my trojan horse in reentering the city as a respectable business man.

Chapter Sixteen
Expropriation And Exit

Jim and I were playing pinochle in the kitchen of the hacienda on the night of March 10th. We had the radio on a Mexico City station that featured the music of the big bands of the era and were enjoying the music and tequila, when the announcer broke in with a special news bulletin.

"Saturnino Cedillo, Minister of Resources was assassinated today while riding in his open car. The assassination occurred three miles west of Zocalo. Both the minister and driver were riddled with bullets and apparently died instantly. There are no suspects at the present time. Minister Cedillo was assassinated today near Zocalo. Now back to the music."

I threw my cards on the table, then hurried to the telephone to place a call to Barbara in Mexico City. After several attempts, the connection was completed and Barbara answered, "I know this is Hugh."

"Yes, I just heard the report. Would you like me to fly over tonight? I know you must feel like you need someone near you who is suffering the loss also."

"Hugh, I wish you would wait until morning as night flying is so dangerous. I'll be alright: I'll appreciate your coming, but please wait until morning."

"Okay, Jim and I'll leave around seven a.m. tomorrow morning. We should be in the city about ten thirty a.m."

"Thank you Hugh, I'll meet you at the airport. I wish to discuss some things with you regarding what I should do. I know you'll advise me wisely. Don't worry about me, I'll be alright. Until tomorrow, good night."

As our plane moved to the parking apron in Mexico City, I could see Cedillo's sedan parked nearby.

Upon reaching the car, I saw Barbara sitting passively in the rear seat. The chauffeur opened the door for my entry. As I settled into the seat Barbara leaned over and placed a friendly, platonic kiss on my cheek. The driver had closed the door quickly behind me then opened the front door for Jim. This action had likely been rearranged in order to assure a degree of privacy for us.

I looked into her eyes—eyes that were reflecting pain from loss. My impulse was to hold her close in an effort to comfort her, but I resisted the urge, then grasped her hand in mine saying, "We're both losers, Barbara. You've lost a gentle man who lived to make you happy, while sharing mutual love and devotion. I've lost one of the two friends I've had in this life. Juan had moved into my psyche as a brother, and that's in addition to his being my close associate. This dual influence has surely etched lasting memories within me and I'm grateful for having known him."

"Thank you Hugh, your expressing of sentiments for Juan serves as solace for my grief. I'm glad you're here!"

She was clutching my fingers in the manner a child frightened by the dark would hold their mother's hand as a shield against fear.

"I must talk to you in private Hugh."

The chauffeur was on the Reforma jousting with audacious, daring operators of vehicles of every type, all aiming their conveyance at any opening occurring in the Phalanx of moving, speeding wheels. I suggested we alight at Chapultepec Park for our conversation, directing the chauffeur and Jim to return for us in an hour.

We found an unoccupied bench a half block off the Reforma, under a canopy of stately oaks, where we sat down. Barbara asked, "Hugh, what shall I do about any money Juan had on deposit in the local bank?"

"Withdraw it today, as soon as possible."

"I really don't have any mercenary desire for anything. At the moment nothing matters with exception of finding someway to find a reason to keep on living. The loss of Juan has brought about my kismet."

"You'll find a reason to live. Remind yourself that nothing is permanent—life survives on change. What we have today will be effected by change resulting from time, tomorrow."

"Nothing is static as the cycle of life undergoing constant change. You'll find a reason to carry on. The mythical greek god, Morpheus gave civilization a tool to use for digging through the rubble of life's losses and disappointments. That tool is the facility to change the mind, the whole being, the human form as we struggle to survive this planet, the planet Earth. By exercising this philosophy we create the insulation to protect us from the jolts rendered by the changes of life. Have no fear Barbara, you'll find the way."

"Have you made the final arrangements regarding, Juan?"

"Yes, he's lying in state, in the Hall of Congress. Requiem Mass is tomorrow at ten a.m. in the Metropolitan Cathedral where we were married."

She stopped talking as her chin began quivering from emotion recalling her wedding, no doubt. Tears, the size of Ceylon pearls, were glistening as they coursed her pained face, each one filled with the brine of sorrow. As I looked at her I found her evident sorrow wracking and tearing my insides, yet the tear, suspended from the tip of her nose, appeared as something of beauty. It was a monument to the true devotion of a love gone ahead.

"Barbara, did Juan reveal the scope of his association with me to you?"

"No. The only comment he made was that he was working closely with you to help you succeed in the Mexico venture. Why do you ask?"

"He was an equal partner in all of my activities in Mexico. That makes you my partner now and I'm sure he'd be pleased to have you carry on. I'd be pleased to program the entire conglomeration for you when you're ready for it."

"Not now Hugh," she almost whispered the words.

"Barbara, after letting you off at home, would you permit your chauffeur to take Jim and me to the Hall of Congress where we can pay our respects to Juan?"

"If you've no objection I'd like to go with you. May I?"

This was a strong woman sitting beside me. I knew her heart and her whole being lay in the casket across the city beneath the cold, high ceiling of a government building, yet she had summoned the composure necessary to accompany me to view the physical body of the man who had offered and given each of us so very much.

"I certainly have no objection if you feel equal to it. I see our car, shall we go?"

We parked at the entrance of the massive structure, then forced our way through a great throng gathered around the portal. The majority of women were bearing the usual signs of grief, red rimmed eyes and revealing sad faces through their mantillas. The men, mostly dressed in black suits and white shirts, were standing quietly as if awaiting some word that Cedillo had arisen and vacated the casket. An official recognized Barbara, then escorted us through the long line of humanity snaking around the immense rotunda.

We moved in beside the open casket where Barbara immediately kneeled, knees on scarlet satin pillows, then gave the sign of the cross. In kneeling position her eyes were level with Juan's silent countenance, where she remained motionless while studying his features before her. Standing beside this man's body gave me a cold surge of feeling insignificant. In death he remained strong enough to look forceful even lying in repose. His face bore an effect of calm confidence, yet his handsome features still beamed the contagious compassion he had always granted those who passed his way, whether they were royalty or peasant, they were all recipients of his beneficence. Yes, he had passed my way and I had learned from him the importance of respecting the dignity of my fellow man. I knew I was a better man for having known him. Barbara arose giving me a smile as fleeting as the whisper of a bat's wings in the night.

"Shall we go?" she asked.

"Yes."

We made our way through the crowd, many of them giving Barbara a respectful nod of the head as she passed. I'm sure this act was in deference of their respect and admiration for Juan, he must have been a popular figure from the mass of people who had gathered to pay their respects.

After we were seated in the car, Barbara turned to me saying, "Why?"

A few moments of pondering her question, I responded with a question, "Why what, Barbara?"

"Why did they kill him?"

"I don't know, but I'd like to know. Let's go by the bank, I'll go in with you, if you wish."

The banker was cooperative in producing information pertaining to Juan's account, this prompted Barbara to request a cashiers check in the amount on deposit. He assured her the check would be delivered to her home by courier the next evening at seven o'clock.

Jim and I spent the night in the Alameda Hotel, then attended the Requiem Mass and final service the next day. After the burial rites, Barbara called me aside to tell me she had found a letter in the wall safe at home. The letter addressed to her was hand written by Cedillo, dated the date of their marriage. It contained instructions and information of things to do, and the way to carry them out. She felt Juan foresaw his untimely death when writing the letter, but he did not express any fear of it occurring.

Barbara directed the chauffeured limousine to take us to the airport where she convinced me my presence was more important in Tampico than remaining in Mexico City. She appeared to have her emotional loss of Juan controlled and agreed to call me when and if she needed my assistance. As we became airborne I saw her waving a handkerchief bidding us good-bye, as we were enveloped in a low floating cloud. We turned and headed for Tampico, we arrived at dusk.

Unlocking the office door the next morning, the phone began ringing. I crossed the room and answered it to hear Hester's jovial voice, "Mr. McCulloch, how do you like the progress on the refinery?"

"Wonderful, and I'll be glad when we can put it on the line. Keep up the good work. Why do you ask?"

"Well—it's time to shake the tree again, that twenty-four hour a day work schedule exhausts money faster than Congress gorging on appropriation funds. We have to tap you for another million to keep those Mexicans sweating."

They are not the only ones you have to sweat. I'll transfer it today. You keep the ball rolling as I'm accumulating quite a pond of oil waiting for completion of that job. The storage tanks are full and I'm selling the bulk of the production to coastwise tankers. I have twelve ground storage ponds and don't mind telling you if an inquiring bolt of lightning touched down on one of them, there would be hell to pay. The money will be available within the next thirty minutes. Anything else on your mind?"

"No, that's all, except I wish all our clients were as pleasant to work with as you've been."

"Mr. Hester, the imperative need for that refinery contributes greatly toward my pleasant attitude. Frankly I'm a bastard under normal circumstances. Keep it moving."

Terminating the conversation with Hester I immediately called my banker in Houston to transfer the million.

"Mr. McMillan, McCulloch here. I want you to transfer a million over to the refinery account. All the overtime gobbles funds like dropping fish in an oversize walrus, but speed in completion takes precedence over cost. I'm over a barrel until it's in operation."

"One moment, Hugh," this was followed by a shuffling of papers, the sound emitting clearly from the receiver, "I'll shift it at once. Let me apprise you of the state of the construction account. After the million shift, the balance will be one hundred fifty thousand."

"I may have to get more from the bank before completion. I can give you a second mortgage on the hotel for collateral," he interrupted me with, "Mr. McCulloch, our bank never enters any financial transaction involving a second mortgage, and for a very good reason. The courts in Texas view a second mortgage as valuable as a three dollar bill. However when your need arises, if it does, we can probably work out something in addition to the existing two million loan. Good luck!"

I dropped the receiver, then placed my hands behind my head and leaned back in the swivel chair, letting my eyes come to rest on the ceiling. I reviewed the conversation with the banker. The austere tone of voice he had shifted to, when addressing me as Mr. McCulloch, created a sudden apprehension—something akin to the first belch of smoke signalling the awakening of a somnolent volcano. He had hoisted a storm flag of concern with his narration on second mortgages. Suddenly I realized the tenuous strand dangling me over the maw of catastrophe could part at anytime. If I expected to get additional funds I had better go for them before they were needed.

The aphorism of nailing bankers when you did not need the money was annealed in the crucible of truth. If one hesitated until more money became a necessity, then the bank's refusal of assistance become a certainty. I made a mental note not to follow up on McMillan's suggestion tomorrow or the following day. He must get my request for additional funding before my account reached a zero balance.

♦ ♦ ♦

Soon after my arrival at the drill tract, Curly drove his truck alongside the car where I sat observing the activity. He came over to me, pushing a paper before my eyes saying, "Take a look at this, Hugh."

I took the sheet from him discovering it contained what appeared to be a test. The paper had twenty sentences printed in Spanish with spaces between each sentence, apparently providing space for written answers.

"Sorry Curly, my Spanish is nonexistent, What is it?"

"Humberto Galvan, Simpson's lead man, was given the paper at the union meeting last night as was everyone in attendance. They are to fill them out and return them within forty-eight hours. Come along, we'll have Humberto translate it for us."

The questionnaire was designed for the purpose of rating the individual qualifications of the union members.

Curly and I stood looking at each other after Humberto had returned to work, Curly spoke, "Well, what do you think is behind it?"

"Damned if I know. It could signify the union is adding the information gleaned, to their arsenal of overblown reasons directed at demands for wage increases. It could result in many things and for the present, I'm dismissing it from my mind. I'll see you later."

The next morning Jim flew me to Houston, where I made a pleasant discovery. My secretary, Lydia, had handled all matters crossing her desk in an efficient manner during my absence, thus reducing the time necessary to dispense with things requiring my attention. After clearing my desk I was ready for a confrontation with banker McMillan for the purpose of floating another million dollar loan to be added to the existing loan of two million.

He gave me a cordial greeting, then in a booming voice blurted, "Sit there Hugh," pointing to a huge leather covered chair situated in front of his massive desk." What can I do for you?"

" I'm in the stretch run and need another million to finish in the money. What can we work out?"

"Hugh, I realize you've gambled big in the Mexico operations and stand to reap a handsome reward for your efforts and money. There is an ugly prospect lurking in the back ground capable of nullifying both your efforts and investments. That being the ogre of expropriation if the Mexican government should decide it would be advantageous to nationalize industry."

"We've heard rumbling of disquiet among the hegemony of Mexico. They accuse foreign operators of squandering their resources and create concern through the banking industry with veiled threats of the take over of industry. If that should come about after I had extended your account another million, I've no doubt this bank would announce a new president! In all fairness I must decline your request for reasons of lack of collateral. I'm sorry."

"Look Mr. McMillian! I have forty-four producing wells in the Clarkwood area west of Corpus Christi. I'll offer the production of these wells as collateral."

"Hugh, you have forty-three producing there. One began flowing salt water two days ago. How do I know this? I anticipated your request for additional funding and took the liberty of sending a loan analyst down to assess your potential. However, one well will not deter our progress in reaching an accord. I'll okay the added million with a lien on the entire production of the Clarkwood field. Is that satisfactory?"

My brain reeled as I considered the enormity of debt I was accumulating and reeled also while I realized how close I was to attaining monolithic financial power upon completion of the refinery, too close to the brass ring to permit a mere million dollars to grind my dream into dust.

"That's an amicable proposal Mr. McMillan. I'll go for it."

The rest of the day was used in touring my hotel from parking lot to penthouse. The beauty of the edifice and the appealing decor served as a balm for my elevated concern over my tremendous debt. The structure seemed animated, no doubt due to the total determination exercised by me to make it a reality. It was the epitome of all my dreams of self-reliance. Dreams created as a result of being evicted from many hotels for many reasons. An obsession to live a life of my own choosing, in my own surroundings, had fanned the flaming determination to build this structure. It was here around me, and it was alive.

The penthouse was a place for breathtaking beauty. As I entered, my ego soared, while I pictured my future life in these surroundings. Smythe had succeeded in creating an aura of mystique with the utilization of mirrors, controlled variegated lighting, and color combinations, all contributed to my intoxication of the moment.

I went through the penthouse trying to view it with a critical eye and found it impossible to find anything I did not like. It was complete—it had everything. No! It did not have everything. There wasn't an Audrey! I flopped on the great bed in the master bedroom and looked at the ceiling. The bed comfort gave illusion of floating on a cirrus cloud. My eye caught sight of the panel near the head of the bed. It contained several toggle switches, each identified by tabs. Selecting the one labelled meditation, I flipped it and turned on my back gazing at the ceiling. The oyster white surface began a transformation. The color was changing in a fluid manner to sky blue—I watched the subtle change progress to the blue-black of the night sky. I was completely relaxed and planet earth was lost in space. I was floating on the cloud observing the night sky when the milky way appeared, followed by the faint glow of the constellation Ursa Major "Great Bear". I don't know how long I was mesmerized. I do know, for the first time in my life, my physical self was totally at rest, and my spirit was on a voyage that brought me absolute tranquility.

I awoke at eleven p.m., astonished I had been out for ten hours! The ceiling had reverted to sky blue during my interlude of deep meditation. As I arose from the bed I reminded myself to congratulate Smythe on his success with controlled effects!

♠ ♠ ♠

We returned to Tampico the following morning where Colonel Rivera awaited my arrival. He intercepted us as we headed for the terminal by saying, "Mr. McCulloch, could I talk with you for a moment?" His voice carried a tone of urgency.

"Certainly, what's on your mind?"

He cast furtive glances to determine no one else was within hearing range, then using an effected stage whisper said, "The rumor is, the government is preparing to seize all foreign owned industry. Have you heard it?"

"Colonel, that rumor has floated around for a year and so far that's all it has been, a rumor."

He picked up his pace beside me continuing, "I certainly hope they don't. It'll put a lot of men out of work due to the government not having people qualified to continue the operations. Persons like you are nice to us and it should not happen."

"Thank you Colonel, perhaps it will not occur." He followed us through the terminal to our parked car. Before entering the auto I turned to Rivera and asked, "Do you know why Minister Cedillo was killed?"

"Madre de Dios! I don't know why! He was admired by all who knew him. I think he was ambushed by order of some foreign power. Maybe some government paid to have him killed, who knows. It was a senseless murder and one that has created much sorrow and anger in my country. He was loved by all, married less than a month. People who have seen his new wife say she is a genteel lady and very pretty. Now she is a pretty widow. Did you see her on any trip to the city?"

"Yes, I can tell you she is a very pretty lady. Crank it up Jim. I'll see you around, Colonel."

We left a small cloud of dust settling on the Colonel as we started for the hacienda.

Alicia met us at the door to tell me Señora Cedillo had called requesting I contact her when I arrived. Closing the door behind me, I placed a call to Barbara. Answering the phone she said, "I know this is Hugh."

"Your E.S.P. is active, Barbara. Can I help you?"

"Hugh, I've received an official government request to vacate our home by the 20th, that's only four days away. What should I do?"

"Barbara, you don't have a choice. You'll have to abide by the request. We are aliens here, and as such have no legal redress in matters involving the government. I'm sorry you have to give up your home."

"I won't suffer any pangs of loss vacating it with Juan having gone. The place is charged with memories of the hours I shared with him here. His strong presence remains affording me both pleasant and painful recall. The memories of the tender touches we shared, gave, and received are pleasing to hold, yet the permanent void he left behind is painful to bear. I think I should leave this house of loneliness just carrying my happy memories with me—leaving the void behind."

"I think you're right Barbara. Would my being there be of any help?"

"No, the bank delivered the cashier's check, and Juan left me legal access as executor of an unknown sum of deposit with the Bank of London. I'll pack my clothing in the Auburn tomorrow and return to Houston to begin anew."

"Would you like me to accompany you? If so, I'll fly over tomorrow morning and drive you to Houston."

"No, no. I'll be alright. I'll call you the day after tomorrow when I arrive. Thank you for your advice and support. Good night."

I fell asleep thinking of Barbara's apparent strength in accepting the loss of Juan as a force majeure; she was worthy of a more lasting happiness.

♠ ♠ ♠

The next morning I stopped in for a chat with Becker. He started talking with evident enthusiasm, "Mr. McCulloch, I've been out to see how your refinery was shaping up, and I'm amazed at the progress. There must be two hundred men working, when do they plan on completion?"

"Perhaps another month." He leaned forward while looking me in the eye, then asked, "Have you heard anything recently about expropriation?"

"No. Just a rumor here and there."

"There must be some basis for the rumor, it brought the big mogul of Gulf down here yesterday. He stayed around most of the day asking questions and keening the wind like an overgrown pointer seeking a pheasant. He was kind of pissed-off at me because I couldn't add anything to what he'd heard."

"Did he offer any comment on anything he picked up?"

"Hell no! I drove him back to the airport, and he was as quiet as a sleeping oyster. But man it would sure play hell for an independent like you, if it does happen, wouldn't it?" I arose saying 'right'. Let's hope it's a rumor, and not fact."

Becker followed me to the door where he clutched my sleeve, then asked, "Mr. McCulloch, do you suppose the killing of Minister Cedillo is tied in with the rumors floating around?"

"I've no idea, Tri-con. Only time will tell."

I drove away pondering the merit of Becker's parting question. Was there a correlation of the rumors and Juan's ambush? My concentration was directed in this vein, the remainder of the day. Darkness came while my mind continued to grope for some tie between Juan's death and the persistent rumors.

After dinner Jim and I opened a quart of tequila—produced the playing cards—then began draw poker at the kitchen table. The radio was tuned to our favorite station, offering the music of the big bands. At nine o'clock the announcer caught our attention by repeating three times, "Señor and Señoras, El Presidente Lazaro Cardenas."

We laid our cards on the table listening to the words of President Cardenas. He started speaking Spanish and delivered his words in a staccato burst of oratory, lasting about five minutes. We sat there without any idea of what he was saying. His words were followed by thunderous applause, this delaying the continuation of his spirited delivery. After about ten minutes of uninterrupted cheer, the president started his speech again, this time in English. He resumed with,

"This declaration of expropriation effective twelve o'clock, midnight this date of March 18th, 1938. Expropriation will include all foreign owned industry dealing with petroleum in any form. The Mexican government will retain all properties—all equipment—all funds now on deposit in Mexico banks. The petroleum industry will be operated by Mexican nationals; henceforth known as Petroleum Mexicanos. The government takes this action with much regret, though the regret is out weighed by the necessity of preserving our dwindling resources of petroleum. All owners, supervisors and personnel of foreign operators will be required to depart Mexico within forty-eight hours of implementation of this declaration, March 20th, 1938, twelve a.m. All investors effected by this proclamation should file a writ of right, setting forth the value of relinquished monies, equipment, and properties. This writ to be filed within sixty days. This will enable our government to follow with restitution in the form of promissory notes in the amount agreed upon losses suffered as a result of this action I am taking tonight. We place ourselves on a high legal and moral plane so that our country may be great and respected. So I say to you, who are effected by expropriation, have no fear of loss, you'll be reimbursed, Good night!"

Jim was looking at me with questioning eyes. Several moments passed, then he exclaimed, "The thieving bastards. Can they get by with this, Hugh?"

My head seemed to contain a kaleidoscope wheeling and tumbling, showing oil derricks, miles of pipes, the hotel, the refinery, all were spinning in a vortex fading to nothingness. I was away from reality. The mental picture was changing back to normal when I said, "Deal the cards!"

Jim was surprised at my feigned poise and expressed it with, "You're some gambler, Hugh McCulloch!"

He did not refer to my misfortune again, even though we played poker until the last shot of tequila was consumed at one a.m.

We retired without comment on the Cardenas speech, but sleep wouldn't come to me. I laid in the darkness awake, my head in a roar from a state of confusion, the uncertainty of the future engulfed me. Where and how, would I recoup the financial loss suffered here?

The enormity of the loss produced a crushing impact on my self-confidence and plans for the future. Was I capable of staging a comeback? The influence and material assistance Justin Brent had given me, had contributed greatly to meteoric rise in the field of petroleum. If I succeeded in escaping from the pit of financial chaos, it would be accomplished without the influence of Justin this time.

The face to face confrontation with defeat of all my dreams of power from wealth would be a bitter experience. In the still of this night, I needed the presence of Audrey so very much. Her warmth would chase the chill of despair and her word of encouragement would booster my sagging self-confidence.

♦ ♦ ♦

Dawn came before sleep, and I arose to start the long journey back to a secure financial position. I drove to the producing wells where I was confronted by a score of federal troops burdened with backpacks, and bearing rifles with fixed bayonets.

As I turned the car onto the road traversing our drilling tract, the soldiers immediately formed in battle array directly across my intended path. An officer stepped forward to inform me in broken English,

"No one is permitted on this property."

I realized any argument was futile so turning the car around, I drove to Tampico.

Enroute I passed dozens of army trucks all loaded with armed troops. The Tampico streets were clogged with military vehicles and were peppered with soldiers in pairs; all bearing rifles slung across their shoulders.

The entire refinery site was surrounded with scores of troops. Surely this massing of military might was a show of symbolism, and not due to any anticipated resistance on the part of foreigners.

At the hacienda I found Jim eating breakfast.

"Jim, the Mexico operation is finished. I've been to the drilling site and refinery. Both are teeming with soldiers. We must find the whereabouts of Curly and the others. They're not on location. I expect to find them jailed. After breakfast we'll load our clothing in the car, go into town to locate the men and get out of here as soon as possible."

"Suits me. I don't like being around trigger happy soldiers."

I told Alicia she was free to leave at any time. We loaded our belongings in the car, then sought out the Tampico jail. The officer-in-charge confirmed the accuracy of my guess by telling me the men had been confined because they had resisted federal troops. Curly defined their "resistance" as refusing to be pushed from the derrick floor like reluctant cattle, at bayonet point.

After much dialogue exchanged between the officer and myself that neither of us understood, I produced the most efficient interpreter—money, in the form of a fifty dollar bill. He fastened his eye on the bill, then pulled it from my fingers as he barked some words in Spanish to a subordinate. The soldier quickly unlocked the cell door throwing it open. My crew filed out of the cage as Simpson asked, "Hugh, what's next?"

"Breakfast for you men, then it's off we go. We are ordered out of Mexico."

Colonel Rivera met me as we entered the terminal building,

"Mr. MCulloch, I'm truly regretful about what is happening here. The oil people have been a blessing to our country and a lot of my people will suffer due to loss of work. I must tell you, you've been a source of pleasure by my contact with you. I wish you didn't have to leave."

"I understand, Colonel. We regret the actions of your government, just as you do. I've left the car you've let me use, parked out front. I appreciate your association, the help you've given me—this will express my thanks."

I tucked a hundred dollar bill into his shirt pocket, "Goodbye and good luck. Thanks again!"

We left him standing there as we started to the plane.

We began to taxi for the runway, when I looked toward the terminal. The Colonel had walked outside to see our takeoff. As he stood, I saw him remove the bill from his pocket, look at it, then start waving a renewed farewell, he was still waving as Jim banked the plane. The Colonel faded into oblivion.

Enroute to Corpus Christi I invited each of the men to visit the hotel anytime after April 15th, where they would receive a weeks lodging, free food and drink. The invitation was tendered to express my gratitude for their service in Mexico.

Curly asked, "Does that invitation include our wives?"

"Did any of you get married in Mexico?" Silence prevailed, no one answered.

"So, no one was married in Mexico? Then I must be talking to a group of single men! I'll extend the invitation to include one accomplice for each of you. Is that more to your liking."

They whooped and jollied as they expressed their delight at my offer, creating a din similar to that of a dog kennel at feeding time.

Curly and the men deplaned at Corpus Christi, where I beckoned Curly aside to tell him to find a place for these men until the lease was exhausted, even though it would mean laying off some who remained in the Clarkwood field.

Jim and I touched down at the Houston airport at four o'clock, where Jim taxied the plane into the hangar. We unloaded our possessions, then as we stood beside the car I said, "Jim, I want you to know my intentions regarding the future. Due to spacing regulations, the Clarkwood drilling is near completion. At this time I haven't any other leases or options on leases to develop. As you know the opening of my hotel is set for the 15th of April. I have a penthouse atop the hotel ready for occupancy. If you wish, you may move into the first room available, which I'm sure is ready now.

"I intend to retain your services as long as you wish to work for me, I hope you'll stay on as there is a probability I'll venture into wildcatting in Venezuela. If I do, the agreement will have to be one that contains a safeguard against any repetition of what just occurred in Mexico. In the interim, when we're not flying, you can help with the opening of the hotel. Meet me there tomorrow morning at ten."

Lydia had left for the day when I arrived at the office. My desk had two neat stacks of correspondence awaiting my attention, plus several notations of incoming calls.

I riffled the telephone memos and found one from Audrey McCulloch, requesting the call be returned. While studying the memo, I found myself trying to guess her motive in calling me.

"Brent residence," Audrey answered.

The blood was pulsating in my temples and I was exerting much effort to erase any croak in my voice before talking. The sound of her voice dissipated any trace of sophistication in me.

"Audrey, I'm returning your call." When I uttered this opening, it had come out as redundant—the statement of a jackass. The sound of her voice had not let my brain synchronize with my voice. I made a new start.

"Audrey, I'm sorry I was out when you called, I hope there isn't anything wrong."

"No, Hugh. I wanted to discuss your unfortunate experience in Mexico. You have my concern about your losses. I had read accounts of your varied investments and I feel sure you had suffered severe financial loss as a result of the expropriation."

"The loss is great enough to have wiped me out. I want you to know it means a great deal to me to have your concern and sympathy. But I'll rise from the ashes of failure just as the Phoenix arose and started anew. I'll not let this reversal stifle my ambition."

"I'm glad to hear you talk that way. I remarked to dad when we heard the news, Hugh would not quit, ever. He agreed, you were too much of a fighter to let it break your spirit."

"How is Justin's health?"

He's walking a tight rope from day to day, never knowing when his heart will give up the fight. He never complains, just maintains a cheerful attitude in spite of his condition.

"Hugh, please forgive me for this probing question, do you still control the new hotel? I ask it only because of my interest in your well being."

"Yes, the opening date will be the 15th of April and I extend to both of you an invitation to attend the ceremony. You would enjoy it I'm sure. There'll be a dance in the main ballroom opening night, with the flowing music of Jan Garber, also the presence of three major movie stars. I'll send a car for you, with Hugh McCulloch driving, if you and Justin will accept."

"I must decline for Justin, as for me—I must consider the invitation a few days before acceptance or rejection. There are many facets of our past association to be considered as well as Justin's view on the matter. I cannot pursue any action that might tend to regress his condition, and I'm sure you understand my delay in giving you an answer. Your invitation is rather sudden."

"Yes I understand. Will you have dinner with me tomorrow evening?"

The next few moments were filled with silence. A silence so deep I felt I was connected with a constellation twinkling from a galaxy.

She gave a deep throaty chuckle, then, "Hugh, you keep pushing don't you. Yes, I'll have dinner with you."

"Eight o'clock. Thank you for being concerned enough to call. It means a lot to me."

After cradling the receiver I attacked the stack of correspondence with a positive attitude. One hour later, having disposed of the last item, I swiveled my chair to face Audrey's portrait. I caught her giving me a faint smile, one that I returned saying, "You're smiling because of the happiness your call gave me. I wish I could thank you for the many dreams of consolation you've provided me. Just having you as my wife has given me towering inspiration, that was necessary in converting me from an automation powered by a source of greed, insatiable ambition and egotism. Now I know the importance of the consideration for the feelings of others—the nebulous comfort provided with the vapor of wealth. Yes, Audrey these are intrinsic values your influence has given me. I need your daily presence to keep them alive and thriving. Please believe, I'm no longer the same man that trampled your dreams of a happy lasting marriage. Your absence has been an iconoclastic teacher. Come back to my side, come back!"

If anyone had heard me talking to her portrait, surely they would have insisted that I be committed to a padded cell. They could not know the soaring happiness engulfing me at this time, happiness due to Audrey's acceptance of my invitation to dinner.

I began to interrogate my self-control. I left the office thirty minutes later, still questioning my ability at stemming the tide of remorse surging within me. Tomorrow's dinner with Audrey must find me projecting myself in the most attractive manner possible, not the self-centered boor she had divorced.

Entering the lobby of the Rice Hotel intending to vacate my room, I was slowed by the sight of an acquaintance slouched on one of the huge leather chairs. He acknowledged my presence with a big smile, then motioned me to come over. I had not seen this man for a year, and I had a mental struggle trying to recall his name. He arose, holding out his hand, two steps from him, his name came to me. "Harry Mumphery, you old goat, it's nice to see you again."

"Same here, Hugh. I hear you've been down in Mexico."

"Just returned this afternoon. Anything going on around here?"

"Some action starting at eight—room 815."

"Fine, I'm in the mood," glancing at my watch I said, "We have an hour, come have dinner with me."

"Thanks, Hugh, but I've already eaten. You go while I study the racing form."

As I awaited my selection of dinner, I was thinking of the easy carefree life Mumphrey coasted through. He was about forty, always groomed to perfection, over six feet, slender as spaghetti, with a head fronting the face of a cherub. He could survey one with his cobalt blue eyes, never showing a trace of emotion. He could study a person in such an intent manner, his features bore the unflinching stare of a cadaver. It was not uncommon when he held the financial fate of a man within his grasp. He could produce both delight and despair with a flip of the wrist.

Harry Mumphery was a professional card dealer. He had been dealing high rolling games for ten years, and was known to be the best in the business. He never participated in the poker games, he served only as dealer, banker and referee while removing five percent of every pot. This percent provided him an above average income, affording him an enviable status in the community. Saturday was his night off, permitting him a good night's sleep to assist in preparing for Sunday.

He occupied a seat on the board of deacons for a local church and passed the collection plate at the Sunday services. He contributed ten percent of his earnings of the previous week.

The pastor naturally regarded Harry as a pillar of consecration as did the congregation, this arrangement provided solace for all concerned. Harry was salving his conscience while the church received a handsome gratuity.

The game started on time. Harry shuffled the cards with the calm, deliberate motion of the professional while I reminded myself this was the first poker game I had engaged in due to necessity. I had always played to experience the gamut of emotions poker provide me; this time I had need of a substantial winning.

Five hours and many hands later, my losses were over fifty-thousand dollars. I was dealt aces and jacks the next hand, opening the betting with a two-thousand bet, which was raised two times before Harry cast his cold, blue eyes on me and asked, "You staying?"

I spaced out twenty-five thousand in chips, pushing them to the center of the table. Harry droned, "The pot is right, cards?"

"One."

He flipped me a card face down, then looked questionably at the first raise.

"Two."

Two cards flashed across the pile of chips to land directly atop those the third player had retained.

The remaining player said in a quiet modulated voice,

"Two, please."

The dealer flipped two cards to the player, then looked at me. I peeked at the last card dealt to me and discovered I had filled up with another ace.

"The bet is still two thousand," I was pushing the chips out thinking, "Boy! I'll sandbag them this time."

I sat back in my chair to study the reaction of the two players.

The next bettor remarked, "I didn't get in this pot by calling, I'll raise you twenty-five thousand."

The last bettor called and raised another twenty-five thousand. Harry looked at me, I peeked at the full house, added fifty thousand to the pot—then waited until the bettor to my left called the raise. I flipped the cards face up saying.

"Aces full over jacks."

Upon seeing my cards the first raise tossed his hand into the discards with a look of resignation. The player, who kicked the bet twice gave me a smile likened to one a mortician might cast on some miserable soul seeking a way out with Russian roulette.

He turned up four kings, as my stomach turned-up a well of bitter bile within! My luck was nonexistent. The time had come for parting from this game!

"Harry, tally up my markers, please."

I left the game a loser by one-hundred-thirty thousand.

I found sleep by consoling myself with the pleasant response Audrey had given my invitation to dinner. The possibility of regaining her respect gave me a refreshing exhilaration as I greeted the new day. The morning found me anticipating the eight p.m. dinner date with her, this excitement serving as a sedation for my sizable loss of the night before.

I vacated my room in the hotel after loading my possessions into the Cord, then drove to my penthouse! The Cord rolled to a stop in front of the main entrance of the Capri!

The entrance offered an air of welcome, enhanced by the unique foyer; the brain child of Smythe. I sat savoring the pleasant effects the entry provided, studying the murals covering the walls. The artist from Mexico City had enjoyed a month long stay on the Isle of Capri at my expense, the visit suggested by Smythe the architect.

The artist had a photographic mind, plus the rare talent of transferring mental scenes to an inanimate surface via the artists brush. The results were astounding. The stark realism of the Faraglioni Rocks towering high above the shimmering blue coastal waters provided the viewer the pungent scent of marine life, as well as the imaginary screech of the gulls pictured wheeling over and around the realistic rocks.

This was my first view of this impressive artistry. Truly the artist had brought a portion of the tranquil, exquisite isle to my hotel and planted it in the entry for all to see! Jim interrupted my admiration, "Hugh, I've been here thirty minutes studying these murals; they're truly the results of a master!"

"They certainly offer a dramatic effect. Let's go and locate a room of your preference, then I'll take you through the penthouse."

After finding Jim a room to his liking, we toured the hotel. He assisted with my occupancy of the penthouse where we discovered a well-stocked bar. Smythe was thorough in his planning, leaving nothing to be desired.

Workmen were scurrying around the site, the bustle being a race against time. We encountered Smythe in the main lobby.

"What do you think of her, Mr. McCulloch?"

"Beautiful and impressive, you've succeeded in producing exactly what I had in mind the day we met in McMillan's office. Congratulations for accomplishing the impossible!'

"Thank you. I'd like to discuss a matter with you when you have the time."

I nodded to Jim, indicating Smythe and I desired privacy. Jim left saying, "See you later."

I turned to Smythe saying, "Any problems?"

"No, none, except the perpetual problem of funding. I was running a trial total of projected expenses before I left the office, expenses necessary to wrap it up plus money required to carry out the extravaganza scheduled for the official opening; it will entail between three and four-hundred thousand more."

"Okay, let's not dilute the impact of our planned opening with trying to shave a few bucks. Hell! I'm like the rabbit scampering for the briar patch, I have to make it! The money will be available today. Don't let anything stand in the way of executing every plan we have made." With that I left, driving to my office.

Upon entering, Lydia greeted me in an enthusiastic manner, "It's good to see you Mr. McCulloch. I'm sorry about the turn of events in Mexico, she paused apparently awaiting a comment from me.

"Yes Lydia, it's a crushing turn of events, but I intend to survive. I came in late yesterday but took care of the calls and correspondence. I like the way you classify your work."

"Thank you, you had a call about fifteen minutes ago from Barbara. She had just driven in from Mexico. She wants you to call. She's at her mothers."

"Please get her for me." I went to my office, closed the door—a few seconds later the call came through.

"Hugh, I drove in about an hour ago, the first thing on my mind was calling you to let you know I'd made the trip safely."

"Did you have any difficulty with the Mexican officials?"

"None whatsoever."

"That's good. What are your plans?"

"I intend to go back to work as soon as possible."

"I would like to have you back here, though it wouldn't be right to dismiss Lydia. Perhaps I can find you a place in the bank if you think the work would appeal to you."

"I'd like that. Why don't you call me, maybe we could have dinner some evening."

"Great I'll call you soon. I'm glad you're back."

As I leaned back a review of the words between Barbara and me, filled my thoughts, a feeling hard to define. My conscience entered my musing, reminding me of my sordid behavior—so repugnant it dissolved my marriage.

I made a silent vow to avoid seeing Barbara since the chance of a reconciliation with Audrey had emerged. The acute pain of losing Audrey was with me still, and I was undertaking a crusade to secure her love and respect once more. This goal didn't leave any room for mistakes; mistakes like stumbling into a situation involving another woman. If another chance to grab the golden ring of happiness came my way, I'd surely be conditioned to snatch it on the fly! I promised myself a life of denial, the denial of partaking of any female perquisites as long as Audrey could be reached.

♠ ♠ ♠

I rang the doorbell at eight sharp. Audrey came out closing the door behind her. She was smiling as she held out her hand to me, "Right on time," she remarked as she clutched my arm while steering me off the porch.

Damn! I was hoping she would ask me in for a few minutes, I wanted to see Justin. The quick closing of the door, coupled with our hasty departure, told me it was planned. Someone didn't want me in the house, who?

We spent the evening dining and dancing atop the Rice Hotel. While conversing between dances she asked me, "Hugh, have you been tempted to remarry?"

I looked her in the eye, "Yes, constantly."

"My! That was a quick answer! Do I know her, your secretary?"

I knew she was thinking of Barbara, so I made haste to dispel the fallacy.

"You know her—she's not my secretary. She happens to be you. Tell me, have you considered marriage?"

"I"ll put it this way. I would consider it if the right man offered himself at the right time. The right time can not arise as long as dad is so dependent on me, and possibly other restraints would have to be considered."

"I'm the right man," I was getting bolder.

"Perhaps. You were at one time—no doubt about it. Maybe you can become the right man again, only time will tell!"

"I wanted to talk with Justin when I came for you tonight. Why did you hustle me off so quickly?"

"Dad had asked me to keep you out. Don't be offended. He'll have to make the decision when he wants to see you. We can't push it. He doesn't like you. He bears no ill will toward you but he's hurt over your cavalier attitude and your disdain of the tenets he considers to be the criteria of human behavior. Many times he's expressed an opinion of your good points. He believes you need to be polished with the abrasive action the mistakes we make in life provide. Do you intend to devote full time to the operation of the hotel?"

"For awhile, then perhaps I'll get into a deal with the government of Venezuela if it can be worked out. The expropriation in Mexico has taken all my reserves. The hotel and four rigs represent the only liquid assets I have.

"I'll rise again—you can rely on it. Maybe I'll fly to Venezuela, before the opening of the hotel, to sound out the possibilities there. They've made two offers permitting me the exploration of government owned land. It merits consideration."

While bidding Audrey good night at her door, I sensed her desire to confine our "good night" to the realm of the platonic. I had conducted a verbal joust with her during the past four hours; she unhorsed me several times during the evening with adroit feints of words; like answering a question with a question—changing topics in mid-sentence. She had won this bout. I turned to leave, it was then she planted a warm kiss on my cheek, then ducked away through the door. Walking to the car I consoled my feelings with, "A half a loaf is better than none."

Chapter Seventeen
Venezuela: A Chance To Regroup And Recoup

The next three weeks were busy ones for me. Details for the opening ceremony of the hotel, plus the winding down of drilling operations in the Clarkwood field occupied my time.

Audrey accepted my invitation to attend the opening, though Justin declined for health reasons. The three newspapers in Houston carried front page details of the gala affair.

Two of them ran articles presenting the opening as a news happening, but one did not resist the opportunity to inject a play on words highlighting some of the more sordid escapades of my past. The writer of the third article did present the hotel in a complimentary vein as well as commenting it was the plushest hotel south of New York. He was articulate as well as vindicative when he added, "It's hoped Mr. McCulloch will use the service elevator while going up to, or leaving his ornate penthouse perched atop this impressive edifice, the Capri Hotel. Hugh McCulloch presents an enigma that defies the imagination.

"He is personable, yet can be intractable and as ruthless as Genghis Khan. The local blue bloods view McCulloch in the same light as they do Genghis Khan; they prefer to stay a safe distance from him. This forced isolation of McCulloch resulted in him finally obtaining a place to live that is insulated against eviction —his own penthouse. This is why he should use the service elevator. Doing so, he cannot be responsible for the loss of any guests vacating because of Hugh McCulloch's boorish conduct. Good luck as an innkeeper, Hugh!"

After reading the article, I contacted my attorney to probe the possibility of a lawsuit against the newspaper charging character damage. The attorney infuriated me by laughing at my suggestion, pointing out the article was in fact accurate; it could stand the test of malicious intent and could possibly damage me to a greater degree if I chose to press the issue of character damage. He closed our conversation by saying, "Hugh, for fear of sounding pious, I must remind you the scripture warns, 'Be sure your sins will find you out,' my advice is to forget it."

"Okay, I pay you for advice, but I think the writer has a punch coming on the jaw. He took a cheap shot at me!"

"Forget it, Hugh!"

The hotel opening was carried out as planned. Two days later the occupancy rate was eighty percent. This rate remained constant during the first three months, then fell off to around seventy-five percent.

August found me squirming under the pressure of inadequate finances to placate the demands of Rhone and Hester, the refinery contractors. As a result, the expropriation had experienced an overrun of two hundred thousand dollars above the construction account funds and were corresponding with me through their attorneys; the letters containing the veiled, legal verbiage lawyers usually resort to when flogging a prospective defendant of a lawsuit. I was feeling a sense of insecurity.

Adding to my dilemma, the producing wells in the Clarkwood field were presenting problems. To date a total of five wells had begun flowing salt water—this development demanded immediate attention if the field was to be salvaged A gas reinjection system would offer the best insurance against the same happening to more wells. I had delayed the installation of the system due to the exorbitant expense it would entail, then I too had been turned down for credit to facilitate the system.

The financial world having a process of communicating far more effective than the drum signals passed through the rain forests of the Amazon. He had tagged me as being a bad risk for further credit. I was being buffeted by the domino theory of financial collapse; one failure spawns another.

The situation was nearing total disaster when September came. It was then I made the decision to contact the Chairman of Natural Resources (Fossil) of Venezuela, one Ramundo Alvarez, my objective being to open dialogue which might lead to my exploring Venezuela's petroleum possibilities. Chairman Alvarez responded quickly to my inquiry, inviting me down as soon as possible.

Jim and I flew out of Houston on September 10th, our destination Caracas, Venezuela. We stayed overnight in Merida,

Mexico, taking off early the next morning. Jim set the plane down on the Caracas strip at two p.m.

We checked into the Norte Americano hotel, then sought out the dark recess of a bar situated off the lobby. After downing three highballs, I asked the desk clerk to get Señor Ramundo Alvarez on the telephone.

Alvarez seemed pleased I had arrived and suggested we meet in the lobby at six p.m. for dinner, where we could discuss the business of exploration.

Returning to the bar I said to Jim, "Let's make a wager of ten bucks."

"On what?"

"I bet Señor Alvarez instructs room service to deliver warm señoritas to our rooms tonight."

"You're kidding, Hugh. We couldn't be that lucky again, unless he told you he'd provide them."

"No. He hinted nothing of the kind, so the bet is on."

"Okay. This is a sucker bet, I'll win even if I lose," he chuckled and rubbed his knees as if savoring the possibility of losing.

We played the game of guessing the physical description of Alvarez. Jim guessed him to be middle aged, rather tall and bulky. I picked him to be short, maybe roly poly and near sixty years old.

At five thirty p.m. I asked Jim if he was feeling his drinks. "You can bet on it!" he said smiling sheepishly.

"So am I, let's knock if off, I've business to discuss. We'll wait for him in the lobby."

Finding an inviting sofa we plopped down to await Señor Alvarez.

I glanced at my watch a short time later. It was five fifty-five p.m. The revolving door was activated by a tall angular man dressed in a black suit. He entered the lobby, cast his eyes with darting glances all around, then stepped beside the door with his arms folded across his chest. Two pearl grey Yorkshires trotted into the lobby held on a leash by a short, rotund man dressed in a pearl grey suit with a carnation riding the left lapel. This fellow seemed to be rolling behind the two dogs as they strained at the leash while crossing the lobby, pulling the wheezing fat man at a fast pace.

Jim turned to me saying, "The dogs seem to be taking him for a walk!"

I could hardly repress a smile as I viewed the activity being like a scene from a movie, "That's my man Jim, short, fat and sixty!"

The tall man in the black suit had stridden quickly to the desk clerk, no doubt to have him identify Hugh McCulloch. He soon was in front of us.

"Are you Mr. McCulloch?"

Arising I answered, "Yes."

"Will you follow me please? Señor Alvarez is here to see you."

I followed him across the lobby where he drew himself to full height in front of the short man and announced in a strong voice, "Mr. McCulloch, here is Chairman Alvarez," then bowed.

I shook the hand of Alvarez and was surprised at his apparent strength. He smiled, "Mr. McCulloch, how nice of you to come down. Welcome to Venezuela. Come let's have dinner."

He headed for the dining room with fast mincing steps, as the dogs led at a fast pace. I was thinking as we crossed the lobby what he would do with the dogs while we dined. I found out very soon. The maitre d' awaited our entrance where he gave an exaggerated bow, then beamed a welcoming smile and said, "This way gentlemen."

We followed him to an elaborately set table. He pulled out our chairs, taking the leash from Alvarez tied it to a leg of the table we were occupying. The two dogs flattened on the floor like two frogs, placed their head between their front paws and directed a pleading look at me. The maitre d' and the Yorkshires had evidently been through this routine many times, the dogs were seemingly settled for the evening, placid and contented.

I knew I could not enjoy my food while two dogs watched every bite with hungry eyes. It was a disturbing prospect.

"Well now, Mr. McCulloch, I want you to order anything you wish, but you must try the milk fed squab, please try it with whatever else you wish to order."

"Alright, I'll have the squab and filet mignon with button mushrooms."

"Bueno! That's good, I'll have the same."

The waiter had placed a bottle of chilled burgundy on the table then filled two sparkling glasses with the rich red liquid. Having taken our order he retreated to the kitchen.

"Mr. McCulloch, a toast!" he raised the glass then intoned, "Man is the master of his fate, when the powers so desire, I wish for each of us our heart aflame. Now I suppose you've been assigned a proper room, and I hope it's to your liking."

"Yes?"

"We have nice rooms, my pilot and I."

"My government has grappled with a problem for several years that I feel you can resolve if the proposal appeals to you. The problem is getting someone to explore, wildcat for oil in unproven areas, namely the area surrounding Lake Maracaibo. The oil companies have refused to develop any area out of the lake.

"Have you seen Lake Maracaibo?"

"No."

"It's almost solid with derricks and we feel the need to develop new areas. Our geologists have assured us oil can be found in other regions. This is what I want you to develop—new fields. How many drilling rigs can you devote to this program?"

"I can start with four rigs, then add to the number as the need arises."

"That's good! Here's what I'm authorized to offer you."

He was interrupted by one of the dogs whining, he looked down at the pooch then suggested I pet the one whimpering. I reached down, stroked the hair on the dog's head, the dog stood up and moved over to lie on the floor beside me where I continued to pet him.

"Louis likes you, Mr. McCulloch. This pleases me. Louis is my fool proof tester of men, that's why I brought the dogs with me tonight. I've learned to avoid anyone to whom Louis does not respond. The animal has the instinct to repel affection from people who've proved themselves not worthy of trust. Yes, Louis the XIVth, is infallible at judging character," he leaned back while casting a smile.

I was thinking if he chose to gauge his trust of people upon the reaction of a Yorksire dog, that was his concern. It was his privilege and his dog; even though the dog bore an illustrious name. I'd prefer to rely on my own judgment rather than that of an animal.

Alvarez continued, "My government will pay transportation costs for your equipment; you'll bear all expenses necessary to conduct the exploration. You'll receive fifteen percent of all production your strikes produce—my government will retain eight-five percent of the production you're credited with." He ceased talking awaiting a response.

"Señor Alvarez I must have some type of insurance protecting me against loss of equipment and/or production due to any act of seizure on the part of the Venezuelan government. A sum equal to the value of my equipment placed in trust in a U.S. bank, plus a sum representing nine percent of production. This sum to be computed monthly, based on well head flow at the prevailing price of crude.

"This escrow fund will require the signatures of two co-signers to effect a withdrawal. Naturally, I'll be one of the co-signers. Due to a recent loss resulting from an act of expropriation, I find myself adamant in making this stipulation before entering into any agreement."

I had made my proposal and patiently awaited his reaction. He pursed his lips as he considered my counter proposal. His round, rosy cheeks resembled a pink balloon with his mouth the inflation nipple. He was a refreshing little man to observe; his face as innocent looking as a chubby cupid. I refused to be beguiled by his counterfeit expression of innocence. This man had not reached his position of Chairman of Resources by exercising a policy of naivete—his facial expression was as deceiving and dangerous as a male Lorelei.

"We have a deal, Mr. McCulloch!" The waiter had placed our dinner on the table and withdrew. Alvarez spoke, "Let's enjoy our food, then talk more over dessert."

After dinner he suggested we fly to Lake Maracaibo the next morning to observe the general area. I agreed to the suggestion then asked, "Señor Alvarez I know a geologist who could expedite my getting started successfully and designate the drilling sites most likely to produce oil. I can get him down here if your government will pay his usual fee plus expenses."

"I'll approve that."

"That's good. Any money used for his services will be money well spent."

Alvarez bid me good night and promised to send a driver for us at nine a.m.

Jim came over to view the act required to get Alvarez and the lively Yorkshires swallowed up in the spinning door and out onto the street! He turned to me asking, "Are you ready to turn in?"

"We might as well. We are flying over to Maracaibo at nine in the morning."

"I want to get up to my room and learn if I lost my bet."

I left the elevator on the third floor, Jim rode up to the fifth. I walked down the hall to room 317. While turning the key I noticed a ray of light escaping the bottom of the door, it prompted me to open the door cautiously as my eyes swept the room for an intruder.

Closing the door quietly, I scanned the room thoroughly expecting to find someone responsible for turning the light on. My quarters were a suite, consisting of the large living room I was standing in, a hall leading to a dressing room and a huge bedroom. I entered the dressing room where I discovered my unknown guest sitting facing the circular mirror of the dressing table. It was circled with lights and its illumination revealed my visitor to be a very attractive female who, at the moment, appeared to be admiring her beauty reflected in the huge mirror.

I leaned against the door frame while studying this interesting specimen who had now lifted a powder puff and was patting her pretty cheeks. She was ignoring my presence as she proceeded with her makeup. Her aloof attitude had begun to irritate me, after a few moments of silence I said, "Dearie, one of us is lost. Do you belong to this room or do I?"

She placed the powder puff in her bag with a planned, deliberate movement, snapped the bag then turned slowly to face me asking, "Do you have a cigarette?"

She was stunning in her wine colored gown; a gown displaying creamy white shoulders flowing into a neck as graceful and intriguing as that of a swan. This gown was formed to the contour of her exciting body and was surely the creation of an artisan who designed it in a shop on the Rue de la Paix.

She surely was one of Alvarez's private kittens farmed out for the night. I produced a cigar case from my jacket pocket flicking it open as I offered it to her saying, "Have a cigar."

I was astonished as she selected a corona with graceful movement of her fingers, then placed it between her lips saying, "Light please."

I scratched the lighter and placed the flame beneath the tip of the cigar expecting her to reject the light. She puffed on the cigar a few times, then leaned back to look me over from head to foot while a twisting wisp of cigar smoke curled upward from her nostrils. This was the first time I had watched a woman smoke a cigar and she was carrying it off with aplomb and grace. Strangely, she did not appear crude or uncouth. She gave me a level gaze as if weighing a question before asking, "Are you Hugh McCulloch?"

"Yes and who are you? Why are you in my room?"

She smiled, puffed the cigar, blowing several perfect smoke rings that floated directly into my face causing me to step aside to avoid them. This dame had the finesse of a timber wolf as she sat there judging me and puffing my cigar. I said,

"Well?"

"My name is Tina."

"Go on, answer my question."

"I'm here to make love and sleep with you."

"That's interesting. Tell me, are you assigned to the room or to me? Who pays you, the hotel or am I to compensate?"

"Señor Alvarez sent me."

"Well, that's just dandy. We're expected to go to bed; I just climb aboard like riding a bus then later you return to where you came from like a cleaning woman returning home after a night of toil."

I will never know for sure the cause of my resentment; it was not created by her appearance—she would have been an asset to any bed. Audrey had suddenly filled my thoughts allowing my sense of reason to emerge; this resulted in me saying,

"I mean no ill feeling toward you Tina when I decline your company tonight, and neither do I fault Señor Alvarez's intentions or his selectivity. I must ask you to leave as I haven't any desire to subject my will to an all night struggle with temptation."

As she came near I detected the titillating fragrance of gardenias. This gave me a fleeting moment of doubt—maybe I hadn't exercised good judgment in spurning her goodies. As she passed through the threshold she paused, then blew cigar smoke in my face. Her act of petulance served both of us well—she the privilege of saving her bruised ego; for me, reward that comes from guessing right. Once in bed I fell asleep quickly.

♦ ♦ ♦

The seven o'clock call from the desk roused me the following morning reminding me today could bring about a cure to my financial ills, if all went well. The elevator door opened into the lobby where I found Jim sitting casually observing the people surrounding him. He saw me approaching, stood to greeted me, "How's everything, Hugh?"

"Fine. How about some breakfast?"

We were seated in a window booth overlooking a bustling street crawling with broken columns of people all struggling to make their way against the oncoming tide of humanity. We observed the activity for a few moments when it became apparent to me they were all pushing and shoving in their efforts to make progress. I remarked to Jim, "It's puzzling how half appear headed in one direction. The rest are trying to go the other way, yet they get the most resistance from the bodies headed the same way they're trying to go."

Jim looked at me and said, "That statement confuses me as much as the action on the street. You said it and I suppose you know what you mean. Here's the ten I lost!" he offered me a ten dollar bill.

"Did you have company last night?"

"Sure did, just like you predicted. Mr. Señor Chairman Alvarez's stable doesn't have the thoroughbreds Cedillo's offered. That filly in Monterrey was really something compared to last night's offering; I'm not complaining, I'd never knock a free ride."

The waiter set two cups of steaming coffee before us. I raised mine and said, "Here's to good health!"

Jim shifted his position as if uncomfortable and grinned, "You're a kill joy, Hugh."

We finished our breakfast and were watching the activity on the street when the waiter asked, "Are either of you Mr. McCulloch?"

"I'm McCulloch."

He turned motioning a man standing in the entrance to the restaurant. The stranger approached our booth saying, "I'm Tony Galvan, pilot for Chairman Alvarez. He's waiting in the car. I'll pilot the flight to Maracaibo. Are you gentlemen ready?"

"Yes, we're ready, I'm Hugh McCulloch, this is Jim Harris, my pilot. We're pleased to meet you."

Alvarez greeted us warmly. We motored several miles to reach the plane. I waited for Alvarez to make some mention of my ejecting the woman from the room, but he avoided the subject. I assumed she had not made any contact with him. I was pleased to avoid any explanation for my act.

We boarded an amphibious plane that bore the official flag of Venezuela painted on the doors. The engines roared as the pilot maneuvered the craft for open water—he then gave it full throttle. The engines acknowledged the full flow of gas with a deafening roar thrusting the plane faster and faster. The noisy thump of waves pummeled the bottom of the aircraft as it struggled to tear free from the grasp of the water.

This was my first flight in an amphibian machine. I found the deafening roar of the engines, coupled with the intense vibration of the craft, produced a state of apprehension that engulfed me until the plane finally brought Maracaibo into view, five thousand feet below.

We descended to a two thousand foot altitude where the pilot crisscrossed the lake several times while Alvarez pointed out various holdings of major oil companies. The lake was a mass of derricks, walkways and platforms all linking hundreds of houses resting on stilts sunk into the lake.

The lush green forest was poised on the bank of the lake and reached as far as the eye could see to the south—the green vegetation of Colombia covered the west. The unpredictable waters of the Caribbean Sea reflected the sun as we looked to the north. The forest below was so dense and green, it appeared to be a huge sea of emerald slime.

Alvarez pointed out the area south of the lake as the region the government would like developed. I was gazing down at the world below deciding it did not matter where I wildcatted, it was all a green hell. After circling the area for thirty minutes we headed for Caracas. As we flew back Alverez outlined the work agreement we had arrived at; thus, making the next move mine. I was ready to begin salvaging what remained of my future in petroleum.

♦ ♦ ♦

The following week involved the legal paper work necessary to set up the deal we had agreed upon. I had set a twenty-five thousand dollar value on each of the four rigs I was shipping down; Alvarez had accepted this as a fair assessed value and he had cemented the contract by depositing one hundred fifty thousand dollars in the Chemical National Bank of Houston as my safeguard against any future expropriation.

Curly Ward proved to be indispensable in getting the crews together and expediting the condensation of the rigs, plus the needed miscellaneous supplies. He had this mass of steel and pig iron, plus two trucks on the pier in Corpus Christi at noon Friday, awaiting shipment. The machinery was scheduled to be loaded aboard a Luckenbach freighter Sunday or Monday, destination Maracaibo. The crew went as passengers on the same ship.

I reached Joe Bob Miller, explained the set up to him requesting he be at the airport Sunday morning at eight o'clock ready for the flight down. He rebelled on the basis of too short a notice. I was insistent enough to beat down his objection, he retorted, "Damn Hugh, you're not asking me, you're telling me."

"That's about right Joe Bob, I need you far more than whoever has you engaged at this time. See you Sunday!"

"Alright—it's going to cost them."

"Okay! The wheel has agreed to approve your fee and expenses, Sunday, eight a.m."

"Right."

Jim, Joe Bob and I landed in Caracas at five thirty p.m. Sunday. We checked into the North American Hotel where I contacted Alvarez by phone.

"Señor Alvartez, McCulloch here. I'm in the hotel prepared to get started tomorrow. The geologist I mentioned is here ready to give readings for drilling sites. Can you go over tomorrow morning and designate the area I'm authorized to explore, giving me some boundaries?"

"Mr. McCulloch, I have a deputy minister living near Maracaibo who's been instructed to give you any assistance you may need. I can have him meet you at the airport anytime tomorrow that's convenient for you. We intend to do our part in making this a profitable venture for you."

"Thank you, sir. Have your man meet us at the airport around eleven a.m. and we'll start moving."

"Very good, I'll be over later this week to check your progress. Good night."

We moved into the bar after dinner to observe the activity surrounding a very enthusiastic group of musicians. They were offering listenable music in the tempos of rhumba, calypso and tangos.

The couples were a pleasure to watch as they moved with fluid motion to the exotic heat of the music. The heady tempos, blended with the pungent sweet odor of marijuana hanging over the scene had a captivating effect. I found myself being projected from a stolid civilized state of mind to a reckless realm of fantasy.

Three attractive "B girls" had keened the scent of the American dollars at the sight of three gringos, and moved in quickly to tell us in broken English they were thirsty. At some prearranged signal, the three of them slid on our laps as they wrapped an arm around each of our necks. At that moment I was paged for a telephone call. When I arose, Jim and Joe Bob did likewise, following me out of the crowd leaving the three chattering and throwing uncomplimentary remarks at our backs. They were cursing us with combination of Spanish and Portuguese venom. The call was from Alvarez telling me his deputy would meet us at eleven a.m. and he also had a house available; recently vacated by an oil company official.

"I do appreciate the thoughtfulness, thank you for calling."

We retired early. I fell asleep thinking of Audrey hoping to persuade her to be my wife once again.

The flight to Maracaibo was uneventful; we landed under an overcast sky. We had rolled to a stop and were unloading our luggage when a man approached asking, "Did Mr. McCulloch come in on a plane?"

He was wearing spotless khaki clothing bearing creases as sharp as a knife blade.

"I'm Mr. McCulloch."

"Good morning! I'm deputy Minister Ramon Cordoba. Welcome to Maracaibo."

As we shook hands I was making an effort to analyze this man—his cooperation was essential to my success; I liked his manner. Cordoba drove us around the rest of the day covering the details in which I'd be involved. The house was satisfactory, just recently painted; it was owned by a friend of Cordoba. He loaned me a truck to use until ours arrived, then we drove to the south edge of town where we looked upon a barrier of green forest; my challenge to overcome if I wanted to succeed.

The next morning men and machines were carving a swath twenty feet wide and a mile deep into the thick growth of mahogany, mangroves and palmetto. This would be my starting point if I could overcome the resistance offered by poisonous snakes, huge lizards, mosquitos soaring like bats and millions of ants that stung like scorpions. I found myself asking, "What the hell am I doing here?"

'The first leg of the road was completed at noon Friday, as were four cleared areas spaced a fourth mile apart, all adjacent to the road; these were the first drilling sites. Saturday afternoon the four rigs were piled on their respective clearings and Sunday the forest was echoing the sound and fury of men cursing and sweating as they wrestled resisting heavy steel into place. These were the sounds that signaled man's eventual destruction of the salient cathedrals of nature; the native jungle.

Jim and I flew back to Houston on Thursday. Lydia informed me Mr. McMillan had called three days in succession. I knew he wanted to hold my feet to the fire in an effort to exact the past due quarterly payment on the two million dollar loan. Friday morning I called McMillian with the hope of getting an extension.

"Mr. McMillan, Hugh McCulloch here."

"Yes Mr. McCulloch, you're a hard man to catch."

The words and tone of his voice blasted my hope of an extension.

"I've been out of town. I'll need an extension on my loan. Can you handle it?"

"Mr. McCulloch the bank must operate in a manner insuring it's depositors against loss of funds. This bank has always adhered to a course of sound business practices in order to keep the trust of our investors; we've been successful, and hope to retain that status."

"The board met last week—a majority vote opposed the granting of any extension and I must tell you we're prepared to exercise our legal right by claiming all future production from the Clarkwood field effective tomorrow. This action will be taken unless you can handle the past due payment, plus interest today!"

His denial of the extension tolled the bell of doom!

I countered with, "If that's a board decision I can understand your position and I'll have to go along with it. I'm engaged in a venture that should relieve me of financial stress within ninety days. At that time I'll be in a position to bring the account up to a current status and will expect the production to be transferred to it's rightful owner, me!"

"Mr. McCulloch! We're sequestering the production as legal owners; your inference is distasteful to say the least, I assume you cannot meet the obligation today. Is that right?"

"No way can I pay it. You haven't eliminated me—I'll be back on the top, then you'll be insisting I borrow money! Good Day Mr. McMillan!"

I dropped the receiver, then realized my whole body was quivering from pent up wrath composed of disappointment, self-pity and a bleak failure looking at me head on. The trap was sprung—my head was in it. Suddenly I was the proverbial rat in that trap. I no longer gave a damn for the cheese—I just wanted my head out. I needed money to conduct the Venezuela venture—I needed it now! Hazardous situations merited perilous action; I took it by calling Frank Diamond, my C.P.A.

"Frank, Hugh here. Effective Monday you'll transfer all money in excess of operating expense for the hotel, to my personal account at the First National Bank, understand?"

"I understand, First National, where?"

"Here in Houston, you know Main and Preston."

"Okay, I got it. How are things going in Central America?"

"Just getting ready to challenge the thickest forest imaginable, you'd have to see it to believe it!"

"I wish you luck, Hugh. By God, you're entitled to some after Mexico."

"Thanks Frank, take care of that transfer for me and I'll see you in a month or so."

I leaned back to ponder the action I had just started. If I hit series of dry holes while siphoning off the hotel revenues to finance them, I'd be in one hell of a mess. Damn it! I refused to think of failure. The phone buzzer sounded, Lydia told me,

"Audrey McCulloch is on the line."

"Hello Audrey! I was just thinking of calling you. How are you and Justin?"

"Hugh, Justin has suffered a relapse. He's back in Methodist Hospital—the doctor is not very encouraging about his prospects of survival. I'm worried sick that he won't come out of it this time; I believe he knows it too, because he's asked to see you. Can you come?"

"Certainly. I should be there in twenty minutes. What room?"

"Room 410. Please hurry!"

Chapter Eighteen
Making Amends: Searching For Answers

Audrey was standing outside the door awaiting my arrival. I took her hand in mine then pulled her to me with my arm around her shoulders, she tilted her head up and fastened her gaze into my eyes saying softly,

"I love him so much, please don't say anything unkind to him regardless of what he says."

"I'll say nothing unkind to him, I promise."

She squeezed my hand then led me into the cold sterile room where Justin lay under an oxygen tent. The element of impending death had not vanquished his look of nobility. His silver hair shone with light of a halo against the backdrop of his white pillow. His eyes were closed, giving the appearance he was slumbering peacefully. I stood looking down at the man who had influenced my life so very much. He had ignited my inner drive by encouraging me to surge ahead —bowl over obstacles—accept nothing short of total success. He had been the catalyst for what could have propelled me to dizzy heights in the petroleum world. He had sired the woman who had brought the sunlight to my dark egocentric existence and lighted the path to love; something I had not known before.

He did not realize his influence and encouragement would create a power mad, rakehell of a man who would eventually thank him by shaming the Brent name and trampling the ideals of his daughter. Audrey called softly, "Dad—dad, Hugh is here."

Justin opened his eyes then smiled faintly at me as he reached for my hand. He squeezed my forefinger gently as I leaned down to hear him whisper.

"I'm glad you came."

"I'm happy you wanted me."

"Hugh—we have missed you since you went out of our lives. I had always wished for a son then you came . . ." He stopped, breathing deeply several times continuing, "You were all I had longed for in a son of my own. You were intelligent, direct and articulate. I recognized these traits in you the first time you came to our home, you won my admiration."

He had stopped talking for several seconds in an effort to command breath enough to continue. He started again, this time with his eyes closed.

"You were human and had the usual balance of traits, one good for one bad. I was too small a man to accept you for what you were—a diamond in the rough. I wish now I'd been a bigger man, and assumed the task of helping you correct your bad points. I turned you away at a time I'm sure you needed the counsel of an older man."

He had loosed his grip of my finger and was quiet, eyes closed. Audrey thought he was dying. She ran from the room for a nurse while I stood motionless watching him. The seconds ticked by—there wasn't any breathing motion of his chest. I too thought he had slipped out leaving an unfinished message.

A nurse hurried into the room, she lifted Justin's hand seeking a pulse, at that moment he opened his eyes, smiled slightly and resumed his whispered monologue, "I let my bad traits rule me when I turned you away. If you'll forgive me for neglecting you I can go to sleep now, I love you like a son."

His head rolled to the side and somehow I knew his soul was vacating the body before us, making ready for the journey to another world—another plane.

Audrey was pressing her face against my chest, her sobs of anguish pushing her hot breath through my clothing. She sobbed for two or three minutes then gazed at me through tearful eyes saying, "You've made three people very happy by being here. Thank you, thank you."

"Come with me," I was turning her toward the door. We walked slowly along the corridor to the elevators, "Wait here just a moment,"

I walked over to the nurses station to leave instructions for the hospital to contact the funeral home. I specified the best known mortuary in the Houston area.

As the elevator stopped at the street floor level I asked Audrey if I might accompany her home and stay overnight. She gently but firmly declined my suggestion, backing her refusal with the explanation she should start tonight conditioning herself to face the absence of Justin.

"I'll be alright, Hugh. I appreciate what you're trying to do. Please call me in the morning." She turned and walked across the parking area toward her car.

I watched her every step as the distance widened—my heart flooded with compassion; sympathy for this strong woman I knew was suffering from intense grief and loneliness while she entered her car and drove away, leaving me standing in the yellow glare of a floodlight.

After getting in my car, I sat half an hour in the semi-darkness before starting the motor. This period was spent in trying to determine if I was doing the right thing by letting Audrey spend the night alone. Should I have insisted on going with her? Why did she reject my suggestion so quickly? Maybe time would give me the answer.

I drove to the penthouse where I stood in the center of the glass walled living room surveying my surroundings while unbuttoning my shirt. The city lights were reflected by a low cloud cover giving the illusion of a well lighted theater entrance. Glancing around me I made a mental inventory of the expensive furnishings, the deep pile carpet, the unique lighting system; the many man hours of labor it represented. For what? Tonight I was surely the loneliest man in the world. My much sought after affluence surrounded me, taunting me, making a mockery of all I had held dear. I laid on my back in the entrance of my bedroom floor and began a mental scan of my past—the present—the future. Somewhere the seed of discontent had germinated to the point of scrambling life's priorities for me. My values were in a state of flux. My needs of yesterday were no longer of paramount value. I fell asleep on the floor.

♦ ♦ ♦

I awoke the next morning still in the throes of discontent. After showering I called Audrey.

"Audrey, I'd like to come over."

"No Hugh, let me meet you. I want to get out of the house."

"Would you care to have breakfast with me in the penthouse?"

"Yes, I'd like that, you know I've never been there."

"Yes, I know. Can you meet me in the lobby at nine?"

"I'll be there. I want you to go to the funeral home with me to make the arrangements."

"Thank you for asking me. I'll see you at nine."

While eating breakfast Audrey asked, "Hugh, your penthouse is elegant but I'm curious; are you happy living here?"

Her motive in asking the question was foremost in my mind as I stalled several seconds before answering, "No, I'm not happy here or anywhere else since you and I've been apart."

She sat toying with her cup gazing down as she turned it around several times. I said nothing to break the silence; it was evident she was in deep thought. Many seconds passed—I wished I could read her thoughts. She raised her eyes to mine, "We should be going to the funeral home. They requested I come before eleven."

After making the arrangements for Justin's services, Audrey suggested I drive her back to the hotel where she had parked her car.

"Do you wish to return home this soon, I was planning a day of being together?"

"Thank you for your consideration but I feel I must start today getting used to Justin's absence. It's best this way."

"Maybe I could come by later?"

"I'd rather you wouldn't; please don't ask me why."

Two days later Justin was buried in Memorial Cemetery. Audrey was apparently accepting his death with control of all outward emotion. She was truly a person of much self-discipline and strong will.

I suggested I accompany her home as we started for our cars after the burial service, but she declined my suggestion. She was determined I stay away. Her attitude was arbitrary but I didn't raise the point for fear it would antagonize her.

She seemed very casual when she suggested I call her sometime. Then she drove away. I stood watching the car disappear around a curve in the drive. I was baffled and frustrated from her rebuff. She was tearing me apart mentally with her lack of interest in encouraging our association.

I contacted Jim that afternoon making plans for flying to Venezuela. We met at the airport at eight a.m. the next morning. Jim asked, "Have you heard about the tropical disturbance in the Atlantic?"

"No, where is it located?"

"At eight o'clock last night it was moving in the direction of Central America at a speed of fifteen miles per hour. Located two hundred miles east of Venezuela and packing winds of sixty miles an hour. It's expected to pick up its intensity as it moves into the Caribbean."

"Can we make it to Merida?"

"I see no reason why we can't."

"Let's go, I want to get out of Houston."

As we passed the Tampico area we entered the usual scudding clouds that precede tropical storms. We were getting much static on the radio making it hard to hear the reports. The latest on the storm had classed it as a hurricane due to an increase in the winds. The announcer predicted the storm would cross Central America near Panama around eight that night.

It got pretty rough before we landed at Merida in a blinding rain. We spent the night in a hangar at the airport due to high water closing the road into town.

The next morning broke with bright sunshine. We refueled, then headed for Maracaibo arriving in the early afternoon. Señor Cordoba stopped by the house, an hour after our arrival, to let me know he had found us a good cook and housekeeper. He also said my crews had started drilling on two locations the day before and complimented me on the efficiency of the men.

The rain from the hurricane had saturated Maracaibo making the streets nearly impassable as Jim and I started for the drilling sites the next morning. We found the newly cleared road to be a quagmire and decided the truck would sink in the morass, so we left it at the edge of the forest and walked to the rigs. As we trudged the road the mud came up to our knees making our progress slow and tiring. Jim remarked, "There isn't a truck that can get over this today."

" I doubt it." We had reached the first rig where we climbed the steps to the floor. We found Curly and the crew in a happy frame of mind as a result of making good depth so far. Curly's voice rang out above the noise of the rig, "Welcome to McCulloch #1! Glad to see you back!"

"How do you men like Venezuela?" I asked. Elliott looked around then replied, "It sure has a lot of mud and trees."

Curly broke in with, "And snakes!"

Come here Hugh, I want to show you a visitor we found on the derrick floor when we came out yesterday," he led me over to the edge of the floor pointing, "Down there."

"Look right there," he was pointing my finger with his hand. This time I detected a ten foot snake stretched out on the ground. The reptile was difficult to see due to its color and skin marking, being the same size of brown leaves effecting a perfect camouflage.

"Damn! Was that thing up here on the floor?"

"It sure as hell was. When we came up here he acted like he didn't want our company. He squirmed, turned and slid all over the floor with head raised about a foot giving us a mean ferocious look as he flicked a foot long tongue at us.

"He was a scary looking son-of-a-bitch until one of the native workers dropped a ten foot length of four by four across him and stood on it to pin him down. A guy on each end of the timber held him while another pounded the intruder on the head with a chain tong. I'd hate for the bastard to slide in bed with me some night, especially after I had put away a fifth of bourbon. I believe that would make me swear off drinking!"

"Looks like you've two crews rolling, Curly."

"Yep, we should get plenty of action as they have already cooked up a rivalry over which crew will hit oil first. Some of the native workers have placed bets on the outcome."

"When can we expect to get the other two rigs in operation?"

"Tomorrow at the latest."

"That's my boy!" I patted Curly on the back," Do you think Jim can push a crew?"

"Hell yes. He was ready in Mexico 'til the bastards ran us out. I've already got the men lined up; with Señor Cordoba's assistance. He's been extremely helpful."

"Let's keep him on our side; we'll need his assistance and good will in the future if we get this jungle to give us what we're seeking. The oil pool under the lake had been tapped around the eight thousand foot depth."

Five weeks of drilling had put two of our rigs around the eighty-five hundred foot depth with no traces of oil sand as of yet. I had to make the decision to go deeper or move to another location. I discussed the situation with Curly. Our decision was to abandon the hole if we had no oil signs at nine thousand. I made arrangements for a road to be cleared from the existing one for a half mile penetration to the east; this being the advice Joe Bob had given if the first sites proved to be dry holes. They were! The results at this point were both distressing and expensive. We moved the two rigs one half mile east to continue the search for the elusive black gold. Curly was apologetic, but I replied, "Dry holes are some of the hazards a wildcatter must learn to accept, they're part of the gamble."

It had been six weeks since we had departed Houston. The mail from Lydia indicated my presence was needed there immediately to satisfy the demands of the insurance company; the firm holding the mortgage on the hotel.

As we were taking off for Houston, I was concentrating on the strategy I'd use to wangle another extension for the second quarterly mortgage payment now past due. They had given an extension on the first one after I had outlined the many expenses necessary to open the hotel; then I hammered on the unfortunate loss suffered in Mexico. My two pages of poor mouthing had produced the desired results at the time; I was now facing a second confrontation armed with nothing but effrontery disarmed with the stigma of "bad credit risk".

I went directly to the office from the airport where I found neat stacks of correspondence awaiting my attention, also several telephone memos. I went through the stacks extracting the letters bearing the return address of the insurance company. There were eight. I shuffled through them selecting the one bearing the latest post date. I could avoid the barrage of preliminary threats contained in the first seven!

The latest missile was postmarked the day before and was quite lengthy. I settled back in my chair to read the two pages. The first paragraph sealed my fate with its impersonal summation of the legal mayhem. I could expect as a result of my violation of the mortgage contract agreement, namely default. The balance of the two pages was a narrative devoted to elongating the generous consideration the company had bestowed upon me; how I had betrayed their trust to a degree of flagrancy that merited only the most strenuous action on the part of the company; the act of foreclosure.

The last paragraph offered the condemned, "me" an avenue of escaping the claws of legality by paying the two past due installments plus interest, both amounting to one-hundred twelve thousand dollars. The sum to be delivered to the Houston office on or before four o'clock, the 10th day of October. That was the missile that blew me out of the hotel business; this day being the 8th of October.

Crossing my arms, I put them on the desk then laid my head down. Dusk was approaching, the office was almost dark. I closed my eyes, it was then I felt the horrible effects of failure. My whole world was collapsing—my financial power had become nothing—fate was stripping me to the nakedness of a new born infant; my life had come full circle—I was back again admiring the beauty of the secondhand Cord automobile—the day I returned to Houston from Kilgore with thirty-five hundred dollars bloating my youthful enthusiasm. Maybe I was dreaming. A voice inside my head said quietly, "It isn't a dream. Get out of here. You're wallowing in self-pity. You can rise to the top. Go back to Venezuela," this inner voice frightened me into action. I arose, groped my way to the door and went through the outer office to the elevator.

Thirty minutes later I was sitting in Kelly's Steak House having dinner and bubbling with enthusiasm to get back to Venezuela. I was charged with the same inner drive that had propelled me to get started eight years before. I had the feeling I had been encouraged by some occult force to forget my losses and concentrate on the future the Venezuelan jungle offered.

I retired about ten o'clock finding myself considering the sale of my River Oaks home as a means of getting additional money. I fell asleep trying to estimate its saleable value. Morning came with the sale of the house still on my mind; I decided to contact a real estate broker when I reached the office.

Lydia was standing on a chair straightening a picture adorning the wall as I entered the office. She had her back to me when suddenly I had recall of having witnessed this scene before. She was aligning the picture Barbara was adjusting the day I had walked over and lifted her from the chair and brought her body close to mine; the ensuing minutes had resulted in a highly volatile interlude—the interlude developing into an event that contributed greatly to the erosion of my marriage to Audrey.

"Hello Mr. McCulloch!, " she turned facing me then stepped down from the chair, "I'm glad to see you."

"Same here, Lydia. I see you've been keeping things in line. I appreciate your assistance."

"Thank you, how are things in Venezuela?"

"So far nothing concrete to boast about, but time will change that."

I went to my office where I called the real estate firm that had handled my purchase of the house. The owner of the firm expressed the opinion it would sell for about one hundred thousand considering the depressed market prevailing at this time.

"I'll get back to you if I decide to sell. Thank you."

I reached a decision—I'd not sell the home. The amount received would not turn the tide of my fortunes now or in the future. The house was symbolic of a common bond Audrey and I had, I'd keep it ready for the day we might live there once more.

I checked my personal account with First National Bank to learn it had a balance of two hundred twenty-five thousand dollars. This sum in addition to the amount the C.P.A. could deposit before legally being halted via foreclosure represented the limit of my finances. I must find oil soon.

I placed several calls for Audrey during the day and evening but she did not answer; I decided she must be out of the city.

The morning of the 10th I moved my clothing and other possessions from the penthouse to my house. While making the transfer, the torment of giving up the hotel depressed me to the extent of seeking surcease with a quart of Chivas Regal. By mid-afternoon I reached the deceiving state of euphoria alcohol provides when one is seeking causes and cures for whatever ails them. The whiskey served as an anesthetic, dulling the pain of my ignominious loss of the hotel.

During the course of the day, I had reviewed my life several times and the same conclusion always emerged: I was in no way responsible for my present plight; the Mexican government had ruined me financially. The erratic thinking produced by the whiskey was filling my mind with wishes to seek revenge. If I had the money to finance a revolution I'd do it gladly to satisfy my desire to seek retribution.

I entered the hotel about dusk more than slightly intoxicated—Jim was sitting, observing the usual activity of a hotel lobby. He saw me enter, meeting me in the center of the lobby saying, "Hugh, when are we going back to Venezuela?"

"Tomorrow. We'll leave here at eight."

"Good! I'm anxious to get back on a drilling rig. I really like that kind of work. What are you up to now? Shall we go into the bar for a few snorts?"

"No Jim, I'm drunk and I want to go to bed. I'll see you in the morning."

As I entered the penthouse I paused in the doorway, glanced around the huge living room—thinking this could be the last night I'd spend here. It caused me regret to realize I was losing this grandeur: it scalded my pride. I went to bed . . . numb.

♦ ♦ ♦

Jim and I were airborne at five minutes after nine the next morning. He was feeling cheerful, while I felt terrible from a hangover. Ten minutes later he gave an ear splitting, "Y-a-a-a-a H-o-o-o-o! we're going down there Hugh and drill nothing but gushers, no dry holes!"

"Damn! Jim, have mercy on my aching head, please."

"Sorry, Boss."

During my absence Curly had moved the third and fourth rigs east, after going through the nine thousand foot depth in their original locations. That totaled four successive dry holes.

Three weeks later we had moved rigs one and two for the second time, after failing to get oil before ninety-five hundred feet. This pattern of drilling a series of dry holes had been costly for me; it was imperative that my luck change, and soon!

The mail from Houston on the 20th of October contained an official legal notice of the hotel passing from my possession to the insurance company. The company had levied their claim; it was effective October 15th. This information came the same day our number two rig brought in our first producing well. This eased my tension somewhat; I responded by having the off crews that night at the Driftwood Bar for an evening of drinks to celebrate the loss of our Venezuelan 'maiden-head'. The McCulloch Enterprise was no longer a jungle virgin. We continued to drill east of our original site by extending the road from time to time.

By January 1st I had a total of nine producing wells flowing into the pipeline; my luck had changed! We were bringing these wells in at depth of forty-two hundred feet; we were setting atop the pool. The next three months Curly and the four rigs were averaging a producing well every two weeks.

During this period Señor Cordoba had been a valuable ally for me. He supplied my rigs with efficient, experienced workers and had been of great service to the whole operation. As I associated with the man, from day to day, I was constantly surprised by his frequent remarks that only a literate man could deliver; yet he had received less than a high school education in a remote village of Venezuela.

He had a beautiful philosophy of life and the people he contacted benefited from having known him. Cordoba gave me much encouragement in the beginning of our friendship. It was during this period he revealed the source of his philosophy. He had suffered great tragedy, yet was sitting beside me able to tell me about it.

"I started working on oil rigs when I was fifteen. This work paid enough so I was considering marriage by the time I was seventeen to the beautiful Rita, sixteen, who lived across the lake in the community of Cabimos. We were married on my seventeenth birthday. We had two lovely baby girls before I was nineteen. I tell you this dramatic summary of my life to disclose the causative factors that brought me in contact with my blessed teacher of life, the revered Carmen Bolivar. My first contact with Carmen came about as a result of the tragic and bizarre occurrences that followed the untimely death of my much loved wife, Rita.

"She had been visiting her parents, who lived a quarter mile down the lane from our little white cottage. She started the trek home, carrying the baby and keeping a watchful eye on little Donna prancing along in front, brushing her hands on the waist high reeds lining the path. The curtain of dark was falling quickly since the sun had submerged in the Pacific, and Rita was hurrying home to prepare the evening meal. This is the way I pictured her last minutes on earth."

"I was standing on the small porch awaiting the return of my little family. Their absences brought a chill to the semidarkness—I was getting lonely for them. It was then I heard the anguished cry of little Donna. I leaped from the porch running into the dark path—my heart pounding as I ran toward the cry. I collided with Donna, knocking her into the reeds where I fell to my knees groping around feeling for my little girl. Her sobbing had increased, it was then I heard the baby cry for the first time. I lifted Donna, carrying her under my arm and ran to the sound of the whimpering baby. I was calling, 'Rita, Rita, please answer'.

"I kneeled down to comfort the baby and saw the silent, motionless form of Rita stretched out in the reeds. I reached for her, slipped my arm under her shoulders and raised her up against me—something warm was tickling down my chest under my shirt. As I reached the light of our home I looked down at my wife. My God! her throat was sliced from ear to ear, her blood had saturated my shirt and trousers. She was dead!

"Investigation resulted in many suspects being questioned. The human animal had struck in the dark; ravished the young mother and wife, then slinked away to his lair. The rapist and murderer was never caught.

"This tragedy threw me into a state of shock, I was powerless to overthrow it. Three months later I was sitting at the kitchen table, alone, preparing to write a suicide note. With a .44 calibre pistol laid on the checkered tablecloth, I sat trying to summon the words that would in some way tell about the terrible loneliness gnawing my sanity away.

"I picked up the pencil, poised over the paper and waited for the first word to enter my mind. My hand started moving with a circular motion—the pencil was not touching the paper but the pencil began to write, not the words from my mind—my mind was blank. It wrote, 'Go to Cabimos to Carmen Bolivar. Go to Carmen Bolivar', the writing was getting faster, faster and faster. I had no control of my hand. Then the moving hand stopped.

"I leaped to my feet, threw the pencil on the table, put the pistol away in a dresser drawer and ran out the door. I ran the two miles to Cabimos, entering the village shouting, 'Carmen Bolivar, Carmen Bolivar'! A native pointed out the shack where she lived—he volunteered the information that Carmen was a witch, but an acceptable witch.

"I called through her door for admittance; she questioned me about my reason for the night visit. I explained the startling experience with the writing; she promptly admitted me. Under her prying questions I admitted I was on the verge of committing suicide when the strange writing interrupted my plans.

"Carmen broke in saying, 'You're the man whose wife was murdered, right?' Yes, how did you know? Are you really a witch?

"She nodded, 'Yes, some call me a witch while others call me doctor of minds and mender of broken hearts'.

"I was hypnotized by her eyes. They were staring into mine—hers were a radiant yellow—she was studying me intently in an unblinking gaze. 'Sit down Ramon', she pointed to a chair made of woven reed placed at a small table. I pulled the chair out and sat down with my mind in a very uneasy state; how the hell did she know my name?"

"She sat across from me, leaned forward blowing out the lamp in the center of the table. The blackness swallowed us creating a mysterious silence. The only sound was Carmen's labored breathing. After a full minute of silence she began speaking in a soft whisper. I could not make out her words even though she was whispering louder and louder until the whisper became a voice; a man's voice. I rose from my chair with the changing voice.

"Do not be alarmed Ramon, I'm your teacher!"

"Who are you? Where do you come from?"

"My name is Plinius Secundus. I was best known as Pliney the Elder during my life on the earth plane, that was from 23 to 79 A.D. I was best known, as an author and teacher of natural science during that incarnation. I've advanced to the fifth plane where I had the good fortune of studying under Plato as well as Aristotle. I'm your teacher to call upon when you're in need of spiritual help as you are now.

"You must realize your beloved Rita was taken from you, not in vain, but to advance the workings of the Universal Law. She will exert her presence on you and the children from an unseen vantage. When I depart and you leave here tonight return to your home. You'll go with a heart no longer heavy with grief and despair, but with a heart and mind lighter from understanding—a knowledge that I'm imparting to you now even though you're not aware you're receiving it. I must go, but will return in the future when you need my counsel as you have tonight. Good night, may God bless you."

"During the time the voice was speaking, it seemed to come from a round ball of faint light about the size of a coconut, having originally appeared before me when the voice had changed. The faint light melted away when the voice ceased.

"Mr. McCulloch, this is truly what I saw and heard.

"A few moments passed then Carmen resumed speaking softly in a language I had never heard before, or since, except when I go to her from time to time. She spoke a few sentences of the unknown language, then suddenly asked me in our native tongue, 'Do you feel better, Ramon?'"

"I can't explain it Mr. McCulloch, but she saved my life by giving me a philosophy to live by that gave me a reason, a cause for living. This is why I revere Carmen Bolivar. Can you blame me?"

"No, I can't. You've had an inexplicable experience. No doubt about it. I'm intrigued by the apparent results you received. Do you go to her often?"

"No, but over the years when I was faced with problems or when I felt the need of strengthening my spiritual or moral being, the aid was given me through the appearance of Pliney, my teacher."

"You mean you've had more than one contact with him?"

"Yes, I've had many contacts with him, always through Carmen."

"Have you ever suspected that Carmen might be a man capable of controlling his voice."

"Mr. McCulloch, if you could see Carmen she would erase any doubt of her being a woman. Believe me she has all the physical attributes of a very attractive female. She is certainly a woman. A good looking one too."

"My curiosity is jumping; I'd love to see this Carmen. Could you arrange it?"

"I believe it can be arranged, I'll let you know in a day or two.

The mail that day brought a letter from Lydia. She was getting married and hadn't any intention of working after marriage. Her letter was a resignation effective as soon as I could return to Houston to hire a replacement for her. Jim and I took off for Houston the next morning at six o'clock.

We checked into the Rice Hotel that night due to a strong tailwind during our flight. The next morning I went to the office convinced I'd close it out since it didn't serve any useful purpose as long as my activities were centered in Venezuela. Maybe I'd reopen a Houston office later.

The urge to talk to Andrey prompted me to call. Her sweet "hello" gave me a thrill.

"This is Hugh, is everything all right with you?"

"I'm doing fine, Hugh. I still miss dad very much, but I've reconciled myself to living without him even though it's still painful."

"Could we have dinner tonight?" A long silence elapsed then Audrey replied,

"I don't think so Hugh. Really there isn't any point in it, I think you'll agree."

"No, I won't agree. Yes, there is a point—that being the fact I love you very much. I've missed you every hour of every day we've been apart." I paused to get her reaction to this declaration; she responded quickly, "I must say I find that hard to believe. You didn't seem to miss me so much in the past. Why the sudden change?"

"There's been no sudden change. I was missing you the first day we were separated. The longing has become unbearable these past three years. This is why there is a point in our meeting. Can you understand that?"

"Not really, though I must admit you did sound sincere. Maybe the time will come when you can convince me you really and truly need me, and want me. I doubt the time is now."

"Audrey, is there someone else?"

"You haven't any right to ask that question Hugh, remember I'm a single woman. I must go now. I wish you the best of everything and hope for your sake you'll eventually become convinced you haven't any right to subject others to your inconsiderate whims. In short, I'd like very much for you to convince me of a transformation. A mending of your ways. Thank you for calling."

By God! She had practically hung up on me. I put the receiver down and reviewed her words. She was showing a penchant for maintaining the status quo and she gave no indication of missing me—she said nothing that expressed any desire to see me.

I was put down; dismissed in a cold methodical manner. I was hurt. Lydia arrived—I congratulated her on her upcoming marriage then told her of my decision to close the office.

"I hope I'm not placing you in a bind by resigning, Mr. McCulloch."

"Not at all Lydia. Maybe when I reopen in Houston, you'll be ready to return to work."

"Maybe. Right now, I don't think so."

"I'll give you a month's pay—let it be a combined wedding gift and severance pay."

She was appreciative of my gesture and showed it by pitching in and helping me close out the office. We worked until nine that evening then parted for the time being. She was an efficient helper, I'd try to rehire her when I reopened in Houston.

♠ ♠ ♠

Two days later Jim and I were back in Maracaibo. We learned from an employee at the airport hangar that a well had blown out somewhere on the other side of the lake. My heart sank at this disclosure as the memory of the Clarkwood holocaust which was still a vivid memory in my mind; I was not ready for a repetition of that misfortune. I called Cordoba from the airport, "Ramon, this is McCulloch. I've just returned from Houston. A man told me about a well blowing out."

He interrupted me with, "Yes, Mr. McCulloch it's your rig. So far there isn't any fire. I'll come for you. Ward is busy at the blowout."

"Thanks, but that won't be necessary, I have a pickup here. I'll take care of things. Thank you."

I placed a call to Myron Kinley in Houston requesting a blowout crew as soon as possible. He was quite calm as he assured me he'd be on site the next day.

He calmed my nerves immediately. He was the best in his business and his confidence was contagious. I felt much better when I dropped the receiver then said to Jim, "Let's get out there and see what we're up against."

Forty-five minutes later we parked a quarter mile from the source of the terrifying screech. The sound was punishing to our ears—making it impossible to converse as we walked nearer.

The only light was a flood light Curly had rigged up to a tree located a hundred feet from the howling hole in the earth. Curly had drawn upon his invaluable experience and followed all the precautionary measures possible to avoid the flaming of the well. He and several of the crew were standing beneath the flood light watching the derrick floor intently; hoping for the best. He wasn't aware of our presence until I tapped him on the shoulder. He turned his head then gave a gesture indicating his inability to help the situation. He pointed to a large drilling valve laying about twenty-five feet from the derrick in the outer edge of the light beam, then made a motion with his hands as if turning the hand wheel of a valve, then threw his arms upward indicating the valve had blown off. I could picture the scene from his pantomime as clearly as if I had been there.

He would not leave around midnight when I made a motion I was headed for the bed. Curly remained all night to make damn sure no one got foolish and tried to smoke; a spark would have resulted in an inferno.

Curly had shut down the boilers on the other rigs as a fire preventive measure—the pungent fumes of gas were heavy in the immediate area, and I found myself asking for divine assistance in avoiding another Clarkwood occurrence.

Jim and I arrived at the blowout early the next morning to find Curly still there, alert but leaning against a tree, his eyes fastened on the well. The sound had not diminished during the night indicating the drill bit had penetrated an enormous gas reserve below the tropical jungle.

Kinley and crew arrived around four p.m. with a rented truck bearing the materials and sophisticated tools designed for their highly specialized work; also highly dangerous!

Five hours later they had succeeded in shutting off the dangerous gush of gas. Two hours after Kinley and crew finished Curly had the other three rigs in operation—things were back to normal.

A few days later I received a letter from Joe Bob Miller outlining a venture he was considering as an investment. He wanted me as a partner if I was interested. The proposition was the construction as well as ownership of a pipeline that would carry oil from the west Texas fields to the Houston ship channel, where several major oil refineries were situated.

The project had appeal if the right people got involved, so I sent a reply to Joe Bob telling him I'd be in Houston the following week letting him know my decision.

Money being the prime mover of all industry forced me to fly to Caracas where I could learn the current value of my oil production account. Jim and I flew over, contacting Alvarez.

"You're doing well, Mr. McCulloch. What brings you to Caracas?"

"I'd like to determine the amount of money to date in my production account. Did you hear about the well blowout Señor Alvarez?"

"Indeed I did. How did you shut it in?"

"Myron Kinley flew from Houston."

"Good! When you receive his statement forward it on to me as the government will pay the cost."

"Thank you, that's most generous."

The Simon Bolivar National Bank was staffed with courteous people. Upon learning my identity, the employees showered me with attention. It was evident the bank president had not heard of my financial collapse or I wouldn't have been invited to his inner sanctum to await the cashier's tally of my account. The perfecto the president had given me was exquisite, as was the fragrant red Rosé he poured in beautiful cut crystal. I snuggled into the plush chair where I savored every minute of the fawning attention I was getting. Maybe I could set this bank up for a future loan provided they were not apprised of my credit rating in the meantime.

The cashier appeared, handed me several sheets of figures saying, "Here you are Mr. McCulloch. We hope you'll find our service to your liking."

"I surely do like your bank—perfecto—the wine—your courtesy. Thank you."

In flight to Maracaibo the time was used in studying the production with which my account was credited—the estimated increase for the future; trying to locate any error in the tally, and estimating the amount of money available to invest in the pipeline.

After looking the financial report over I made the decision to make an initial investment not to exceed two hundred thousand in the pipeline. As we landed in Maracaibo I said to Jim, "We'll be flying to Houston on Monday."

"Okay, Boss."

Monday evening I called Joe Bob from the hotel to tell him I was in town and ready to talk about his proposal. He agreed to meet me in Kelley's Steak House at nine p.m. where we would go over the deal.

Before me I was watching the foam on a cold mug of freshly drawn beer awaiting the arrival of Joe Bob. The crowd around me seemed to all be talking all at once, the din gave one the impression of chattering monkeys.

"Are you still winning at poker?" The voice and the question had come from behind—I turned to see my inquisitor. He was probing my face with a pair of eyes expressing hatred, he was wearing an expensive suit and was about my size. He looked vaguely familiar. His jaw muscles were flexing rapidly; tight, relaxed—tight, relaxed. His cheeks were undulating like a squirrel's working on a hickory nut. His mouth was curled at the corners, twisted like that of a perverted gargoyle. He was not a pretty sight poised there glaring at me.

I gleaned a message of recognition; this was the man who accused me of cheating in the game at the Petroleum Club, his accusation resulting in me having to pay several hundred dollars for damages to the club—he had contributed to my being ostracized from the club. Anger was building up in me from recalling these unpleasant facts. We were face to face engaged in a battle of wills.

The atmosphere presented a sequel to our previous encounter. Vengeance! More violence! The bar patrons had suddenly moved away.

Joe Bob entered the door pacing over to me, threw his arm around my shoulder, "Hugh, you reprobate you. I'm glad to see you."

We were shaking hands now, "How are things in Venezuela?"

"Couldn't be better, how is it with you?"

"Fine, let's go to the dining room, I'm starved."

When I passed my antagonist I was prepared to retaliate if he tried to get a sneak punch. My concern was unfounded, as he stepped aside to permit Joe Bob and I clear passage, he had lost his desire for revenge, at least for the moment.

During dinner Joe Bob explained his plans for the pipeline. He had done his homework well, as proved by his command of all the facts pertaining to the construction, the right-of-way, the expected revenue when oil began coursing the line, the cost. He layed it all out in a very comprehensive manner. I found he was whetting my interest with every disclosure, in addition his cost estimate had given me an inward sigh of relief; the initial costs for each of us would be a hundred fifty thousand.

"Foresight beats hindsight," he remarked. "I've made arrangements for bank financing to finish the construction when we have two hundred miles of pipe in the ground with the right-of-way guaranteed for the distance to the ship channel. What do you think of it, Hugh?"

His enthusiasm was contagious; he was looking at me awaiting my reply—his eyes were sparkling like diamonds swinging from a dowager's ears.

"When do we start?" I gave him a big grin.

"Hot Damn! We're partners again. I always knew we'd be together again ever since you shucked the lease business. Boy! I can see the sign now, "Miller & McCulloch Transmission Corporation", we'll be in high grass in a couple of years, wait and see."

"When do we start?" I asked again.

"If you can stay around for two or three days we can get it moving."

"I can stay."

We parted to meet at nine a.m. the next morning in the coffee shop of the Rice Hotel. I found myself questioning my quick decision when I retired for the night.

Chapter Nineteen

Pipeline To Profit And Cedillo's Gift

The morning found my thoughts in a positive vein and I was convinced the pipeline would be a good investment. Oil was being produced in the west Texas and New Mexico region, which had to be transported to refineries. The pipeline operation did not rely on the possible uncertainties encountered when drilling wildcat wells.

Joe Bob was drinking coffee while reading the morning paper; the paper was propped up against a vase of flowers on the table. I pulled out a chair joining him.

"Good morning, partner," he said, as he folded the paper. "I hope all is well with you this fine morning."

"It is. Have you had breakfast?"

"No, I was waiting for you. Let's eat!"

I had speared a slice of ham with my fork when Joe Bob said, "Hugh, I wonder if that guy lost his ear."

"What guy?"

"The one you clobbered with the chair in the beer joint, you remember that, don't you?"

"Yes I remember. If he did lose it I'm sorry; he forced that on me, I had no choice after he kicked my ass."

"That's right, you didn't. When we finish breakfast we'll go talk to an acquaintance of mine who is a pipeline contractor out on Navigation Boulevard."

We went into the office where a secretary asked us to be seated while Mr. Tucker completed a telephone call. I picked up a magazine from the end table and flipped the page carelessly. It opened to a picture of the Capri Hotel. I closed it on my finger to learn the name of the magazine. It was the Oil Land Gas Journal, March 'thirty-eight issue'. I remembered it to be one of the publications in which I had advertised the opening of the hotel.

"Mr. Miller!" A booming voice bounced off the walls. I glanced up to see the source of this robust greeting; the speaker was none other than "Houdini" the entrepreneur—the wildcatter turned muleskinner the night we stole the drill pipe near Conroe. The magazine fell from my hand surprised at seeing him. Tucker. . . Tucker . . . By God! That was his name, Tucker. I stood facing him. He was resplendent as usual, the way I remembered him; the charcoal gray suit mated with his frame perfectly. He was reaching to shake my hand as Joe Bob said, "Frank Tucker meet Hugh McCulloch." I grasped his hand.

"Frank and I've met before."

Tucker suddenly became wary of my presence. I could sense it—it was like the electrical tension that occurs between dogs and cats.

"Your face is familiar and your voice is too. Where in the hell did I know you?"

I knew his animated state was a result of his fear that perhaps I had been a victim of his skulduggery in the distant past; fear of a past sin rising to plague him. I laughed, it was time to lift him off the hook of apprehension.

"You're a poet too, along with your other talents. I started out as a "boll weevil" with you on a rig near Pistol Hill in 'thirty one. Perhaps you well recall our "borrowing" drill pipe from a neighboring rig. The mules were unusual in that they could not see in bright sunlight—making it necessary to move the pipe to our rig under the protection of night—the mules could see better than we. Remember?"

"Oh yes! How well I remember. Tell me, are you Hugh McCulloch, the hell raiser, the debaucher of women, the guy who built that swanky hotel on South Main?"

"Yes, I built a hotel. The Capri."

Joe Bob broke in, "Mr. Tucker we're here to discuss a pipeline job with you."

Tucker came back, "Just call me Frank. Come into my office." We followed him to his private domain where he closed the door and told us to take a seat. He went around the end of a massive desk to seat himself in the big upholstered, swivel chair facing us.

"Now gentlemen what are we discussing here?"

Joe Bob spoke, "We intend to build a sixteen inch line with entry in the Midland-Odessa area—a line extending to the

Houston ship channel. We'd like you to construct it—if you want the job."

Frank shot back, "I want the job."

"We'll see if you want the job by the offer you make us," Joe Bob retorted.

Frank walked over to a large wall map of New Mexico, Texas and Louisiana, lifted a cloth strip measuring device, stretched the tape across the area under discussion then said, "We're looking at five hundred long miles," he returned to his desk where he started figuring on a scratchpad, his brow creased from thought.

I broke the silence with, "Those five hundred miles are flat ones, that should hold the cost within reason."

Tucker shifted his eyes to me where he held my gaze for several moments. I had the feeling he suddenly remembered me being adamant in demanding a cashiers check for payment of my labor in Kilgore when he had cashed Harry Benbow and me out of the well we had worked on.

He dropped his eyes to the pad and continued to figure. A few minutes later he said, "I'll lay the line, furnish all labor, insurance, and materials necessary for the completion of the project—guarantee to have it pass all the tests before I cover it for the sum of three hundred fifty thousand dollars. You'll pay the cost of the sixteen inch pipe plus paying me one hundred twenty thousand when we have tested and covered the first one hundred seventy-five miles, another one hundred twenty thousand when we have three hundred fifty miles completed—the balance of one hundred ten thousand to be paid at the terminus. I'd like a decision as soon as possible, as I could avoid a lengthy move of equipment if you can reach a decision within the next forty-eight hours. That's it gentlemen."

He placed the palms of his hands behind his head then rocked back in his expensive chair giving us the look of a man who had just doubled the raise in a high stakes poker game.

Joe Bob looked at me, trying I knew to read my reaction to the price Tucker had quoted. He asked, "What do you say, partner?"

"Sounds reasonable to me—I'm ready if you are."

Joe Bob turned to Tucker, "When can you start?"

"Next week."

"Have your secretary draw up the agreement for us to sign. We're in business."

Miller agreed to set up credit for the pipe; to handle all legal work necessary for connecting to the sources around Midland-Odessa and carry out all action to get the project started.

My duties were to get an office set up in Houston at once. The following day I leased a very attractive one in the Mullen Tower, purchased new furniture, hired a secretary-receptionist named Diana Krist.

I called Audrey to ask her to have dinner with me. She was courteous by expressing interest in my pipeline venture and wishing me good luck but declined the invitation politely switching the conversation to my Venezuela activity. I found her cool attitude very discouraging. If only she would show interest in finding out whether or not I had changed. The way she handled my attempts of trying to show her the new side of me only resulted in making her unreachable. I was confused by her tactics; hurt by her indifference, as well as developing a feeling of futility. We fenced verbally for several minutes with me committing various thrusts at her armor of indifference; she had parried with effective ripostes making my efforts come over as an exercise of futility. The impasse was clear. I quit the fight by saying, "I'll call you again, maybe you'll be in a better mood."

"Do that. Good-bye."

I remained in Houston for ten days getting the operation set up. During this same period Jim had flown Joe Bob out to Midland three times.

Before flying back to Maracaibo I made another attempt at establishing a rapport with Audrey; she was on my mind constantly. I left Houston feeling my chances with her were not encouraging.

♠ ♠ ♠

My luck was running high in the Venezuelan operation; the jungle had given us forty-one consecutive wells. My eighteen percent of this production placed me once more in the position of having financial strength—the news of my new found fortune was trickling back to the states. The newspapers of Houston had seized upon the opportunity by unleashing a barrage of items: feature stories giving me a thrashing by way of slanted opinions, and review of the sordid details surrounding my rise and fall in the world of petroleum.

When the papers arrived in Maracaibo, always several days after publication, the local oil men would pounce on any scandal revealed concerning me. I now had the dubious distinction of being the most discussed person in Venezuela.

My good fortune developed some good aspects to offset the bad press; being the restoration of my triple-A-rating with Dunn and Bradstreet. I was once more being offered the many investment opportunities a man of financial stature is exposed to.

My time was divided between Houston and Venezuela, although I was transferring more responsibility to Curly Ward as the months passed. He was elevated to the position of liaison man between McCulloch Enterprises and the local government.

I had gone to Carmen Bolivar for advice several times since Ramon had introduced her to me. I'd sit at the small table across from her; after a few minutes her voice would become masculine, telling me what I had on my mind. She would then proceed to suggest the action I should follow to gain success over my problem.

She—he—had given me very accurate solutions in the past. Several months back she had instructed me to start drilling at a right angle from the eastern most well and continue drilling in that direction until we reached the first dry hole, then start at another right angle. The accuracy of this suggestion had proved to be on target. It was uncanny. She had suggested I invest in pipelines.

I awakened one morning with the jolting occurrence of the previous night—had it really happened or was it a dream? I had gone to seek advice on whether or not I should follow up on a feeler I had received from the Colombian government regarding me developing their unproven oil reserves.

We had sat down at the table; the light had turned to dark immediately. The female voice spoke a few words in the strange language breaking the heavy silence. A minute passed then, "Hello, Hugh!" the man' s voice jolted me with surprise.

The voice was of someone I knew well; Curly's no. Ramon's no. Where had I known the voice?

"Hugh this is Juan, your friend. Do not be alarmed at hearing me, I've been trying to make contact with you for several months. Tonight your faith and my strength have at last made connection."

"What the hell is going on here?" I arose from the table then said, "Who's trying to make a jackass of me?"

"Listen to me, Hugh!" The voice was strident—it was demanding my attention.

"I'm the spirit of Juan. I'll prove it to you, then I'll get on with why I was willing to exhaust so much of my spirit strength to come here tonight. Sit down for starters, the first time we met we were in the lobby of the Ambassador in Monterrey, right?"

"Yes," my voice was shaky from this experience.

"You and I were partners in oil in Mexico, until I was ambushed. You no doubt have wondered why I was assassinated; it was to eliminate my opposition to the expropriation. I was prepared to fight the take over in a very effective manner, the president feared I'd be successful; that's why I'm here in spirit only. How is my dear Barbara? I loved that woman very much. I loved you as a brother, Hugh. That's why I'll do something to make amends for your losses in Mexico.

"The hacienda you leased at Tampico; the huge stone fireplace, it's very important to you."

"Go to Tampico as soon as possible. Enlist the aid of Colonel Rivera in following my instructions. Ask him to drive you to the hacienda. He can order any occupants of the house to leave for one hour. He has the military authority to carry it out. Reach up inside the fireplace, the front inner wall. Two feet up you'll feel an oblong stone projecting out from the wall surface. Grasp the stone and remove it. Reach as far toward the front of the wall as you can. There you'll find a metal box; remove it. Do not open it in Rivera's presence."

"Just one minute. Why are you so sure Rivera will co-operate with me?"

"Because he has always liked you and he, like I, feel you were literally robbed by the expropriation.

"Your generosity affected him greatly, the day you left you gave him a hundred dollar bill. He has not forgotten. I must go now my dear friend, my strength is failing.

"Please tell Barbara how great was the love I shared with her. The contents of the box should bring you several million.

"Juan, please tell me what is in the box."

"The box was left in my grandmother's care during the war between the forces of Maximillian and Benito Juarez."

"What is in the box?"

"Carlotta's jewels."

"Juan, why me?"

The silence was broken with the female voice of Carmen asking, "Did you receive an answer to your problem?'

"Yes, thank you—thank you." I arose and started walking to the door, the experience of the past half hour had been a mystifying one.

Carmen spoke, "Mr. McCulloch I wish to give you something of appreciation for the kindness and friendship you've given our mutual friend, Ramon Cordoba."

She walked to a shelf on which was a wooden box, she raised the lid, reached in and lifted a small cloth pouch, handed it to me saying, "Take this, Mr. McCulloch."

I squeezed it lightly, curious of its contents, "What is this?"

She smiled as she replied, "Life is a procession of problems, the struggle we know as life sometimes overpowers our will to fight. This pouch contains a substance when chewed it will erase all awareness of your surroundings. The mental state that follows the chewing will take you from the present to the past. Your life will pass in review while in this state, but the experience will leave you with a clear mind. The problems will have become less of a burden."

"What is the substance?"

"The bark of the Cauca tree; you chew a bit for each journey into the past. It will not harm you; take it with my blessings. Good night."

I left her house questioning my senses. Had they betrayed me? Did I experience the occult, or was my imagination running rampant?

I laid in bed several hours before sleep relieved my mental struggles. As I surrendered to sleep I decided to accept the hearing of Juan Cedillo's voice as factual. It was his voice, he had spoke of incidents unique to our association. The credibility of his statements could not be shaken; my sixth sense told me to carry out Juan's suggestion.

♦ ♦ ♦

I wakened the next morning feeling an urgency to fly to Tampico in search of conclusive proof I had experienced a contact with the dead: the finding of the box in the chimney.

I was reluctant to reveal the purpose of the Tampico flight to Jim for fear it might not be there, even though I was driven by a confident belief that it would be.

"We're flying to Tampico, Jim."

"When Hugh?"

"As soon as we have breakfast."

We touched down in Tampico around two o'clock. After coming to a stop near the terminal entrance we saw Colonel Rivera coming out to greet us. He was smiling happily as he embraced me, then said, "Mr. McCulloch I'm so happy to see you, and you too, Mr. Harris."

"You're looking fine, Colonel. I've missed our association and have thought of you many times since we left."

"Mr. McCulloch, please have Jim put your plane in the hangar where it won't be seen."

Jim heard the request and taxied the plane into the open hangar. When he climbed out the Colonel closed the doors saying, "I feel all is much safer now. How long are you staying?"

"Colonel, I must ask a favor of you."

"Anything you wish Mr. McCulloch."

"Can you drive us out to my former hacienda?"

"Yes, my pleasure. Come, let's go."

"One moment Colonel! When we get there can you persuade the people who happen to be in the house to leave for thirty minutes? There is something there that belongs to me; I'd like to recover it."

The Colonel rubbed his chin as he pondered my request, then replied, "If anyone who happens to be there refuses to leave I'll resort to my military rank by ordering them out, but I don't expect any resistance. It's likely we'll find only the housekeeper. Let's go."

He headed for his car in a fast, determined walk. The Studebaker came to a quick stop, the sound of squealing brakes accompanied by a cloud of dust announced our arrival.

As we climbed from the car I noticed a brown face peering out the front window. It disappeared behind the curtain as we mounted the steps. The Colonel pulled the huge pistol riding his hip, then rapped on the big door using the butt of the weapon for a knocker. A wizened faced, middle-aged woman opened the door; her wide brown eyes were fastened on the Colonel with a frightened, questioning look, "Si Señor?"

Rivera shifted to his voice of authority barking a steady stream of Spanish for a half minute. The woman nodded in assent; came out and walked to the car where she sat in the front seat.

The Colonel said, "Okay there's no one else here, go in."

"Jim you stay out here to keep an eye on the woman." I entered saying, "I want you to come with me, Colonel."

We walked to the fireplace. I found my knees rubbery and unsteady from a combination of excitement and anticipation. I found it difficult to keep my composure as I stood quivering in the presence of Rivera who was observing me closely. Little did I know what the next minute would produce. I was staring at the opening in the huge fireplace, my state of mind swinging like a pendulum. Would the fireplace produce an occult enigma, would it produce conclusive proof that my imagination had controlled me? I kneeled on the hearth—my knees shaking, my chest heaving. I looked at the Colonel. He was watching me through curious slitted eyes. The moment of truth was now. I reached up, my fingers groping for the projecting stone. Sliding my fingers up, oblivious to the shower of soot cascading down my arm—I touched it! There it was! I grasped the stone and started pulling outward while rocking it back and forth. Big globules of sweat were streaming into my eyes.

There! I had the stone in my hand. In my haste to probe for the box I dropped it producing an explosion of ashes and soot as it struck the pile of cinders below. The soot obscured my vision. I made a swipe across my eyes with my free hand while I explored the hole with the other. My fingers brushed an object. The feel of cool metal was in my grasp. I was holding a small box between my thumb and fingers—I drew the box from the opening then lowered it to my knee. My body was blocking Rivera's view. I stood, turned to face him and said, "Here it is, I thought it would be safe here."

"Good! I'm glad you recovered it. Let's get out of here."

Riding back to the airport I was a sorry sight covered with soot. Jim laughed at me saying, You look like Al Jolson, Hugh."

I was fighting a powerful urge to see the contents of the box but Juan's words of caution not to open it in the presence of Rivera gave me the power to resist the temptation.

After wheeling the plane from the hangar we were bidding the Colonel good-bye when I thought of giving him a tip for his valuable assistance. I pressed two one hundred dollar bills into his hand and told him I'd pay his expenses if he could ever come to Houston for a visit. He assured me he would look forward to coming.

I breathed a sigh of relief as the plane became airborne. I was losing my tautness of nerves as Tampico receded from sight. I was gripping the small metal box from fear it would escape my clutches when Jim asked, "Hugh, did you forget the box when we left so hurriedly after being ordered out?"

"I didn't actually forget it that morning. I was considering the possibility of having our possessions confiscated at the airport. That's why I left it there."

"You must've hidden it in the fireplace."

"That is exactly where it was concealed.

"Now that we are fifty miles away I can tell you I was scared when you mentioned flying to Tampico. I could see you and I languishing in some crummy jail counting cockroaches for pastime. Yes, I'll admit my ass was sucking wind all the time we were there, but I'm glad you retrieved your box."

We landed at Maracaibo about midnight; as we left the airport Jim suggested we eat something before turning in. I lied when I said I had a headache, so I asked him to drive me to the house then he could return for something to eat.

Damn it! I had to see the contents of the box—my curiosity was tearing me apart. When we reached the front of the house I jumped out saying, "See you in the morning."

I watched the tail lights disappear from view then vaulted the steps anxious to get to the privacy of my room. After lowering all the shades and locking the door I sat in the middle of the floor.

The box lid was secured with small snap catches. I flipped them up—slowly lifted the hinged cover to discover a folded paper yellow from time concealing whatever lay beneath. I lifted the paper; before my eyes were about fifty magnificent rubies, all the size of common marbles. I turned the box upside down ridding it of it contents. Fifty or more shimmering, flashing diamonds the size of pecans were shining their magic beauty against the backdrop of the maroon carpet. I was mesmerized by the brilliancy of them; each demanding impassioned reverence from the viewer with their twinkling flash of colors. Some were beaming a constant shaft the hue of arctic ice—some winking with glowing saffron eyes—some emitting the intriguing glow of planet Mars. It was like viewing a kaleidoscope made of diamonds.

The allurement before me was making me dizzy after staring at the gems for half an hour. I turned my attention to a pendant strung on a chain of hammered yellow gold. The links were square rather than the usual round. I lifted the chain, started passing the links between my thumb and forefinger working toward the lavaliere. It turned lazily revealing an oval shaped diamond at least an inch long and about an inch at it widest point. As it turned suspended from the chain, it bombarded me with a myriad of blue-white shafts of breath-taking beauty. Audrey would wear this! I placed the gems in the box, then picked up the folded paper. After unfolding it I read the writing. It was written with bold strokes of the pen using purple ink. It read:

The bearer of this letter is the lawful, legal owner of this collection of diamonds and rubies. The bearer is authorized to sell or transfer ownership at the bearer's discretion. The diamond lavaliere is a part of this collection of gem stones.

Carlotta Maximillian,
this day 26th of February, 1867

I folded the paper, placed it on the top of the gems, turned out the light and sat in the darkness until my eyes grew accustomed to it. I then went outside carrying a large heavy knife with me to dig a hiding place for the box. I put it underground near the steps at the rear of the house. My excitement over the stones finally subsided and I found sleep.

The next morning I casually strolled around the house to check the hiding place. The ground showed no visible signs of having been disturbed, I went on my way. A week later I transferred the box to Houston where I placed it in a safe deposit vault.

Chapter Twenty
Reunion And The Big Surprise

The Houston office was in good shape thanks to the diligence of Diana. Due to my buying an existing pipeline that ran from Conroe to Houston the workload had increased to the point where a legal secretary was essential. The Midland pipeline was in operation adding to the paperwork that came through the office. In addition to the Venezuelan production, I had bought three used rigs from a wildcatter turned politician. These rigs were searching for oil in the Del Rio area.

Joe Bob had received and accepted an attractive offer of a big salary, expenses and part owner of a new company in the Trinidad-Tobago area. He felt it would be to his advantage to dispose of his interest in the pipeline and offer me first chance at buying him out.

I bought his interest for the sum of one million dollars; a nice profit for him and a good buy for me.

Multimillionaire; that had a nice sound to it. By mid-nineteen forty I had reached that plateau again. This time around I was settled in the category as a sedate businessman who had once acquired the Midas touch. Every project I touched became a source of more profit. It seemed I could not lose.

I had broken the bank on three occasions in Galveston's leading gambling spot; each winning exceeding the half million mark. I was winning at everything except the one thing I wanted most. More than power—more than money; I wanted Audrey to take me back. This was the elusive butterfly of my life; our reconciliation always winnowed by her memories of my escapades of the past—THE PAST—THE PAST—the past . . .

I raised my head from my arms folded on the desk, my neck muscles seemed very tired. The office was dark. I swiveled the chair to face the window. There were lights twinkling from the

Gulf Building. I crossed the office, flipped the light switch then glanced at my watch, it was nine o'clock! I had entered my office around five, four hours ago! I walked back to my desk; the small pouch of Cauca bark was laying where I had placed it after removing a small portion which I had chewed. My head was very clear; I experienced a peace of mind I had never had before just as Carmen Bolivar had predicted. I placed the pouch in the bottom drawer of my desk; the bark not only gave one a refreshed feeling, it speeded up the passing of time! Four hours, it was unbelievable! I noticed a memo on the desk, it was from Diana reminding me of Harry Benbow's call. She had added a P.S—"You were sleeping so peacefully with your head on your arms at your desk, I didn't have the heart to waken you! Signed Diana, five thirty p.m.

I went to my apartment where I sat in a chair for two hours, the time being spent in trying to analyze what had really occurred during the four hours in my office. The results of chewing the Cauca bark had actually channelled my mind to another plane making it separate and apart from my physical self. Yes, it was becoming clear to me now—six hours later. My mind had been privileged to experience the realm of the occult. It was indeed an enlightening venture into an advanced dimension. Twenty years of my life had passed before me, beamed on a screen so gigantic I witnessed the chronology of my life in four dimensions. The cinematics were in natural color—the sounds surrounding the twenty years of life—the tangy taste of the wines—the sense of feel had been prevalent throughout the viewing. It had been a ride on a magic carpet. I must soar away again sometime!

As I entered the office the next morning, Diana intercepted me to inquire if I had slept very long the evening before. She had been preparing to lock the door when she could not recall my leaving. She had entered to check on me after getting no response from the buzzer. There she had found me fast asleep; head and arms on the desk.

She said she had been a little concerned wondering if I felt all right but surmised I was exhausted from travel.

"Did you return Mr. Benbow's call?"

"No, I didn't, will you place a call to him now, please."

I stuck my head in Penelope's office, "Hi! Penelope, any new developments in the field of romance?"

"Now, Mr. McCulloch you know I've better things on my mind than romance!"

"God Almighty, woman! Is there something better?"

She waved her arms in a manner of dismissing me and started typing. Diana followed a ritual of placing the morning paper on my desk before my arrival, then served me a cup of black coffee as soon as I came in. She appeared with the steaming coffee, then informed me there wasn't any response from the number Harry Benbow had left.

"Thank you Diana."

She had turned and started walking to the outer office; as usual my masculine leer was focused on her tight, firm buttocks. As she closed the door I shot a parting stare at her well turned legs. I thought, "There goes a world of excitement."

War—rumors of war filled the front page of the Post. I turned the page, read an interesting article about Kentucky Derby winner, War Admiral. He was ensconced on a Kentucky horse farm enjoying his retirement. The writer pointed out War Admiral's duties consisted of eating and taking advantage of willing mares. Some life!

My eyes fell next on the name Audrey McCulloch! The item read:

"Mrs. Audrey McCulloch is in flight today, racing to Mayo Clinic, Rochester Minnesota where she is taking her four year old son, Hugh McCulloch Jr. in a race against time and possible death. Young Hugh suffered injuries in an auto accident two days ago. He was rushed to a local hospital for treatment. He was administered a blood transfusion and was thought to be on the road to recovery when his condition worsened. After exhaustive tests to determine the cause of his sudden change, it was discovered young Hugh's blood type was RH negative. He had received Blood type RH positive. This combination of blood types can be fatal if the blood supply is allowed to remain in the victim. The Mayo Clinic is equipped with a machine capable of rendering the change of the blood supply. Young McCulloch's condition was termed as critical when the chartered plane took off for Rochester at eight fifteen this morning."

My mind was spinning like a pinwheel as I dropped the paper on the desk. The realization I had a four year old son struck me the same instant of his serious condition. Why had Audrey kept his birth and life from me for four long years? The combination of confusion, compassion, and shock had put me into a stupor. Life was showering me with mind boggling revelations, experiences and surprises the past ten days. A dead man had talked to me; the proof was in the safe deposit vault. And now, I had become an instant father just reading the paper!

I collected my wits and asked Diana to call Jim Harris at the hotel. The buzzer sounded.

"Jim, we're flying to Rochester, Minnesota."

"When?"

"Right now! I'll tell you about it when I pick you up. Bring enough clothing for several days. I'll pick you up at the Texas Avenue entrance in ten minutes. Be there!"

I hurried to Diana, "I'll be out of the city for several days."

"Shall I send the mail to Venezuela?"

"Hell no! I'm going to Minnesota." Diana raised an eyebrow and gave me a questioning look.

"I'm going to Minnesota to pick up my son and my wife.

She looked at me, "In that order?"

"Honey, I don't have time for an explanation now. You can learn all about it from an item on page two of the paper on my desk."

I raced out the door for the elevator. Ten minutes later I pulled into the guest loading curb on the Texas Avenue side of the hotel. Damn it! I could not see Jim.

A few seconds later he came swinging out the door and literally jumped into the car, threw his bag in the rear seat and asked, "I didn't hold you up much, did I?"

"No Jim, I had just arrived."

After we were well on our way to the airport, I realized I should tell him what had happened to prompt this speedy departure.

"Jim, I learned this morning I'm the father of a four year old son."

"The hell you say! How did you find it out?"

"Reading an article in this morning's Post. He's being flown today to the Mayo Clinic in Rochester, Minnesota.

"He is in critical condition from being given the wrong type of blood. His mother and I were divorced over four years ago; she was pregnant then, but chose to keep the fact from me. I know now why she has refused to permit me to come to her home; she was keeping the boy a secret."

"I'll bet this all came as a shock, didn't it?"

"You're damn right it did. I'm still shaking inside."

We fueled the plane. When we became airborne Jim set a course for Rochester. I was nervous and irritable as we cruised northerly.

"Is this as fast as this crate will go?" I asked him.

"I can full throttle if you say so, but it'll be a hell of a strain on the plane."

"Get it open, if she shakes to pieces we'll buy a better one."

At nine thirty p.m. I was standing before the information desk of St. Mary's Hospital in Rochester; my son was in room 511. I left Jim waiting in the lobby. As I entered the elevator I suffered my first element of doubt; Audrey might refuse to approve my presence. The door opened silently—I stepped out. The hall was clear of people; one nurse was studying medical charts at her station. Hearing my approach, she looked up and asked, "May I help you?"

"Yes, please. Do you know if Mrs. McCulloch is in the room with her son, Hugh?"

"I'm sure she's still there—down the hall to your left."

The door was slightly ajar; this permitted me to enter quietly. Audrey was sitting in a chair; her back to me. I called softly, "Audrey." At the sound of my voice she sprang to her feet, turned to me with a look of astonishment on her face. She placed her face against my chest, then started sobbing. A few moments passed as I held her close to me. Gaining her composure she said softly, "Thank you for coming. We need you so much." She sighed then nodded toward the bed, "Do you want to see your son?"

She was pulling me by the hand toward the bed where the quiet form lay motionless. I looked down at a beautiful sight; my son! He was so appealing lying there, his dark curly hair accenting the freckled, puckish face. As I studied his calm features, I was overcome with both pride and alarm. I was filled with alarm and concern for his life!

This was a momentous occasion in my life—the next moment I was silently praying, not only for little Hugh's complete recovery, but for help from above for myself to be worthy of the role of father and husband. God had been a stranger most of my life but I'd see about changing that too. I leaned down and kissed the sleeping boy lightly on the tip of his nose.

Audrey had been watching me intently the past few minutes, as if I were a jigsaw puzzle and she was trying to fit the pieces together. I nodded to her indicating that we leave the room. She followed me out to the hall where I turned to her and said, "Audrey, I read about our son in this morning's paper. I flew up here with two objectives in mind. To see you and Hugh through this, and to take you both back to Houston."

"Do you forgive me for keeping it from you?"

"Yes darling, I know why you did it—I understand."

"Thank you, Hugh. I don't feel alone anymore."

"Audrey you've a choice; you can marry me here in Rochester, or as soon as we arrive in Houston. Which will it be?"

She gave me a big smile then replied, "I'm sure we can find a willing minister before we leave Minnesota, my love!"

We sealed the agreement with a long delayed kiss. We went back to our son's room with her clutching my arm the way she once had done. It was a glorious feeling to have the chance to make amends for a lot of misdeeds.

I went down to the lobby of the hospital interrupting Jim's reading of a National Geographic. I told him I'd be spending the night in the room with my son, but he should seek a room nearby for the night, returning around nine the next morning as we would need him for a witness if Audrey and I found it possible to arrange our marriage.

I returned to the room where I sat down in a chair situated across the bed from where Audrey was sitting. I had leaned forward for a closer study of Hugh Jr.'s facial features. After studying his boyish face for two or three minutes I remarked, "He looks just like me."

I resumed studying the sleeping boy; spellbound from the realization that he was a part of me. Audrey brought her chair around the bed and placed it beside me, she then grasped my hand in hers as she said, "He's a fine lad, isn't he! I know he'll accept you quickly as I've told him every day of his life he had a wonderful father; a father who would return to be his teacher and companion. I have told him all about you—you do have many good points, Hugh."

We fell asleep shoulder to shoulder with our heads together. We were wakened by the sound of subdued conversation between two nurses. I raised my head—started turning it from side to side hoping to rid myself of a stiff neck. I glanced at my watch, it was seven a.m. One nurse greeted my awakening, "Good morning!" By now Audrey had awakened and was rubbing her neck too, then looked at me and said, "It's not a dream, you're really here, darling."

"Yes, I'm here to stay, sweetheart."

"You must be the father. Little Hugh looks just like you."

"Thank you and may I add I'm proud of that fact."

The smaller nurse was bending over Hugh Jr. wiping his brow gently with a damp cloth to awaken him slowly. He rolled his curly head from side to side, then his eyes opened. He immediately started rubbing them with his chubby little fists. He turned his head at the sound of Audrey's voice then focused his sleepy eyes on me. I grinned at him but said nothing. He held a steady gaze on me for a full minute then his mouth curled into the most lovable, endearing smile I'd ever seen. He shifted his eyes to Audrey standing beside me and asked, "Is he my daddy, mommy?"

"He's your daddy, honey. I told you he'd come sometime, didn't I. What do you think of your daddy, Hugh?"

He gave an impish grin that made his freckles seem to crawl, then looked at me saying, "He's so big, mommy. Big like King Kong."

Audrey looked at me, "What shall we do with him? He's such a teaser, don't be surprised at anything he says."

The nurse interrupted, "Come along Hugh we're going to let you play with a big toy that has a lot of flashing lights. Will you like that?"

"Flashing lights! A big toy! I'll like that." She picked him up and laid him on the O.R. table setting beside the bed and fluffed the pillow up for him asking, "Are you ready, Hugh?"

"Yes, ma'am."

As she wheeled him out the door he sang out in his child-like voice, "Don't go away, daddy."

His plaintive request told me I'd never part from him or his mother. I had found the quiet, peaceful harbor my ship of soul had been seeking. I had dropped anchor—the anchor to the sought after, elusive, peace of mind.

The doctor who was supervising the blood transfer appeared in the door where he assured us Hugh Jr. would experience no difficulty from his eight hour hook up with the machine. He would no doubt be released from the hospital two days later.

The doctor left us saying, "I know you'd like to visit him during the eight hour procedure but we found a child cooperates better if his parents are not around. We hope you'll understand." He looked at his watch, "He'll be back in his room around four thirty p.m." The doctor disappeared into the elevator.

I turned to Audrey, "Come along Beautiful, we'll have breakfast then find a marriage license and a preacher, in that order. We'll begin the first day of a glorious lifetime of happiness—that is, if you haven't changed your mind." I looked at her with a questioning gaze.

She gave a musical laugh, "You can't avoid my clutches by offering me suggestions of how to escape Mr. McCulloch. When you entered the room last night, the fly "you", had become entangled in the spider's web "me."

She grasped my arm to guide me to the elevator as she said, "It's off to Eden we go!"

We picked up Jim who was waiting in the lobby, then had breakfast.

♠ ♠ ♠

"I now pronounce you man and wife," the minister had intoned the words at eleven ten a.m. in the living room of his home. He had summoned a neighbor to fill the quota of witnesses necessary to make the marriage legal. Audrey and I ended the marriage kiss, grudgingly, at eleven fifteen a.m. The kiss had thrilled me far more than my first automobile.

We spent our wedding night in a hotel located near the hospital, having left as soon as our son had fallen asleep. The imminent prospect of conjugal experiences were foremost in my mind as I undressed. Foremost because this time my attitude was entirely different than it was on the wedding night of our first marriage. The memory of how I approached the act of love, in such an insensitive, callous manner—seeking only self-gratification, not feeling any consideration for the attitude of my mate. She had responded to my bungling just as if I were the world's greatest exponent of, "How to please your mate on your wedding night."

Tonight I was filled with the warm desire to touch her lightly at first—with flicking, tantalizing caresses; each telegraphing the message of true love crying release. Tonight I'd be true to myself.

When I came from the shower she was in bed, in total darkness. I did not need the fragrance of Chanel to serve as a beacon to guide me to her, as my built-in homing instinct was still accurate. I rolled gently on the bed and found her out stretched arm under my neck. She quickly pulled me against her hot body—a body pulsating with anticipation and desire. I whispered, "Honey, can you ever forgive me?" She bit my ear lobe lightly and hissed in my ear, "Please Hugh, no talking, let our instincts do it!" Neither of us said a word until seven a.m. the next morning when I was awakened by my aching left arm. She had slept on it and I'd be damned if I'd move it before she woke.

I heard her whisper, "My man is back." She turned and kissed me passionately as she said, "Thank you, my man."

"And thank you my woman. We'd better get over to the hospital to see about our little boy."

Hugh Jr. was sitting up in bed awaiting our arrival and squealed, "Hi, mommy! I'm glad you didn't let daddy get away." He hugged both of us—his childish hug meant more to me than he could ever know.

We took off for Houston the following morning—our patient fully recovered and showing it by exploring every foot of the plane—laughing with childish glee with each new discovery. Thirty minutes after take off Jim called him, "Hugh, would you like to help Uncle Jim fly the plane?"

"Yes, yes," he scampered in Jim's lap where he stayed the rest of the flight.

Audrey asked, "Where do you wish to live—our home or the Brent house?"

"Do you have a preference?"

"Yes, I always loved our home. I'd like to go back there to live."

"That's my preference too, Honey."

Audrey was searching in her purse; she produced a small box. It was wrapped in plain white paper and tied with twine. She held it out to me,

"Hugh this is something I found when going through dad's personal belongings after his death. It was wrapped loosely in bond paper with a note attached. The note instructed me to give you this box when you returned to me and Hugh Jr. He wrote the words in a positive vein as if he knew you'd return someday. I have no idea what it is—anyway I'm following his wish. Here!"

she said, pushing it in my hand. I untied the knot, removed the paper wrapping then discovered some writing on the back side of it. I unfolded it to read:

"Hugh, I'm happy you've come back to Audrey and little Hugh. I always knew the good in you would eventually prevail, as exhibited by your return to where you're needed and loved.

"I offer this token in recognition of your honesty and goodness. Justin."

I could barely hold back the tears after reading his words, I had a terrific struggle facing me if I succeeded in living up to the standards he had stressed. I opened the small cardboard box and there before me was the diamond pin I had found and returned to Justin. Audrey picked it up, turned it around in her fingers saying,

"His love for you was great—this pin proves it."

We landed in Houston at eleven p.m., transferred our bags to the car and started our thirty minute drive. We let Jim out at the Rice Hotel.

We were driving on Polk Avenue with Hugh Jr. wide awake, standing up in the rear viewing everything around him. He was a bubbly intelligent little rascal.

"Daddy look at the people coming out of that building."

I looked where he was pointing—a neighborhood theater where the last show patrons were spilling onto the sidewalk. The marquee of the theater was flashing off and on the feature being shown.

"Edward G. Robinson"
in
"Dead Men Don't Talk"

Without thinking I muttered, "They sure as hell do!"